Also by Ellen Hopkins

Crank

Burned

Impulse

Glass

Identical

Tricks

Perfect

Tilt

Margaret K. McElderry Books

Ellen Hopkins

Margaret K. McElderry Books

NEW YORK LONDON TORONTO SYDNEY NEW DELHI

MARGARET K. MCELDERRY BOOKS

An imprint of Simon & Schuster Children's Publishing Division

1230 Avenue of the Americas, New York, New York 10020

MARGARET K. MCELDERRY BOOKS is a trademark of Simon & Schuster, Inc.

For information about special discounts for bulk purchases, please contact Simon & Schuster Special Sales at 1-866-506-1949 or business@simonandschuster.com.

The Simon & Schuster Speakers Bureau can bring authors to your live event. For more information or to book an event, contact the Simon & Schuster Speakers Bureau at 1-866-248-3049 or visit our website at www.simonspeakers.com.

Also available in a Margaret K. McElderry Books hardcover edition

This Margaret K. McElderry paperback edition August 2013

Book design by Mike Rosamilia

The text for this book is set in Trade Gothic Condensed No. 18.

Manufactured in the United States of America

First Margaret K. McElderry Books paperback edition September 2012

10 9 8

The Library of Congress has cataloged the hardcover edition as follows:

Hopkins, Ellen.

Fallout / Ellen Hopkins.

p. cm.

Summary: Written in free verse, explores how three teenagers try to cope with the consequences of their mother's addiction to crystal meth and its effects on their lives.

ISBN 978-1-4169-5009-7 (hardcover)

[1. Novels in verse. 2. Drug abuse—Fiction. 3. Emotional problems—Fiction. 4. Family problems—Fiction. 5. Brothers and sisters—Fiction. 6. Mothers—Fiction.] I. Title.

PZ7.5.H67Fal 2010

[Fic]—dc22

2009048408

ISBN 978-1-4424-7180-1 (paperback)

ISBN 978-1-4424-0945-3 (eBook)

For Orion, Jade, Heaven, Clyde, Eli, and Kalob, always in my heart. For Jason, Cristal, and Kelly, always my children, wherever they are. For John, always my own forever love. And with sincerest love and respect for my editor, Emma Dryden, who enriches my books with her wisdom and enriches my life with her friendship.

With a special nod to Jude Mandell, whose keen insight allowed me to see the direction I needed to go with this book. Many, many thanks, Jude!

RENO GAZETTE-JOURNAL

RENO—Local author Marie Haskins's fifteenth novel, *Submission*, debuted at the number one spot on the *New York Times* bestseller list. But this time, Haskins writes about a different kind of monster.

"This is a complete departure from my previous books," Haskins said. "I have finally fulfilled a very old dream and taken the plunge into horror."

It remains to be seen whether or not her fans will take the plunge with her, as the poems go beyond free verse, into the realm of formal poetry, specifically sonnets. Fortunately for Haskins, a number of words rhyme with "suck."

"I have long wanted to write about vampires, but chose to wait until the subject was no longer a staple of every publisher's list," Haskins said. "My vampires are sophisticated and totally sexy, but set in a future world. Sort of like *Dracula* meets *Star Trek*."

We Hear

That life was good
before she
met

                the monster,

but those page flips
went down before
our collective
cognition. Kristina

                wrote

that chapter of her
history before we
were even whispers
in her womb.

The monster shaped

                our

lives, without our ever
touching it. Read on
if you dare. This

                memoir

isn't pretty.

Hunter Seth Haskins

SO YOU WANT TO KNOW

All about her. Who

she

really is. (Was?) Why
she swerved off
the high road. Hard

left

to nowhere,
recklessly
indifferent to

me,

Hunter Seth Haskins,
her firstborn
son. I've been

choking

that down for
nineteen years.
Why did she go

on

her mindless way,
leaving me spinning
in a whirlwind of

her dust?

IF YOU DON'T KNOW

Her story, I'll try
my best to enlighten

you, though I'm not sure
of every word of it myself.

I suppose I should know
more. I mean, it has been

recorded for eternity—
a bestselling fictionalization,

so the world wouldn't see
precisely who we are—

my mixed-up, messed-
up family, a convoluted

collection of mostly regular
people, somehow strengthened

by indissoluble love, despite
an ever-present undercurrent

of pain. The saga started here:

FOREWORD

Kristina Georgia Snow
gave me life in her seventeenth
year. She's my mother,

but never bothered to be
my mom. That job fell
to her mother, my grandmother,

Marie, whose unfailing love
made her Mom even before
she and Dad (Kristina's stepfather,

> Scott) adopted me. *That was*
> *really your decision,* Mom claims.
> *You were three when you started*

> *calling us Mama and Papa.*
> *The other kids in your playgroup*
> *had them. You wanted them too.*

We became an official
legal family when I was four.
My memory of that day is hazy

at best, but if I reach way,
way back, I can almost see
the lady judge, perched

like an eagle, way high above
little me. I think she was
sniffling. Crying, maybe?

Her voice was gentle. *I want
to thank you, Mr. and Mrs.
Haskins, for loving this child*

*as he deserves to be loved.
Please accept this small gift,
which represents that love.*

I don't really remember all
those words, but Mom repeats
them sometimes, usually

when she stares at the crystal
heart, catching morning sun
through the kitchen window.

That part of Kristina's story
always makes Mom sad.
Here's a little more of the saga.

CHAPTER ONE

It started with a court-ordered
summer visit to Kristina's
druggie dad. Genetically,

that makes him my grandfather,
not that he takes much interest
in the role. Supposedly he stopped

by once or twice when I was still
bopping around in diapers.
Mom says he wandered in late

to my baptism, dragging
Kristina along, both of them
wearing the stench of monster

sweat. Monster, meaning crystal
meth. They'd been up all night,
catching a monstrous buzz.

It wasn't the first time
they'd partied together. That
was in Albuquerque, where dear

old Gramps lives, and where
Kristina met the guy who popped
her just-say-no-to-drugs cherry.

Our lives were never the same
again, Mom often says. *That
was the beginning of six years*

*of hell. I'm not sure how we all
survived it. Thank God you were
born safe and sound. . . .*

All my fingers, toes, and a fully
functional brain. Yadda, yadda . . .
Well, I *am* glad about the brain.

Except when Mom gives me
the old, *What is* up *with you?
You're a brilliant kid. Why do*

*you refuse to perform like one?
A C-plus in English? If you would
just apply yourself . . .*

Yeah, yeah. Heard it before.
Apply myself? To what?
And what the hell for?

I KIND OF ENJOY

My underachiever status.
          I've found the harder you
                    work, the more people expect

of you. I'd much rather fly
          way low under the radar.
                    That was one of Kristina's

biggest mistakes, I think—
          insisting on being right-up-
                    in-your-face irresponsible.

Anyway, your first couple years
          of college are supposed to be
                    about having fun, not about

deciding what you want to do
          with the rest of your life. Plenty
                    of time for all that whenever.

I decided on UNR—University
        of Nevada, Reno—not so much
                because it was always a goal,

but because Mom and Dad
        did this prepaid tuition thing,
                and I never had Ivy League

ambitions or the need to venture
        too far from home. School is school.
                I'll get my BA in communications,

then figure out what to do with it.
        I've got a part-time radio gig at
                the X, an allowance for incidentals,

and I live at home. What more
        could a guy need? Especially
                when he's got a girl like Nikki:

PICTURE THE IDEAL GIRL

And you've got Nikki.
She's sweet. Smart. Cute. Oh,
yes, and then there's her body.
I'm not sure what perfect
measurements are, but
Nikki's got them,

all wrapped up in skin
like wheat-colored suede.
Delicious, from lips to ankles,
and she's mine. Mine to touch,
mine to hold. Mine to kiss
all over her flawless

deliciousness. Plus,
she's got her own place,
a sweet little house near campus,
where I can do all that kissing—not
to mention what comes after
the kissing—in private.

I'm done with classes
for the day and on my way
to Nikki's, with a little extra fun
tucked inside my pocket. Yeah, I
know getting high isn't so
smart. Ask me if I care.

I AM GENETICALLY PREDISPOSED

To addiction. At least that's what
they tell me, over and over.

The theory has been hammered
into my head since before I could

even define the word "addiction."
Your grandfather is an addict and

*your mother is an addict, so it's
likely you will become an addict*

*too, unless you basically "just say
no."* Much easier said than done,

especially when you're predisposed
to saying, "Hell, yeah!" Anyway,

I'm more of a dabbler than a dedicated
fuckup. A little weed, a little coke.

Never tried meth. Don't think I ought
to take a chance on that monster.

Catching a buzz is one thing. Yanking
the devil's tail is just plain stupid.

NIKKI ISN'T HOME YET

I let myself in with the key
she leaves stashed under the plastic
rock by the door. Good thing

she doesn't own much in the way
of expensive stuff, something
I'm sure the neighbors are well

aware of. This isn't a bad street,
but it's heavily stocked with students,
many of whom have forgotten

the Golden Rule, if they ever knew
it to begin with. Inside, the window
shades are cracked enough so light

filters through. A thin beam
splashes against the hallway mirror,
lures my attention. When I turn

to find it, the eyes reflected
in the glass are completely unique.
"Piebald," Mom calls them.

Green-dappled gray. Definitely
not Kristina's eyes. What I want
to know now, as always, is whose?

I'VE ASKED THE QUESTION BEFORE

"If Kristina is my biological
mother, who fathered me?"

Who

was her man of the month?
I've been told she slept
with more than a few,
but which

was

the one whose lucky
sperm connected with
the proper egg? Whose
genes sculpted the relief of

my

cheekbones, the stack
of my shoulders, the stretch
of my legs? Do the eyes staring
back at me now belong to my

father?

IN MOM'S BOOK

The story goes Kristina was

　　　　　date-raped by some low-life

druggie lifeguard dealer.

　　　　　When I asked if that was true,

Mom would only say that

　　　　　the book is fiction, *based* on

fact, and that they aren't one

　　　　　hundred percent sure about

my paternity. But I think she

　　　　　was trying to spare my feelings.

Who wants to believe they

　　　　　were conceived of a rape, even

if the rape might have been

　　　　　somehow solicited? What kind

of guy keeps going when

　　　　　a girl says no way? And if a guy

like that really is my father,

　　　　　could I have inherited a rape gene?

NOT THAT I'VE EVER ONCE

Insisted "yes" when a girl said *no*.
I'm not that kind of guy.

I'm smart.
>   (Except when loaded.
>   Then I can be kind of stupid.
>   At least till the buzz wears off.)

I'm witty.
>   (Except when I don't get
>   enough sleep, which is often.
>   Then I lose my sense of humor.)

I'm compassionate.
>   (Except when someone
>   acts like a complete idiot.
>   Especially in my face.)

I'm understanding.
>   (Except when it means I can't
>   have my way, so I try to avoid
>   people who won't let me have it.)

I'm kind.
>   (Except for those days
>   when, for no apparent reason,
>   I hate pretty much everyone.)

I'VE GOT A LITTLE PROBLEM

And I'm not really sure
how to fix it. Not really sure

I need to. Not really sure I could.

Life is pretty good. But once
in a while, uninvited and

uninitiated, anger invades me.

It starts, a tiny gnaw
at the back of my brain. Like

a migraine, except without pain.

They say headaches
blossom, but this isn't so

much a blooming as a bleeding.

Irritation bleeds into
rage, seethes into fury.

An ulcer, emptying hatred

inside me. And I don't
know why. Life is pretty good.

So, what the hell?

AS I PONDER THE QUESTION

A key turns uselessly in the lock—
          uselessly because I neglected

          to secure the door behind me.
Nikki peeks cautiously around

it, jumps back like she's been
          bitten. Guess she didn't expect

          to find some guy standing here.
"Hey," I yell, "it's only me."

          Nikki slams back across
              the threshold, almost knocks

              me over. *Hunter! You scared*
the heebie-jeebies out of me!

Heebie-jeebies. She's totally
          cute. I pull her into my arms,

          happy to concentrate on her slate
blue eyes, instead of the green ones

in the mirror. "Sorry," I say,
          meaning it. And to prove

just how much, I give her one
of my world-famous kisses.

Okay, maybe that's a bit of
an exaggeration, but I have been

told I'm an exceptional kisser.
I give it my all, and Nikki responds.

Her kiss is like a sudden fever—
white-hot, unplanned, contagious.

Too quickly, she cools, pulls away.
Apology accepted. But no smile,

and she never doesn't smile. I study
her face harder, find anger, concrete

in the set of her jaw, but eiderdown
sorrow in her eyes. "What's wrong?"

She slumps against me, takes
refuge as her sadness flows, wet,

in steady tears. *My dad walked out
on my mom. He wants a divorce.*

THAT'S IT?

I'd like to feel sorry for her, console
her, tell her it's all a huge mistake.

But what I really want to say
is, "Big effin' deal. Divorce?

At least they were together
while you were growing up.

At least you'll get to see him
almost as much as you do now.

At least you know just who
in the bloody hell your father is!"

But that would take Nikki-Complete.
What I hold here is Nikki-in-Tatters.

So I take her hand, lead her
into the kitchen, sit her at the table.

"I brought a little something
that will make you feel better."

I twist one up, half expecting her
to say no. She only smokes weed

on special occasions. Apparently
this occasion qualifies, however.

She takes a big drag, fights not
to cough. Fails, and that makes

      the tears fall harder. He—hack—
      is such a prick. I ca-can't—hack—

      believe he could just up and leave
      Mom. N-not—hack—f-f-for . . . her!

"Who?" None of my business,
of course. But, hey, she brought it up.

      His goddamn boss! You know,
      the bitch who owns the company?

      She's old. Rich, yeah, but old . . .
      Her voice is tinged with hysteria.

      After almost twenty-five years,
      he leaves Mom for . . . for her?

"Here." I pass her the J. "Take
another hit. A little one this time."

      She doesn't cough, but she does ask,
      You'd never cheat on me, would you?

I BITE DOWN HARD

On the impending lie.
Fact is, I've already
cheated on Nikki,
though I'm not sure
why. It was an awful

        mistake, and it only
        happened once, post-
        football-game beer
        binge. God, that girl—
        a Vegas Rebels fan,

and so a rival meant
to be jeered at, not laid—
was a real piece of work.
Anorexic as hell, but
high-horsepower motor,

        revved to the max . . .
        Nikki stares at me,
        waiting for an answer.
        Say something quick,
        idiot. I reach across

the table, take possession
of her hand, look into
the depths of her tear-
glittered eyes. "You
are my one and only."

AS THE WORDS

Slide out of my mouth,
I wish I could mean them.
She is so beautiful, just there.

A fairy seeking wings, and
when she finds them, I know
she'll fly far, far away.

                              Love is like that.

Suddenly I want her more
than anything. Like some
conceit-driven Grimm

Brothers king, I need to
capture my sprite with
trembling hands. Except

                              I could crush her.

Wonder how many small
things of beauty—flowers,
seashells, dragonflies—

have met such a demise.
Wonder how much fragile
love has collapsed

                              beneath the weight of confession.

ENOUGH ALREADY

One too many lit classes,

I guess. A little too much poetry,

dredged up at all the wrong times.

Thanks so much for that, Mom.

      You've got a poet's soul, she told

      me once. *And an old soul at that.*

Whatever that means. I don't feel

so old, for the most part. I do like

words, but this is not the time

for them, nor is it the time for

confessions. There is invitation

in Nikki's eyes. It's time for that.

THE WOOD

In her room is cherry—deep
reddish brown. Elegant.

The sheets on her bed are black
satin. Slick beneath desire-

dampened skin. Her hair is like
a sunburst against the onyx-

colored pillowcase. Its perfume
spices the air with ginger

and some exotic bloom.
The scent fuels my hunger

for her body. I want to own
it, merge with it, become part

        of her. *Hurry,* she urges. But
        the tease is almost the best

part of the game, so I bring her
close and closer with my hands

and mouth and finally I am inside
her. I can't get enough, so we go

and go until the only thing left
is to finish. And still I want more.

Autumn Rose Shepherd
SOMETIMES I SEE FACES

Somehow familiar,
but I don't know why.

I cannot label them,
no matter how intently

I try. They are nameless.
And yet not strangers.

Like Alamo ghosts, they
emerge from deep

of night, materialize
from darkness, deny

my sleep. I would call them
dreams. But that's too easy.

I SUSPECT

One of those faces belongs
          to my mother. It is young, not

much older than mine, but weary,
          with cheeks like stark coastal

cliffs and hollow blue eyes, framed
          with drifts of mink-colored hair.

I don't look very much like her.
          My hair curls, auburn, around

a full, heart-shaped face, and
          my eyes are brown. Or, to be

more creative, burnt umber. Nothing
          like hers, so maybe I'm mistaken

about her identity. Is she my mother?
          Is she the one who christened me

Autumn Rose Shepherd? Pretty
          name. Wish I could live up to it.

AUNT CORA INSISTS

I am pretty. But Aunt Cora
is a one-woman cheering section.
Thank goodness the grandstands
aren't completely empty.

I'm kind of a lone wolf, except
for Cherie, and she's what you
might call a part-time friend.
We hang out sometimes, but

only if she's got nothing better
going on. Meaning no ballet recitals
or play rehearsals or guy-of-the-day
to distract her from those.

But Aunt Cora is always there,
someone I can count on, *through
chowder or broth,* as Grandfather says.
Old Texas talk for "thick or thin."

GENERALLY

Things feel

about the consistency
of milky oatmeal.
With honey.
Raisins.
Nuts.

Most days,

I wake up relatively
happy. Eat breakfast.
Go to school.
Come home.
Dinner.
Homework.
Bed.

Blah, blah, blah.

But sometimes,

for no reason beyond
a loud noise or leather
cleaner smell, I am afraid.
It's like yanking myself
from a nightmare only,
even wide awake,
I can't unstick myself
from the fear of the dream.

I don't want to
leave my room.

CAN'T BEAR THE THOUGHT

Of people staring, I'm sure
they will. Sure they'll know.
Sure they'll think I'm crazy.

The only person I can talk to
is Aunt Cora. I can go to her
all freaked out. Can scream,
"What's the matter with me?"

And she'll open her arms, let me
cry and rant, and never once
has she called me crazy. One

time she said, *Things happened*
when you were little. Things you
don't remember now, and don't want
to. But they need to escape,

need to worm their way out
of that dark place in your brain
where you keep them stashed.

THAT FELT RIGHT

And now, when that
unexplained dread
boxes me in, I take
deep breaths, try to

        free those bad things,
        whatever they are. It
        doesn't always work.
        But sometimes it does.

    And always, always,
    I thank Aunt Cora for
    giving me some smidgen
    of understanding about

        who I am and what
        surprises life might
        have In store for me.
        I swear, without her

I probably would
have jumped off
a bridge the first
time I got my period.

        Yeah, we'd had the basic
        You're a Woman Now
        video and discussion
        in sixth grade. But

    textbook "birds
    and bees" cannot
    even prepare you for
    what that really means.

I HATE WHEN I BLEED

Can't tell my period when to start,
how many hours to make me
miserable. Can't tell it not to come

at all. I have zero control over
any of that, and that really,
really bothers me. See, I've got

a little thing called OCD.
Obsessive-compulsive disorder
is something people make fun of.

But when it's something
you've got, there's nothing
funny about it. First off,

you know you have it, know
some little piece of your brain
is totally out of whack. Nothing

you can do about that, either.
Not without therapy, and that
means telling someone you know

you're just a tiny bit crazy.
How do you admit that without
giving up every bit of power

you have finally managed to grasp?
Some people have it worse than I do,
I guess. I mean I don't wash my hands

seventeen times a day or count
every step I take, then take a couple
more until the exact number from

here to there is divisible by three.
My compulsion is simply order.
Everything in its place, and spaced

exactly so—one inch, no more, no less,
between hairbrush and comb. Two
inches, no more, no less, between pairs

of shoes on my closet floor. Black socks,
upper left corner of my top right dresser
drawer; white socks in the lower right.

I doubt Grandfather has even noticed
how every can in the cupboards is
organized alphabetically, labels out,

or that cleaning supplies beneath
the sink are arranged by color.
But Aunt Cora definitely has.

SHE DOESN'T TAKE IT SERIOUSLY

She thinks it's funny, and funnier
still to mess with my mind by moving

my shoes   farther apart
or puttingmycombinsidemybrush
or arranging a can of
                    yams
                    in front
                       of the
                          applesauce.

She says I should lighten up, quit
beating myself up mentally. I know
she only wants what's best for me,
but sometimes she makes me mad.

If it were easy to throw
                    my
                    clothes
                              into
                    a heap
        on the floor,

of course I'd rather do that than
spend hours
folding them
p r e c i s e l y
right. Right?

I AM IN THE DEN

Arranging Grandfather's
eclectic collection of
paperbacks alphabetically
by author—Graham, Billy;
Grey, Zane; Grisham, John—

when the telephone rings.
I've got it! Grandfather
yells from the kitchen.
I peek at the caller ID.
NV St Prsn—Nevada

State Prison. The collect
calls from Trey come once
in a while. Usually, to listen
to Grandfather's raves,
when his prison account

needs a cash recharge.
Little SOB wants me
*to pay for his cigarettes
and soap? Does he think
I'm made of money?*

Still, he always sends it.
Three times convicted
felon or not, Trey will
always be his son. His son.
And my convict father.

I SLIP QUIETLY

Along the linoleum. Grandfather
does not appreciate me listening in.

But for some reason, my radar
is blipping. There's something

different about this call. Maybe
it's the tone of Grandfather's voice

tipping me off. It's not exactly
hard to hear him. He's yelling.

But despite the high volume, a tremor
makes him sound downright old.

> *I don't give a damn what you want.*
> *You are not welcome in this house.*

> *I told you that when you went away,*
> *and I haven't changed my mind.*

"Went away," meaning he was locked up
by the State of Nevada. Again. That was

eight years ago. I remember he called to
share the news while we were planning

my ninth birthday party. I had no
idea what "five to fifteen" meant.

But it sure seemed to take all the fun
out of talking about balloons and cake.

Apparently it's working out to "more
than five, less than fifteen." At least,

> that's what I'm hearing from the kitchen.
> *You may have paid your debt to society,*
>
> *but you haven't paid your debt to me.*
> *Not to mention to your daughter. She*
>
> *doesn't even know who you are, and*
> *neither do I. Car thief? Drug addict?*
>
> *You just stay the hell away from here.*
> *I don't need that kind of worry.*
>
> *This call is costing an arm and a leg.*
> *I'm going to hang up now.*

AND HE DOES

The phone slams against the table,
        loud enough for me to hear it
        from here. I scoot away from
        the door, down the hall, just as
Grandfather exits the kitchen.

        He looks at me, anger smoking,
                black, in his already dark eyes.
                I suppose you heard all that.
                I hate talking ill about your father,
        but that boy is doomed to go

        straight on down to the devil
                when he dies. He moves toward
                me, trembling slightly. *I should'a*
                beat that boy more. He never
        did have an ounce of respect

        or caring for anyone except for
                himself. Not even for your mama,
                I'm guessing. I told Maureen
                he was gonna end up badly
        if she didn't . . . never mind.

GRANDFATHER IS STERN

To put it too mildly. I love him,
of course. How could I not
love someone who gathered me
in, offered a home and his unique

brand of love? It's hard for him
to love, I think. He has been divorced.
Remarried. Widowed. Left to live
mostly alone until Aunt Cora

reappeared, with little toddler me
tucked haphazardly under one arm.
I *do* love him. But sometimes he's harsh.
"Mean" might be more accurate.

He reminds me of a cop walking
the beat too long, in a bad part
of the city—creased and bitter-
eyed and too early gray. He yells.

Rants. Every once in a while,
he leaves a bruise, no apology.
For my own good, he says, *So you
don't end up like your father.*

More than once I've heard him try to
blame Trey's mom for her son turning
out bad. *Maureen never understood
that kids need discipline, or they'll ride*

*roughshod over you. A good switching
by a loving hand never hurt no one.*
Quoted directly from his own father
would be my guess, and the oxymoronic

bite of the statement slipped
his notice completely, right along
with the bigger issue he insists
on ignoring: Maureen left him because

of his own drug habit and the reasons
behind it. The pills he pops like Tic Tacs
are legal. Prescribed to moderate
sleep problems and anger problems

and mood problems that swing him
from suicidal to crazy happy in
the space of a few hours. All I can
say is thank God for modern medicine.

SOMETIMES, WHEN IT'S JUST

Grandfather and me, if he's downed
the exact right combination
of pills and brew, he'll talk

about growing up in a little
backwater town maybe
six hours north of here.

Sweetwater may not be so
very far from San Antonio,
but it's a wide world apart.

We were possum poor and not
exactly unhappy being that way.
'Course we didn't know better.

My pa was a born-again Baptist,
and Sunday was the best day
of the week because Baptists

respect the Sabbath. Weren't
no cotton rows hoed on Sunday,
that's for sure. Not a single one.

His accent is honey-thick Texas.
But Aunt Cora's is a mild imitation.
She moved to California young,

when Maureen divorced Grandfather.
Still, she carries a hint of Good
Ol' Boy (Girl?) in her inflection.

Me? I'm fighting it, though it may
be a losing battle. Still, despite
living in Texas for most of my life,

somehow it isn't Home. And
the really messed-up part of that
is, I have no clear idea where

Home might be. It's not here
in San Antonio. Not with Grandfather
or Aunt Cora, though it really

should feel that way. Not with
Trey, wherever he might settle
down if they actually let him go.

No, Home is somewhere else.
I don't know if it's a place
I've already been, or one

I've yet to find. But I'm pretty
sure the answer is tangled up
in Where I Came From.

AND WHERE I CAME FROM

Is tangled up
                    in those faces

        I see. At least,
                        I'm pretty sure

it is. No one here
                    will tell me much

        about why I'm here.
                            Other than the jail

            thing, which I get.

                        But I know I must

                            have more family
        somewhere. Why

                        have they never
    tried to get hold
                            of me? It's all so

                    confusing, especially
    when the people
                    I do have insist
                            on keeping secrets.

43

I HAVE MANAGED

To learn a handful
of assorted details
about the jigsaw

        puzzle

that is my beginning.
Nothing what you'd
call solid. Bits and

        pieces.

I know I was born
in Nevada. Reno,
I'm told. But I

        don't

know if my mother
still lives there.
When I ask, I

        always

get the standard
answer: *You don't really
want to try and*

        connect

with her, do you?
Well, what if I do?

        Do they

think if I found her,
I'd love them less?

ALL THINGS CONSIDERED

I'm not sure if I want to connect
with her or not. And even if I do,
I have no idea where to start. Not
like Grandfather will share information.

Reno? Maybe. But it's a big place,
and Nevada is bigger. And why
think she still lives there? Besides,
I don't even know her name.

I wonder
         if she
                remembers mine.

Maybe she's dead. Disabled.
Brain fried too crispy to even try
to stop by and say hello for fifteen
years. I was two when Aunt Cora

took custody of me, which was just
about the time the State of Nevada
took custody of my parents. Locked
them up that time for a couple of years.

Aunt Cora says
         the monster
                swallowed them.

THE MONSTER

Is what they called their crystal.
We learned about it in school.

How it messes up your brain.
            Makes your teeth go rotten.
Blasts caustic chemicals
            through arteries and veins.

How just a little spoonful
            keeps you up for days,
no desire for food, high
            until you crash. Nosedive.

How using once or twice
            can hook you. Take your mind
captive. Agitate cerebral cells
            until you wind up psychotic.

What they didn't say is how
the monster chews up families.

MINE ISN'T THE ONLY ONE

But it's the only one I'm qualified
to talk about. I don't know if my parents

    were ever in love, but for argument's
    sake, I'll imagine they were.

        So along comes the monster. Then what?
        Sex, obviously, or I wouldn't be here.

    Good sex? Bad sex? Group sex?
    All of the above? I mean, why did any

of that have to change because they
decided to get high together? I don't

    understand. Did they both go gay in
    lockup? Decide they liked same-sex

        sex better than sex with each other?
        Did they ever even try to put things

right with each other after they got out?
Did they ever even once think about me?

Summer Lily Kenwood
SCREAMING

I learned not to
                    scream
a long time ago.
Learned to
                    bite
down hard
against pain,
                    keep
my little mouth
wedged shut.
                    Fighting
back was useless,
anyway. I was
                    fragile
at three, and Zoe
was a hammer.
                    Girls
are stinkier than
boys when they
                    get
dirty, she'd say,
scrubbing until I
                    hurt.
And if I cried
out, I hurt
                    worse.

I'M FIFTEEN NOW

And though Zoe is no longer
    Dad's lay of the day, I'll never
        forget her or how he closed
            his eyes to the ugly things
                she did to me regularly.

He never said a word about
    the swollen red places. Never
        told her to stop. He had to know,
            and if he didn't, she must have
                been one magical piece of ass.

Cynical? Me? Yeah, maybe
    I am, but then, why wouldn't
        I be? Since the day I was born,
            I've been passed around. Pushed
                around. Drop-kicked around.

The most totally messed-up
    part of that is the more it
        happens, the less I care. Anyway,
            as foster homes go, this one is
                okay. Except for the screaming.

SCREAMING, AGAIN

It's Darla's favorite method
of communication, and not
really the best one for a foster

parent. I mean, aren't they
supposed to *guide us gently*?

> Her shrill falsetto saws through
> the hollow-core bedroom door.
>
> *Ashante! How many times*
> *do I have to tell you to make*
> *your goddamn bed? It's a rule!*

Jeez, man. Ashante is only
seven, and she hasn't even
been here a week. Darla

really should get an actual job,
leave the fostering to Phil,

who is patient and kind-eyed
and willing enough to smile.
Plus, he's not bad-looking

for a guy in his late forties.
And I've yet to hear him scream.

DARLA IS A DIFFERENT STORY

Here it comes, directed at me.
> *Summer! Is your homework finished?*

Hours ago, but I call, "Almost."
> *Well, hurry it up, for God's sake.*

Like God needs to be involved. "Okay."
> *I need some help with dinner.*

Three other girls live here too.
> *And turn down that stupid music.*

The music belongs to one of them.
> *I can barely hear myself think.*

She thinks? "It's Erica's music."
> *Well, tell her to turn it down, please.*

Whatever. At least she said please.
> *And would you please stop yelling?*

GAWD!

My neck flares, collarbone
to earlobes. Like Erica
couldn't hear her scream?

I fling myself off the bed,
cross my room and the hall
just beyond in mere seconds.

"Erica!" (Shit, I *am* yelling.)
"Can't you . . . ?" But when
I push through the door,

the music on the other side
slams into me hard. No
way could she have heard

the commotion. "Great
song, but Darla wants you
to turn it down. What is it?"

Erica reaches for the volume.
"Bad Girlfriend." By Theory of a Dead-
man. I just downloaded it today.

She looks at me, and her eyes
repeat a too-familiar story.
Erica is wired. Treed, in fact.

I TOTALLY KNOW TREED

In sixth grade, the D.A.R.E.
dorks came in, spouting stats
to scare us into staying straight.
But by then, I knew more than
they did about the monster
because of my dad and his women,

including my so-called mom.
Her ex, too, and his sister and cousin.
Plus a whole network of stoners
connecting them all. The funny
thing is, none of them have a fricking
clue that I am so enlightened.

Tweakers always think no one
knows. Just like Erica right now.
"Shit, girl. You go to dinner lit
like that, you're so busted.
Darla may be a bitch. But she's
not stupid, and neither is Phil."

        Here comes the denial.
        Her shoulders go stiff and
        her head starts twisting
        side to side. But she doesn't
        dare let her eyes meet mine.
        What are you talking about?

"Hey, no prob. I'm not a spy,
and it's all your life anyway.
I'm just saying you might
as well be wearing a sign
that says 'I Like Ice.' If
I were you, I'd skip dinner."

I turn, start for the door,
and Erica's voice stops me.
It's just so hard to feel good,
you know? I do know. And
more than that, it's just
so incredibly hard to feel.

MAYBE THAT'S WHY

I have also felt the gnawing desire to try
crystal, despite knowing what it did

        to
        Barely There Dad

        to
        Rarely Here Mom.

Maybe they were just trying to feel
something too. Something besides

        heat
        for each other

        hate
        for each other.

It's too bad they hooked up at all. Because
the only things they have in common

        are
        giving me life

        and
        tearing my life apart.

MY MOTHER

Gifts me with a visit once, maybe
twice, a year. Our conversations
seesaw between inane and trite:

> How's school?

"Okay, I guess."

> Still running track?

"Not for a while."

> Extracurricular stuff?

"Not really, no."

How they *should* go is like this:

> How's school?

"Better than could be
expected, considering
I only have foster parents
to make sure I'm there
on time, with breakfast in my
belly, encouraging my rather
outstanding performance,
despite the fact that no
one really gives a shit."

Still running track?
"Not since the day a wind
sprint almost sent me to
the hospital because my
asthma (which can no doubt
be attributed to your
tweaking during the first
trimester you were pregnant
with me, and smoking the entire
nine months) kicked in so
hard I could barely suck
enough air to keep my
face from turning blue."

Extracurricular stuff?
"Sure, because I've been
encouraged so regularly
to explore my unique set
of talents, huh? And, like,
I've got parents who'd
come watch me perform
even if I could sing or act
or dance or whatever.
No, Mother. My only
extracurricular stuff has
to do with making out."

I COULDN'T SAY THAT, THOUGH

Because then she'd feel validated
about her other regular line of inquiry:

> *Boyfriends? No?*
> *Girlfriends, then?*
> *Either way, it's all*
> *good with me.*

I hate that she thinks sex
is the only thing on my mind.

The last time she went there,
she was taking me back to Darla

and Phil's, after a long weekend
of not-quite-bonding at her tacky

> Vegas apartment. *Any news on*
> *the boyfriend front? Getting a little?*

Like I'd confide in her if I was.
"Who do you think I am? You?"

Sometimes, I guess, I'm snappish.
But doesn't she deserve snap?

> Her comeback was immediate,
> not to mention completely lame.

Summer Lily Kenwood!
Why are you so angry?

"Let's start with my name.
Like my life is so full of sunshine,

and like you didn't know how
crappy it would be the day you

named me. And then there's
you, who chose to go ahead

and have me, even though
you didn't want me. . . ."

> She jerked her piece-of-crap car
> over against the curb. Lit a new
>
> cigarette off the one already
> irritating my asthma. *Shut your*
>
> *mouth. I did want you. Still want you.*
> *I just don't have enough resources. . . .*

"God, Mother. You sound like
an investment banker instead of

a total loser tweaker. Resources?
What you don't have is enough love."

IT WAS NASTY

Mean.
In your face.
Designed for
overt reaction.
And it got zero.

She pulled away
from the curb, exhaling
nicotine poison, regardless
of my little brothers, chilling
in the backseat. Drove me home,
dropped me off without a single word.

I don't know
if she was stunned
into silence, or if her
meth-mangled brain couldn't
grasp what I said. Either way, we

haven't spoken
in months. I'm pretty
sure she was straight that
day. Pretty sure she's been
straight every time I've seen her.

Always, she's chain-
smoking anxious. Often,
she's angry. I've never seen
her happy. Was she ever happy?
Was she ever happy when not using?

GODDAMN METH

Has ruined
so many lives.

       Her life.
          Dad's life.
             My life.

             Friends' lives,
             because they use
             or because people
             they love use.

                They don't call it
                the monster for
                nothing. It chews
                people up, spits 'em
                out, often unsalvageable.

So why have I been even
a little tempted to take
a spin with the monster?

IT'S NOT HARD TO FIND

Here in Bakersfield. In fact,
    California's central valleys
        are fertile ground for more
            than pistachios and wheat.

They are, in fact, a sort
    of monster lair. Bikers
        have busily built labs
            in the area for many years.

And while law enforcement
    has been busy too, there's
        a lot of "nothing" out here.
            They can't be everywhere.

I know all this because
    my boyfriend's Gramps
        was an original Hells
            Angel manufacturer.

He's in prison too. Not for
        cooking it or transporting
                it, but for stabbing a guy
                        in a bar fight while high on it.

That's not something Matt
        is proud of. In fact, he hates
                meth, and what it's done
                        to his family. If he knew

the idea of trying it had
        even crossed my mind,
                he would not be happy.
                        And if he had the slightest

notion that his best friend,
        Kyle, is the one who keeps
                offering it, Matt might end
                        up just like his grandfather.

SO FAR

I've refused.

>Refused the meth.
>Refused the scene.
>Refused Kyle's kiss.

Well, sort of.

>Once he cornered me.
>Once he held me close.
>Once our lips connected.

Matt was gone.

>Away from school.
>Away from town.
>Away from me.

I almost gave in.

>Almost relented.
>Almost submitted.
>Almost said okay.

But I remembered.

>Kyle is a stoner.
>Kyle is a player.
>Kyle is Matt's best friend.

I THINK OF THEM BOTH

As I lie in bed, body
asking for sleep
while my brain insists on

            flashing

cerebral photographs.
Phffft. Matt and me,
last summer, making

            out

like there was no tomorrow.
Love that phrase. Because
without tomorrow,
what's wrong with

            some

spectacular today? *Phffft.*
Kyle, touching me,
in a totally different

            kind

of way than Matt could
even imagine. *Phffft.*
Matt, a solid dream

            of a

guy telling me, *I love
you,* as we lie together
in a tall field of wheat.

            Warning!

The next photo is X-rated.
And when I wake, I am still
warm from the night before.

MAYBE WHAT I NEED TO DO

Is make us a threesome.
        If I belonged to some weird
                religious sect, that's what
                        I'd do. Except don't all those
                weird religious sects expect
        two girls to a guy, instead of
the obviously better way to go?

What is wrong with women,
        anyway? Two dudes. One you.
                Yeah, baby. That's what I'm
                        talking about. It's stupid
                as hell to think that way,
        but WTF? It's my effing
daydream, isn't it? I keep

dreaming it right through
        breakfast. On the short bus
                ride to school. But then, as
                        I pace the sidewalk, waiting,
                a sudden realization hits. Two
        guys. One girl. Can't do that.
If I did, I would be my mother.

I WATCH THE PAIR

Of them now, coming up the walk, cutting
through the herd trying to make first bell.

Matt is two inches taller. So why does Kyle
loom larger? Why should that matter at all?

Kyle spots me first, waves. There is much
in his smile that Matt can't see. But I can.

Matt says something to Kyle, slaps his shoulder,
turns away from him, heads toward me.

I love the confidence in his stride,
goal in sight, no hint of hesitation

> until he reaches it. Reaches me. *Hey.*
> Not exactly eloquent, but that's okay.

> Lips have better uses. The kiss they bring
> is autumn rain—wet, warm, wished for.

Matt bracelets me with strong arms.
He smells clean, but not perfumed,

like Tide detergent and Ivory soap.
I am safe here against his chest,

where his heart thumps desire.
This is all any girl could want.

So why do my open eyes stray over
his shoulders? And why am I satisfied

to see Kyle staring back at me?
He gives a little shrug, continues

        inside, just as the first bell blares.
        Matt pulls away reluctantly. *Guess*

        that's our cue, huh? He gives me
        another quick kiss, slides his arm

around my waist, hustles me toward
the door and the long row of lockers

just beyond. At the far end, Sierra
Freeman has cornered Kyle. Only

his body language loudly says he's
not exactly frantic to get away.

MATT WALKS ME

To my first-period class—
        AP English. Thank God
        for advanced placement.
        The regular curriculum
would drive me bonkers.

I taught myself to read
        before kindergarten.
        I lived with Grandma Jean
        and Grandpa Carl then,
and books were everywhere.

Grandpa helped me learn
        to count. After that, math
        was easy. Two grandparents,
        take away one (goddamn
cigarettes got him too young)

leaves one. And when that
        one goes just a little crazy
        having lost her husband
        of thirty-nine years,
two grandparents take away

one equals zero. Anyway,
      words and numbers have
      always been easy for me.
      And even without people
who care, my grades rock.

      Matt, who is clueless
            about much more than
            my relatively curvy
            exterior, likes to tease
      me. *Who knew a brainiac*

      could be so much fun?
            is one of his favorite
            lines. "Fun," meaning
            I let him cop regular
      feels of those curves.

He knows I take all AP
      classes, but somehow
      has no real idea just
      how brainy I am. Okay
by me. It's an advantage.

Hunter

SATURDAY

The alarm blares again.
Second snooze cycle?
Third? Behind my eyelids,
morning is bright. Eightish?
I roll over and open one eye.
Almost nine. Damn. Up I go.

I've got to land an earlier
air shift, at least if I have
to keep doing remotes.
Live broadcasts are fun.
But it's not good to do them
with bags under your eyes.

Not if you want to look
like a radio star. Okay,
maybe I haven't reached
"star" status. The stars do
morning or afternoon
drives. I pull ten p.m. to two

a.m. twice a week. But
they *are* weekend nights,
so at least a few people
are up late, listening.
I even have groupies.
Hey, maybe I *am* a star.

THE REMOTE

Is at the football game.
The UNR Wolf Pack versus

the Boise State Broncos.
Boise is a powerhouse

team and generally cleans
our clock, but UNR has got

one radical quarterback
this season, plus an all-state

running back. Never know.
We just might take 'em.

Wolf Pack fans are ready to howl.
The game should be packed.

Which means I'd better
get a move on. Traffic

will be a bitch. A glance
out the window confirms

it's a crystal-edged October
day. Perfect football weather.

I shave. Shower. No time
for breakfast, a quick brush

to excise morning mouth.
Jeans. Long-sleeved blue tee

sporting the X logo. It's a little
wrinkled, but the black leather

bomber will camouflage that.
Socks. Socks? My sock drawer

is empty. Oh, well. Yesterday's
shouldn't be too bad. Mom's always

> griping about my dirty laundry.
> *All you have to do is get it from*
>
> *your room to the laundry room.*
> *Twenty-five steps total. How hard*
>
> *could that be?* The word isn't "hard."
> It's "organized." Not my best thing.

Yesterday's socks it is. New pair
of Nikes, barely scuffed at all.

Out the door in twenty minutes.
If I'm lucky, I won't be late.

IT'S A HALF-HOUR DRIVE

To the station. Another forty
        minutes to load the remote
        broadcasting equipment
into the company van.

Just about the time
        I'm ready to roll,
        a beater Pontiac burps
into the parking lot.

Oh, no. It's Montana.
        Her real name is Corrine,
        but she wanted her air
name to play off

        Hannah Montana.
            Don't ask me why.
            Morning, she breathes,
        in her best "I'm trying

        not to sound like
            the dingbat I am" voice.
            (Not that it works.)
        Awesome day, huh?

"Uh, yeah." I load
        the last speaker. "Well,
        I'm about ready. As soon
as Rick gets here . . ."

Montana's head swings
             side to side. *Didn't you*
             get the message? Rick
has a major flu bug.

She moves closer. Too
             close. Her lips are four
             inches from mine when
she says, *It's me and you.*

No, no, no! It's bad
             enough working a remote
             with Rick the Brick Denio,
whose "I'm God's gift

to the world" attitude
             has thirty years in radio
             to back it up. Montana's
"hey, I'm the shit" pose

comes from bottled
             blond hair and way-
             too-round-to-be-real
36DDs. And, fake or

no, those babies were
             designed for Montana
             Disney (no lie!) to steal
the show wherever she goes.

ESPECIALLY FOOTBALL GAMES

Especially with those DDs
encased in a gray angora sweater,
and her equally impressive ass

advertised by a short, tight navy
skirt. Wolf Pack colors are silver
and blue. She's a one-of-a-kind fan,

one every guy walking by can't help
but notice. It's irritating, but what
really pisses me off is how she just

stands there, flaunting fuzzy silver
and tight navy blue, while I do all
the work, setting up the X tailgate

party. Even Rick would have helped.
At least we have a designated
parking spot in the alumni lot. People

are parked down the hill, a half mile
or more away. By the time they reach
us, they're huffing and puffing.

Montana sympathizes. *Long walk?*
Well, come on over here and have
a hot dog and soda, on the X.

MOST OF THEM

Are already drinking beer.
But they take the dog, if only

for the chance to stand that
close to those amazing ta-tas.

I have to admit, Montana
is great advertising, if a mediocre

on-air personality. She knows
jack about music. She'll probably

go on to fame and fortune as
a spokesmodel or something.

Anyway, I watch her work
the mostly male crowd until,

    finally, a couple of cute girls
    wiggle up to me. *Are you Hunter*

    Haskins? says the curvy redhead.
    'Cause I really *love your show!*

    Yeah, agrees the slender brunette.
    I listen every weekend. You're good.

My turn to flirt. "Sweetheart,
I am so much better than good."

Then I remember, "Hey, are you
interested in a hot dog?"

The girls dissolve into laughter,
and I realize how that sounded.

I flush, hot despite the nip in the air.
"Uh, I meant a Polish sausage."

        That makes Red laugh even
        harder. *Is Haskins a Polish name?*

        The brunette's eyes are watering.
        And just how big is that sausage?

Wow. Obnoxious. So why does
the thought of a threesome

cross my perverted mind?
"I've never had a complaint,

if that's what you mean." A gasp
behind me makes me turn. . . .

AND THERE IS NIKKI

And not only that,
            but there is Nikki with
                        her parents, UNR alumni

and rabid Pack fans.
            But not exactly fans
                        of Hunter Haskins.

Surely they realize this
            is part of the radio
                        personality game?

"Oh, hey!" I reach for
            Nikki, who shrinks
                        back a little. "Great

to see you all here.
            How about a . . ."
                        Shit. If I say hot dog,

my groupies are gonna
            howl. I turn my back
                        on them completely.

"Want some lunch?"
            I gesture toward
                        the gathered X fans

all happily munching
            Polish sausages. Nikki,
                        red-faced, shakes her head.

Her mom, all stuck-up,
                slides her arm around
                            Nikki's shoulder. *No.*

                    Her dad looks slightly
                            amused, but his voice
                                    is stiff. *We already ate.*

"Oh. Okay." How do
            I make this right? "Nik,
                    can I talk to you a sec?"

She starts to say no,
                but if I don't fix this
                            now, it might be unfixable.

"Please?" I take her
            arm, pull her away
                    from her mother's grasp

and off to one side. "Hey.
                Those girls are listeners.
                        You are the one I love."

I NOTICE HER MOM AND DAD

Watching us. Standing
a couple of feet apart,
as if they want nothing
to do with each other.

And I remember. "So,
are your parents back
together?" I know her
answer before she says,

> *Not really. He claims*
> *he wants to come home,*
> *but he still wants to work*
> *with . . . with* her.

His boss. And maybe
the woman he loves
more than he loves
his wife and daughter.

> *There's a big alumni*
> *party today. They only*
> *came together to keep up*
> *appearances.* She starts

to tear up again, and
I pull her into my arms.
Kiss her forehead softly.
"It will all work out. I promise."

WHY DO I PROMISE

Shit like that?
Then again, it

        will

all work out.
Just not necessarily
the way she wants

        it

to. I look at her
mom, rigid as iron,
suspicion written

        all

over her face. And
why not? Her husband
has blatantly

        come out

about falling for
someone else. Why
would she want him
back, anyway?

        In the

final analysis, their
marriage will forever
be stained. In the long
run, stay or go, it's a

        wash.

IN MY ARMS

Nikki sways, relaxes
just the slightest bit.

I take the opportunity
to repeat, "I love you."

   Love you, too. Her whisper
   is shaky, like aspen leaves

   in a bold autumn breeze.
   They're waiting for me.

"I know. But I'll see you later,
right?" Her answer is slow

   coming. Finally she gives
   me a lukewarm, *I guess so.*

We turn back toward the X
lunch line. My groupies, thank

God, have wandered off.
Nikki's mom watches us

with relentless eyes, unlike
her dad, who is focused on Montana.

   That fact does not escape
   Nikki. *God. He's such a dog.*

HE DOES KIND OF LOOK

Like one—a basset hound,
maybe, or a cocker spaniel.
A dog with dopey eyes.

Nikki pulls away from me,
pushes between her parents,
forms a three-link chain.

They start toward the gate
just as the cannon fires,
signaling first kickoff.

Hot dogs in hand, the X fans
disperse, leaving Montana
and me to watch the stragglers.

        After a while, Montana turns
        to me. *Pretty girlfriend*, she says.
        You two serious, or what?

Without my telling them to,
my shoulders hunch into a shrug.
"We're not, like, getting married

or anything. But I like her a lot."
Her question was out of left field,
my answer bordering on evasive.

Looked more like love to me.
Meaning, I guess, that she was looking.
Mind if I give you a little advice?

Advice? Who does she think
she is? Dr. Phil in drag? But
what the hell. "Uh, guess not."

Radio is entertainment, or should
be, anyway. Your jock persona
should feel real to your listeners.

But never forget that it's fabricated,
created in the name of entertainment.
Once you start thinking it's real,

start taking the fake you too seriously,
the truly important things in your
life will vanish. Believe me, I know.

I do believe her. But why?
Montana is schlock to the nth
degree. "Do you want to elaborate?"

Her smile, sad, makes her pretty.
Maybe someday. For now, I'll
just say I used to be married.

MARRIED?

          Hard to believe.
Divorced?
          Even harder.
          She's either
older
          than she looks,
          or she's lived
faster
          than most.
          Probably the latter.

          But why do I think
          that? To be
honest,
          I don't know her at all.
          She could be PhD
smart,
          might trump Rick Denio
          when it comes to being
witty.

          If I dug deep enough
          beneath the facade,
who
          would I find? Is Corrine
          standing beside me? Or
is she
          really Montana?

AS I PACK UP THE VAN

I think back to when
I was a kid, trying too
hard to be "just like
everyone else," when
I felt totally different.

Not an outcast, exactly.
Just different. I tried
so hard to look normal
that everybody noticed.
And bullies pounced.

I entered public school
late to the game, after
a couple of years
of parochial torture.
So I didn't start third

grade with solid buddies
to back me up. When
someone picked on me,
I crumbled at first. Then,
when I got tired of it,

I learned to push back.
Being about the biggest
kid in my class helped.
But I never wanted to
fight. I wanted friends.

MAYBE CORRINE

Just wanted friends,
        and that's why she turned

        into Montana. Maybe she
wanted revenge. Wonder

why her marriage sank.
        Stupid question. No way

        were people meant to be
monogamous. Not human

behavior. Human behavior
        of the nonmonogamous

        type is all around me here.
Guys smooching on girls,

obviously "their" girls, yet
        checking out other girls

        walking by. Girls aren't
a whole lot better, and this

is only the "checking" out
        stuff. The actually "doing"

        stuff behind each other's
backs is almost as bad.

FOR EXAMPLE

In the distance, a couple arrives
very late to the game. Not long

> ago, the cannon boomed the start
> of the second quarter. The man walks

quickly, two steps in front of the woman,
up the steep hill from the east parking lot.

> His near lope and the solid set
> of his shoulders tell me he's pissed,

or at least determined to reach
the gate before she does. She, on

> the other hand, seems just as resolute
> to continue at her own measured speed.

Way to go, lady. Don't let him stress
you out. Whoa. Wait. As the man

> crowns the hill, stomps into view,
> his silhouette becomes very familiar.

I know him. Know him well, in fact.
It's my dad. And she, I assume, is my mom.

THAT DETAIL IS CONFIRMED

As they get closer, as is another
assumption I made earlier. Dad
is definitely not happy. His scowl
creases his face, makes him look

a decade older than his fifty-seven
years. I wave to draw his attention.
When he sees me, his expression
softens, but only a modicum.

Like from "ready to kick someone's
ass" to "maybe I'll just mess him up
a little." I'd like to say I've never
seen him like this before, but why

lie? Dad possesses a temper,
and patience isn't his best thing.
Mom says I take after him that way.
I have no idea what she means.

"Hey, Dad," I say as he pulls even.
"What's going on?" Mom chugs
up after him, and I add, "Hi, Mom.
Sorry I missed breakfast."

On Saturdays, if Mom is home
instead of book touring, she tries
to make breakfast special. There
was a time when I wouldn't miss one.

Mom smiles, and in kind of a polar
opposite way to Dad, the crinkles
around her eyes plump up. *No prob.*
Sometimes sleep trumps food.

Dad snorts impatiently. *We're*
late. "Circumstances beyond
our control" and all. Can we talk
at dinner? Still pissy. Poor Mom.

He starts off, leaving Mom
standing here. Once his back
is solidly pointed at me,
I whisper, "What's wrong?"

She shrugs. *Nothing you need*
to worry about. Kristina's latest
scheme is all. She not-quite-hugs
me. *I'd better catch up. TTFN.*

KRISTINA, SCHEME QUEEN

That could be her epitaph.
And her obit could contain
the following resume:

Job Title: Drug manufacturer and trafficker.
Job Description: Make easy money cooking meth
                    and moving it, Point A to Point B.
                    (Caveat: Ingredients are volatile.)

Job Title: Prison inmate.
Job Description: Get paid thirty-six cents per hour
                    painting murals on cafeteria walls.
                    (Caveat: Goes toward restitution.)

Job Title: Boy toy.
Job Description: Low pay, but all the sex you can ask
                    for. Just lay back and spread your legs.
                    (Caveat: Unprotected sex equals babies.)

Job Title: Newspaper saleslady.
Job Description: Pyramid possibilities if you form
                    a crew of loser teenagers.
                    (Caveat: High school dropouts are lazy.)

Job Title: Used car saleslady.
Job Description: No salary, but decent commission
                    for offing overpriced lemons.
                    (Caveat: Lots of used car lots; few suckers.)

Job Title:	Rap video extra.
Job Description:	Major bucks for slinking around on set, pretending to fawn over rap star. (Caveat: Some rap stars are phonies.)
Job Title:	Stage mother.
Job Description:	Shuttle your kid from casting call to casting call, hoping *he'll* get paid something someday. (Caveat: You and thousands of stage mothers.)
Job Title:	Mail-order minister.
Job Description:	Perform cheap outdoor weddings for tips because you can't afford to own a chapel. (Caveat: Most couples prefer a hokey chapel.)
Job Title:	Golf tournament caddie.
Job Description:	Great tips for wearing short shorts and lugging older men's heavy clubs hole to hole. (Caveat: Not always talking golf clubs.)
Job Title:	Part-time limo driver.
Job Description:	Long hours on call, unless you're ballsy enough to work the airport and dredge up biz. (Caveat: Might as well drive a taxi.)
Job Title:	Mother.
Job Description:	Not really sure what that is.

CYNICAL?

You bet. But the truth
is, for Kristina, the next
"amazing opportunity"
is always within sight.

        Why can't she ever
        get things right?

Dad believes she came
into the world hungry
to break rules, argue.
Instigate a fight.

        She has a short fuse
        too easy to ignite.

Mom, who is gentler,
and carried her for nine
months, thinks of Kristina
in a different light.

        She was a special child.
        Beautiful. Talented. Bright.

I mostly only see her on
holidays. She has a truck-
driver mouth. Smokes too
much, is wound too tight.

        Like a hummingbird,
        denied the freedom of flight.

Autumn
CHANGE IS COMING

The surety of that has augered
its way into my brain, stirring up

all those buried childhood fears. I
deal with the uncertainty of tomorrow

by über-controlling today.
Which means getting up an hour

early to make double sure
my room is spotless—fresh

sheets and pillowcase; no
dirty clothes in the hamper;

trash emptied; furniture
dusted; carpet vacuumed—

before I even think about
heading out the door to school.

This morning is in perfect order.
We'll see what evening brings.

AUNT CORA

Doesn't seem to notice
the scent of change in the air.
She sings as she busies herself

in the kitchen, making breakfast.
Usually we all just settle for cereal,
but today I smell a hot griddle.

Pancakes? Something is definitely
going on. The domestic goddess
thing so isn't her. "Morning."

> Her back is to me, and she jumps
> a little before turning, red-faced.
> *You scared me half to death!*

But she's laughing, and I can't
help but laugh too. "Kind of
an overstatement, don't you think?

And what's up with the pancakes?
Going Rachael Ray on us, or what?"
I watch her ladle thick, lumpy batter.

> *Rachael Ray? Ha-ha. Don't think*
> *so. Still, it never hurts to brush*
> *up on your culinary skills, does it?*

She flips a hotcake like a pro.
The weird thing is, I can only
remember her ever making them

maybe two or three times in
the past. "So what's *really* going
on with you? Something to do

with all the late nights out the past
few weeks?" She's been gone a lot
lately, and I'm pretty sure there's more

to it than her working part-time at
Olé Tex-Mex and going to school
three days a week to learn massage

> therapy. *Better late than never,*
> she told Grandfather and me when
> she embarked on her new career path.
>
> *I don't want to wait tables forever.*
> What she didn't say was she doesn't
> want to stay single forever either.

SHE DOESN'T SAY THAT NOW

But she does say, *Well, you never*
            know. I just might want to make
            pancakes for someone special
someday. Uh . . . not that you're

not special. I mean . . . If her face
            was red before, it's pickled
            beet purple now. The look
on my own face must communicate

something loud and clear, because
            her shoulders slump slightly. *Okay,*
            might as well confess. I met this
guy. He's my teacher, actually,

and he is incredible. She spits
            out a list of attributes: *tall,*
            gorgeous, smart, professional.
Then, a major ding: *divorced.*

Divorced? Like with alimony
            and child support? How old
            is the guy, anyway? Might as
well ask. "How old is he, anyway?"

I expect her to say forty-five,
              maybe even fifty. So it comes
              as a major surprise when she
answers, *Thirty-one. I know it's*

              kind of weird to think about
                     going out with someone
                     who's younger. But stranger
              things happen every day, right?

She said *think about going*
              out with . . . So . . . "Does
              that mean you aren't going
out with him yet, or what?"

Not sure why the idea of her
              dating this guy bothers me so
              much. He's not like her first
or anything. But something seems

              different. *No . . . yes . . . uh . . .*
                     Not like real dates. No movies
                     or dancing or anything. Just
              coffee and stuff. But I hope . . .

SHE PAUSES

At the *thump . . . th-thump*
of Grandfather lumbering
like an old bear up the hall.

        His question precedes him
        through the doorway. *What is that*
        I'm smelling? A hot breakfast?

Aunt Cora puts a finger to her lips,
but it is the uneasiness in her eyes
that swears me to secrecy.

        Yep, she says. *I must have dreamed*
        about pancakes, because I woke
        up half-desperate for them.

Thump . . . th-thump . . . thump.
Slower than usual. He must
have had a toss-n-turn night.

        Pull up a chair, instructs Aunt
        Cora. *They're just about ready.*
        Apple butter or maple syrup?

The only answer is both. I watch
Grandfather ease into a chair.
Aunt Cora sets a heaping plate

in front him. He inhales buttery
steam, takes a big bite. *Hope you
dream about breakfast more often.*

He gives her a funny look, one
I can only interpret as sensing
something different about her.

She's not about to fill him in.
*If we had pancakes too often, you
wouldn't appreciate them so much.*

Grandfather downs a short stack,
then he says to me, *I have to run
an errand. Want a ride to school?*

Unusual. He hardly ever
goes anywhere. But what
else can I say? "Uh, sure."

THE FIFTEEN-MINUTE RIDE

Seems to take an hour. Unlike Aunt Cora,
Grandfather is definitely fishing the same

tide of anxiety I find myself trolling.
He is taut as a tug-of-war rope. Impossible

to slacken, despite the fact that lately he's been
downing bourbon instead of beer, along

with bigger and bigger doses of meds. He falls
asleep in his chair every night around eight.

Even now, with coffee rather than booze
chasing his mood fixers, his voice is muddy

      when he finally cracks the wall of silence.
      Your father is getting out next week.

Just the way he says it—all quivery
and ice-cold—sends shivers through me.

"I thought it might be soon. I heard
you on the phone the other day."

      He says he wants to see you. How
      do you feel about that? He turns

a corner and the school pops into
view. Trey wants to see me? What for?

And how do I feel about seeing
him after eight years in prison,

eight more years of him being nothing
to me but sporadic collect calls?

"I don't know," I tell Grandfather
as he turns into the passenger drop-

off zone, pulls over against the curb.
"I'll have to think about it." I get out

of the car. What I said was a lie. I know
exactly how I think about it. I hate Trey

for leaving me. Wish I could love him,
but don't have a clear idea how.

Do I want to see him? Part of me does.
The other part thinks he ought to take

a flying leap off a very short pier. Maybe
"I don't know" wasn't a lie after all.

I'LL NEVER FORGET

The last time Trey blew back
into my life. I was almost five,
and he was on parole after

serving two years for fraud.
It was not his first time in lockup.

When he came to the door, I had no
idea who he was. Grandfather and
Aunt Cora don't keep many photos

of him, and the ones they do have
are from long before he ever

started messing around
with meth. He is handsome
in those pictures—tall and strong,

with dark hair and curious gray
eyes and a killer smile. The guy

who came to Grandfather's door
looked like a derelict. I clung
to Aunt Cora's skirt as if I were

sewn to the hem. It was a safe
place I knew all too well.

Hey, sis! Trey planted a big
not-brotherly kiss on her lips.
Then he spotted me. *Autumn?*

His voice held need, and his
eyes were steel. *Come to Daddy.*

Daddy? No. I didn't have one
of those. A big ol' twister
started up in my gut. I backed

behind Aunt Cora, burrowed
deeper. Trey reached for me.

"Noooo!" I screamed, and
turned to run. But not quick
enough. Bark-rough hands

clamped around my waist.
"Please don't hurt me."

Here now, soothed Trey.
*I would never hurt my little
girl.* He petted me as he might

a nervous pup, but that did little
to quell the tornado inside me.

SOMEHOW HE DIDN'T GET

Not

my

cup

of

poison

That, despite his probable
relationship to me,
I wasn't his little girl.

then and not now.
He has never even pretended
to play father to me.
With a little help from

grandfather, Aunt Cora raised
me, though she was only
seventeen when I was born.
What an amazing

of blessing! She could
have just let me fall into
the system, instead

giving up her own party
years to take care of me.
Or she could have left
me to suffer Grandfather's

alone.

INSTEAD, SHE STAYED

Played the "mom" role, and played
it well. Thank God I've got a female
    someone in my life. I'd like to say

I've got tons of girlfriends, but nope.
    Not exactly sure why, but I have
never been what you could call

        popular. Aunt Cora says it's my aura.
    I see them, you know. Yours is dark.
        Sort of like black coffee, although

    it fluctuates. Sometimes there are
        little flecks of gold. If you could
    make those coalesce, turn your

        aura more toffee than coffee,
    things would be different. Let me
        give you some exercises. . . .

Everyone needs a mystic aunt for a
    surrogate mom. Sometimes it's hard
to believe she's only thirty-four.

    I swear she must be reincarnated.
Some ancient witch, burned at the stake,
    returned for a shot at redemption.

WHATEVER SHE IS

Witch or gypsy,
                    I don't have time
to think about it
                    now. I summon as
many gold flecks
                    as I can, hope they
turn me toffee-er,
                    point myself toward
Ms. Carol's room.
                    Cherie feels generous
today, or maybe
                    she's got something
to brag on. She's
                    waiting by her locker,
which is two down
                    from mine. I don't
really want to talk
                    to her, or anyone.
So much for gold
                    flecks. I'm black coffee.

I SHOULDN'T HAVE WORRIED

About not feeling like talking.
Cherie can talk enough for
both of us. And she does.

> *Guess what? Billy Burke*
> *asked me to Homecoming.*

"Great," I say, even though
I think Billy is disgusting.
Why would she want to go
out with that loser, anyway?
Coffee. Coffee. Coffee.

> *Wanna help me shop for*
> *my dress? I'm thinking blue,*
> *or maybe green, but I'm not sure.*
> *Is blue the wrong color for*
> *fall? Because all I'm seeing*
> *in magazines is, like, plum and*
> *apricot and that custard yellow. . . .*

She goes on and on about
fashion, all the way to Ms. Carol's
classroom. I nod and smile
and do my very best to
conjure up toffee.

WHEN WE WALK THROUGH THE DOOR

I really hope I've managed
to glom onto a few gold flecks

because there's a new guy,
sitting across from my regular

seat. He's not like model pretty
or anything, but he is extremely

cute in a boy-next-door sort
of way, with sun-streaked hair

and dark eyes and cheeks that
dimple when he smiles. Smiles.

At me. My face goes hot as I slide
into my chair, wishing I had the slightest

clue how to flirt. I don't. Never tried
it. I can barely manage to smile back.

> And when his grin widens at my obvious
> discomfort and he whispers, *Hi*, I think

I might just curl up in a little ball,
roll away into a corner, and die.

IT'S NOT LIKE

I've never been attracted
to a guy before. I'm a normal,
healthy heterosexual girl.

Okay, not totally normal,
which is why guys aren't exactly
fighting over me. Pretty much

everyone here knows my tale
of woe. Who wants to date a loser
who uses words like "woe," and lives

with her grandfather because
her parents shuffle in and out
of jail, for cripes' sake?

Aunt Cora says if I'd just carry
myself with more dignity, things
would be different. She claims

I overthink stuff, and maybe
I'm overthinking stuff right now.
Maybe the new guy is just

being nice because we have
to sit next to each other.
Maybe he is smiling at Cherie,

not me at all. Or maybe he is
only smiling because I blushed
like the idiot I am. Or maybe . . .

Suddenly I notice that the room
is silent, and everyone's looking at
me. Ms. Carol is up front, taking roll.

> *Autumn? Are you here, or what?*
> Now everyone laughs, because
> obviously I'm *not* here,

despite being present. Still, I lie,
"Um. Yes. Here." I slump down into
my seat, but once everything goes

quiet, I chance a glance at the new
guy, too cute in a leather bomber.
He's still smiling. Definitely at me.

TIME

Slows to a crawl, each grain of sand
in the hourglass suspended
midair before finally
dropping through.
American history
isn't the most
exciting class
anyway, but there
is no way I can possibly
concentrate on the Industrial
Revolution. The boredom is crushing.

I feel like a vacuum is sucking the air
from my lungs. My heart races.
My wrists throb. There's
a gushing in my ears.
I could die. Right
here. Right
now. I close my
eyes, breathe. Breathe
to fight the burgeoning panic.
No! Damn it. I won't give in. *Not*
here. *Not* now. Not when I'm so close.

SO CLOSE

To feeling like
maybe, just maybe
I have a chance
at being okay.

So close
to feeling normal.
Regular. Not a misfit
at all, but someone
worthy of a friend,
and not only a friend,

but
a boyfriend. Breathe.
Deep. The threat of
suffocation recedes.
The all-encompassing
terror falls far,

far away.
I am, in fact, okay.
For the moment.

I HAVEN'T HAD

A panic attack in quite a while.
I had my first one when I started
middle school. I really thought
I was going to die that day.

My arms and legs went all tingly.
Then my heart beat so insanely
hard, I thought it would explode,
rip my chest wide open.

No one understood what was
happening, not even the school
nurse, who called paramedics.
It took a savvy ER tech to explain

that my heart didn't have a problem.
My messed-up brain did. Okay,
he didn't say it was messed up.
I figured out that part myself.

Since then, there have been
other attacks. Other days when
I felt like I didn't dare leave
my room. I've done my homework.

I know anxiety causes them, just
like it causes my OCD. You can find
the easy fix in pharmacies, but
I don't want to be like Grandfather.

Or worse, end up like my parents—
a slave to addiction, and legal drugs
are often as addictive as controlled
substances. (Shouldn't those really be

called uncontrollable substances?)
I learned how to mostly cope without
medication, thanks to Aunt Cora,
yoga-meister, who showed me

how the right kind of breathing
can pull my brain out of the "how
now seems" into the "what really is."
Score one more for Aunt Cora.

THE BELL RINGS

Ms. Carol shouts out
our homework assignment
as the mass exodus

begins. I gather my stuff,
look around for Cherie,
but the only person still

in the room is the new guy.
OMG. Is he waiting for me?
Hi, he says in an accent-free

voice. California smooth.
*I'm Bryce. We just moved
here from—*

"California." My fingers
are tingling. No. No. No!
Breathe deep. Breathe.

He grins. *Yeah. How did
you know? You psychic,
or something like that?*

He is just so cute. Why
me? Whatever the reason,
I actually smile back at him.

"Nope. Not psychic. But
I know California when I
hear it." How am I doing this?

> We start walking. Together.
> *You ever been to California?*
> Through the door. Together.

"Yeah. My dad used to live
there. And my aunt. I live
with her now." Too much info.

> But he doesn't ask for more.
> *Oh. Do you like San Antonio?*
> Down the hall. Together.

"It's okay. It's really all I
remember." Too much, again.
"Someday I'll go back."

> He knows what I mean. *Me*
> *too. You can take the kid out*
> *of California, but . . .*

I know what he means. At
least, I think I do. California.
Huh. "Exactly." Still together.

Summer

ROUSED

From sleep.
Someone is . . .

crying somewhere
in the darkness

blanketing me.
"Who's there?"

> The voice is tiny,
> frail as a promise

> when it stutters, *N-no*
> *one. Just . . . m-me.*

Not quite all
the way awake,

still I know who
it is. "Ashante?

What's wrong?"
I reach for the lamp

beside my bed,
fumble for the switch. . . .

AMBER LIGHT

Spills in a narrow
   stream across my
     bed to the floor
      beyond. Ashante
       crouches in the
        corner by the door,
         arms crossed tightly
          against her chest.
She is a storm
   cloud—puffs of
    ebon skin fringing
     her soiled white
      cotton nightgown.
       And the repulsion
        glimmering cold in
         her eyes is familiar
because it is some-
   thing I have seen
    staring back at me
     from the glacier ice
      of my mirror. I already
       suspect the answer
        when I ask, "What in
         the hell happened?"

I OPEN MY ARMS

Her eyes grow wide, and she shakes
her head. Tears streak her cherub cheeks.
I slip out of my bed, move toward her,
and she shrinks back against the wall.

"It's okay," I soothe. "I won't hurt you."
I approach her as I would a cornered dog,
crazy wild with fear. I force my voice low
and calm. "Now tell me what happened."

> This time when I reach gently for her,
> she tips forward into my arms. *Sh-she*
> *m-m-made me do something b-b-bad.*
> *I told her n-no, but she said I h-had to.*

She? Darla? What kind of bad?
"Who, honey? Did she hurt you?"
Ashante hesitates, trembling. I insist,
"What did she make you do?"

> Finally she admits, *It was Erica.*
> *She made me touch her in bad places.*
> *It didn't hurt me, though. But she said*
> *if I told, she'd make me be sorry.*

A MEMORY SLAMS INTO ME

A different room.
A different house.
A different town.
            I was young.
            I was small.
            I was afraid.
                        He was big.
                        He was strong.
                        He was supposed

                                    to keep me safe.
                                    No one saw when
                                    he came to me,
                                    put his hand over
                                    my mouth, and said,
                                    *If you tell, I'll make
                                    you sorry. Understand?*

                        He was all over me.
                        He was on top of me.
                        He was inside me.
            I never told.
            I never screamed.
            I never healed.
A different night.
A different place.
A different girl.

I NEVER TOLD

I'd already been
pushed aside by

> my mother
> and my father.

I'd already lost

> my Grandpa Carl
> and Grandma Jean.

I'd already been
shuffled through

> one foster home,
> another, one more.

That was the fourth.

> Why didn't anyone want me?
> What was wrong with me?

What if that place
was my last chance?

> Was that what it took
> for someone to care?

No, I never told.
Another girl did.

My BODY

Healed quickly. But the wound
to my psyche was deep.
Wide. First aid, too little, too late,
left me hemorrhaging inside,
the blood unstaunched by psychological
bandage or love's healing magic.

Eventually it scabbed over,
a thick, ugly welt of memory.
I work to conceal it, but no matter
how hard I try, once in a while
something makes me pick at it
until the scarring bleeds.

In my arms, Ashante cries,
innocence ripped apart
by circumstance. Bloodied by
inhuman will. Time will prove
a tourniquet. But she will always
be at risk of infection.

ANGER MUSHROOMS

Inside me, swells to fill every crack, every pore,

every cell until I burn fury. I carry Ashante to

the bed, throw back the blanket, cocoon her with it.

"Stay here." She starts to protest, but whatever

she sees in my eyes makes her acquiesce. "Don't

worry," I soothe. "She won't ever touch you again."

Not as long as I have anything to say about it.

My head throbs. My hands shake, sweat.

It's hard to open the door. When I do, I notice

the silent hallway, remember the hour. Don't really

care. Light trickles from beneath Erica's door.

She's wide awake when I storm through it,

into her room. "What the fuck have you done?"

SHE STARES AT ME

With meth-emptied eyes,
and when she smiles in silent
defiance, she is death, grinning.

I want to shake her. Want to
kick her ass. But what for?
She's not even here. Still,

I can't let it go. Girl. Man. Mostly
dead or no, a predator is a predator.
You can't let it roam unshackled.

"What did you do to Ashante?"
I demand, stomping right up
in front of her and grabbing

her by her hair. I expect her
to jerk away, swing at me, or
something. But she just sits

> there like a mannequin.
> *I didn't do anything to her,*
> *but she did plenty for me.*

ZERO REMORSE

Zero guilt. Zero emotion.
She really is evil, or at
least what she smoked
this afternoon is. I can't
take it. I want her to hurt.

I swing a stiff backhand,
slap her face. Hard.
She animates suddenly
and we are on the floor.
She is stronger than I thought.

Her right hand connects.
Fingernails bite into my
cheek, sink through my skin.
All the hate and pain and fear
I've ever felt in my life ball

up into one vicious biting,
scratching beast. "Fuck you,
bitch!" I scream. She is Zoe.
She is my mother. She is . . .
him. Stop. I have to stop. Can't . . .

SUDDENLY, I AM JERKED

Into the air,
                kicking,
        swinging.
Strong bands
                of muscle
        encircle me,
pin my arms
                against my side.

                        What in the hell
                                        are you doing,
                                Summer?

                        It's Phil. Of course.
                                        Have you
                                totally flipped?

"No! It's not me!"
                "It's her!" I yell,
        nodding toward
Erica. "She did it,
                not me!" But
        even as the words
spit from my mouth,
                I know I look like
        the crazy one.

I MAKE MYSELF GO LIMP

What happens next
can go a number of ways,
I realize. Darla has pulled
Erica off to one side of the room.
Surely Darla notices the state of her high
or the stench of meth sweat.

Ashante stands in the doorway,
holding my blanket and sucking her thumb.
"Tell them," I plead. "Tell them what
she did to you." Her eyes look like
they'll pop right out of her face.

Suddenly I notice crimson
drip-dripping onto my shirt. I try
to reach up, find the source,
but Phil still has a death grip
on my arms. "Am I bleeding?"

His squeeze relaxes some.
Let me see. He spins me around,
draws in his breath. *Uh, yeah.*
You'd better clean that up. He lets
go of me. *Come right back, okay?*

THAT BAD, HUH?

I go to the bathroom,
           flip on the light switch.
                      Aagh! No wonder
                                 Ashante looked so
                                            scared. This is ugly.
Striping the right side
           of my face from eyebrow
                      to cheek is a long, narrow
                                 gash. Not a scratch.
                                            Too deep, carved by
something critically
           sharp. A ring? Closer
                      inspection makes
                                 me slightly queasy.
                                            This will leave a scar.
Soap. Water, hot as
           I can stand it. Pain
                      can be a good thing.
                                 Sometimes it means
                                            killing germs, and if this
gets infected . . . well,
           I'm not sure exactly what,
                      but I'm positive I don't want
                                 that to happen. The bleeding
                                            slows, but the wound puffs up.

The girl in the mirror
        looks like a total freak,
                with one side of her face
                        swollen. Ugly. Deformed.
                                She starts to cry. Shit!
No fair. No fucking
        fair. It wasn't even
                any of my business
                        what Erica did. Was it?
                                And what if Ashante
won't tell what she did?
        Who will take the fall?
                Erica? Or me? If I tell,
                        will they believe me?
                                And how much do I tell?
Everything could come
        crashing to the ground.
                It's like trying to cross
                        a raging river on a rope
                                bridge—fairly stable until
you reach the middle,
        and then it all starts
                to sway, and you know
                        you shouldn't look down.
                                But you can't help yourself.

DARLA COMES INTO THE BATHROOM

She approaches slowly, warily,
as if she's cornered a killer tiger

or something. I snort. "No worries.
One attack per day is my max."

> But her expression shows concern,
> not fear, and I realize it's my face

> she's worried about. *That looks bad.*
> *Maybe we should take you to the ER.*

ER? They'll want to know what
happened. Take a report. Send

it off to my caseworker. Bye-
bye, Darla and Phil. "No. I'm okay."

> *That's going to leave a nasty*
> *scar, Summer. Unless . . . we*

> *could try the Liquid Band-Aid*
> *stuff. It stings like crazy, but . . .*

"I can handle it." I follow her
to the other bathroom, watch

her dig through her medicine
cabinet. Finally she finds the bottle.

>   *This is a good antiseptic, too.*
>   *That's why it stings so much.*

>   The smell is almost enough
>   to knock me over. *Hang on.*

Sting? It's liquid fire, welding
my skin together. "Holy crap!"

But it lasts only a few seconds.
And I've felt worse pain.

>   Darla looks at me with sympathetic
>   eyes. But then she says, *Okay,*

>   *now that you're going to live, will*
>   *you please tell me what happened?*

IF I TELL

Things could go
from bad to worse.
It's been stable here,
few real surprises. But

                  if I tell,

the status quo will be
ruptured. The system
isn't famous for
equitable fixes.

                  Things could

go from worse to
unbearable. But if I don't
tell, Erica will get away
with her disgusting act
and Ashante will

                  go

without the help
she needs right now.
If I don't tell, things
could definitely go

                  straight to hell.

MY MOUTH OPENS

Like a floodgate,
cascading words
doubtless better left
dammed up inside.
But every ugly detail
comes splashing out.
As I talk, Darla's eyes
grow wide. She didn't
suspect a thing. How is
it possible to take care
of problem kids and not
maintain a semi-constant
vigil for problems? Is she lazy?
Ignorant? Or maybe she doesn't
really care about anything
except the monthly stipends.
If that's the case, too bad, so
sad. I'm betting one or more
of those is about to disappear.

DESPITE DRAGGING

My rear on three hours' sleep;
despite my swollen cheek
being sort of stitched together
by a substance resembling dried

nail polish; despite the drama
I've jump-started, then left in my
exhaust, I am sent to school.

While I wait for Matt, people take
one look, swing wide around me,
as if the condition of my face
might be contagious or something.

I seriously need a major dose
of Matt. Need to feel cared for.
Loved. So far, though, no Matt.

But here comes Kyle. Solo.
Odd. He and Matt always ride
together. He notices me, and
even from here I can see his face

                    light up. But when he pushes
                    near, he pales. *Oh my God.*
                    What happened to you?

I launch a condensed version
of the lurid story, and as I talk,
he reaches out, gently traces
the contour of the wound.

The move is unexpected.
Uncharacteristic. Unbelievably
tender. No one has ever touched

me quite this way. I look up
into his eyes, find invitation.
That isn't new. But this feels
different. My own hand lifts,

covers his, rides along as it
travels my cheek again, this
time all the way down to

the corner of my lips. I kiss
his fingertips before yanking
myself out of the moment.
"Uh . . . where's Matt, anyway?"

> I let my hand drop. His should
> too. But it doesn't. *He'll be here
> later. Dentist appointment.*

My Actions

Imply regret, but we both know
I'm not sorry for what just happened.

Hastily withdrawn affection or no,
we both understand I want to touch

Kyle again. Almost as much as I want
him to touch me again. I need to

say something, but can find
no words to convey the burst

of emotions I'm feeling. Guilt.
Lust. Remorse. Intrigue. Perhaps

most of all, I have an intense
desire to see where Kyle's small

gesture of concern might lead.
But what should I do now?

Best answer: nothing. Pretend
it didn't happen. "Bell's gonna ring."

> *I'll walk you to your locker.*
> He keeps his body very close.

Protectively close. Almost
as if I belong to him. Hmm.

MATT FINDS ME

At lunch, sitting on the lawn,
absorbing cool autumn sun.
Thinking about the other guy.

> He comes up behind me and
> when I turn, reacts immediately.
> *Holy crap. That's fucking nasty.*

It is pretty swollen and in a few
small places, the adhesive has
come unstuck. I dabbed blood

a few times this morning.
Unlike Kyle, Matt is not
inclined to touch the thing.

> In fact, he looks kind of nauseated
> when he says, *Hope whoever did
> that to you looks worse than you do.*

Ouch. I'd chalk that up to being
a male reaction, if not for the one
I got earlier from— Stop already.

"I dunno. Haven't seen her this
morning." Come to think of it,
she wasn't in chemistry today.

*Oh. Well, do you want to tell me
what happened?* The tone of his
voice says he doesn't really care.

He is just voyeuristic
enough to enjoy the bitch
fight part. But that isn't what

matters, and if he enjoyed
hearing the other part, it
would piss me off. "Not really."

                    Okay then. Skip it. I'd kiss you—
                    he gives me a grossed out look—
                    but I wouldn't want to hurt you.

I don't know if it's because
he doesn't seem to care,
or because someone else

cared so much, but suddenly
I'm pissed all over again. I jump
to my feet. "Don't bother!"

                    I head for the nearest building,
                    ignoring his confusion-soaked question.
                    Damn, Summer. What did I say?

FOR THE MOST PART

I keep my temper in
        check. Rarely does
anger get the best of me.
        The past twenty-four
hours have used up my
        pissed-off allowance
for the rest of the year!

I sit in Spanish. Thinking
        about the *puta* who
messed up my *cara*, and
        the *cabrón* who doesn't
really care about my face. Not
        that I learned the Spanish

words for whore or bastard
        from Señor Gonzales.
I learned those in my last
        foster home. One of the girls
there was pretty much a *chola*.
        That's a *gringa* word for

gangbanger. Anyway, I did
        learn a couple of *palabras*
here with Señor Gonzales:
        amor and *nuevo*. If you
put them together, what do
        you get? Answer: new love.

I'M NOT REALLY IN LOVE

With Kyle. I'm not really in love
with Matt, either. Falling in

            love

with someone is the surest
highway to hurt that I know.
When the door to love

            opens,

the window to control closes.
I have little enough power
over my life as it is.

            The portal

to pain is caring too deeply
about anyone. That includes
me, myself, and I. It's scary

            to

think I might never take a deep
drink of forever love. Scarier
still to gag on yet another

            deception.

Too many lies in this frozen
world. And too few destined
mergers of the heart.

I DO BELIEVE THAT

So why, after class,
when I spy Kyle at
the far end of the corridor,
does my heart quicken?

Why do I feel like I can
barely catch my breath
(and it has nothing to do
with my asthma)?

Why does a glimpse
of his crooked smile
threaten to melt the ice
dam encircling my heart?

Why do I even halfway
buy into the ridiculous
idea of a remote
possibility of love?

NEVADA APPEAL

CARSON CITY—Former Pink Pussycat madam Robyn Rosselli moved one step closer to the Nevada state legislature today when her opponent, Greg Cappelini, dropped out of the race.

Cappelini's ties to the nuclear power industry have plagued him since tentative plans to go forward with the Yucca Mountain project were recently revealed.

"At least I'm an *ex*-whore," joked Rosselli. "But seriously, if Nevada voters place their faith in me, they can be assured that I will do everything in my power to kill Yucca Mountain once and for all."

Rosselli worked at the Pink Pussycat for fifteen years, before returning to college to earn her BA in political science. "Running a ranch is all about politics," she said. "Courting voters isn't much different than courting johns."

Rosselli, who has admitted a youthful flirtation with crystal meth, was a vocal supporter of the new requirement for legal prostitutes to pass regular drug tests.

Cappelini was not available for comment.

Hunter

NEVADA DAY

Not sure how many
other states make a big deal
about the day they were admitted
to the Union. But God bless
the Silver State for Nevada Day.

Three-day weekends rock.

Especially when they mean
you can spend Friday morning
sleeping in late, then waking
the beautiful lady dozing next
to you for an extra-long go-round.

Ambitious sex totally rocks.

Especially when it leaves
her damp hair splayed in silk
cords across your chest,
and each of her breaths lifts
the cherry tips of perfect breasts.

Another go-round rocks exponentially.

WHEN WE FINISH

We're pretty much wrecked.
Nikki slips out from between

the ruined sheets, heads toward
the bathroom and a hot shower.

          But not before confirming,
          I love you, Hunter.

"You too," I say, mesmerized
by the sway of her narrow hips.

She leaves the door cracked open.
I hear water splash against tile,

and soon ginger-scented mist drifts
into the room. Heaven must be

a whole lot like this. A sigh escapes
as I roll onto my side, notice my cell

phone flashing. Good thing I had
it on "silent." I punch voice mail.

          The message is from Jude, the
          X program director. *Snagged*

          those David Cook tickets for you.
          I'll leave them in your mailbox.

MOM IS AN *AMERICAN IDOL* DEVOTEE

And a huge David Cook fan.
When he was on the show,
she bugged me every week
to call in and vote for him.

So when I heard the Brewery
Arts Center was bringing him
in for Halloween, I asked Jude
for tickets. The station gets them

for just about every concert.
I don't ask for them often,
but Mom and Dad have been
totally stressed lately. Being

around them is like tiptoeing
on broken glass, razor-sharp
slivers aiming for the soles
of my feet. Sometimes

I wonder how their lives
would be if I had never
been born. It's not like
they asked to start over.

Sometimes I wonder if I am
           the reason they don't hold
                     hands anymore, rarely kiss
                               in public. If I am to blame

                     for the emotional distance
           between them, an expanding
rift that seems to grow wider
when I am home, near them.

Mom insists they're still
           best friends, and I guess
                     that's true. She says it's
                               normal for passion to cool.

                     Is all love so predictable
           or is it, in fact, my fault?
           I don't mind so much when
Dad gets mad at me. I'm pretty

sure that's a testosterone thing.
           But I can't stand it when Mom
                     goes all silent and frozen.
                               I hope David Cook can thaw her.

THIS MUST BE

How Santa feels on
Christmas Eve morning,
sleigh clean, reindeer
fed, presents wrapped,
loaded and ready to go.
It's not like I've never

given Mom and Dad
gifts, and nice ones at
that. But this one feels
so special—practically
custom-made for Mom.
(Not to mention free!)

I punch the speed dial
on my phone, wait for
Mom to pick up at home.
Ring. Ring. Ring. Ring.
No one's here to take
your call right now . . .

Hmmm. Mom said they
were staying home this
weekend. I try her cell.
No answer. Dad's cell?
All he has to do is say
Hello for me to know . . .

SOMETHING'S WRONG

"Hey, Dad. Where are you
guys?" Something nasty
seethes in my gut, acid.

*I just dropped your mom
off at the airport.* His voice
trembles. Anger? Worry?

*Kristina is in the hospital.
That bastard beat her up.
Like what else is new, huh?*

"Who beat her up? Ron?"
An ex-boyfriend, in and out
of her life because he is (or

believes he is) the father
of her two youngest kids.
"I thought he was locked up."

*Those places don't keep 'em
forever. Not cost effective.
Like it's cheaper in the long*

*run to turn them loose and
deal with the mayhem later.
You'd think they'd learn.*

Ron has caused more than
his fair share of mayhem, mostly
when he's off his meds and

the voices only he can hear
whisper evil in his ear. "Uh . . .
is Kristina going to be okay?"

*She has a couple of broken
ribs, and I guess he smashed
her face pretty good. They're*

*taking her in for X-rays and
an MRI. . . . He pauses. Tsks.
She'll never be okay.*

Sadness peppers his voice.
Usually when he talks about
her, it's with anger. It hits me

like an unexpected wind
that he cares about her. In
fact, he might even love her.

THE REVELATION

Throws me, but I'm not
sure why. Dad came into
Kristina's life when she
was only five. It was he

        who picked her up,

put her on his shoulders
to "see the world from way
up high," just like he later
did for me. It was he who

        put her on her feet

when she took a spill
off her bicycle, not
Grandpa Who's-it in
Albuquerque. The story
goes it was Mom who

        told her to leave home,

because she had turned
all our lives inside out
and we wanted them right
again. It was Mom who

        said a sad but firm good-bye.

So why has it always
seemed to me that it
was Dad who so firmly
and irrevocably

        closed the door behind her?

I REALIZE SUDDENLY

That Dad is waiting for me
            to say something. Why did
            I call again? Oh, yeah. Tickets.
"How long will Mom be in Vegas?"

                    Not sure, he says. *The kids*
                            need someone to take care
                            of them. That's why she had to
                    drop everything and go. Why?

"Uh . . ." Santa's sleigh just
            crashed. "Nothing. I thought
            I might see you guys at the parade
tomorrow is all. I've got a remote."

                    Not this year. Sorry. You know
                            how Nevada Day traffic is,
                            and I want to be available
                    in case your mom needs me.

"No prob, Dad. I understand.
            Tell Mom I love her, okay?"
            And, not quite an afterthought,
"Hey, Dad? Love you, too."

A WARM GINGER FOG

Spills across the floor. Nikki
trails it into the blind-darkened

room, drying her long golden hair.
Backlit by the bathroom glow,

her silhouette belongs to an angel.
A Victoria's Secret angel, but still . . .

> Her voice holds a hint of incredulity.
> *Did you just tell your dad you love him?*

My eyes burn, but I force a laugh.
"Why? Does that surprise you?"

> *Not the loving him part. The telling him*
> *part.* She sits on the bed. *What's wrong?*

I don't like to discuss the Kristina
crumbs of my life. Not even with Nikki.

"I scored some David Cook tickets for
tomorrow night. Mom is a fan. But she had

to go to Vegas, spur of the moment."
Segue to . . . "So, you wanna go with me?"

To Vegas or David Cook? Okay, bad
segue. *Either way, I can't. I have to*

work. Nevada Day weekend is Big Tip
Weekend at Bully's, you know?

Especially for a cocktail waitress
with Nikki's attributes. "Gotcha."

She's not done with me yet, though.
Why did your mom have to go to Vegas?

I could lie. Omit. Make a joke. Too
much work. "Why else? Kristina."

She knows enough to know that's not
good. *Your mother's in trouble again.*

"Previous mother," I correct. "Or
the uterus I once spent nine months in."

Nikki smiles, but asks with concern,
Is your previous mother okay?

I shake my head, echo Dad's earlier
words. "Kristina will never be okay."

I'M SORT OF AMBIVALENT

About that. I should feel
bad, right? I mean, some
jerk beat her bloody. No
one deserves that, right?

So why, when Nikki asks,
What happened to her?

do I shrug and say, "Guess
she walked into her ex's
fist," with pretty much
zero emotion attached?

And why, when she says,
Oh, no! That's terrible!

do I respond, "Her fault, really.
The only guys she ever invites
into her life are felons, failed
AAers, and other assorted losers"?

And why, when she says, *But
no woman deserves to be hit,*

do I dare voice my opinion
that, "Not true. Some women
damn well beg for it"? I bite
down on the copper taste of anger.

Nikki takes a step back,
as if I might think she had
damn well begged for it.
But I could never hurt her.

   So why, oh why, when she
   asks, *How can you be so cold?*

do I walk toward Nikki, flexing
my fingers? "Look. If Kristina
doesn't kill herself, some guy
will probably do it for her."

   And why, when she says,
   You are just plain mean,

do I let loose a tsunami? "And
you know what? If something
bad did happen to Kristina,
I'm not sure I would care."

   Disbelief floods her eyes.
   You can't feel that way.

Rage-fueled words froth
from my mouth. "That's
exactly how I feel, and if
you don't like it, fuck you."

NIKKI'S EYES

Go wide, and I realize what
I just said. "I'm sorry," I try.
I reach for her, but she slaps

my hand away. She stands,
goes to the closet for clothes.
Her voice is dead calm

> when she says, *You never tell*
> *me how you feel about anything,*
> *Hunter. You never communicate*
>
> *at all. In fact, you might want*
> *to rethink your major. And while*
> *you're doing that, you'd better rethink*
>
> *you and me. If we can't talk about*
> *things like your "previous mother,"*
> *we don't have much of a future together.*

I don't know what to say.
All this because of Kristina?
I watch Nikki slip into jeans,

a curve-hugging jade green
sweater. For the millionth time,
I think how beautiful she is.

But what is it with women
and talking? Some things were
meant to stay private, right?

> She comes over to me, touches
> my cheek. *Still nothing to say?*
> *Goddamn it, I hate when you just*
>
> *stare at me like that.* Her hand
> jerks away and her eyes harden,
> morgue-cold with anger. *Fine.*
>
> *Fuck you too, then. Take your shit,*
> *get out, and don't come back.*
> *I can't deal with this anymore.*

She storms from the room, slams
the door so hard a picture rocks
off the dresser, falls to the floor.

WHAT, EXACTLY, DID I DO?

I mean, yeah, I told her, "Fuck you."
        But that was heat of the moment,
                and I said I was sorry. I can't
                        believe she has such a short fuse.

She'll cool off and it will all be
        fine, right? First things first.
                I need a shower. The bathroom
                        is so Nikki—green and yellow

and messy and smelling of ginger.
        The water heater is old and Nikki's
                shampoo-condition-and-shave
                        routine pretty well emptied it.

I am barely rinsed by the time
        the H_2O fades from lukewarm
                to frigid. Any other day, I'd be
                        mad. Today, all I can do is laugh.

I towel off giant goose bumps,
        borrow a couple of swipes
                of Nikki's deodorant, use
                        her brush to spike my hair.

The face in the mirror is mine.
Yet somehow I feel disconnected
from the person wearing it. Nikki's
words come back to me: *I don't know*

who you are. So I ask Mirror
Man, "Who are you?" But he
just stares stupidly back at me.
Who am I? Don't have a clue.

But I don't have to figure
that out right now. I'm cold.
I have my own drawer in
Nikki's dresser, where I keep

a few things for sleepovers.
I choose boxers. Wranglers.
A red long-sleeved tee. *Take*
your shit. No way. She'll change

her mind. I leave the rest in
place, retrieve the fallen photo—
Nikki and me boarding at Mt. Rose.
Great day. There have to be more.

MIGHT AS WELL

Go home for a few hours,
I guess. It's a twenty-five-
minute ride, so I twist one
up and by the time I pull
into the driveway, I feel
a whole helluva lot better.

At least until I go inside,
only to overhear Dad on
the phone. *You can't be
serious, Marie. We've
discussed this a dozen
times. . . . Stop yelling at
me, please. Of course I
understand. I'm not stupid. . . .*

See? The minute I walk in
the door, they're arguing.
There goes my nice little
buzz. I sneak past Dad's
office into the kitchen. Sex
and stress—not to mention
weed—make a guy hungry.
And thirsty. I consider
snagging a beer, but Dad's
already in a snit. Better stick
with a sandwich and root beer.

GOOD PLAN

Dad comes into the kitchen
while I'm still slopping
mayonnaise on the bread.

Hunter! Didn't hear you
come in. He reaches into
the fridge for one of the three

remaining Miller Lights.
"You were on the phone.
So what's up in Vegas?"

He shakes his head. *A lot.*
None of it good. In addition
to the ribs, Kristina's jaw

is fractured. And the MRI
showed something unusual
in her brain. They have to do

more tests. Plus, the cops
went to her apartment, looking
for Ron. The manager

let them in. They didn't find
Ron, but they did find
three grams of crystal meth,

sitting right out in the open
on top of her dresser. Kristina
claims it must be Ron's,

but it was in her apartment
and he wasn't. She could be
in some serious trouble.

Uh, yeah. A twice-convicted
felon in possession of
a substantial amount of ice?

Even if she's telling the truth,
who's going to believe her?
The question now arises,

"What about Donald and
David?" Kristina's youngest
kids, ages eleven and seven.

Well, there is a major problem,
isn't there? If they catch Ron,
he's going away. This is felony

assault, on top of his record.
Kristina may be going away
too, and even if she isn't, it will

be weeks before she'll be
in a position to play mother
to those kids. So it basically

comes down to foster care,
or . . . His jaw clenches, and
every discernable muscle tenses.

"Or you and Mom take them
in." No wonder they were
arguing. Impossible situation.

He nods. *Marie wants to bring*
them home. It makes me so angry!
We both swore we'd never do it

again—not that we resent having
you, but we're too old to be parents
of young children. The only alternative

I can think of is Jake and Misty.
But after what happened last time,
it's not really fair to ask them.

THERE'S AN UNDERSTATEMENT

Uncle Jake owns a bigger heart
          than any man should, because
hearts are too easily broken.

          He gave a big chunk of his heart
to me, playing babysitter while
          most of his buddies were focused

on trying to score girls. The rest
          of his heart (minus what belongs
to Mom and Dad) went to Misty

          in high school. They married soon
after graduation, even though
          everyone said they were too young.

So far, they've proved everyone
          wrong. School. Work. Paying bills.
They've waded through, together.

          Then, when Kristina got pregnant
with David and decided she
          couldn't put up with four-year-old

Donald's hardcore behavior
          problems, Jake volunteered to
take him in. He and Misty dealt

patiently with biting. Head
banging. Scream-punctuated
      tantrums. Purposeful destruction.

Not his fault, Jake claimed.
            She never taught him better.
Truth is, he was wild as a bobcat.

      With nurturing and love, Jake
and Misty tamed him. Taught
      him the meaning of "no," how

to say "please" and "thank you."
            Then, of course, Kristina wanted
him back. *Sort of like sending*

      your puppy out to be house-
broken, was Dad's comment.
            Donald did return to Kristina,

better for the experience. But he
            has regressed some over time.
Let's just say there's rarely

      a dull moment when Kristina
and her brood come round
            for holidays and family reunions.

AND NOW THE BROOD

Might be moving in? No
                                    wonder Dad's feeling
                    a little anxious.
            A little pressured.
                            A little concerned
that his comfortable
                                    retirement might become
                    decidedly uncomfortable.

Everything at home
                    has been relatively
                            stable for a long time.
The drama for the most
                    part has remained
                            housed in Las Vegas.
Kristina has kept semi-
                    steadily employed,
                            and maintained a couple
of semi-steady relationships.
                    Of course, Ron was always
                            lurking in the shadows,
                    ready to pounce,
        ready to maim,
                            ready to bring her down.
And Kristina never
                            played smart, never
            played the game like
                            it was for real.
                    Easier to play victim.

SPEAKING OF PLAYING

The last time Donald came
to visit, he fried my brand-new
Xbox. "Uh . . . So where are
the demon kids going to sleep?"

> Apparently Dad hasn't bothered
> much with the minutiae. *I don't*
> *know. Haven't really thought*
> *about it. The guest room?*

I snort. "Mom's white on white
with white trim guest room?
You've got to be kidding, right?"
He thinks it over for a second,

> has to laugh, too. *We could*
> *give them permanent markers*
> *to decorate the walls, I suppose.*
> *Or there's always . . .*

I was afraid of that. Hmm.
Well, if I take everything of value
with me, "Maybe I could stay
with Nik." Then I remember.

> *Take your shit, get out,*
> *and don't come back.*
> Ah, no worries. Surely
> she's cooled off by now.

I STASH ANY RESIDUAL WORRY

In a dark closet inside my brain
while I do my air shift.
Can't let my listeners know

I've just been kicked out
of my bedroom, not to mention
maybe out of my girlfriend's bed.

Celebrities don't get kicked
out of places, right? I slip into
Biggest Little City radio star mode.

"What's up, Reno? If your
Nevada Day was anything like
mine, I know what was up

this morning. Hope your
evening rocks just as hard. Coming
up, White Tie Affair and

Sugarcult. But let's get things
started with Three Days Grace."
Cool as ice cream.

A LITTLE AFTER MIDNIGHT

One of my groupies calls and I offer
her the David Cook tickets, which, as

> promised, were in my in-box. *For
> real? What can I give you for them?*

I get her meaning, but pretend
innocence. "Nothing but love,

honey, nothing but love. Track me
down at the parade tomorrow."

The pimply overnight geek comes
in ten minutes late. I don't say a word

as I vacate the booth. The night
squeezes me with icy fingers, chills

me all the way through. When I get
to Nikki's, the house is dark.

Her car is gone. All the stuff I left
is in two paper bags on the porch.

I reach beneath the fake rock. But I
already know the key isn't there.

Autumn

A COLD RAIN

Is falling this morning.
Not unusual for October.
It rains a lot in San Antonio.

                            Warm

rain. Cool rain. Steamy
hot rain in the summer.
That part of my life, at least,
has stayed constant. Not

                            like

the rest of it has. Aunt
Cora, who has fallen out
of her senses in love,
is absent much too often.

                            I've

met Liam and understand
why she wants to spend
time with him. But I need
to talk, and I could

                            never

ask Grandfather the kind
of stuff I need to know.
I recently entered unfamiliar
territory. A place I've never

                            been before.

AN OLD MAXIM GOES

Love is in the   air. Seems like
the October   air was heavy
with it. Aunt Cora inhaled a
big whiff. And somewhat
incredibly, so did I.
It's totally crazy.
I'm scared.

I don't know   enough about
being in love   to insist that I
really am. But I definitely feel
something for Bryce, and
I'm almost positive he
feels something
for me.

But how do I   know for sure
if what I feel is   anything more
than gratitude   for him paying
attention to me? And how can
I tell if he feels anything
more than sorry
for me?

CHERIE SAYS

Don't overthink things.
Go with the flow, see

where it takes you. Love
is unpredictable, you know.

Not that I listen much
to what Cherie has to say,

and not that I've really
discussed my feelings

with her, except to half
answer her nosy questions.

He's really cute, isn't he?
You really like him, huh?

Well, duh and duh. But I say,
"Yeah, he is. And wouldn't you?"

Did he ask you out yet?
Did he kiss you yet?

"No and no." Just thinking
about kissing him makes me

nervous. All I know about kissing
is what I've seen in the movies.

Still, I have to admit the idea
does intrigue me more than a little.

I try to look nonchalant about
how I feel. But it must be obvious

to anyone with eyes how
I can't keep my own eyes

off Bryce. It's like my irises
are made of iron and

he's a head-to-toe magnet.
That's not hard to understand.

He's adorable. Smart. Funny.
What I really don't get

at all, though, is why
the attraction is mutual.

Bryce is caviar. I am
more like canned sardines.

MAYBE I'M WRONG

About the attraction
       being mutual after all.
As always lately, when I get

to school, I immediately
       scan the halls for Bryce,
and when I finally spot him,

he is nose to nose with
       Tiffany Garcia. My cheeks
flame. Is everybody looking?

Tick-tick-tick-tick goes
       my heart. Fast. Faster.
My fingers start to tingle.

No. Not now. Everybody
       is looking, and if I freak
out, I'm completely ruined.

       As I take deep and deeper
              breaths, a voice falls over
       my shoulder. *What's up with that?*

Cherie. Just perfect. Inhale.
       "I really don't know." It's all
I can find enough air to say.

I JERK MY LOCKER OPEN

Hard. Too Hard.
  The neat stacks spill
    into each other, onto
      the floor. Now everyone
        is gawking my way for sure.

          Are you okay?
          Cherie's question
          is laced with concern.
          I must look ready to pass
          out or die or something.
And maybe I am.
  "Yes . . . No. Uh-uh-
    uh . . ." Great. Let's
    add stuttering to my list.
      "I don't know. I mean . . ."

          I'd be mad too.
          Tiffany is a total
          slut. Almost every guy
          here has gone all the way
          around the world with her!
Okay, it's a slight
  exaggeration, but
    I'm in no mood to
      disagree. "It doesn't
        matter. Not like I own him."

The truth of that
   stings. My eyes tear
      up, and I wish Cherie
         would just go away, let me
            wallow alone in my misery pit.

               As if reading,
                  my mind, she says,
                     There's Billy. I need to
                        ask him something. I'll be
                           back in a few minutes, okay?
"I'm fine, Cherie.
   Go on." At least
      my locker door is
         between me and Bryce.
            Except there, on the ugly

               brown linoleum,
                  my history book and
                     chemistry notebook
                        huddle, open-covered.
                           I'll have to pull my face
out from behind
   the rusting metal
      to get hold of them.
         Tick-tick-tick-tick-tick!
         Blood whooshes in my ears.

WITH MY BACK TOWARD

The disturbing melodrama,
I squat, reach for my mess.

> Now a different voice
> settles like fog around me.

> *Here. Let me help you.*
> I know without looking

who's speaking. The stupid
thing is, I somehow feel grateful

Bryce is talking to me at all.
Still, I protest, "No, thanks.

I've got it." My tone is not
Christmas fudge sweet.

> He holds out a hand, which
> I ignore. *What's wrong?*

What is wrong? Not like
I can confess what I'm feeling.

"Uh, nothing. Something
happened at home is all."

He watches me reorganize
my stacks. *You never talk*

much about home. Why not?
Don't you trust me?

I shut my locker, turn to
look him in the eye. "Not

a whole lot to talk about,
really." I leave the rest hanging.

Over his shoulder, I notice
Tiffany, now nose to nose

with Billy Burke. Cherie would
flip! "What's up with her today?"

The question slips out, slick
as Quaker State. Bryce rotates

on one heel. *Who? Tiffany?*
She got new green contacts.

I guess she's showing them
off to anyone who'll notice.

MORTIFIED

That pretty much sums up
how I feel right this minute.
Mortified and relieved.

"Oh," is all I can manage.

I finish lining up my spare
pens and pencils by color,
just as the bell rings.

> *Do you like football?*

Bryce falls in step at my shoulder.
He's warm and clean scented,
like rain and fresh-cut apples.

"Playing or watching?"

Dumb thing to say! Of
course he didn't mean
playing. *Tick-tick-tick.*

> *You like to play football?*

> He sounds really pleased.
> *Actually, I meant watching.*
> *There's a game tomorrow?*

"I . . . uh . . . love football."

It's a slight exaggeration.
Aunt Cora loves football,
so I tolerate it. Hours of it.

Bryce grins. *Want to go with me?*

He's asking me to the game?
Like a "sit next to him in the stands,
knee touching knee" kind of date?

Tick-tick. Stay cool. "Sure."

Suddenly I'm acutely aware
of his body, pressed up against
mine. It feels proprietary. I like it.

Cool. I'll see you at lunch.

Before he turns away, he leans
into me, and his lips brush
the pulse just below my ear.

Tick-tick-tick-tick-TICK!

I THINK

I just might go ahead and die

    right here, right now. How

    could anything be better than

the way I'm feeling this moment?

Ms. Dzumba blathers on

    and on about amoebas, and all

    I can think about is Bryce's

kiss. It *was* a kiss, wasn't it?

God, what if it was just an

    accident? Was I supposed

    to respond? What if that's

the only kiss I ever get?

Worse, what if it's not?

        What if we go to the game

        and he wants to kiss for real?

Like lips, with me kissing back?

What if I try to kiss back

        and I totally blow it? Like

        bump teeth or bite tongue?

Wait. Tongue? What about that?

What if I freak out completely?

        Oh my God. Why did I say

        okay? I can't. I'm just not

a "go to the game" kind of girl.

HOW DO I BACK OUT GRACEFULLY?

Think, Autumn. Excuses
aren't that hard to come by.

I'm sick.
        Too close to the truth.

I broke my leg.
        Too easy to disprove.

I have a toothache.
        The dentist? On Saturday?

Work called me in.
        When did you get a job?

I need to study.
        There's always Sunday.

I'm going in for
green contacts.
        There's a novel idea.

Grandfather won't
let me go.
        The biggest kicker of all.
        What if he won't?

BY THE TIME

The bell rings for lunch, I still
haven't figured out what to say.

Then I see Bryce. Every ounce
of doubt melts away beneath
the warmth of his smile.

By the time I have stashed
my books, he is at my side.

> Almost unbelievably, I feel
> his arm slide around my waist.
> *Hungry? Come on. Let's go.*

I am not even a little bit hungry.
At least, not for food. Usually

I grab a quick bite at the snack
bar, sit on the lawn or in the quad
to nibble and read. But not today.

Bryce guides me out the door,
along the damp sidewalk to

the parking lot. He stops beside
a pretty emerald green Acura,
opens the passenger door.

I've never ridden in some
random car before. I slip inside,

vaguely uncomfortable, as if
I'm doing something wrong.
I kind of like the feeling, though.

　　　　Bryce takes the driver's seat, glances
　　　　my way. *Penny for your thoughts.*

My brain stutter must show.
How not to sound like a total
dweeb? "I was just checking out

your stereo." True enough.
It's a Bose. Cost a pretty penny.

　　　　Nice, huh? My brother gave it to
　　　　me for Christmas. He starts the car
　　　　and the CD player kicks in. Incubus.

Interesting information. He has
a brother. A brother with money.

I realize suddenly that I know as little
about Bryce as he does about me.
Who has the biggest surprises in store?

SURPRISE NUMBER ONE

I expect him to drive to McDonald's
or Burger King. Instead he high-
tails it several blocks away, pulls
into a strip mall parking lot.

Esperanza's is a great little taqueria,
one of Aunt Cora's favorite "hidden
hot spots." Apparently it's one
of Bryce's favorites too.

> He pulls up in front. *They have
> killer burritos here. Oh, hey,
> you* do *like Mexican food, don't
> you? Wow, this place is rocking.*

"Well, yeah. It *is* lunchtime.
And yes, I do, in fact, like Mexican
food. We'd better hurry, though,
or we'll be late back to school."

We go inside, squeeze our way
through the crowded tables
to the takeout counter. Bryce
orders his burrito. I ask for

a chicken soft taco before
I discover, "Oh, no. I didn't
bring any money." I must have
left it in yesterday's jeans.

> Bryce doesn't miss a beat.
> *I've got it. I invited you to lunch,*
> *remember?* Surprise number two.
> Some guys are still gentlemen.

We eat in the car, listening
to music I could never play
at home, at least not without
headphones, at least not

when Grandfather is around.
He isn't big on metal. Bryce
downs his giant burrito faster
than I can finish my taco. I grin.

> *What?* he says. But he knows
> why I'm smiling. He shrugs.
> *Guess I was hungrier than*
> *I thought. Must be hormones.*

THAT MAKES ME LAUGH

Unfortunately, my mouth is full.
I lift my hand, barely in time

to save the windshield from
a spray of chicken taco.

> *Hey, now!* he says, laughing too.
> *I just detailed this car, you know.*

> He starts the Acura, aims it toward
> school. *And anyway, what's so funny?*

Somehow, I manage to swallow what's
left of my lunch. I shake my head.

"It's just the hormone thing reminded
me of something Aunt Cora might say."

> *Why do you live with your aunt?*
> The blunt question catches me

by surprise. "Uh . . . actually,
we both live with my grandfather. . . ."

> But that's not what he wants to know.
> *What happened to your parents?*

I SHOULD HAVE AN ANSWER READY

But I never expected
              I'd need one. I pretty
                            much figured Bryce
would lose interest
              in me long before
                            asking that question.
Chunks of truth thump
              round in my brain like rocks
                            in a tumbler: They were
too young, clueless,
              selfish. Hell-bent
                            to party, to fight,
to find trouble. Mired
              heart-deep in love,
                            in pain, in addiction.
But I don't want to talk
              about the monster, don't
                            have the courage to say
"prison." These words
              define me as a freak.
                            And so, as Bryce turns
into the designated
              student parking lot,
                            pulls into a space, a lie
(at least I think it's a lie)
              leaks from my mouth.
                            "My parents are dead."

TEARS POOL IN MY EYES

Bryce mistakes embarrassment
for sadness. He reaches for me,
pulls me against the comforting

       beat of his heart. *Oh, baby,*
       he whispers. *I'm so sorry.*

"I don't . . . I just . . . never
talk about it." That part is true.

       You don't have to talk about
       it. Sorry I brought it up.

He kisses my forehead, down
my left temple, the corner of
my eye. Some weird instinct

I never knew I possessed turns
my face into his, and suddenly

we're kissing a for-real, deadly
serious kiss. His lips are soft.
Warm. Yielding. His tongue,

when it comes, is gentle. Inviting.
My own tongue is accepting and . . .

SURPRISE NUMBER THREE

Some totally foreign parts
of my body awaken suddenly.
Oh my God. That's what it's all

about! We are kissing. Tongue
on tongue. I can't believe it's
so easy. So wondrously,

perfectly, impossibly *me*.
I am breathless, but I don't
want to fight the sensation. For

once, *not* breathing feels right.
I am tingling, too. But in
all the right places.

I DARE

To open my eyes, only to find
Bryce staring at me.

> *Wow. You know the old saying,*
> *"You're beautiful when you cry"?*
> *Well, you definitely are.*

"I'm not cry—," I start, but when
his hand brushes my cheekbone,
his fingers come away wet.

"I guess I am, huh? I'm sorry,
I . . . uh . . ." He stops me with

> one tear-damp finger against
> my lips. *Shh. Nothing to be sorry*
> *about.* He kisses me again,

and this one is even sweeter,
despite a lingering essence

of Esperanza's world-famous
salsa. Not to mention a spicy
taste in my own mouth. Guilt.

Summer

CRAZY

If I had to use one word
to sum up my life now,
that's what it would be.

                Insane,
pure and simple. Here
I try to do the right thing,
attempt to be one of the

                heroes.
What does it get me?
A life tossed into turmoil,
any pretense of stability
shattered. It takes

                super-
human strength to get
through the day when
evening might bring pain

                or
worse, love, only to have
that love stolen away.
I hold tight to my heart,

                otherwise
it might get broken into
tiny little pieces. Taking
a chance on that would
mean you definitely

                have to be crazy.

THAT KIND OF DENIAL

Of course means
I must be in love.

> Fighting that love
> as best I can.

It's a hopeless battle.
I'm already heart-deep.

> Don't want to be.
> Love scares me.

Do want to be.
Love summons me.

> Don't want to be.
> It's an illusion.

Do want to be.
It's pure magic.

> Don't want to be.
> He will smother me.

Do want to be.
He takes my breath away.

WHETHER OR NOT

I want to love Kyle, I do. I have
been avoiding Matt, and he doesn't
know why. He's hurt and I should
confess, but I have no clue how
to say good-bye. All I know

is that the only splinter of happiness
I find in each day is when Kyle
is near me. Life is currently a vortex.
The incident with Erica exploded
completely. Human shrapnel

flew. Our mutual caseworker,
Mrs. Shreeveport, is still trying
to sort things out. She yanked
us both out of there immediately.
Ah, but just where to put us?

There was only one foster care
opening—so many messed-up kids,
so few places for them. Erica posed
the biggest risk right then. What to
do with a possible sexual offender?

Now, though, I hear they may send
her back to Darla and Phil's.
Ashante is too scared to tell
what really happened. Poor little kid.
So begins the end of innocence.

AND ME?

Too bad, so sad. Nowhere else close
to send me, I ended up back with my dad,
at least for now. I can't stand it here.

I mean, at least foster homes are required
to maintain a certain level of cleanliness.
Not like Dad's deteriorating single-wide

on a dirt road near a dairy farm at the far
edge of town. Everything here is layered
in tobacco smoke and cow shit dust

and carries a lingering scent of human
piss because neither Dad nor his latest lay,
Kortni, knows how to use a toilet brush.

My first instinct upon arrival was to pick
up the litter on the floor, toss the food,
molding in the fridge. Then it struck me.

Why do any of that? If I do, they'll expect it,
maybe think God returned me from foster
care to become their designated housekeeper.

I hope I'm not here long enough for the trash
to gross me out completely. Bad enough
I have to lay my head on the same old pillow

I used when Zoe still lived here with us.
It was clean then. Everything was—Zoe
reigned as scrub queen. Something to do

with the little bugs she imagined everywhere,
including under her skin. Meth addicts
pick those nonexistent bugs into sores.

Pretty sure Dad doesn't do meth anymore.
You can't eat like he does or wear such
a big belly while dancing with the monster.

He cleaned up when Grandma Jean
and Grandpa Carl took him to court over me.
Guess, win or lose, he decided to stay ice free.

Noticed I didn't say bad habit free. He chugs
cheap beer, and the smell of weed
has become a daily welcome home

in the two weeks since I've been back.
He even asked if I wanted a hit once, but the idea
of smoking with my dad seemed messed up.

I hate that he made that offer to me. Hate
that he doesn't think better of me.
Hate him for not really wanting me here.

ONE OKAY THING

About being here. Neither Dad
          nor Kortni really cares about
          when, if, or how I come or go.
          They barely take notice at all.
Other than school, I'm free.

The main problem is transportation.
          It's a long way to civilization,
          if you can call anything about
          Bakersfield civilized. To find
something to do on this Sunday

morning, I need a ride into town.
          Dad is still sleeping off too much
          Saturday night fun. I should
          call Matt. Have him come get
me, apologize for being so cold.

He's such a nice guy, at least
          for the most part. I mean, pretty
          much every guy is about feeling
          you up when he can, right?
But Matt's never pushed me to go

all the way. Never once raised
          his voice to me. Never once
          made me feel less because
          of where I came from. And
somehow that makes him boring.

SO INSTEAD

Of calling Matt, when I pick up
the phone, the numbers I punch
in add up to Kyle. *B-r-r-n-g.*

Why am I doing this? *B-r-r-n-g.*
He won't be home anyway.
B-r-r-n-g. He's out having fun—

> *H-hello?* Definitely Kyle on
> the other end. Was he sleeping?

"Oh, hey. It's me. Did I wake you
up?" The long pause that follows makes
me wonder, "Do you know who this is?"

> *Of course.* Wide awake now.
> *What's up? Everything okay?*

Nerves strike suddenly, try to
shut me up. "I-I'm fine. I just
have some free time today and . . ."

And what, Summer? "And thought
maybe you could pick me up. . . ."
Bad choice of words. "Uh, come

get me. Maybe hang out for
a while? I'm at my dad's, and
claustrophobia is making me insane."

THERE, SAID IT

This time there is no hesitation.
*Thought you'd never ask. Give
me about a half hour, okay?*

Over and out. It's a very long
thirty minutes, watching for dust
clouds blowing this direction.
Finally, though, a big puff of gray
signals Kyle's F-250 is coming
this way. My pulse picks up speed.

I leave a note: *Went into town
with a friend. Back before dark.*
Not sure why I bother. Dad
and Kortni will probably
just be rousing around then.
Hey, maybe they're vampires.

On the more likely chance that
they're not, I grab my hoodie
and head out the door. No need
for verbal explanations when
a written one will do. Kyle skids
his truck to a stop in the gravel.

He slides across the seat,
opens the passenger door.
Get in, he says. *Where to?*

FAIR QUESTION

After all, this was my idea.
        But I don't have a destination
in mind. I shrug. "Anywhere."

                        He grins. *Anywhere it is.*
                He starts the truck, which
                        hums gently. Well-tuned.

We bump down the dirt
        track, turn onto the blacktop
away from town, toward

                                the state park. The road
                        winds along the Kern River.
                                Ever rafted this section?

I shake my head. "Heard
        it's fast through here." I don't
mention my water paranoia.

                                I'll take you in the spring.
                        It's more than fast. It's ball-
                                shrinking crazy. And cold.

I laugh. "I'll take your word
        for it." I look over at him,
can't help but stare at his

incredible physique. Only
problem is, he catches me.
What? Something wrong?

"No." Is he kidding? Just
being here so close to him
makes everything, "Perfect."

It's close to an invitation.
Kyle takes the opportunity
to ask, *So what got into you?*

I understand the question,
but pretend I don't. "What do
you mean? Got into me how?"

We've been traveling at
a good clip. He slows down
now. *Why did you call me?*

A direct question deserves
an equally direct answer.
"I wanted to be with you."

Well, if that's the case . . .
His hand finds my thigh,
pulls. *Come over here.*

I'VE BEEN THIS CLOSE

To Kyle before, but never with the same
intention. Not sure where he'll decide

to park, but I do know when we get there
everything will be different between us.

We will no longer be two sides of a triangle.
We will be adjacent parallel lines.

My own hand travels the length of his leg,
from knee to groin, memorizing the cut

> of his muscles. *You're driving me crazy,*
> he says breathlessly. *But then you've*
>
> *been driving me crazy for a while.*
> *I just have to know: Why? Why now?*

"I don't know. I love Matt, really I do.
But more like a friend. Not like . . . this."

> At the mention of Matt, Kyle tenses.
> *Matt. Right. He's going to be pissed.*

I pull my hand away. Slide over a little.
"It's not too late. We don't have to . . ."

> *Yes, we do.* He pulls me against him again.
> *Put your hand back where it belongs.*

HE TURNS OFF THE MAIN ROAD

Onto a narrow strip of potholed
        pavement. It leads to a small parking

                area. River access, and this time
                        of year, there's no one else here.

My heart beats against my chest
        like eagle wings against heavy air.

                Kyle throws the shifter into park,
                        pushes me over enough to slide

out from beneath the steering
        wheel. In almost the same motion,

                he yanks me into his lap and our
                        lips weld together. Heated. Urgent.

This is not a kiss of friendship.
        This is a kiss born of lust, and I have

                never known anything like it.
                        This is unstoppable, no holds

barred. This is beautiful.
        Crazy. A beginning. Betrayal.

                Addictive. Aggressive. Alive.
                        This is something to be afraid of.

I AM CERTAIN OF THAT

Yet even as my brain cries, "Slow down,"
my body insists, "Give me more." Kyle's
hands move over me and his touch

is nothing like Matt's clumsy
investigation. Somehow, these
hands have intimate knowledge

of the heights and depths of my body.
Their skin is unimaginably soft.
But they are not gentle. "Easy . . . ,"

I start, but as the word leaves
my mouth, I realize I don't want
it easy. And Kyle knows it too.

> *Shush,* he commands. *Don't tell me*
> *what to do. I know what you want*
> *and I'm going to give it to you.*

His words bring a rush of fear
and, worse, excitement. He lifts
my shirt up over my head, kisses

> down my neck to the deep V
> between my breasts. Pauses.
> *You are incredible. Beautiful.*

I look down into his upturned
eyes, and though he doesn't say
so, I know he wants my permission.

In answer, I unclasp my bra, offer
myself to his mouth, his tongue,
his teeth. This is already more

than I've given Matt, or ever will.
Superego whispers, "How far are you
willing to go?" But I don't have to

answer that question yet. I place
my hands on Kyle's cheeks, lift
his face toward mine. He pulls

away reluctantly, like an infant
intent on dinner. But he lets me
kiss him softly, cool the inferno.

"I didn't come here with you
because I want to have sex
with you." I kiss him again,

> feel the heat of his response
> beneath me. Still, he asks reasonably,
> *Why did you come here with me?*

A BATTLE BEGINS

Inside me. Head versus
heart. Logic versus emotion.
And every synaptic surge of

        logic

is telling me not to let
my mouth spill
the words my heart

        insists

are true. Any girl ever
stung in this common
manner would agree

        it's

a bad move to confess
such a strong emotion
so quickly. In fact, it's

        idiocy.

So okay. I'm stupid.
I don't stop myself,
but rather rush

        to say,

"I know I shouldn't tell
you this, but I wanted to
be with you because . . .

        I love you."

I EXPECT HIM

To laugh. Snort. Push me
away. What I don't expect

> is for him to knit his fingers into
> mine and say, *I love you, too.*
>
> *God, Summer, don't you realize*
> *how hard it's been to feel like this*
>
> *about my best friend's girl? How*
> *it hurts to see you with him?*
>
> *It's torture. I've wanted a day*
> *like today for a long, long time.*

One hand rises to touch my still
exposed right breast. This time

he is gentle. I close my eyes, give
myself to the dizzying sensation.

"So what are we going to do?
About Matt, I mean." The hand

> falls away. *We tell him. Tomorrow.*
> *You're mine now. Nothing can*
>
> *come between us, especially*
> *not Matt. Understand?*

SUDDENLY I'M UNCOMFORTABLE

But it's not the tone of his voice—
inflexible, with jealous undertones—
that makes me that way. It's how
I've been kneeling, legs spread
across his lap, for twenty minutes.

> When I try to move, he stops
> me. *No. Not till you say you*
> *understand. You and Matt*
> *are finished, right?* He sounds
> mean, but his eyes are pleading.

"I love *you*, Kyle. Not Matt.
I could never be with him
again." His grip does not
loosen, so I quickly add,
"But my knees are killing me."

> Everything about him relaxes,
> and he laughs. *Why didn't you*
> *say so?* As I slide to one side,
> he suddenly gets the picture. *Gain*
> *an amazing girl. Lose a best friend.*

THAT MAKES HIM WANT

A cigarette. He reaches into
        the glove box for a pack
                of Marlboros. *Want one?*

I shake my head. "Don't
        smoke. It's seriously
                bad for my asthma."

He looks at the cigarette
        he's about to light up.
                Asthma? Does he think

it's a test? "Yeah. But go
        ahead if you need to.
                Not like it's anything new."

He thinks about it for
        a second or two. *Put your
                shirt on. Let's take a walk.*

It's a brisk fifty degrees
        outside—by Bakersfield
                standards, a cool fall day.

Kyle lights his cancer
        stick, takes my hand,
                and steers me along

the riverbank. Summer-
     fried grass chatters
          beneath our feet, and

the water mutters along.
     Smoke bothering you?
          Kyle asks, blowing it

downwind, away from me.
     "Not at all." He finishes
          his cigarette, stubs it out,

pulls me down into a soft
     tuft, sits close, and leans
          his face into my hair. Sighs.

Tobacco breath escapes
     his mouth, yet somehow
          it doesn't make me gag,

and when he lays me back
     to see the sky, I find myself
          very near heaven. *Kiss me.*

It's more order than request,
     but I don't care. All I want
          to do is lose myself in him.

I'M SO LOST

I barely notice when my shirt
comes off again, or how the cool
breeze plays strange melodies
up and down superheated skin.

The sharp tang of Kyle's desire
rises into the chuffing wind,
and when my lips journey
his body, they come away

with a thin lick of salt. We are
moving quickly toward what
I didn't come here for, but I am
powerless to stop him from

unzipping my jeans and peeling
them off me before sliding out of
his own. Am I ready for this after
all? The only things in the way

of "all the way" are red cotton
boxers and a pair of barely there
panties. Ninety-eight percent
of me is ready to say okay.

I close my eyes against the azure
glare. Kyle moves over me,
expertly tries to convince the last
two percent. Riffs of pleasure

trill through my veins. Excite
me. Frighten me. Delight me.
Off go the boxers. On goes
the latex. But just as he pulls

at the panties, I remember
that other girl, in that other
town, how she watched, terrified,
as the man who was supposed

to protect her chose instead
to harm her. My muscles go
rigid. I never told anyone. Now
someone will know. "Wait."

> He pauses, confused at jumbled
> signals—my body screaming
> yes, while my mouth says no.
> *It's okay. I won't hurt you.*

My eyes sting. "I want to. I do.
But . . ." My face heats to flush.
I don't want him to know. Don't
want anyone to know. Tears spill.

> Kyle brushes them gently away.
> *What's wrong?* The answer
> he waits for is painful. But for
> us to work, I have to tell him.

AN INTENSE

Shiver

    quakes me, initiates teeth
    chatter. Kyle hands me my shirt
    like an offering. Waits,

silent,

    as I launch the lurid account.
    I can't look at him while I recite
    it. Instead I focus on a skinny

sapling

    wearing a single crimson leaf.
    I am the fledgling tree, weighted
    not by wind, but by memory. I

bend

    but refuse to break. I finish
    with a plea. "I've never told
    this story to anyone

before.

    Can we just keep it between
    you and me?" The question
    floats, a fallen red leaf in

the breeze.

KYLE HAS LISTENED

Without comment. Finally he says,
Who would I tell? He cocks his head,

looks at me in an assessing way.
That's why you never did it with Matt?

"Not with Matt or anyone else. But
how do you know we never did?"

He grins. *Because Matt isn't the type
to get laid and not brag about it.*

*I, on the other hand, am very good
at keeping secrets.* He moves closer,

puts his arm around my shoulder.
I'm sorry that happened to you.

*But it doesn't change how I feel.
I love you. And if you really love*

me, you have to trust me. In one
swift motion, he shifts his body

and I am again reclining in autumn
gold grass. I learned a long time ago

not to place my trust in anyone.
You always get screwed in the end.

But when Kyle lowers himself over me,
the kiss that finds my lips is brimming

with promise. He lifts my wrists above
my head, pins them purposefully to the ground

with one strong hand, as if I might complain
about his other hand, voyaging over

my body, lingering in all the right places.
It already knows me. Such intimate

awareness deserves trust, and so I open
myself to it. And to Kyle. He takes complete

control. Instinct or experience? No matter.
My body surrenders. Reacts. Invites.

He is not gentle. But I am not afraid.
And as we rise and rise in symphony,

each note completely new to me, I think
I might never be frightened again.

AWASH

In love's pastel afterglow,
we drive slowly back toward
town. Back toward Matt. Still

wondering what I'll tell him, but
worrying less about his reaction.

> As we turn down the dirt track
> toward home, Kyle pulls over.
> He gives me a long kiss, then

> says, *I'll pick you up tomorrow,*
> *okay? We'll deal with Matt together.*

He puts the truck in gear, and
as we near the trailer, I notice
Dad sitting outside, smoking.

When he sees who I'm riding
with, his body straightens.

> Kyle stiffens a bit himself. I can
> almost smell the testosterone
> exchange. *Is that, like, your* father?

"Well, yeah." Who else would
it be? "Come say hello."

We get out of the truck, but
Dad doesn't budge, just sits
staring. Kyle offers his hand.

> *Hey, Mr. Kenwood. I'm Kyle.*
> *Good to meet you.* Quite polite.

> At least Dad shakes his hand.
> *Uh . . . yeah . . . same here.*
> Dad's majorly checking Kyle out,

and it's making him uncomfortable.
Better go. See you tomorrow.

> We watch him leave, and once
> the dust dissolves, Dad asks, *Who*
> *was that? Your boyfriend?*

"Not exactly," I lie. "And why
were you staring at him like that?"

> Dad shrugs. *He kind of reminded*
> *me of someone I used to know.*
> When I ask who, his answer

> feels somehow a little evasive.
> *Just an old friend of mine. Trey.*

VARIETY

HOLLYWOOD—Citing the usual "irreconcilable differences," producer Chase Wagner split with Amanda Haynes, his wife of almost twenty years. Haynes, however, said those differences have everything to do with Wagner's frequent dalliances.

"A marriage simply can't survive the pain that comes from this sort of deceit," Haynes said. "I thought I could make him love me. Guess I was wrong."

Wagner has lately been spotted with Sara Leander, star of his upcoming *Nevada Heat.* But former fling Merri Childs maintained the relationship is likely doomed.

"Chase never quite got over his first love," Childs said. "He only mentioned her once, but when he did, oh the sadness in his eyes! She was his high school sweetheart in Reno. No wonder he never wanted to film on location there."

Wagner and Haynes will share custody of their three minor children. Their oldest son, Kristopher, is a sophomore at USC, where he follows in his father's film-major footsteps.

Hunter

CONFUCIUS SAY

The more things change,
the more they stay the same.

Okay, it probably
wasn't Confucius
who said it, but
whoever it was had
it all wrong. In my
humble opinion,
the saying should go:

The more things change, the more
you wish they would stay the same.

I like things on track.
A railroad track, in
fact. Humming right
along, buzzing with
a regular rhythm. Slip
in a little adventure,
sure. But don't flip
a switch and send me
down a different rail.

The more things change,
the less I like my direction.

CHANGES

Donald and David have
taken up residence in my bedroom
at home. Despite Dad's objections,

there wasn't a better choice.
They just started Pleasant Valley
Elementary, the same school I went

to at their age. The transition has
been difficult. Okay, that's putting
it mildly. Vegas to Reno is like Palm

Springs to Placerville. Low desert
heat to foothill chill. And that's just
the beginning. After mostly running

roughshod over Kristina, adapting
to Mom and Dad's rules is sort of like
a homeless guy going through boot camp.

I am, in turn, sorry for them and pissed
as hell that they have no idea how
to take care of my stuff—the stuff

I had to leave behind when I moved
in with Nikki. I knew I could talk
her into it. I'm a born politician.

THE NIGHT SHE THOUGHT

She kicked me out, I sat in the dark on
her porch, waiting for her to come
home. It was a long, cold wait. But
I wasn't about to let us flame out
because of a little fight.
Especially not
one about my
previous mom.
So I zipped up
my jacket and
waited her out. When she
finally showed, I stowed
all trace of ego, begged
her to take me back.
My apology
was sincere.
But then, when
I threw in the
part about my
little brothers
needing my
room, and the
reasons why,
Nikki couldn't
say no. Even so,   **ORGIVENESS hasn't come easy.**

THE FIRST FEW NIGHTS

She made me sleep on the couch.
        Refused to touch me. Barely
                spoke in complete sentences.
I wormed my way back into
        her good graces like any guy
                with half a brain might—flowers.

Supermarket flowers, true,
        but I half filled the house
                with them. She came home
from work to find sunflowers
        in the kitchen. Lilies, tulips,
                carnations, and phlox on end

tables and windowsills. African
        violets in the bathroom. Roses
                (what else?) in the bedroom.
The place smelled like a florist
        shop (or funeral, depending
                on where your head is at).

She was completely stunned,
        and helpless against my kiss.
                When she kissed me back,
I delivered the coup de grâce,
        making love to her on a bed
                blanketed thickly with petals.

OUR TRUCE

Has been an uneasy one, exacerbated
by, of all things, Thanksgiving
tomorrow. Never let a woman

watch the cooking channel.
Especially not as the holiday
season approaches. After one

Saturday marathon, Nikki got
it in her head that she was going
to make a turducken. Not only

that, but she wanted to host the day
for her dad (who, I'm pretty sure,
would much rather spend it boinking

his boss), her mom (whose method
of drowning out that soap opera
is a pricey bottle of scotch), and me.

Now even if I wanted to deal with all
of the above, which I soooo don't,
my mom expects my presence at

her dinner table. It's like being married,
only worse because I'm *not* married,
but have to act like I am anyway.

THE COMPROMISE?

Woo-hoo. Oh, yeah. Get this.
Mom invited Nikki to roast
her turducken at our house.
Mom's doing side dishes, pies,
and a prime rib (*just in case!*).

Best of all, with the probable
exception of Nikki's dad's girlfriend,
the entire extended family plans
to come. No wonder I feel married.
Which explains why, fifteen hours

until total insanity, I'm well on
my way to a major buzz, here at
my buddy Jason's. We're talking
Jäger, Heineken, and some fat
blunts. It's one hell of a party.

Nikki's at work, so I'm basically
on my own, surrounded by stoners
smoking weed. And, in a big bowl
on the coffee table, are assorted meds,
confiscated from who-knows-where.

It's a regular designer potpourri of sleep
inducers, mood enhancers, pain reducers,
and, for all I know, laxatives. Everyone
is welcome to play the pharm game. Only
one rule applies: You have to take three.

I TRIED TO RESIST

Really I did. For one thing,
        I'm supposed to pull a morning
air shift tomorrow. Another change:

I've been promoted. Still
        working weekends, and assorted
holidays, when the so-called

stars would rather sleep in.
        But no more late nights. I've
moved to the six to eleven a.m. slot.

Yeah, it's a little more money.
        But it also means I have to be
up at five a.m. to get to the station

on time, wide-awake and
        prepared to help listeners
"Start your day, the X way."

I entertain myself for a while,
        watching other people's various
stages of inebriation and half

listening to the argument
        in my head—the smart side
of my brain saying, "Leave

the damn bowl alone," while
	the dimwit half asks, "What harm
could three little pills do?"

To pharm or not to pharm? Ah,
	what the hell? I close my eyes,
reach into the capsule stew,

grab three anonymous pills.
	But before I can pop them into
my mouth, my cell buzzes.

		Nikki texts: *Can u pick me up?*
				Car won't start. Dead batt.
		So much for pharming. At least

for tonight. I reach into my
	pocket, fish around for some-
thing paper, find a receipt to

wrap the still unidentified pills
	in. Who knows when I might
need them? I text back: *On my way,*

chug my beer. Why waste
	good brew? "Gotta go," I say.
As if anyone really cares.

THE ALARM BLARES

Five a.m. Five? Oh, crap. I knew
working mornings was going to
suck. It's still dark outside, for
cripe's sake. Dark, and the bed
is warm. Warm with Nikki.
Might as well wake her up too.

She comes out of her dreams,
into my arms, and I already know
waking her will be the very best
part of this day. "I love you,"
I tell her, once and again, as
a hint of pale morning appears.

        Nikki stays in bed as I go to
        shower, turn the water hot to fight
        the house's chill. I'm shivering
        into a towel when she calls,
        Hey. What about my car?
        As she waits for an answer,

anger blossoms. Not her fault,
though. Car. What *about* her car?
It's Thanksgiving. Everything
will be closed. No batteries,
and even if there were, I have
to be at the station. Really soon.

I could pick her up after work,
but I know she's anxious to get
busy on the duckurken thing.
"Get dressed. You can drop me
off, then take my car. Just don't
forget to pick me up later, okay?"

I swear, relationships are labor-
intensive. All about compromise.
Yada. Yada. But when Nikki
comes into the bathroom, all
mussed from sleep and our
early morning rendezvous,

she looks at me in the mirror,
and her eyes hold so much love
that every ounce of resentment
melts away like butter on a hot
griddle. I relinquish the sink,
go into the bedroom, slip into

the jeans lying on the floor.
They're a little wrinkled, but
clean enough and worn to
the point of real comfort.
A whole lot like the bond
between Nikki and me.

FOR A REFRESHING CHANGE

The pimply overnight guy has to wait
        for me. I'm through the door at six
oh three, which means he had to play
        the station call. Damn. Hope he did it.

FCC rules demand it, and a station
        can get fined if it doesn't identify
itself close to top of the hour. Oh,
        well. Not my problem now, I guess.

        The dude comes skulking down the hall,
                muttering mostly under his breath. *Sure.*
        Promote the half-ass guy and keep me
                doing nights. He slams on out the door.

Half-ass? Me? And just what
        does that make him? A company
man? I head on into the booth,
        just as the last spot of the break finishes.

Perfect timing, man. Half-ass?
        I don't think so. I punch up the next
song on the playlist, zero seconds
        to spare. Yeah, I should have been

here earlier. Most morning guys
        get in at least an hour before their
show begins, to dig up some witty
        repartee and be solidly prepared.

Maybe tomorrow, right? Anyway,
        I can do this gig with my eyes closed.
Witty is my middle name. And I know
        the playlist inside out. Lenny Kravitz

finishes up. "Hey, Reno, happy
        Thanksgiving. If you're up this
early on a holiday, what's wrong
        with you, anyway? The turducken

can wait for an hour or two. Go
        back to bed, say hi to your wife,
and get a little for me." Okay,
        that was a wee bit crude, but that's

the name of the morning show
        game: Crude. Rude. Ear-catching
entertainment. Rick the Brick
        Denio ain't got a thing on me.

I'M MOST OF THE WAY

Through my shift when the studio
telephone rings. "You got the X."

> *Is this Hunter Haskins?* The husky
> voice is somehow familiar.

"Uh, yes it is. And who am I speaking
with?" I have almost placed her

> when she says, *You remember
> me, right? You gave me those Dave*

> *Cook tickets. It was a really great
> show, you know. So thank you.*

Oh, yeah. Red. Actually, Leah.
"No problem. Glad you liked it."

> *I was just wondering if you're on
> mornings now or what. Cuz I think*

> *you're really good. And I was also
> wondering when I can see you again.*

Despite everything with Nikki
this morning, Leah's breathy

innuendo holds immense appeal.
I allow myself a short fantasy—

me, popping buttons, exposing
soft white flesh . . . stop it, Hunter.

Rein it in. You will not be exposing
anything, unless it belongs to Nik.

"Uh. The next remote I'm scheduled
for is the Sparks Hometowne Christmas

Parade." Two weeks, two days. "I'll
be announcing with Montana."

> *Oh. So long? Well, I guess I can wait.*
> *I've got a little something for you.*

The girl is persistent. "Nice. Hang
on . . ." I put her on hold, dig into

my brain for a little Bob Marley trivia,
pass it on to my listeners. "You still there?"

Doubtless. "Well, you have a good
Thanksgiving. See you in Sparks."

I'M STILL MUSING

About "celebrity" perks when Big
Leon comes in to take over. "Hey,
dude," I say. I'd ask his opinion
on the matter, but his air name

refers not so much to his height
as to his three-hundred-pound
girth. Pretty sure he's never been
offered a fine little piece just by

virtue of his "not exactly a star"
status. I gather my stuff, head
out to the parking lot, look for
my Nissan. Not there. Damn.

I should have called Nikki to
remind her. But then I notice
Mom's Jeep, with a familiar
face behind the windshield.

She gives me a major smile
as I climb into the passenger seat.
"Hey, Aunt Leigh. Great to see
you. Uh, my car's okay, right?"

> She laughs, reaches over to
> give me a hug. *It's safe. Poor*
> *Nikki is just up to her elbows*
> *in three varieties of stuffing.*

"Yeah, right. Hopefully one
is plain cornbread. Where's
Katie? Didn't she want to escape
the madcap feast preparations?"

Leigh's smile vanishes. She sighs.
*Katie and I broke up. Crap timing,
huh? Least she could have done
was wait until after the holidays.*

"Oh. I'm sorry." We drive home,
Leigh droning on about "different
backgrounds" and "different dreams."
I truly am sorry. She and Katie have

been a thing for more than six years.
We all thought this was "the one,"
especially Leigh, who seemed so happy
when they were here last Christmas.

I look at her tightly sculpted face,
softened some by the shallow tendrils
at the corners of her eyes. Almost
forty, still beautiful. And single again.

WE GET TO THE HOUSE

A little before noon. Cars line up along

the driveway single file, like half of Noah's

beasts—Dad's mostly restored Willys Wagon,

my Nissan (parked crooked, thanks so much, Nik),

Jake and Misty's dirt-crusted blue Subaru,

Nikki's mom's showroom-clean Audi Quattro.

Her dad's car—an amazing '09 Z06 Corvette—

is conspicuously absent, but I wouldn't expect

him to show this early, considering dinner

isn't supposed to be served until late afternoon.

He's probably six inches deep in his boss right now.

Poor Nikki's mom. Guys are dogs. Woof, woof.

THIS DOG STARTS SALIVATING

As soon as the front door opens.
If the chiduckey tastes even half
as good as it already smells,

Nikki is going to get an extra,
extra special thank-you tonight.
Maybe that cooking show paid

off after all. Dad and Jake are
in the living room, watching Big
Ten football and slurping brew.

I poke my head through
the archway, feign interest. "Hey,
honey, I'm home. What's the score?"

Jake stands, offers his right
hand. *All tied up, three-three.*
Grab a beer and come sit down.

"Sure. Give me a few." I follow
the drift of sage and rosemary
toward the kitchen, where

the women have gathered like
ravens to watch Mom crust
the prime rib with fresh ground

pepper and rock salt. Marie Haskins
doesn't need cooking shows.
Experience trumps experiments.

It's a scene right out of a movie.
Five women, all beautiful
within their own stages of life,

talking and laughing and drinking
wine. Golden-shelled pies decorate
the granite countertops, leak

scented steam, hinting at their
anonymous fillings. Bread
dough rises in yeasty grandeur,

and a chorus line of foil-wrapped
potatoes await their own turn in
the oven. It's a scene right out

of a movie, okay. Artificial.
Look into any of these ladies'
eyes, I guarantee you'll find

some manner of hurt. Something
to deny feasting and celebration.
Something to deny Thanksgiving.

CALL ME A CYNIC

You wouldn't be inaccurate.
Then, again, neither is my assessment.

Conspicuously absent is one female
member of this family. Kristina

should be here for her kids.
And speaking of the demonic duo,

wonder what manner of evil David
and Donald are perpetrating right now.

Upstairs. In my former room.
I'll check it out in a few. Meanwhile,

I probably should be social. "Hello,
ladies. Need any help?"

> Mom says, *Don't think so. But thanks.*
> Misty says, *How sweet of you to offer.*

Leigh snorts, knowing the offer was
mostly empty. Nikki's mom

turns rheumy eyes at me. Whoa.
How much wine has she sloshed already?

Nikki, sweet Nikki, sidles over, clearly
wanting to kiss me. Except

her mom is standing there staring.
Like I care. I reach, pull her right

up against me. "Your turkey thing smells
really good." Then I whisper,

"But not as good as you," and
I give her a giant lip smack, despite four

pairs of eyes pointed directly at the two
of us. Voyeurs deserve what they see.

Nikki smiles, but extricates herself
from my grasp and goes to be one

of the girls. Guess that's my cue
to go be one of the guys.

I grab a beer from the fridge.
"Well, call if you need anything," I lie.

When I turn, I notice David outside
the window playing with . . .

A NEW PUPPY

"Hey. No one told me you got
a new pup." It's been a few
months since Moxie died, at the ripe
old age of fourteen. Downright
elderly for a German shepherd.

> *Too quiet around here without*
> *a dog,* Mom says. *Besides, we*
> *thought it might be good for*
> *the boys to have something*
> *to love and take care of.*

Or to dislike and mutilate.
Cynically speaking, of course.
David actually seems
to be enjoying the pup's
company. I was just a little

younger when Moxie came
to us, all wiggly and yappy.
She grew into a straight-up
incredible dog, and I took
a fair amount of credit for that.

This puppy—Sasha, I'm told—
may be just the thing to bring
David and Donald out of
their shells. Only Donald, like
his mother, is obviously elsewhere.

I AM ON MY WAY

To check on his whereabouts
when the telephone rings. No
one else bothers, so I answer.

> *Hello? Who the fuck is this?*
> The always pleasant Ron.
> *I want to talk to Kristina.*

"Uh, this is Hunter." Wonder
if he even knows who I am.
"And Kristina isn't here."

> I swear I can almost hear anger
> swelling, pewter, in the silence.
> *Well, where the fuck is she?*

My own temper kindles.
"I don't know where she is,
Ron. She's not my prob—"

> *She's out fucking around on
> me, isn't she? Who is she with?
> I swear, I'll kick her ass.*

"You already did that, dude.
Look. She isn't here. I haven't
seen her since last Christmas."

Don't lie to me, you little shit,
or I'll kick your ass too. His
voice is a cougar's sharp hiss.

His threat doesn't scare me,
but it does piss me off. "You're
going back to jail, you know. . . ."

Dad materializes beside me,
takes the phone, calmly says,
Kristina isn't here, Ron.

If you can't find her, that's
too bad, but it's really not
our concern. What does *concern*

me is your ruining our holiday.
I'm going to hang up now.
Don't call back. Today or ever.

Dad follows through, hangs
up, and that might be that except
around here, nothing ever is.

A LOUD GASP

On the stairs makes Dad
and me wheel in unison. Donald.

Was that my dad? he shouts.
Why didn't you let me talk to him?

My dad remains calm. *Your father
didn't ask to talk to you, Donald.*

*So? I wanted to talk to him.
You can't keep me away from him.*

Dad's voice rises, ever so slightly.
No one's trying to keep you away—

*Yes, you are. I hate you. I hate
it here. I want to go home. . . .*

The poor kid totally breaks
down. *Please. Let me go home.*

Dad drops his voice a notch.
Look, son, you can't go back there.

Liftoff again. *Shut up. Shut up.
Yes, I can.* Suddenly, something

flies by my face, barely clearing
my cheek before crashing into the wall.

"What the . . . ?" I retrieve the now
        useless thing, formerly my Wii controller.

                Donald thumps up the stairs,
                        into his (my) room, slams the door.

        Dad follows, and all of a sudden
                a whole flock of women appears,

        clucking like hens. We can all hear
                Dad ask calmly, *Please let me in.*

Just another day (holiday) in
        paradise, huh? Still holding most

ot my beer, I go to join Jake,
        cheer for no team in particular.

        Upstairs, Dad's plea becomes
                a demand. *Open this damn door!*

In the hallway, the hens are
        still clucking away. And . . .

"Hey," I yell. "Is something
        burning?" *Cluck-cluck-cluck. Bwoik!*

I'm thinking a serious buzz
        is in order. Beer will not do.

WHAT MAY DO

Is the pill potpourri
still in my pocket.
Who knows what
they might really do,   if anything. I reach
                for possible Nirvana,
                swallow it down with
                two gulps of beer. Wait.

      I plop on the plush
      leather sofa, fake cheer
      when Wisconsin scores,
      slug down more beer.   Wait. About the time
                I think I must have
                gagged down placebos,
                my brain goes fuzzy

and my tongue thickens
in my mouth. Behind
my forehead, a *zzzzzz*
sound lifts, like bees   swarming, and my ears
                feel like I'm diving
                deep. Pressure. I close
                my eyes, try to shut out

      football. Shouting. Crying.
      Clucking. Burnt butter
      smell. Dinner should be
      interesting. To say the least.

WE'VE ALWAYS KEPT

Thanksgiving relatively low-key.
      Grandfather. Aunt Cora. And me.
            We spend the day cooking. Tasting.
                  Eating. Getting way too full. Just us.
But not this year. This year
      we're going to a big schmooze
            at Liam's parents' house in Austin.
                  Aunt Cora wants to introduce us.
Not sure why she needed
      to make the big intros today.
            She knows how I feel about
                  breaking bread with total strangers.
Grandfather isn't a whole
      lot happier about it than I am.
            But Aunt Cora can be pretty
                  convincing when she's honey sweet.
It's a skill I'm working hard on,
      especially where Grandfather
            is concerned. I've tried and tried
                  to get him to loosen my reins, at least
a little. It's hard to maintain
      a romance when most every
            move is monitored. Grandfather
                  doesn't trust me, which another time

I might find sort of funny. Me?
   In need of watching? I mean,
     considering his distrust took
       root in a past defined by my father,
it's not really fair to me.
   Then again, considering
     I'm not exactly anxious for
       him to know any details about Bryce
and me, some people might
   say I've earned it to some
     degree. But, hey, a month
       of secrets in seventeen years?
I'd say that's not so bad.
   And a month of romance
     in all that time means I've got
       a fair amount of catching up to do.

I HAVEN'T CAUGHT ALL THE WAY

Up yet. Haven't gone all the way
"there," not that he's asked to.

Part of me really likes that—
that he respects me enough

not to pressure me into something
I'm probably not ready for. Part

of me wonders if I'm not good
enough for him to even want to try.

It's warped. So am I. Although
I have to say, with Bryce in my life

I feel a little less distorted than
I used to. He grounds me. Not only

that, but for once, people at school
don't look at me like I'm a complete freak.

Not with Bryce's arm around my waist
as he walks me to class. Not when they see

us steal kisses (you're not supposed
to swap spit in the hallways). Not when

they see us come and go in his car,
stereo blaring. Sometimes grunge,

sometimes country. I'm happy to listen
to Three Days Grace. And, with some

coaxing, he'll agree to Toby Keith,
though I haven't quite convinced him

Toby's music is rock with a Texas
drawl. On weekends we manage

to steal some time together, if I can
talk Grandfather into letting me go

to a game, the mall, or the library. Bryce
will meet me and we'll cheer our team,

window shop, or make out behind the stacks.
I must say, I've become a pretty good kisser.

And I'm starting to like how that makes me feel
in places I've always refused to think about.

YEAH, I KNEW I HAD THEM

I took sex ed twice
in middle school.
I totally get the
mechanics, and
when it comes
to spelling the
names for those
places, hey, I'm a
regular champ. But
up until now, the
idea of putting
that knowledge
to genuine use
seemed way too
complicated to
consider. Not to
mention more than
just a little messy.
Okay, when it comes to   E X, I'm retarded. But
                              better late than never.

IF YOU BELIEVE THE HYPE

Pretty much everyone my age
has been doing it since puberty
claimed them. I have no idea   how

accurate that is, but think it must
be a gross exaggeration.
In health class, Mr. Vega said
most self-proclaimed virgins   will

resort to self-satisfaction. Just his
saying the word "masturbation" out
loud bellowed embers in my face.   I

have never . . . could never . . .
At least I'm pretty sure I could
never. Mr. Vega also said
that the best way to   know

what you like is to experiment
without a partner. What I like?
That's up to me? And anyway,   I'm

afraid if I happen to figure out
what I like, I might never stop
doing it. OCD masturbation.
The world is definitely not   ready for that.

WONDER WHO THINKS I DO

Aunt Cora? Maybe, maybe not.
         Seems like satisfaction of any type

         would make one's little gold flecks
multiply like jackrabbits. My aura

would sparkle like an Oscar-
         night Yves St. Laurent. And anyway,

         Aunt Cora is probably too busy
basking in her own satisfaction

to worry too much about mine.
         Cherie? She thinks I do, of course

         she does. She's got a grubby mind.
Grandfather? No way. If he thought

such a thing, for even one
         minute, he'd cure me, Baptist-style.

         The only other person who might
care is Bryce. Oh God, I hope

he doesn't think I do. Hope . . .
         Wait one sec. Maybe I hope he does.

HOPE HE DOES

Because, so sayeth
Mr. Vega, the big M
is normal. I want Bryce
to think I'm normal,
though I suspect he
might guess otherwise.

(Guess otherwise and like me
anyway? What's that about?)

Hope he does because
that would mean Bryce
is putting me and sex
in the same thought,
something I'm pretty
sure no one else has.

(Want—really want—him to think
about me in a sexual way? Weird.)

Hope he does, mostly
because putting me
and sex in the same
thought means he's
got me, Autumn Rose
Shepherd, on his mind.

(Means he's got me on his
mind in any way at all.)

I WISH I WAS SPENDING

Thanksgiving with Bryce. Just the two
of us, plus cornbread-stuffed turkey,
taters, gravy, cranberries, pumpkin
pie. Skip the green bean casserole.
Aunt Cora loves that stuff. Claims
it's her specialty. Special? Uh . . .

Anyway, it's my fantasy, so
excise the French cuts, smothered
in mushroom soup. Start with
Bryce and me nibbling each other
for appetizers while the bird
roasts and the pies cool
on the counter, perfuming

the kitchen with cinnamon and
nutmeg. Bryce leans me back
over the Formica . . . scratch that.
Fantasy, remember? Leans me
back over the shiny black granite,
kisses me. And not in a nice way.

And I kiss him back, with every
fiber of me screaming, "Go ahead.
Say okay. You know you want to.
Beg him to—" Except a buzzer
goes off. The turkey's done. Taters,
too. Gosh darn food fantasies.

TURNS OUT

The buzz isn't fantasy. It's my cell,
insisting I've got a text message.
Bryce. Wonder if he was reading
my warped mind long-distance.

        He's in San Diego, spending
        the holiday with his grandparents.
        Hey u. CA wud be prettier if u
        wur here. 'S cold w/o u.

Abbreviations irritate me. I text
back without resorting to shortcuts.
"Hey, you. Texas is always warm. But
Thanksgiving would definitely be

a lot more fun if you were here.
I'd even cook for you." I hit
the send button, fall back into
my kitchen fantasy. But not for long.

        My cell buzzes again. *Wish u wur*
        cooking 4 me. Gram's cooking
        mostly suks. Hey, are u a good
        cook? Cuz if u r, I think I luv u.

DID HE MEAN

He loves me? Like for real?
Or was he just being funny?

My stomach flip-flops. How
should I answer? Should I answer

at all? OMG. Because I think
I love him, too. But do I dare

tell him that? What if he didn't
mean it? I might scare him away.

But what if he did and I don't
let him know I feel the same way?

Why doesn't love come with
an owner's manual? Maybe I should

try "funny" too. I text, "No matter
what kind of cook you are, I think

I love you, too." My finger hesitates
over the send button. I reread

his message. Reread mine, too.
Ah, what the heck? Here goes.

OFF

Through
cyberspace
the declaration
travels. Byte
by byte.
I wait.

One minute.
Two. No answer.
Please, Bryce?
Seconds tick
by. Damn!
Joke.

Just a joke,
Bryce. Please
don't be mad.
Please don't
dump me.
Buzz!

I jump. Afraid
to look. But
glad when I do.
Good. C u
Sunday.

I SOAR

Up, up, dangerously close
to heaven, and I'm not
the slightest bit afraid.

                  I

have never even once in
my life felt like this before.
Like anything is possible.
No matter how messed up I

                  am,

this amazing guy cares
about me. Maybe even
loves me. That's seriously

                  crazy.

My aura must be all the way
past toffee, to coppery.
Gold, even. I have an

                  in-

sane urge to tell someone
about this. But even Aunt
Cora would have a hard
time believing I'm really in

                  love.

I CRASH

Back to earth. Back to reality.
Back to Thanksgiving with strangers.

      Aunt Cora swore all would be well.
      You'll love Liam's family, she promised.
      And you'll feel right at home. I'm even
      making my green bean casserole.

Yeah, boy. Thanksgiving would not
be the same without it. Everyone's

      supposed to bring something.
      How about your special cranberry
      sauce? asked Aunt Cora, when I
      claimed I didn't know what to make.

I use two secret ingredients—
orange and cinnamon. It's easy

but tedious, and three hours until
we're supposed to ring the doorbell,
I should get to getting, as Grandfather
says. Aunt Cora usually helps me, but

she's already at the Cregans', dousing
green beans with cream o' shrooms.

I DON'T NEED HER HELP

I've made this recipe twice a year

(Christmas, too) since I could tell

the difference between a saucepan

and a skillet. It just seems strange,

going through the familiar motions

laughter free. The kitchen throbs

silence. The sound of my sock-padded

footsteps echoes, wall to wall to wall.

I yank open the cupboard, grab

the necessary utensils, clanging them

cacophonously. Noise to battle

the hush-edged aloneness.

Then I line up ingredients in correct order.

Cinnamon. Cranberries. Oranges. Sugar.

CRANBERRIES SIMMERED

Sugar, orange peel, and cinnamon
added. Everything in a pretty glass
bowl, gelling rich red in the fridge,

it occurs to me that contributing
to the eardrum-slicing quiet is the fact
that Grandfather has not yet appeared.

We should leave before too very
long. I explore. Living room? Empty.
Hall? No sign of anything living.

Foreboding strikes suddenly. I march
right up to Grandfather's bedroom door.
Knock, half expecting no answer.

> But on the far side, a drawer closes.
> The sound precedes footsteps
> across the complaining wood floor.

> *Coming,* Grandfather calls. *Coming.*
> Twice, as if convincing himself
> he really needs to get a move on.

I imagine him pajama-clad
and candy-stripe-eyed, but
the grandfather who opens

the door is one I've never, ever
seen before. "Wow. I didn't
know you even owned a suit."

A genuine grin creeps cheekbone
to cheekbone, and his eyes—
clear as a cold-water creek—fill

with delight. *Dug it out of mothballs.*
Today is a special occasion.
Thought Cora might appreciate

you and me dressing to the nines.
Go put on something real pretty.
It's an order. But a gentle one.

THE WHOLE THING

Is so unexpected, I'm halfway
changed into a plum-colored silk

blouse when my fingers start to
tingle and my breath stutters short.

Wait. Why now? Nothing's wrong
except . . . Except for this sudden

feeling like the world just flipped
upside down. South Pole on top.

Santa's lair at the butt end. I close
my eyes, sip in air through clenching

teeth. What is going on with me?
It's just one dinner at the home of total

strangers. One stupid holiday meal,
Grandfather and me putting on the dog

to impress . . . who? One Thanksgiving,
not a commitment, not forever . . . Dread

stuffs itself into my head, and I can't say
why, let alone know how to fight it.

IT'S NOT EXACTLY UNUSUAL

For anxiety to trill suddenly.
        But usually, somewhere in my brain,
                there's a certainty that it's ridiculous.
        This doesn't feel that way. This feels
like a warning of coming chaos.

I finish buttoning my blouse,
        tuck it into the striking tie-dyed skirt
                Aunt Cora gave me on my last birthday.
        I've never worn it before. It seemed
like a treasure. One to hang in

the closet, a safe place to keep
        it. Now that it's on, it's only cloth.
                I finish dressing, brush back my hair,
        tie it loosely with blue velvet ribbon.
Grandfather will be pleased.

But I'm frightened by what
        I see, held completely still in
                the mirror's glass grip. The girl
        captured there, staring back at me,
is someone I don't recognize.

THAT GIRL

Curves softly

inside flounces
of fabric. She looks
like the woman
I'm afraid to grow into.

Lifts her hand

with uncommon grace.
She could pass for
the sophisticate
I'm too clumsy to be.

Touches cheeks

blushed berry in
steep hollows.
I wish I knew who
sculpted her face.

I don't know

that girl. The only
thing familiar about
her is how she wears
fear in her eyes.

IT IS THAT GIRL

Who gets in the car with
Grandfather. That girl who
rides, silent as a ghost, for
ninety-three minutes, barely
even acknowledging her
grandfather's faltering small talk.

That girl who stares out
the window, counting water
tanks and watching big and
bigger American flags flap
in the wind. That girl who
quick-freezes after arrival.

　　　　　　　　Coming? asks Grandfather,
　　　　　　　　exiting the driver's side and
　　　　　　　　then, in a most gentlemanly
　　　　　　　　fashion, circling the car to
　　　　　　　　open the passenger door.
　　　　　　　　What can that girl do but join

her grandfather on the wide
sidewalk? Together, the two
assess the Cregan place—
a huge, upscale tract home.
One of those houses that
resembles its huge, upscale

neighbors to a creepy
degree. The houses come
in three hues—beige, gray,
and not-quite-white. Not much
to distinguish one from another
except the number of stories,

size of the garage, and gravel
color. Even the plants—native
Texas species, known to thrive
in this climate—are the same.
All, no doubt, must be approved
by the homeowners' association.

Part of me likes the conformity.
The order. Part of me wonders
if anything ever disturbs it.
Wind? Rain? Hurricane?
Birth? Divorce? Argument?
What difference does it make?

THE DOOR FLIES OPEN

Before we make the welcome mat.
Some sort of chaos, after all?

But no. It's just a jacked-up Aunt Cora.
Come in! Everyone's here. She snatches

Grandfather's elbow, tugs. *All right,*
he snarls, tugging it back. *I'm working on it.*

Maybe his suave exterior is nothing more
than a barely disguised case of nerves.

I follow, cradling my cranberry surprise
as if it might jump from my arms. Aunt Cora

leads us into the kitchen, where most
of the celebrators have gathered.

She sidles up to Liam, pulls him over
to meet Grandfather, who has yet to

have actually made his acquaintance.
This is my dad, Leroy. Dad, this is Liam.

Grandfather shakes his hand but looks
uncomfortable. *Glad to finally meet you.*

This is only the beginning of a long round
of introductions. We meet Liam's mom and

dad; his brother, Tom; sister, Laurel; two aunts;
three uncles; a cousin or four. And that's just

the ones in the kitchen. I can hear voices
in some other unidentified room. I don't think

I made nearly enough cranberry sauce.
Throughout the entire process, Aunt Cora

hangs on to Liam as if letting go might make
some imaginary tower tumble. Finally, all of

us not quite knowing one another's names,
Aunt Cora's eyes stop traveling the room

long enough for her to notice. *Oh.*
You wore the skirt. It looks amazing.

Suddenly everyone is looking at me.
My palms start to tingle. Before I can lose

my breath, I excuse myself. "I could use"—
blood jackhammers my brain—"some air."

I START TOWARD THE FRONT DOOR

But someone catches my arm.
Come on out here, he says.
The backyard is real pretty.

It's one of Liam's cousins. Beau?
Michael? Whichever, he is a couple
of years older than me and wears

Irish good looks in long, straight
black walnut hair, white linen skin,
and eyes the color of violets.

I catch my breath, shadow him out
into a miniature botanical garden,
with ponds and statuary and trees

in full autumn dress. It's stunning.
Very Zen. My heartbeat slows in
appreciation of the almost solitude.

Almost, but for what's-his-name.
You okay now? His voice is satin.
You looked right about ready to bolt.

"I'm good, thanks. I, uh . . . sorry.
Can't remember your name.
Too many thrown at me at once."

He grins, showing perfect pearl
teeth. *Micah. This is a big family,
okay. And we're not even all here.*

Mi*cah*, not Mi*chael*. Good name.
But why is he being so nice?
"Funny. Our family *is* all here."

Not exactly accurate. But close
enough to the truth, I guess.
Family is about connection.

>   *Nothing wrong with a, uh,
>   compact family. Long as
>   you're good to each other.*

Are we good to each other?
Not bad, I suppose. But all
I can do in response is nod.

>   Silence closes in, squeezes.
>   Micah releases its grip. *You* do
>   *look pretty in that skirt, you know.*

Cheeks flaming, I stutter
something like, "Thanks," just
as someone inside calls out,   *Dinner!*

A GIANT FEAST

Is laid out, buffet-style, on the long kitchen counters.

We form a line, help ourselves, then find places to sit.

The older adults claim the formal dining room, leaving

us younger people to choose our seats at folding

tables in the kitchen. I fill my plate sparingly, pick

a chair, wait to see if Aunt Cora will join me. She doesn't.

But Micah does, sitting beside me. *Do you mind?*

I shake my head, making his recent compliment rattle

around inside my brain: *Pretty in that skirt . . . pretty . . .*

In the next room, Mr. Cregan recites grace and

before the amen, Micah's thigh leans gently against

mine. This can't be happening! But it is, and it's warm,

and all those newly discovered body parts alert.

The conversation around me blurs to a buzz. I do

my best to tune out and eat my turkey and stuffing

without dripping gravy on my blouse or (pretty!) skirt.

This is just dumb. Not four hours ago, I was fantasizing

about a private Thanksgiving with Bryce. Now here

I am surrounded by Cregans and, for some unfathomable

reason, leg-to-leg with probably the best-looking member

of the clan. This cannot be happening. Maybe I'm asleep

and this is all a dream. Blood whooshes in my ears,

damping a gush of laughter. Somebody told a joke?

Suddenly metal clinks against glass, like a bell.

All attention turns toward the dining room, where

> Aunt Cora and Liam are standing. *Excuse us, but*
>
> *we have some happy news,* says Liam. Aunt Cora
>
> catches my eye, smiles. *We're getting married.*

DAD'S IDEA

Of a Thanksgiving meal,

    Turkey Day treats, in his

vernacular, is going out

    to my all-time favorite place,

(are you ready for this?)

    Carrows. Best burgers, ever.

Burgers for Thanksgiving?

    Poultry gives me the trots.

No pumpkin pie, either?

    Bet Carrows will have it.

Carrows pumpkin pie?
Think I'll skip it. Burgers?
Maybe they have turkey
burgers. Jeez, man. Even
foster homes celebrate
Thanksgiving, trying to
make up for real parents
who aren't real parents.

    Hey, I've never been much
    of a cook. And Kortni?
    Let her do a turkey, we'll all
    get the trots. And anyway,
    the important thing is being
    together, right? Thankful
    we can be like a real family.

OPERATIVE WORD:

"Like" a real family. I've never
       actually had one of those, and
                I'm not exactly sure what I'd do

with one if I got one. Don't even
       know if I want one of my own
                creation. Marriage? Children?

Sounds like a double whammy
       to me. You don't even see that
                happily-ever-after crap on TV

anymore. Death. Divorce.
       Deviance. That pretty well
                describes network television

in the twenty-first century.
       Mostly because it reflects
                contemporary reality. No,

I think I'll stick to steady
       relationships for as long
                as they might reasonably

last. No promises. No "I do's."
       No contributing to global
                overpopulation. Now or ever.

LONG BEFORE

Any Thanksgiving meal at all, a volley
of snores—Dad's and Kortni's—
chase me down the narrow hallway.
I slip out the front door, into the bite
of November, early morning. A day

without seeing Kyle? Not going to
happen. The rutted dirt challenges
my bare feet, but somehow I manage
the short jog. He's there. Parked.
Waiting. Of course he is. I barely

      have the door yanked open and
      we are kissing. *Come up here.*
      He pulls me into the truck and into
      his arms without our mouths unlocking.
      Lip to lip, he manages, *Damn, I love you!*

I slide my arms around his neck,
pull my head back so I can plunge
into the aqua deep of his eyes.
There's something swimming there,
in the dark pools of his pupils.

Something disquieting. Now
that I think about it, I can taste
it too, lingering on his tongue.
It's not quite sweet, and reminds
me of how the chem lab smells.

Crystal. He uses sometimes,
has offered it to me, though
not since we've been together.
"You buzzed?" The thought
half horrifies, half excites me.

        Nah. At my disbelieving look,
        he admits, *Not really. Just did*
        a little. I don't react, and that
        makes him kind of twitchy.
        Why, you want to try some?

Always before, I just said no,
left it solidly there. I waver
now. I want to share everything
with Kyle. Want to know what he
knows, feel what he feels, share

the same space he's in. I almost
say what the hell. In fact, I open
my mouth to do so. But what comes
out is, "N-not today." I hope he thinks
it has to do with Thanksgiving.

        Instead he says, *Chicken?*
        Rather than argue or explain,
        I simply tell him he's right.
        No need for lengthy stories
        about Mom and predisposition.

INSTEAD

I'll try distraction. "Want to go
        somewhere?" I do my best
        to sound sexy, but think
I need to practice. I sounded

more fan girl than vamp.
        Sexy or just plain fanatic,
        I am a little surprised when
Kyle responds by shaking

        his head. *Wish we could . . .*
                To prove it, he touches me
                suggestively in a very intimate
        place. *But I have to get home*

        pretty soon. We're going to
                my Aunt Liz's house in Fresno,
                and Dad wants to leave by nine.
        Just as Kyle knows better

than to argue with his dad,
        I understand pouting will
        not only get me nowhere,
it just might make Kyle mad.

HE INHERITS HIS TEMPER

From his father, he says.
I've only witnessed it on
a couple of occasions. Hope
I never have to see it again.

The last time was when
we told Matt about Kyle and
me. It was at school the day after
we first got together. Matt came

walking toward us in his usual
cheerful way. His smile dissolved
when he noticed us, hands locked
together and eyes wearing worry.

> *Uh, what's going on?* But
> what was going on was obvious.
> Hurt wrinkled his face as if
> he'd suddenly aged thirty years.

My stomach lurched, roller-
coaster-style. "We need to
talk," I started. I was wavering,
and Kyle must have felt it in the way

> my hand trembled. He grabbed
> control. *Dude, you're not going
> to like this, but Summer and
> I hooked up yesterday.*

Matt's reaction was swift.
*What the fuck are you talking
about? Summer? And what
exactly does "hook up" mean?*

My face flared, dry-ice hot, and
I saw Matt's eyes flood with sudden
understanding. "Oh God, I'm so
sorry. I never meant to hurt—"

Kyle totally lost it. *Shut up,
Summer. Don't you dare make
excuses.* Then, to Matt. *That's
right. We did it. And we'll do it*

*again. She's really good, so you
know. And she's mine. Understand?*
Back to me. *You are mine, aren't
you? Didn't you say you loved me?*

I tried to nod, but a vortex of
confusion sucked me in. "Uh . . .
yes. I mean, I guess. I mean . . ."
I wasn't sure about anything.

But even if I'd wanted to change
my mind, it was too late. Matt's hurt
had fanned into full-blown anger.
I guess, I mean, whatever. Fuck

you both. I don't need a whore
like you, Summer. And no one
needs a so-called friend like you.
He was solidly in Kyle's face.

And Kyle reacted badly, shoving
Matt backward. Hard enough
to land Matt on his butt. *Just*
leave us the fuck alone, okay?

I was mortified. Freaked out
that it had gone so badly.
Even more freaked out at how
easily Kyle went off. Crazy.

But that didn't change how I feel.
Didn't make me love him less.
In fact, in some perverted way,
it was sort of a turn-on.

EVEN SO

One thing I do know.
                    I don't ever want to
                                        make him mad at me,

and he does not much
                    care for the "oh, poor
                                        me" routine. So I'll suck

it up. Still, my melting
                    smile must signal
                                        disappointment. "That's

okay. We'll get together
                    tomorrow, right?"
                                        Couldn't keep me away.

He reaches for my shirt,
                    pulls, and not too gently.
                                        Again, we are connected

by the kind of kiss that
                    should be integral
                                        to every single good-bye.

I WATCH THE DUST

Of his retreat lift
into the bitter
blue sky. Not
a single cloud
to catch it.
Clear.
Cold.
Empty.

Like how I feel
right now. Love
is strange. One
minute you're
jungle fever.
The next
you're
Arctic
winter.

I'M GETTING DRESSED

For our like-a-real-family Thanksgiving
Day jaunt to Dad's all-time favorite

Carrows when my cell warbles.
Kyle! I scramble to find the phone

hidden in the chaos that is my dresser.
But no, it's not Kyle. (Why did I think

it would be?) When I see whose number
has in fact materialized on caller ID,

I consider pretending I never heard
the very loud ring tone. Still, it is a holiday.

Guess I should pick up. "Hey, Mom.
Happy Thanksgiving." I expect some

sweet, if bogus, holiday greeting.
Instead she launches verbal mortars.

> *I called Darla and Phil's to say hello*
> *and they told me you're not there*
>
> *anymore. You're living with your dad?*
> *Why didn't you bother to let me know?*

My first instinct is to lob a grenade
right back at her, but something in her

voice says she doesn't want to go to war.
She sounds ready to implode. "You okay?"

That's all it takes to light the fuse.
She's falling bricks. *No. I'm not okay.*

The boys are with your grandparents
in Reno because Ron set me up. . . .

The fifteen-minute rant nets some
pertinent information. Mom's fragile

life has shattered yet again. Ron beat
her up, possibly left a stash of meth

where the cops who came calling
could, or even would, find it. And now

it's up to her, in a couple of weeks,
to try and convince a judge that she,

a proven liar and twice-convicted
felon, is, this time, completely innocent.

Best of luck, mother-of-mine. I don't
believe you. Why should a judge?

BUT THAT'S NOT WHAT SHE WANTS

To hear. So I listen without commentary.
And, I guess, less sympathy than she,
for some stupid reason, expects.

> *Well?* she finishes. *Nothing to say?*

Her supercilious tone irritates me.
"Sucks to be you," is the best I can
do. What does she want from me?

> *How can you be so . . . so mean?*

Now, somehow, it's on me? My turn
to blow. "God, Mom, are you stupid
or what? Why don't you move the fuck

away from there? Go somewhere
Ron can't find you. Start over . . .
Get a real job. Take care of your kids."

> *How would I do that? I don't have—*

"Don't say it. Don't say you don't have
the resources. Grandma Marie would
help. You know that. You're just a . . ."

> *A what?* Her breathing sounds tattered.

289

I should feel sorry for her. But I don't.
I can't. I'm sick of her freaking
excuses. "A goddamn coward.

It's easier to keep on living like you
do. Day-to-day. No thought for
the future or the past. Not caring

about the shit you're always crotch-
deep in. What about the boys,
Mom? What about any of us?"

She is quiet for a very long time.
I hope it's because something I said
actually sliced through her denial.

But no. *Happy Thanksgiving to you, too.*

And she's gone. Suddenly I want
to take it all back. Damn her, anyway.
I love her. I hate her. I wish

I didn't know her. I ache to know
her better. My glass bravado
cracks. Splinters. Crashes down.

I NEVER CRY

Never, ever cry over Mom

        or the charade that is my life.

But tears fall now. And I do

        nothing to try and stop them.

God, how I want to let her in.

        But I know she'd only shut me out.

Doesn't matter why—meth or

        men or something I can't fathom

at all—the fact is, she's incapable

        of loving me like a mother should.

So I can't let myself love her

        like a daughter should. To unlock

myself in such a way would simply

        be an invitation to heartbreak.

ALMOST DONE

Feeling sorry for myself when
a little warning chimes in my head.
Mom is the queen of denial.
Not her meth? Maybe not, but

        odds are

decent she's using again.
Wouldn't be the first time
she jumped off the wagon.
One time she came to visit so

        high

that she didn't realize the guy
she was putting the moves on
happened to be my caseworker.
Not like we all couldn't tell

        she

was lit. Her sweat-sequined skin
leaked a smell like tar remover.
When Darla asked if she wanted
to join us for dinner, Mom

        lied,

claiming a bad case of fast-food
poisoning. And when the cute
clean-cut dude finally mentioned
his official relationship

        to me,

she added disgusting details
about her fabricated illness,
used them to make a hasty
escape. Like anyone believed her.

MEMORY LANE

Is an ugly stroll. I'm working hard
       to turn the corner when Dad finally

               calls, *Let's go, girls. I can hear*
       a big ol' burger mooing my name.

Does he have even the faintest
       idea how stupid that sounded?

               Maybe not. But evidently Kortni
       does. *Burgers don't moo, idiot.*

Idiot. Nice. This little outing should
       go well. I settle into the rotting

       backseat of Dad's decrepit Chevy
Impala. Stinks like cigarette-

tainted armpit drip. Reminds
       me again of Mom. How can

she ruin every holiday (even
       the ones that don't feel much

       like holidays) without even being
there? Why can't I just forget her?

BUT SHE'S ON MY MIND

As Dad weaves down the rutted
dirt toward the highway, Kortni
chattering like an irritated crow.

Unusual, considering the amount
of beer they've apparently consumed
since breakfast. The smell of cheap

brew, mixed with stale tobacco,
gags me slightly. "Uh, Dad.
You sure you're good to drive?"

> *Damn straight. Why wouldn't*
> *I be?* As if to prove he's too
> damn straight, he pulls out

> a joint, hands it to Kortni.
> *Light that, would ya, babe?*
> *Gotta keep my eyes on the road.*

Just perfect. Can I get high
from secondhand pot smoke?
"Uh, Dad? My asthma?"

> Kortni torches the blunt
> anyway. *We'll just open all*
> *the windows. You'll be okay.*

They're smoking. I'm steaming,
despite the fact that it's pretty
damn cold, moving freeway-speed

with all the windows dropped.
Whatever. Usually I don't think
much about Kortni at all.

Right now I'm thinking how
much she resembles a Pekingese,
double-inhaling pot smoke

up her smashed-in nose, snorting
a little with each exhale. I bet
she's one hellacious snorer.

As Dad's girlfriends go, I guess
she isn't the worst. Not that I've met
them all, or wanted to. A couple

were prettier on the outside, evil
ugly inside. Zoe tops that list. Not
sure exactly where that puts Mom.

Old pictures I've seen at Grandma
and Grandpa Haskins's house prove
Kristina's exterior was stunning once

upon a time, in a land before crystal
meth. Amazing how fast that drug
can age you. It's a zombie, sucking

youth right out of you, lifeblood.
Then again, if she hadn't fallen
into that lifestyle, she wouldn't have

met Dad at all. And then there
wouldn't be me. A perverse question
bubbles up. Perverse, because I know

it's going to bug Kortni. Like wheezy
me cares. "So, Dad. How exactly
did you and Mom meet?" We've never

            discussed it. And he doesn't
            really want to now. *Um. Why?*
            You writing an autobiography?

Big word. Wrong word, but big.
"No. That would be *your* memoir,
not mine. I just want to know is all."

            Oh. Here's our exit. We'll talk
            about it later, okay? Saved by
            Carrows. Lucky Dad. For now.

HOLY CRAP

Can't believe this place is so crowded.
       Must have been a whole herd of mooing
              Thanksgiving burgers. We have to wait
                    outside for almost a half hour.
Dad and Kortni smoke. Regular
       cigarettes, thank God. I move upwind,
              stand off to one side. Don't want to
                   think any more about Mom right now.

So I'll think about Kyle instead.
       I'd rather be spending today with
              him, think he probably wishes
                  the same. Poor guy. Dysfunction
pretty much defines his family
       too. His mom died eight years
              ago, a DUI fatality. "DUI" meaning
                  "diving under the influence" into

a fast-running but shallow section
       of the Kern River. The coroner
              ruled it an accident, but Kyle
                  believes the act was purposeful.
       Sick of Dad's shit, he called it.
              The bitch went and left us alone
                  with him. Just goes to show
                    how little she cared about us.

"Us," meaning him and his sister,
          Sadie. Deserted by their mother.
                    Left with an alcoholic father
                              and his own string of girlfriends.
Probably why Kyle and I are
          so good together. The old
                    saying, "takes one to know
                              one," definitely applies to us.

I've got a saying of my own:
          "Takes one to love one." Mom
                    told me something like that once.
                              The topic of discussion was Ron,
who had just left bruises on
          three-year-old Donald. I was
                    on a rant. "How come all the men
                              in your life have been losers?" I asked.

          She barely reacted to the word
                    "loser." *I could never have*
                              a relationship with someone
                                        who didn't understand addiction.
Nice phrasing. Translation:
          She could never be with a guy
                    who wasn't an addict himself.
                              No wonder she can't stay clean.

THERE I GO AGAIN

Thinking about Mom. I have so
got to stop that! Think about Kyle.
Think about Kyle. Think about . . .

> The door opens and a senior-
> citizen-type hostess chirps,
> *Kenwood, party of three.*

Not sure you could call us a party.
Then again, Dad is pretty much
a walking, talking party all by himself.

> *There it is,* he says, opening
> the menu. *The Mile-High Burger.*
> *My mouth is watering already.*

He orders the cholesterol-
ridden nightmare, plus a beer.
Kortni dittoes. I go for the Mile-

High Turkey Stack. Hey, it's got
the requisite (for me, anyway)
poultry, plus some vegetable matter,

on a flaky croissant. Homage
to the day! The beer arrives.
Disappears. A second round

comes before the waitress can
deliver our meal. Dad slams
that one too. By the time

our Mile-High feast hits the table,
he's barely coherent enough to
order another one. "Dad," I warn,

"I know we're celebrating and
everything, but maybe you'd
better slow down a little."

　　　　　　　　Before he can argue, Kortni
　　　　　　　　jumps to his defense. *He's fine.*
　　　　　　　　And anyway, you're not his mother.

If I were Kyle, I'd simply blow.
Being Summer, I'll choose
a more covert route to revenge.

In silence, I pick at my sandwich,
watching Dad and Kortni wolf
theirs down and chase them

with even more beer. I wait until
their mouths are full, then venture,
"So, Dad. Tell me how you met Mom."

HE MANAGES NOT TO CHOKE

But just barely. Kortni shoots
evil eye arrows. Touché, bitch.

> *Well, uh . . . , he beer-sputters.*
> *You know how we met, right?*

"Haven't a clue. Neither of you
has ever really talked about it."

> *Why does he need to discuss this*
> *now? Kortni tries to interfere.*

I look her dead in the eye. "This is not
your business. I want to know."

> *S'all right, slurs Dad. Why not?*
> *This is as good a time as any.*
>
> *Remember I tol' you 'bout my old*
> *buddy Trey? Well, he was married*
>
> *to your mom at the time, and they*
> *had a little girl. Autumn. Pretty thing.*
>
> *I used to take care of her while*
> *Kristina worked. After Trey moved*
>
> *out, of course. Always kind of felt*
> *bad about her coming between us.*

"Wait!" Hunter, me, Donald, David . . .
"Are you saying Mom has another daughter?

And what do you mean, 'coming
between us'? Coming between who?"

> Me and Trey. See, I was just
> supposed to stay a few days.
>
> But God. It was a bottomless
> party, crystal 24-7. Hard to walk
>
> away from that. And you know
> the crystal scene. Shit makes you
>
> horny as hell. Everyone screwing
> everyone. Only when me and Kristina
>
> hooked up, we had chemistry.
> Thought for sure it was love, but
>
> you think all kinds of crazy shit
> when you're tweaking. Trey came
>
> home from a score and found us
> mid-dirty. And that's pretty much
>
> how I met your mom and lost
> my best friend. Now can I eat?

HE WOLFS

The rest of his burger, and since
I'm no longer hungry, I push
my plate across the table, watch
him finish my Thanksgiving dinner.
"Can we please go now?"

> He doesn't seem to understand
> (or maybe just doesn't care) how
> this disclosure (yes, I asked for it)
> has rocked me. Torpedoed me.
> *Can I please finish my beer first?*

I don't look at him or Kortni
as I consider what this means
to me. Why didn't anyone ever
tell me I have a sister somewhere?
Mom never once mentioned her.

And then there's the whole part
about how my dad pretty much
broke up her marriage. Yeah,
the drug scene didn't help, but
how do you just waltz right in and . . .

Oh. My. God. Not only did Dad
waltz right in and break up a marriage,
but Mom waltzed away with him, broke
up a best friendship. I am my mother.
And that is something I just can't be.

I WAIT IN THE CAR

While Dad pays the bill, sunk
very low in the not-plush seat,
digesting. Not food. Information.

Revelation.

Dad sways a bit. Kortni props
him, but she's not in great shape
herself. They look like cartoon drunks.

Caricatures.

Neither of them should take the wheel.
But even if I knew how to drive,
Dad would not admit inebriation.

Impairment.

No one speaks as he starts the car,
backs up, barely missing the truck
behind him. In my belly, knots of worry.

Apprehension.

The knots clench as we weave toward
the on-ramp. Not far, the windows
swirl with red and blue lights.

Spotlights.

Hunter

DAMN COLD

For the first weekend in December
the temperature has trouble climbing

to thirty degrees, and the mountains
look like sugar donuts beneath early snow.

I'm up at first light and off to announce
the Sparks Hometowne Christmas Parade.

As I leave, I hear Nikki's heavy breathing.
Fast asleep, despite my noise. *You've seen*

one parade, you've seen them all, she said
last night, when I asked her to come along.

Sleeping in sounds better. Anyway, you'll
be the star. You won't have time for me.

Okay, that part is mostly true. When you're busy
playing celebrity, you don't have much time

for your tag-along girlfriend. Still, I want her to
be there. I lie down beside her, kiss the warm

pulse at the hollow of her neck. It's enough
to stir her from dreams. Enough to make me

wish I could stay. "Sure you won't change
your mind?" I slide my hand beneath the ginger-

scented blankets, find the satin skin of her thigh,
seduce her into that perfect state of not-quite-all-

the-way-awake. "I want you to be there with
me. You're my good-luck charm, you know."

Nik smiles. *Bet you say that to all the girls.*
Now let me go back to sleep. Love you.

"Love you, too." My hand doesn't want
to go. But the rest of me has to, so it tags

along. "If you decide to come see Santa,
you know where to find me." But her breathing

tells me she's already most of the way back
to dreamland. Wonder who's waiting for her there.

CHARMLESS

It takes forever to find parking,
despite the early hour. The main
drag is cordoned off, leaving
Victorian Avenue car-less except
for the ones soon to be parading.

I park in the Nugget Casino
garage, walk several blocks
to the corner where Montana
and I will announce equestrian
teams, bands, and local dignitaries,

shivering as they wave from
the decks of classic convertibles.
The Shriners will drive funny
little cars and unicycles. Civic
groups will flaunt tractor-pulled

floats. Scout troops will march
in formation, the university
cheerleaders will cartwheel,
clowns will throw candy. And,
bringing up the rear, Santa and

his missus will arrive in a horse-
pulled sleigh so the kids will
know Christmas is coming and
the malls will be open overtime.
Nikki's right. Totally predictable.

PREDICTABLE OR NOT

I've always kind
    of enjoyed the whole
        "it's beginning to look
    a lot like Christmas"
spiel. The parade

serves as a kickoff
    to a month of "loving
        each other so Santa will
    come" kind of feelings.
Christmas should be

all year. Only, then
    we'd go broke. Never
        mind. Actually, this year
    I have a little spending
cash. Think I'll get

Nikki something
    really special. Jewelry,
        maybe. Or better (for me),
    lingerie. Maybe I'll ask
Montana's opinion.

There she is, setting up
    the mics. Women who
        aren't afraid of work rock.
    Especially when it would
be my work otherwise.

THE PARADE BEGINS

At ten on the dot. I've been
practicing my announcer banter.
"Here comes the Reed High School

Marching Band, Montana. As
Ambassadors of the city of Sparks,
the band has traveled throughout

the U.S., as well as to England and
Ireland." Montana waits for the din
of the trumpets to dim before

> saying, *Speaking of Ambassadors,*
> *Hunter, here comes the Reno Rodeo*
> *Flag Girls Drill Team, which represents*

> *Reno Rodeo year-round at events*
> *and drill team competitions. Each year*
> *some one hundred girls try out for fifteen . . .*

And so it goes for well over an hour.
Despite the frigid temps, the bundled-
up crowd is as large as I've ever seen it.

The most amazing thing is that young,
old, or somewhere in between, when
I say something, they actually listen to

                                        me.

SEE, WHEN I WAS A KID

I was not what you'd call
popular. The truth is, other
kids picked on me.

Bullied

me, to the point where
I started to defend myself
before the fact. I'm not
sure why they

harassed

me in such cruel fashion,
but it seemed my teachers
never saw the instigation,
only my sometimes

over-

the-top reaction. How
many recesses I stayed
inside, while the bullies
went out to play!

I don't

remember exactly when
it stopped. Middle school,
I guess. Maybe eighth
grade. Doesn't matter. All I

know

is that eventually some
of my mom's fame
rubbed off on me.

MOM'S FAME

May not have been the most
valid way to gain friends
and win dates. But hey, whatever
works, right? I'll never

forget this one girl. Tori. God,
she was a rabid Marie
Haskins fan. Stalker material.
When she found out

who I was, she threw herself
at my feet. Actually,
a more literal way to put that
is she threw herself on

her knees. Right in front of me.
It may have been my first
oral experience, but she for sure
had a fair bit of practice.

All she asked for in return was
a signed Marie Haskins
book. I told Mom it was for a sick
girl. Not far from the truth.

THE MEMORY

Elicits a lustful smile. Montana
can't help but take notice.

> *Wow. Thinking about*
> *Christmas presents just now?*

"Not Christmas, but definitely
a gift worth remembering."

The grin she returns is knowing,
even if she is only guessing.

> Then she flips back into announcer
> mode. *Speaking of Christmas presents,*
>
> *Hunter, look who's coming down*
> *the street right now!* Anticipation

bloats the crowd. "You mean
that jolly old elf himself, Montana?"

> *That's right. Here comes Santa,*
> *and . . . has he been working out?*

The kids all strain to see svelte
Santa. "I think you're right. Who

would believe it? Santa and the missus
must have a membership at Gold's Gym!"

Gold's Gym, of course, is a sponsor.
Not to mention an X advertiser.

As buff Santa's sleigh rolls off into
the distance, people begin to move

toward their cars or vendor booths.
I turn off my mic, begin to pack up.

A small pair of hands slides around
my waist from behind. Nikki must

have changed her mind, dragged
herself out of bed. "Nik?" But neither

> voice nor hands are a match. *Nope.*
> *Not Nik. It's just me. Hey, Hunter.*

Equal parts disappointment
and exhilaration jab me. Not Nikki.

But not exactly bad, either.
"Leah. All on your own today?"

> *Well, yeah. Remember I told you*
> *I had something for you?*

SHE WINKS

Who knew
    with such
        a small
            gesture

                a girl
                  could look
                      like such
                          a letch?

Can a girl
    even be
        a letch?
            Exactly

                how is
                  "letch"
                    defined?
                      Suddenly

I've got
    a good
        idea of
            what this

                girl has on
                  her dirty
                    little
                      mind.

SHE WAITS IMPATIENTLY

While I help stow the gear.
Am I seriously considering
a stroll down Deviant Lane?

> Montana notices Leah's angsty
> pace. *You looking for trouble?*
> she asks in an underneath voice.

Hard to deny obvious truth.
"Probably. Although I didn't
exactly go looking."

> She reassesses the redhead.
> Shrugs. *Okay, then you're
> pursuing serious trouble.*

This is so not her business.
"What time is the talent show
again?" Montana and I are judges.

> *Go ahead. Change the subject.
> See if I care. One o'clock, main
> stage. And. Do. Not. Be. Late.*

I check my watch. Just
about noon. "No worries.
This shouldn't take long."

I PURSUE SAID TROUBLE

Like a buzzard sniffing after
        roadkill. "Okay, Leah. What do
you have for me?" It's a loaded

question, and she's quick to
        react. She smiles, leans into me,
and I appreciate how beneath

                her unzipped jacket, a low-cut
        black sweater reveals truly
                stunning cleavage. *Let's walk.*

We go five blocks, silent.
        Cut across a hectic parking lot.
Turn down a sleepy street.

                Finally she tugs me to a stop.
                        I scored some amazing smoke.
                Thought you might like a taste.

Smoke? Argh. Tempting.
        I've been out for a while.
Oh, what the hell? "Okay."

                Just keep walking, she says,
                        lighting an already rolled J.
                Pretend it's a cigarette.

I do and she does and somehow
　　　　　we get away with smoking weed
out in the open, on a city street.

I'd be lying if I said it didn't
　　　　　lift my stomach, roller-coaster-
style. Definitely a thrill, getting

away with illicit behavior.
　　　　　More of that is brewing, for sure.
Leah slips her hand into mine,

and my first thought is of Nikki.
　　　　　I suspect where this is headed. So why
am I still going along with Leah's

plan? Stunning cleavage or no,
　　　　　Leah is not the right thing to do,
literally or figuratively, despite

how soft her hand is in mine,
　　　　　or how the jasmine perfume of her
reminds me of a warm June evening.

Stop it, Hunter, stop it. You are
　　　　　not just another guy, lusting after
an easy piece. You are not . . .

BUT APPARENTLY I AM

Leah turns her face up toward mine,
daring me to kiss her. God, she is

luscious, ripe fruit temptation,
serpent coiled in expectation.

    I can hear Nik whisper, *You'd never*
    cheat on me, would you, Hunter?

The snake strikes, and I pull back.
"Leah, I have a girlfriend, you know."

Her hand falls out of mine, and
relief escapes in a long-drawn sigh.

    But she will not so easily be dismissed.
    Her fingers settle gentle on my inner

    thigh, move slowly higher. *Yeah. So?*
    I'm not asking for commitment, and

    I don't want to mess up your life. I just
    want to give you a little piece of me.

She boosts up on tiptoes, looks
into my eyes as she kisses me.

I am pulled into the liquid emerald
of her eyes, the invitation—no, demand—

of her pillowed pout, her experienced
hands. And I'm helpless. Weak. Convinced.

She pulls me down a narrow alleyway,
backs me against a splintered garage door.

I pretend protest, but we both know
claiming I don't want this would be a lie.

> *Shush*, she pleads. *Don't say a word.*
> *Just let me take care of you.* She kisses

me again, encourages my hands
along the hilly contours of her body.

And in one long, sinuous movement,
she is on her knees. In total control.

I CLOSE MY EYES

But what materializes
out of the darkness there
are shadowbox photos of Nikki.
Those, and the snap of December
against uncovered skin

       might be enough to make
       me stop, but when Leah senses
       my wavering, her urgent *please*
       closes around me, pulls me
       in. I look up at the froth

of clouds. Cappuccino sky.
The summer scent of jasmine
lifts from a tide of titian
hair, and there is no hesitation
now, no U-turn, no braking,

only relentless forward motion.
Propulsion. A kaleidoscope
of titian. Jasmine. Cappuccino
clouds. And every trace of Nikki
dissolves in Leah's warm rain.

ONLY AFTER

We are finished,
    clothes zipped up,
        hair smoothed,
            does the thought
                cross my mind
                    that someone
                might have seen.
            Enjoyed watching.
        Got off themselves,
    maybe. My cheeks
burn. Can't say why.

Only after we have
    exited the alley,
        started back along
            the sleepy street,
                toward the hectic
                    parking lot, does
                it occur to me that
            the fame that brought
        me here belongs to
    me, not to my mom.
I like how that feels.

WE WEAVE

Through the thinning crowd.
Some have taken their children
home, out of the crisp morning,
away from the threat of snow.

A stab of intuition makes me
survey the knot of people nearby.
Did Nik decide to come after
all? That could be very bad,

all things considered. But when
I assess faces, the one my eyes
grab hold of does not belong
to Nikki. I do not recognize

the man standing just there,
scanning the human sea. So why
do I think I know him? Someone
ducks in front of him, and I lose

momentary sight, but when his
eyes at last connect with mine,
they are green-dappled gray. Piebald.
He turns away suddenly, as if

whoever he was looking for
found him instead. He melts
into the tide of bodies. Faces.
One of them very much like mine.

ZAPPED

As if by a stun gun,
by the most unexpected
encounter, the entire
top of my head tingles.

                            I stand

trembling, unable to
totally comprehend
what seeing those eyes
might mean to me.

                            Awed.

Frozen in place. Heart
quickstepping. Breath,
a shallow draw.
I am pulverized

                            by

the weight of one fragile
moment. Denial descends,
a threadbare shroud. Maybe
I have it all wrong. But

                            simple

reasoning convinces me
otherwise. I don't know why
I've never seen my father
before, but I reel in the

                            recognition

that I've seen him now.
I just want to know,
who is he?

A SHARP WHINE

Slices through the buzz
in my ears. What? Who?
Oh, yeah. Leah. Right.

She's looking at me like
I've missed something very
important. *So is that okay?*

Freight train slam. "Uh . . .
Sorry. What did you say?"
Repeat, then go away.

*I said I want to give you
my number*, she says, only
a lot annoyed at my inattention.

What I want is to track
down the bastard-maker.
"Um . . . I'm not sure . . ."

*I know you probably won't
ever use it. But just in case.
Or you can give me yours.*

"No, no." The last thing
I need is her calling me.
"Give me yours." I fumble

around in my pocket, finally
fish out my cell phone. Try
to punch in the numbers

she recites. But my mind
is in a whole other place
and I miss one or three.

> *Here. Let me do it, okay?*
> She extricates the phone from
> my hand, programs the correct

> sequence. As she returns my
> cell, she slinks up against me.
> Kisses me. *Hope you had fun.*

"Fun" isn't exactly the word
I would use. "Yeah, sure.
Thanks a lot. I have to go, okay?"

> She pouts at my abruptness,
> but doesn't argue. *Okay. You
> can call me any time, Hunter.*

"Good to know. Bye now."
I turn on my heel, hurry off,
fingers crossed she doesn't follow.

ALMOST TALENT SHOW TIME

I make my way toward the main
stage, checking out every male
face I see. Some of those guys
probably think I'm gay. Sorry,
dudes. Not looking to get laid.
Already did that. Sort of, anyway.

I chug down guilt. Gallons
and gallons of guilt. Why did
I just do that? Not like I needed
it, couldn't get that, and better,
from my Nikki. I'm a total
two-timing jerk. And why?

Okay, Leah would tempt most
any guy with a working pecker.
But you don't have to give in
to temptation, not even bodacious-
breasted, fiery-haired, "won't take
no for an answer" temptation.

I swear I will never do such
an idiotic thing again. Nikki
means too much to me. I stop,
dig out my cell phone, excise
Leah's number from its memory
bank. All's well that ends well.

SPARKS HAS TALENT

So much talent that the city now
        hosts two of these imitation bad
                reality TV shows every year, on

July Fourth and at Hometowne
        Christmas. A group of hopeful
                singers, dancers, and baton twirlers

paces on one side of the stage.
        The audience is likely all friends
                and family members, plus a few

curious onlookers and people
        just trying to get inside, out of the cold.
                Montana is across the room, in deep

conversation with some guy.
        His back is to me, but his posture
                tells me much. The guy thinks a lot

of himself. Montana sees me
        and smiles. The guy turns his
                head to see who she's smiling at,

and before I can even discern
        his eyes, I know they're piebald.
                The question becomes, what next?

COVERING THE SHORT DISTANCE

Across the room makes me
break out in a disagreeable
sweat, despite the chill in
the air. And in my heart.

Coward.

That's what I am. Afraid
to face down my ghosts,
despite hating the way
they haunt my every day.

Idiot.

It strikes me suddenly
that I could be all wrong
about this guy. So what if
his eyes are sort of like mine?

Dimwad.

Totally. What are the odds
that this is my father, anyway?
Much too coincidental, right?
Yet when I close the gap, I'm sure.

Son of a bitch.

MONTANA, IT SEEMS

Knows him pretty well. They stand,
barely touching. Intimate. Casual.
I hate to interrupt. Hate to know.

> *Oh hey, Hunter,* Montana says.
> *This is Brendan.* Bam. The name.
> Is it one I've heard somewhere?

Brendan looks at me, clueless.
Hey, kid, good to . . . He sees . . .
something. Enough to make him pause.

> Montana doesn't notice. *Brendan*
> *just moved back to Sparks. He recently*
> *got out of the army. Four terms in Iraq.*

Her voice is filled with pride and
what I think may be affection.
I notice his outstretched hand.

I know I should shake it, but my own
hand is trembling. Instinct tells me
to run. Far away. Don't look back.

But I have to play this out for sanity's
sake. So I clench my teeth, will
the quaking to stop. "Good to meet you."

PLANNING A WEDDING

Is supposed to be such a happy time.
Okay, Aunt Cora is not only happy.
She's downright demented with
happiness. Crazy in love.
I wish I could share her

joy. But I am crushed
by fear. I've always lived
with seeds of dread, waiting
to burst forth fruit. Apricots, if
I'm lucky. Peaches, sometimes, or

maybe mangoes. But this time,
the fear seeds have grown into
watermelons. Thick-skinned.
Pithy-fleshed. Weighted
with blood-tinted juice.

I can barely breathe with
them swelled up inside me.
Afraid to go out. Afraid to stay
in. Who knows what uncertainty will
strike next or what will happen to me?

IT'S ALL QUITE LOST

On Aunt Cora, who thinks,
>因 because I'm her maid of honor,
>>因 I must be honored. I should tell
>>>因 her how I feel, but I can't bring

>>>因 myself to mute her vibrant aura.
>>因 Even I, a total aura neophyte, can
>因 make out the shimmer. Do all
brides wear an opalescent halo?

Liam's family expected
>因 a June wedding. (How cliché.)
>>因 But Aunt Cora didn't want to
>>>因 wait. What, did she think he'd

>>>因 vanish, or curdle like old milk?
>>因 Or maybe she was worried
>因 he (or she) might have a change
of heart? I don't pretend to

understand. All I know is they
            settled on a Saturday-before-
                        Christmas wedding. So now
                                    she not only ruins the rest of my life,

                        she ruins the Christmas before
            the rest of my life. Not to mention
Thanksgiving. Holidays will never
be the same again. Nothing, in

fact, will ever be the same.
            No more Saturday-morning
                        pancakes or Sundays filled
                                    with too many football games.

                        No more late-night black-and-
            white movies or yoga exercises.
            No more easy laughter. Aunt
Cora is Liam's. And not mine.

SHE DENIES THAT TOTALLY

Whatever the future holds,
I will always be here for you.
I made that commitment a very
long time ago, she claimed.

We were shopping for her wedding
gown. Waiting for the saleslady to bring out another dress
to view. Size six. Off the shoulder.

I could have picked out the dress
she eventually chose without her
even being there. I know her. Too
well. Will I know her next year?

Nothing will really change
that much, she promised. *Except*
I'll be living with Liam, and
I'm kind of doing that now.

True. Other than wedding stuff,
I hardly see her at all. Which gives
me much too much time alone,
thinking about my own future.

ABSORBED BY STATUS QUO

I never really thought very far
beyond the day-to-day. Next year

I'll graduate high school. Then what?
University? Doubtful. Community

college? Maybe. But I still have no
idea what I want to be. Teacher?

I can't imagine spending my days
trying to keep kids in line, let alone

trying to teach them something.
Astronomer? I actually love scouring

the heavens, imagining what might be
out there somewhere. But how do you

make money doing that? Doctor?
Blood makes me sick. Stockbroker?

Yeah, right. Some tedious job seems
the likely road, and routine might work

best for me. But will it bring happiness?
Fulfillment? I don't even know if that matters.

Beyond "what will I do," where will I live?
I can see Grandfather failing, though

he'd never admit it in a million years,
especially not to himself. If he gets sick,

I'll take care of him, like he's taken
care of me. But if he dies . . . what?

My fingers begin to tingle. I'm alone
now, as I'll be alone then, swallowed

by silence. I rasp razor-edged air.
On my own. Don't want to be there.

Can't breathe. On my own. Must.
Breathe. On my own . . .

SUDDEN FOCUS

Buzz. Silence. *Buzz.* Silence.
What? Doorbell. My head clears
with a deep breath. Doorbell?

Bryce. "Just a second," I call
loudly. Don't leave! I'm here.
And now he is here with me.

I go to the door, trying not to
look as pasty faced as I feel.
An exercise in futility.

> *Are you okay?* are the first
> words out of Bryce's mouth.
> *You don't look so good.*

"I'm fine now you're here." I pull
him over the threshold, close
the door quickly, so the neighbors

don't notice I have a visitor. I want
it to be our luscious little secret.
Grandfather and Aunt Cora

are in Austin, scouting Baptist
churches that might be available
for an hour or so on short notice.

With dozens in the phone book,
odds are they'll be gone all day.
Hours, anyway, providing the perfect

opportunity to spend some quality
one-on-one time with Bryce.
We've never been quite so alone

together. His arms surround me,
and I sink into him, grateful for
his warmth. "I love you."

> *And I love you.* His mouth covers
> mine. His lips are soft, and his tongue
> tastes of cinnamon. My heart rockets.

This kiss is somehow different than
all the others. It builds in intensity,
and with no one around to take

notice, I have no reason to slow
the swell. Bryce's apple-rain scent
envelopes me. I gulp it in. Devour it.

Want to devour him. What sorceress
has possessed me, infusing every
nerve ending with intense desire?

SORCERY OR HORMONES

Something *has* possessed me,
and whatever it is, *it* stops
kissing Bryce. But only long
enough to say, "Come on."
It leads him down the hall,
into my bedroom. I think
I should stop *it*. Don't know
if I can. Don't know if I want to.

Autumn (me?) has no control
as *it* invites Bryce onto my bed.
He pushes me back against
my pillow. Peels away his shirt.
Unbuttons mine. Stares down
at me with love (lust) harbored
in his eyes. *Wow*, he says, before
kissing me again. Only this time,

his lips move across my neck,
down over my collarbone. To
the soft mounds beneath. I want
to say, "Wait." But *it* won't let me.
I can barely catch my breath, but
this time for all the right (wrong!)
reasons. My heart jackhammers
in my chest. Bryce must hear!

His lips stop traveling my torso,
long enough to encourage me
out of my jeans. His come off too,
and I might stop to fold everything
correctly, but *it* insists I just leave
our clothes heaped together
and take a good long look at Bryce.
Except for sex ed pictures, I've never
seen a penis before. But I'm def

seeing one now. "No," I want
to say. But *it* reaches out. Touches
Bryce there. Likes how the skin
feels. Likes the heat. "Stop,"
I want to say, but *it* makes Autumn
(me?) do things she doesn't know
how to do. I realize suddenly that
it means to make her go all the way.

This is like watching a movie, only
I can't find the remote. No way
to pause. No way to reverse.
Off go my panties. Now everything
moves slow motion. Finally I find
my voice. "Wait. I'm not sure . . ."
It doesn't let me push him away,
but *it* does let me say, "I'm a virgin."

THAT SLOWS HIM DOWN

But he doesn't want to stop.

Instead he becomes gentle.

You want to, don't you?

I want to say, "Maybe not,"

but *it* maintains control,

kisses him. "Yes. I want to."

I won't hurt you, he promises.

Let me make you ready.

He touches that place.

Kisses that place. *It* moans.

No, Autumn moans. No, I moan.

And I see that *it* is really me.

REALLY ME

Here with Bryce,
wanting to give
him all of me.
I'm scared.

But he has made me ready.

"I love you."
The words spill
from my mouth
just before
a bright flash
of pain.
Breathe.

He is in me when he promises again,

And I love you.
Did it hurt?
Can I keep going?
He waits

for my answer.
"Not too much.
And yes."
He starts to move.
Slowly at first.
Rhythmically.

I follow his lead and together

we move faster.
Into the tornado.
Rocked by an
apple-scented
maelstrom,
skin to skin

with the person I love, every vestige

of doubt vanishes
in white-hot bolts
of lightning.
No pain now.
No sense
of wrong.

Everything is perfect.

WE LIE TOGETHER, SILENT

For a while, legs knotted,
his fingers twisted in my hair.
A foreign scent lifts from our
skin. After-sex perfume.
Not altogether unpleasant.

> Eventually he says, *We should*
> *probably clean up. Ever*
> *showered with a guy before?*

For some crazy reason,
embarrassment attacks.
I've just gone all the way. And
suddenly I'm worried about him
seeing my naked body? "Never."

> Whether it's the tone of my
> voice or the look on my face,
> he grins. *First time for everything.*

The sheets are a mess, and I
am compelled to strip them
immediately. Hope OxyClean
can handle it. Meanwhile,
Bryce has started the shower.

By the time I get there,
the bathroom is rain-forest
steamy. We step into the shower
together. Hot water streams
over my bruised, used body.

> Bryce picks up the soap.
> *You wash my back and I'll*
> *wash yours.* He washes more

than my back. And I do
the same for him. It's all so
decadent, all so someone
other than me. I'd call it fairy-tale,
but it's more like pornography.

> *Would you look at that! It's*
> *ready for more already.*
> *You are some kind of magician.*

I'm not sure how long it usually
takes for it to get ready again,
but it definitely is. I don't think
magic has anything to do with
it. Just a good lather rub. And me.

THE SECOND TIME

Is better than the first. Does
it just keep getting better?

This is probably not the time
to try and find out. Peaks of

afternoon have worn down toward
soft hills of evening. "Guess you'd

better go soon," I say, wishing
he could stay here forever.

        Bryce finishes dressing. *Okay.*
        I'll go. But only under protest.

He always says the right thing.
"Can we get together tomorrow?"

        He smiles. *Can't get enough*
        of me? Well, the feeling is mutual.

Promise infuses the day's last kiss.
That makes it the best one yet.

I AM LOADING

My sheets into the washer

> when a little voice nags,
> *Uh. Hello? Nice time and*
> *all, but I think you forgot*
> *something kind of important.*

Something important, like

> *protection. You know, birth*
> *control. You can get pregnant*
> *the first time, remember?*
> *Or maybe that's what you want?*

Why on earth would I want

> *to get pregnant? Maybe as*
> *a way to keep Bryce attached*
> *to you? A way to make sure*
> *you won't be alone after all.*

But that might make him

> *think you trapped him? Might*
> *drive him away? Nah. He's*
> *the type to stay. Even without*
> *him, you wouldn't be alone.*

THAT LITTLE VOICE

Is crazy. I don't want to get pregnant.
                    (I *don't* want to get pregnant, do I?)

A baby would change my life forever.
                    (Like my life is so perfect right now?)

I'd have to quit school. Be a dropout.
                    (You could finish up via the Web.)

I'd get fat. Have morning sickness.
                    (There are ways around those things.)

Grandfather would disown me.
                    (Grandfather doesn't own me now.)

Aunt Cora would be disappointed.
                    (Aunt Cora has already moved on.)

Marriage is nothing but a trap.
                    (Who said anything about marriage?)

A baby needs a mom and a dad.
                    (Not like Bryce would disappear.)

But what if he did disappear?
                    (Then I'd still have a baby to love.)

A NEW FANTASY

This one can include Bryce and me
in the kitchen, only with a baby,
sleeping soundly in a pink nursery.

A little girl.

I feed Bryce breakfast, kiss him
good-bye. He heads on out the door
to work. The baby wakes.

Wanting her mommy.

I breastfeed her, change her,
put her in a pretty, soft dress.
Take her to the park in a stroller.

Everyone wants to see her.

She's a model baby. Hardly
ever cries. Has my red hair
and Bryce's hazel eyes.

The perfect combo.

AM I NUTS?

I am all about order.

        Dryer buzzes.
        Remove sheets immediately.
        Fold, wrinkle-free, perfect corners.

What is a baby?

        Dirty diapers.
        Messy high chairs.
        Sour spit-up on clothes.

Babies need order too.

        Clean diapers.
        Clean clothes.
        Clean high chairs.

Clean babies are happy babies.

        Smiling babies.
        Cooing babies.
        Cuddling babies.

Cuddling babies fill you up.

        Fill you with happiness.
        Fill you with devotion.
        Fill you with love.

I AM MAKING MY BED

When Grandfather and Aunt Cora
breeze through the door, talking
about details. Wedding talk is details.

> *. . . people on the guest list.*
> *. . . people in the wedding party.*
> *. . . people the church can comfortably hold.*

Even all the way down the hall in
my room, I can hear how Grandfather's
staid voice has bloated with enthusiasm.

> *. . . flowers for the altar.*
> *. . . flowers for bouquets.*
> *. . . flowers for centerpieces.*

Grandfather discussing flowers?
Surreal! They don't even call my name,
sure of the fact I'm here somewhere.

> *. . . reception location.*
> *. . . reception music.*
> *. . . reception food.*

I don't want to think about any
of it. I only want to think about
Bryce. Making love. And babies.

I GO TO JOIN THEM ANYWAY

Mostly because they'll probably
come looking sooner or later.
Just as I reach the kitchen,
I hear a cork pop. Loudly.

> Aunt Cora screeches. *Ah!*
> *Where's my glass?* She turns,
> smiling, as I come into the room.
> *Guess what? We found a church.*

I point to the champagne
bottle, foaming merrily down
its neck into a bubbly puddle
on the counter. "I figured."

> *Want some?* She glances quickly
> at Grandfather, who is scribbling
> notes at the table. He shrugs,
> so she pours three glasses,

before I even say, "Guess so."
I've had champagne a couple
of times. Always very small glasses.
I've never, in fact, gotten drunk.

Glasses raised all around,
Grandfather offers the toast.
*To Cora and Liam, and to two
lives together as one.*

Who knew he was a poet?
As we clink-and-drink, I offer
my own silent toast to Bryce,
me, and new directions.

The champagne goes down
like a froth of hope. Aunt Cora
refills our glasses, but I'm already
feeling a bit on the "sparkly" side.

My brain fuzzes with thoughts
of the afternoon, and when I catch
Grandfather talking about the relative
merits of orchids versus roses,

I laugh. Inappropriately. Aunt
Cora looks at me. Really looks
at me, head cocked like a pup
at a whistle. *Come here a minute.*

SHE PULLS ME INTO THE HALL

Thinks a second, then yanks me
all the way into her bedroom.

> *Okay, give. What's up with you?*

My throat goes thick and my fingers
numb. "What do you mean?"

> *Your aura. It's like . . . ruby.*

Oh my God. Freaking gypsy aunt.
"Um . . ." Can't confess. "I, uh . . ."

> *You're in love. Who is he?*

She's like a little kid at a pony ride.
Me too, on champagne. "B-Bryce."

> *And why haven't you mentioned him?*

Now my brain buzzes anger. "You . . . uh . . ."
Go ahead, say it. "You're never here."

SHE DOESN'T DENY

She deflates. Like someone stuck
her with a pin and the champagne
bubbles escaped. *You're right. I'm sorry.*

"It's okay. I mean, you're getting
married. It's not like you should
be thinking about me, anyway."

Her heads starts to shake. *Getting
married doesn't mean you're not
important too. Tell me about Bryce.*

We sit on her bed and I recite
the basic information, omitting
everything about today. And babies.

He s-sounds great, she sputters,
champagne kicking in. *Do you
want to invite him to the wedding?*

A member of the family already?
"Th-thanks. I'll think about it."
Sputtering a little myself, the first

time I've ever had alcohol go to
my head. Makes me laugh. Makes
me brave. Think I kind of like it.

Summer

STRADDLING A THIN WIRE

Three hundred feet in the air.
That's how I feel.
Safe for the moment.
But not very.

December gray shrouds
the valley.
Nothing new. Except
colder than normal.

I was almost looking forward
to Christmas this year.
Thought maybe
it might be special.

Despite Dad and Kortni.
Because of Kyle.
But now I'm not even sure
where I'll be.

The wire sways in the wind.
Half of me wants
to hold on for dear life.
Half wants to jump.

IT'S BEEN THIS WAY

Since Thanksgiving. The night
Dad got pulled over, less than
half a mile from Carrows.

When the red and blue carousel
started spinning behind us, we
all knew things didn't look good.

> Still, a guy has to give it his best
> try. Dad rolled down the window.
> *Wussup, S . . . Off . . . cer?*

> The cop leaned to look in the car,
> backed up at the smell. *License
> and registration.* As if they were all

he was after. Flashlight illuminating
every move, Dad reached for
the glove box. Instinctively,

> the cop's hand slipped down
> toward his hip, and the extremely
> large pistol poised there. *Slowly.*

> Dad rooted around for ten seconds
> or so. *'S here somewhere. Hang on.*
> Finally he found the requisite paperwork.

356

Expired. All of it. But even if it
hadn't been, Dad was going to jail
after breathing point one two.

A second cop arrived just in time
to help with the breathalyzer.
And, seeing as how Kortni was

also more than a little wobbly, he
ended up driving us home. They
called a tow truck for Dad's car.

And since it was a holiday weekend,
both Dad and car stayed in lockup
for four days. Kortni slept for two

of them. Woke up, ate some cereal,
then jumped back on the beer train.
Kyle was in Fresno until Sunday.

His dad got pissed every time I called,
so I didn't even have phone time for comfort.
I was stark, raving stir-crazy. Almost bored

enough by Saturday to get an early start
on my history essay. Almost enough by
Sunday to call Matt. Instead I called Mom.

CALLED FIRST

Around ten a.m.
No answer.
Left a voice mail.

Tried again
an hour later.
Same results.
Second voice mail.

The old saying
goes, "Third time's
a charm." Whoever said
it didn't know Mom.

She never returned
my calls. But the fifth
time, I guess it was
sometime well after
two, she finally
picked up.

I SUSPECTED

She was using again, not only
because she was asleep (crashed)

at two p.m., but also because
she sounded spun. Her voice

> was clipped. Staccato. *Hello?*
> *Summer? Is that you?*

"Uh, yeah, Mom. How come
you were asleep?" Daring the lie.

> *It's Sunday. I don't work*
> *Sunday. Don't you ever sleep in?*

"Not until two. Anyway, how
was your Thanksgiving?"

> *You called to ask that?*
> *What's wrong with you?*

"Nothing. I'm fine. I mean,
well, Dad had a DUI. . . ."

> *You don't expect me to bail*
> *him out, do you? Does he?*

"Uh, no. I don't . . . I didn't
call about that, Mom. . . ."

WHY DID I CALL?

It wasn't just the boredom.
It was the question that had
been burning inside me for
three days. Mom prompted,

Okay, then. Why did you call?

And out it came, slick as
a baby pig. "Why didn't you
ever tell me how you and Dad
met, and that I have a sister?"

Very long pause. Who told you?

Duh. "Who do you think, Mother?
Anyway, that doesn't matter.
Don't you think I have the right
to know something like that?"

Even longer pause. I guess so.

Anger seethed. "You guess
so? I know we don't talk much,
and when we do, it's usually
all about you, but—"

No pause. Now, wait a minute—

BUT I WAS ON A ROLL

"No, Mother. We usually *do*
only talk about you, and obviously
not about stuff that matters. . . ."

My eyes stung, and the words
I wanted to say tried to stick
in my throat. I coughed them out.

"I have a sister. Where the hell
is she? What's her name?
I already know who her father

is, and how you hooked up with
Dad and all. Have you always
been that way? Don't you ever

feel bad? I mean, for God's sake,
how can you just keep sleeping
around, piling one guy on top

of the next? How can you just
keep making babies, then tossing
them away? How can you . . . ?"

> Right about then I noticed
> she had hung up the phone.

KORTNI BAILED DAD OUT

The next morning.
They might have
just booked him
and let him go,
except for a couple
of pertinent things.

One: Not his first DUI.
He had one less
than two years ago.
Blood alcohol level:
point zero nine.

Two: Weed under
the seat. Less than
an ounce, but not
only fineable, also
contributable to his
condition that night.

He's looking at
thirty days' jail time,
license suspension,
and a big chunk of
change, and if he
can't pay it, more
jail time. He goes
to court this week.

HE'S PRETTY MISERABLE

And I almost feel sorry for him.

       Not that I didn't try to warn him.

And I almost want to comfort him.

       Not that he's often been worthy of that.

And I almost want to give him a hug.

       Not that I want anyone but Kyle to hug me.

And I almost want to say it will all work out.

       Not that I really believe it will, for him. Or me.

And I almost want to tell him I love him.

       Not that I have, since I was a little girl.

And I almost think I should fix that.

       Who knows when I might have another chance?

HE'S ON THE PORCH

Smoking and, of course, sucking
up suds. Who knows when he might
have another chance at a good buzz?

Kortni went to town for groceries.
(She still has her driver's license.)
So there's an empty chair. I sit.

"Hey, Dad. I just want you to know . . ."
Say it. Say it. Say it. Can't. Not yet.
"I'm sorry about what happened."

> He doesn't look at me. Just stares
> across the winter-bared fields.
> *Me too. Sometimes I'm plain stupid.*

All the time. But I don't tell him
I think so. Say it. Say it. Say it.
Ah, what the hell. "Love you, Dad."

> Now he looks at me, eyes drawing
> slowly from the dirt, across dead
> air, to my face. *What did you say?*

He didn't hear? Didn't believe
it? And now I have to repeat it?
"I said, uh . . . that I love you."

I EXPECT

A reciprocal declaration—an "I love
you, too." Or maybe condemnation—

a "Why don't you say it more often?"
Anything, really, but what he does say:

                                        Why?

"What do you mean, why? You're my
dad, right?" Sounds lame, even to me.

                                        So?

His one-word responses are pissing
me off. "Shouldn't I love my father?"

                                Not necessarily.

Two words. Communication.
I realize, however, that he's right.

Loving your parents is not required.
He inhales the last drag of his cigarette.

                                Get me a beer?

WHEN I RETURN

He is ready to talk, as if words
suddenly materialized in his brain.
First, a long drink of brew.

          Then his mouth opens.
          I'm sorry I'm such a shit-
          for-brains. I thought I'd
          be a better dad. Wanted
          to be. Really, I did. But
          then I let my bad habits
          get the better of me.

I watch him pull another long
swallow. Light another cancer
stick. "It's called addiction, Dad."

          I know. Can't stop. And
          to tell you the truth, even
          if I could, I don't want to.
          You're the only good thing
          in my fucked-up life. And I
          couldn't even be thankful
          enough to look after you
          right. They took you away. . . .

I want to shout, "No, you
shoved me away!" Instead
I say, "You're selfish, Dad."

He shakes his head, smoke
escaping side to side from
the corners of his mouth.

> *Not always. Nope. At first*
> *it was all about your mother.*
> *I loved her. God. Never love*
> *someone that much, because*
> *you're sure to end up hurt.*
> *I would have married her.*
> *Would have raised up your*
> *sister like my own. Would*
> *have raised you better. . . .*

This is the most he's ever
spoken to me at one time.
Ever. "So what happened?"

> *When she got pregnant with*
> *you, I told her all that, begged*
> *her to give up the crystal.*
> *To be fair, she tried to clean*
> *up. For you. Tried and mostly*
> *failed. Meth is a mean mother*
> *monster. But even if she could*
> *have given it up, the fact is*
> *she loved Trey more than she*
> *ever loved me. Or anyone.*

LEFT UNSAID:

Even me.
> I always knew
> she chose drugs
> over me. Now I
> find out she chose
> some-guy-not-my-
> father over me too.

Happy as I am
> to have any new
> information that
> imparts insight re:
> what made me, me,
> and why I'm here,

I need more
> answers. Now, while
> he's hopefully stuck
> in verbal mode, is
> the time to strike.
> After we catch our
> collective breath.

Understanding
> my father is suddenly
> important. Not sure
> why. Understanding
> my mother very well
> might be impossible.

BUT I HAVE TO TRY

So here goes. "How did
I end up with you when
Mom went to prison?"
He looks at me like I'm

speaking Chinese. *Hasn't
anyone ever told you this
stuff? Not your mom? Not
my mom? Seriously?*

"If someone had, I wouldn't
be asking, Dad. Not like
I need to have stories
repeated. I'm not a little kid."

He smiles tightly. *Even when
you were little, you never
did want to hear the same
story twice. Buying books*

*for you was a waste of money,
not that we ever had a whole
lot to waste. So, okay, how
much, exactly, do you know?*

"Only what you told me at
Thanksgiving. That she was
married to your old friend, Trey,
and that you broke them up."

HE COCKS HIS HEAD

Reaching way back into his brain,
trying to locate that night.

> *I said that? Guess I was pretty
> buzzed. Don't remember it at all.
> Yes, Trey and I were friends, and I was*
>
> *passing through. Don't remember
> where to, but once I was there a few
> days, I didn't want to leave. Ever.*

"Because of the dope or
because of Mom?"

> *Both. Oh my God. You can't imagine
> how much crystal they were moving.
> And as for your mom, she was skinny*
>
> *as hell, and a total tweaker bitch,
> but I fell for her right off. Something
> in those eyes, and she was wild in b—*

Way TMI, Dad. Still, "Uh, it's okay.
Obviously you guys had sex."

> *It was more than that, at least
> for me. I was flat in love with her.
> Which was a fucked-up thing to be.*

Trey wasn't around much.
Working a little. Dealing a lot.
Kristina and I were tight for a while.

He stops. Lights another cig.
Stares at his empty beer can.

I should get him one. The deadly duo
seems to be fueling his storytelling.

I don't think she ever really loved
me, though. She was crazy about
Trey. She liked making him jealous.

Which was dangerous for both of
us. He did have a temper! When
he found out about us, he freaked.

Dad looks longingly at the empty
again. This time I just go get one.

A very long swig and he begins
again. We got into it pretty good.
But even if I would have beat

the crap out of him, she wouldn't
have chosen me. I got the picture
and left. Didn't know she was pregnant. . . .

PREGNANT WITH ME

Mom never did figure out the birth
control thing. I might be worried

about my paternity, except I look
almost exactly like Dad. Lucky me.

Like most mid-level dealers, they
smoked up the profits, and Denny's tips

didn't exactly cover what they owed
their supplier. Your mom got creative.

And she got busted. She and Trey
had already turned state's evidence

once to get off a trafficking charge.
This time they were going away

for fraud. Check kiting. Identity theft.
They got two years in state prison.

Your mom delivered you the day
before they sent her away. Her mother

took you home from the hospital.
Kept you safe. Until she found me.

I'VE ALWAYS FELT

A strange connection
to Grandma Marie. Strange,
because we don't see each other
all that often. Also a sort
of jealousy because

of Hunter. I mean, she
and Grandpa Scott adopted
him. When I was younger, and
in foster care, I wondered
why him and not me?

And I thought it was
because they didn't have
enough love to go around. Semi-
irrational, I know. I mean, they
couldn't reasonably

take in all of Mom's
kids. And now, it seems,
they *did* take me in, at least for
a little while. But then, how
did I end up with Dad?

BACK TO THE ORIGINAL QUESTION

I wait for him to drop the butt
of his cigarette into the foam
at the bottom of the Pabst can.

Sssss! The sound is snakelike.
Don't much like snakes.

"So did Grandma Marie know
you were my father or what?
Did you know each other?"

> Dad chuckles. *We had met once.*
> *Let's just say it didn't go so well.*
>
> *Your grandmother didn't think much*
> *of me, or of any of Kristina's men.*
> *Can't really say I blame her.*

Me either. Mom's taste in men
is what you might call piss poor.

> *Kristina told her I was your father*
> *and how to get hold of me.*
> *The news came as a total shock.*
>
> *I didn't know what to do. I'd already*
> *hooked up with Zoe by then.*

ZOE

The name is like a punch
in the gut. *Whoomf!* There

goes my air. "So why did
you bring me home, then?"

> Dad gives the smelly beer can
> a wistful look. *First of all, I wanted*
>
> *you. You were part of Kristina*
> *and me. The best part of both*
>
> *of us, as it turns out. Convincing*
> *Zoe of that was something else.*
>
> *But your Grandma Jean and grandpa*
> *made me see I had to try.*

I know the rest of the story,
at least what happened after

that. One thing I still don't know,
though. "So where is my sister?"

> He shrugs. *Trey's sister, Cora,*
> *took her when he and Kristina*

went to prison. I don't have
a clue where they are now.

Your mother might know, or
maybe your Grandma Marie.

But I don't think so. Last I heard,
they'd dropped out of sight.

Dust in the distance signals
Kortni's imminent return. As

the dirt cloud nears and the engine
rumble closes in, I ask one last

burning question. "Did you ever
think maybe you weren't my father?"

No hesitation. *Of course. Not*
like your mom was exactly what

you could call faithful, especially
not with crystal involved. She swore

she'd only been with me, but once
a liar, always a liar. First thing we

did when we brought you home
was get us tested. You're mine.

THAT'S A GOOD THING, RIGHT?

Better to know for sure where
you come from than to go
through life wondering, even
if you're not really certain you
like where you come from. Right?

Something to ponder.

Along with everything Dad
just confessed. Kortni pulls up,
parks, starts unloading bags
of groceries. Dad goes to help,
and I should too.

But I want to talk to Kyle.

I go inside, start toward
the phone, see the answering
machine light is blinking.
Why didn't we hear it ring?
Too absorbed in storytelling?

Whatever. I hit the play button.

It's my caseworker. *This is Alice
Shreeveport. We have been
informed of your unfortunate
incident. We need to discuss
Summer's living situation. Please . . .*

CALL HER

She wants Dad to call her.
>
> To discuss my living situation.

I could erase the message.
>
> Pretend we never got it.

But they'd only come looking.
>
> Sooner or later they would.

New blow to my solar plexus.
>
> This time my asthma kicks in.

I didn't want to live here.
>
> Breathe. Can't. Find. Air.

So what if they take me away?
>
> Breathe. Can't. Find. Air.

Put me in another foster home?
>
> Breathe. Can't. Find. Air.

Send me to a different town?
>
> Breathe. Can't. Find. Air.

Away from Dad. Kortni. Kyle.
>
> Breathe. Must. Find. Inhaler.

NEEDLE-SHARP AIR

Spikes my lungs.
Breathe, damn it.
This means nothing.

I crawl down the hall,
into my room. Dig
in my backpack.

Locate my inhaler.
One big pull. Capillary
expansion. Holy crow.

I hear Dad slam
through the front door.
He and Kortni must

be arguing. They've
done a lot of that
lately. I should tell

him about the message.
But he'll find out
soon enough. Instead

I'll go ahead and call
Kyle. Maybe he'll
know what to do.

AP Associated Press

Miss Nevada, twenty-three-year-old Devon Shepherd, found herself embroiled in yet more controversy after she arrived in an inebriated state for a performance of *The Nutcracker* at the Pioneer Center in Reno.

"It was the anniversary of her sister's death," explained Shepherd's mother and manager, Angela. "Devon and LaTreya were very close. She has had a difficult time coping."

Casino showroom dancer LaTreya Shepherd was killed two years ago, when her fiancé, Robert Cole, shot her in a jealous rage. Shepherd's father, Brad, was later convicted of attempted murder after paying a prison inmate to poison Cole, who survived.

Devon Shepherd previously served as Miss Teen Nevada, as did LaTreya, two years prior. Angela Shepherd has been accused of being the "classic overbearing stage mother," something she strongly denies. "I supported my daughters and their dreams," she said. "And I will continue to support Devon now."

This is not the first time Miss Shepherd's character has been questioned. Only three weeks after winning her Miss Nevada title, she publicly remarked, "This is a major stepping-stone to a career in film. Hopefully not pornography."

She later said, "Obviously, I have poor taste in jokes."

Hunter

SOME SECRETS

Are better left kept.

Sometimes you're better

off thrashing around

on your own in the dark.

Sometimes those things

that percolate in your brain

brew into bitter coffee

once disturbed. Sometimes

it's good to remember

not to go poking in woodpiles

where snakes like to hide

and red-bellied spiders crawl.

Unless you're hoping to

get bit. Lusting for poison.

ALMOST A WEEK

Since I met Brendan.
Dad.
Biologically speaking.
I think.

Still not totally sure, mostly because
I didn't have the balls to confront him.

Just couldn't figure out a way to say,
Hey dude, did you once rape my mother?

Wasn't the right venue.
Wrong place.
Wrong time. Too many
people around.

So instead, it's eating me up from
the inside out. Sounds like a bad plot

thread. Only, instead of some vicious
little monster inside, all I've got is anger.

Anger and the need to know.
Even though
knowing won't change
a single thing.

382

AFTER THE TALENT SHOW

Brendan and Montana left
right away. I don't think he liked
her celebrity status. Didn't like
the groupie need to say hello.

Usually I like it, even though
once in a while it leads to poor
behavior on my part. Witness
my earlier Leah rendezvous.

But that day I exited quickly
too. Needed to let the emotional
dust settle. Needed to work
through what my next move

should be. I called Mom from
my car. Explained the scenario.
Hoped she'd say no way.
Your imagination has run amok.

But she said, *I was never
one hundred percent sure
that he was really your father.
I hoped he wasn't. But I think*

*maybe your instincts are good.
I can't tell you what to do
about it. Listen to your heart.
It generally says the right thing.*

MY HEART SPOKE UP

Told me Brendan is a prick
and that, even more than our mutual

eye art, increases the likelihood
that he is, yes, my father.

Guilt seethed all the way
home. And there was no staunching

it when Nikki greeted me at the door
wearing a sexy red dress.

> *Like it?* she demanded.
> *It's for the station Christmas party.*

"I love it. You'll be the prettiest girl
there, that's for sure."

Without warning, chills
rattled my body. "Cold out today."

> *See? I'm glad I didn't go. Come on,*
> *I'll fix you some cocoa.*

She pulled me off into
the kitchen, prattling on and on

about shopping and malls
and where we'll spend Christmas Day.

Though my eyes couldn't help but admire
her silk-sheathed frame,

my brain could not focus
on what she was saying, something

> she finally took note of. *Hey. Are*
> *you getting sick or what?*

She set the steaming cup
in front of me, and her cool hand felt

> my forehead. *Nope. No fever. That's*
> *good, anyway. So . . .*

> Her look was apologetic,
> like she should have asked sooner.

> *How was your day? See some great*
> *talent? Any randomness?*

I sipped the rich chocolate.
"There were a couple of pretty

good singers. Lots of not-good singers.
Randomness? Some."

NIKKI'S ADVICE

Was typical Nikki.
*Maybe you should just
let it go. You're not sure,
anyway, right?*

I had to admit I wasn't
sure. And also, "Not being
sure about him means
not being sure about me."

She sidled up behind me,
slid her arms around
my neck. *Doesn't matter.*
I'm *sure about you.*

That kind of trite remark
always irritates me. "Easy
for you to say. You know
who your parents are."

Her arms fell away, and
I expected an angry retort,
but her voice carried only
hurt. *Do what you have to.*

SHE WAS MAD

But I was mad too. Not
at her, but that didn't much
matter. Not right then.

In fact, I was mad enough
to let myself not feel too bad
about my little p.m. tryst.

But by bedtime, I felt emptied.
Nervous. Too, too alone.
I watched Nik come from

the shower, skin warm and
hair wet, and I wanted her
with every electron of my being.

Not just her body. All of her.
In bed with me, a piece of me.
No, all of me. Because without her,

I am nothing. I knew it then
and I know it now. And, thank
God, she allowed my hours

of self-pity, then showed me
again what it means to be
in love with an angel.

I WATCH HER NOW

My angel

getting ready for the Christmas
party. Perfuming her arms
and legs with ginger-steeped
lotion. Sliding sleek,

tawny

legs into gartered stockings.
Curling long ripples
into the honey lake of her

hair.

Enhancing already
impossible beauty with
a touch of blush against

flawless

skin. She slips into her
new dress—a seraph robed
in red. Then she turns to

face

me, the question in her eyes
as obvious as my answer:
"You are more than
beautiful. You are

perfection."

BEST OF ALL

She is mine. I am acutely
aware of how other men stare
as we enter the ballroom.
They are not looking at me.

I love her on my arm,
an exquisite piece of jewelry.
A few of the women glare.
Nikki is the ruby

they wish they could
be. Their marble eyes follow
us to our table, leave us
there. I offer a chair

to Nikki. "Stay here.
I'll go get us drinks." The bar
is hosted, and no one
asks to see my ID,

so I order Chardonnay
for Nikki; Jack Daniels and
Coke for me. By the time
I get back to the table,

Rick Denio has closed
in. But star-striking Nikki
won't be nearly as easy as
he expects it to be.

AMUSING TO WATCH, THOUGH

I circle the table, sipping my drink,
liking the whiskey burn. Rick is all

over Nikki, and she looks really
uncomfortable about it. He's a jerk.

"Hey, Rick. Putting the moves
on my girl?" I hand Nik her wine.

>   Rick is in the game. *Your girl?*
>   *Didn't know you had such good taste.*

"There's a lot you don't know
about me. Uh, where's your wife

tonight?" The station buzz is she
ran off. With another woman.

>   Rick's face flames, but he remains
>   calm. *She had another party.*

I can't help but smile at the opening
he just gave me. "A girl party, huh?"

I haven't had a spar-fest for a while.
This one could be fun, but Rick's

>   done playing. *Not sure who all's*
>   *there. Excuse me. There's Montana.*

THERE, INDEED, IS MONTANA

In a bold, backless dress, sparkly
        silver. And with her, all decked
        out in a complementary gray
tux, is . . . "Brendan," I whisper.

        Nikki looks. Looks again.
            Harder. *Oh my God. You* do
            look like him. I can't believe
        it. Hey, you're okay, right?

Okay enough to chug my drink.
        "Yep. Fine and dandy. Except
        I need a refill. You good for now?"
She's barely touched her glass.

Good. I can only carry two
        glasses, anyway. I order twin JDs.
        Doubles. Tip the guy five bucks
so he doesn't reconsider the ID.

When I turn around, I'm only
        half-surprised to see who has
        joined Nikki at our table. Poor
Nik looks positively green.

Goes well with her pretty red
        Christmas dress. Ha. I crack
        myself up. Too bad I'm spoiling
to be in a very unfunny mood.

BEFORE I CAN SIT DOWN

Nikki sees my double-fisted
whiskey and Cokes. She jumps
to her feet, extracts the drinks

> gently from my hands, sets them
> on the table. *I'm starving. Let's get
> some food.* It is not a request.

Anger starts to build, like wasps
daubing mud. But then when
I glance at Montana, her eyes

harbor anxiousness. She wants
the evening to go well. So all
I do for the moment is say,

"Hey, Montana. You look great
tonight." I know I should say
something to Brendan, but all

I can manage is a small wave.
Then I let Nikki steer me
toward the seafood-heavy buffet.

> *When Montana asked if they
> could join us, I didn't know how
> to say no,* apologizes Nikki.

"Not your fault." I concentrate
on loading my plate. Shrimp. Crab
legs. Oriental chicken salad.

Nikki's plate makes mine look
greedy. "Aren't you hungry?
I thought you were starving."

> *I only said that because*
> *I figured you should eat*
> *before drinking all that booze.*

> *The last thing you need to do,*
> *all things considered, is get*
> *blitzed.* She cringes, as if hearing

the wasp daub. I will keep
my temper in check. But I also
plan on drinking whatever

I please. Free drinks don't come
around every day. Still, I will
play her way. "I'll be careful."

I TRY, REALLY I DO

I eat everything on my plate.

                (Chase every bite with a swig.)

Return for alcohol-absorbing pasta.

                (Finish one drink; start second.)

Third trip is to the carving board.

                (Polish off drink two. Back to bar.)

Finally, dessert. Chocolate cheesecake.

                (Work on third—really fourth—JD.)

I think I'm doing pretty well.

                (No way to converse when imbibing.)

And then Brendan starts talking.

                (About how Sparks has grown. Swallow.)

Reminiscing about Wild Waters.

                (His lifeguard days. Single-gulp glass drain.)

THE WASP BUZZ INTENSIFIES

Only Nikki seems to notice.
She shoots me a warning
glance. But it's too late.
I stop Brendan midsentence.

"So . . . do y-you 'member
a girl name Kr-Kristina?" Damn
booze. Damn mud daubing.
I want to be coherent.

> Brendan's forehead wrinkles.
> He thinks a minute, finally replies,
> *Kristina? Sounds familiar.*
> *Why? Should I know her?*

Nikki's hand lights gently
on my arm. I swat it away,
one of those bees. "You might
have known her as Bree."

> Bam! Recognition floods
> his eyes. *Bree. Yes. I knew her.*
> Clearly, he doesn't want to say
> more. *That was a long time ago.*

> Nikki is close to panic.
> *Uh, hon, would you get me*
> *another glass of wine? Please?*
> She looks at me helplessly.

Buzz. Buzz. "Just a minute,
okay?" *Buzzzzz.* The entire
table is staring now. Good.
This deserves an audience.

"I don't suppose you remember
a certain night, up on Mount Rose.
Just you and her and a little
crank . . ." Loud. Too loud.

> But he definitely remembers.
> *Now, look. That was a long,*
> *long time ago and—wait.*
> *What do you know about it?*

"Dude, the whole world—well,
a lot of it, anyway—knows
what you did to her that night.
I know because . . ." The rest

sticks like tar in my throat.
My face is hot and my eyes
sting and oh my God, I will
not cry. Nikki is on her feet.

Montana is too. Brendan just
stares stupidly, waiting for me
to finish. So here goes, "I know
because I'm her son and . . ."

CAN'T CONFESS EVERYTHING

I just can't. But I can still
          accuse. "She said you raped
her, you son of a bitch."

My hands clench, but I'm not
          going to hit him. Not now.
Not here. Instead I start across

the wide expanse of floor.
          I expect Nikki to come, but it
is not her butterfly hand that lights

                    on my shoulder just as I exit
                              the big ballroom doors. *Hold
                    on. I think we should talk.*

I whip around, dislodging
          myself from his grip. *Buzz.*
"What the fuck do you want?"

                    People stare. But Brendan
                              doesn't care. *Come on.
                    Let's sit over there, okay?*

He knows better than to
          touch me again. For some
insane reason, I follow him.

The casino carpet is purple
        with wavy green lines, and
it's making me seasick.

I will myself not to puke,
        and we sit in some eggplant-
colored chairs at the far end

                        of the foyer. I can't look at him
                                as he launches his story. *Yes,*
                        I knew Bree . . . Kristina. We went

                        out a few times, and we did
                                a lot of crank together. All true.
                        That night—the one you mentioned—

                        we were messed up. Wasted, in
                                fact. Now, I don't know . . .
                        Have you ever done meth?

I have no choice but to
        look him straight in the eye.
I shake my head. "Never."

                        Well, here's the deal with meth.
                                You're not always in control,
                        and that night everything got out

of hand. I'm not proud of what
happened, but the truth is,
she kind of asked for it. . . .

Bzzzzzzz. My face flames.
  "Is that what you wanted
to tell me? Because it's not

good enough. You forced
  yourself on her when she
said no and that's rape."

        His turn to shake his head.
          Like I said, I don't take pride
        in it, or in much of my life

        at that time. I did drugs.
          Did girls. Stole. Cheated.
        Lied. The reason I joined

        the army? A judge gave me
          the choice—military or a long
        time in jail. I'm glad now.

        I got clean. Disciplined. Did
          my time and went back, hoping
        to maybe make up for before.

I WANT TO KEEP HATING HIM

But he sounds
        reasonable
        honest
        apologetic.

I want to keep blaming him.

But somehow I
        believe him
        relate to him
        almost forgive him.

I want to keep berating him.

But words don't
        make sense
        seem wise
        matter anyway.

I want to keep thinking he's the enemy.

But suddenly he's
        just a man
        not a monster
        no longer a stranger.

        My father.

THE BUZZ QUIETS

Blood pressure drops.
Anger dissipates, ghostlike.

But I'm still just this side
of wasted drunk. Enough

for me to open my mouth
and say, "Did you know

Kristina got pregnant that
night?" I think surprise

> should surface in his eyes.
> Instead he says, *Actually, yes.*
>
> *She sort of blackmailed*
> *me into abortion money.*

A half laugh stutters out.
"You still don't get it, do you?

I'm that baby. And you, quite
probably, are my biological father."

HIS JAW PLUMMETS

And that alone is almost worth
every emotion I've lately
sorted through. "Really.

I mean, hello. Have you
not noticed a resemblance?
Did it not cross your mind?"

His eyes—my eyes—scan
my face. *It never occurred—
I mean, I saw her mom with a baby,*

*once. You, I guess. But I thought he—
you—she said—Oh my God.
Why didn't anyone ever tell me?*

"Why? What would you
have done? Married her and
played house for a while?

Look, I don't expect anything
from you. My grandparents
adopted me, gave me a great

childhood. Better than you
or Kristina ever could have.
I just thought you ought to know."

OUR EYES LOCK

Green-marbled gray
to green-marbled gray.
But really, there's not
a whole lot more to say,
except, "Why did you
come back here?"

He shrugs. *This is home.*
My mom died two
years ago, but my dad
still lives in Fernley.
Blood is thick, you know?
He chokes on the sentence.

I have a grandfather
in Fernley. Maybe we'll
meet one day. Maybe he
listens to me on the radio.
Oh. He's old. Probably
not exactly an X listener.

Brendan gets to his feet,
and I notice that Montana
and Nikki are standing
a respectful distance away.
Uh, look. This is kind of
a lot to absorb and . . .

I stand too. "Like I said,
I don't expect anything
at all from you. So no
worries about blood tests.
I'm an adult, and I can
take care of myself."

We start toward the girls.
Montana looks wary.
*Guess I have to tell
the story twice, huh?
Oh, well. Relationships
shouldn't have secrets.*

Suddenly I notice
Nikki's stance. She's
pissed. Maybe even
more than pissed.
Because of what just
happened? It's all good.

EXCEPT IT'S NOT

Brendan shakes my hand,
        takes Montana's arm, and they
return to the party. I reach for
        Nikki, but she yanks away.

    She hands me my jacket,
            which I left on a chair,
    holds out my cell phone
            between two fingers,

    like it's poison. *Heard it*
            ring and thought it might
    be important. By the time
            I dug it out of your jacket

    it had gone to voice mail.
            Her own voice crackles.
    Sorry, but I went ahead and
            picked up the message.

    She straightens, squares
            her shoulders, and I know
    I'm in trouble. *It was from*
            some girl named Leah. . . .

Autumn
ONE DAY

Until the wedding. One week
until Christmas, such as it will be.
School just let out for vacation.
And there's so much to do.

Shopping. Manicure. Rehearsal
dinner tonight. More shopping.
Hair appointment. Studio
portrait. More shopping.

I wish I could be excited
about it. But all I want to do
is hole up in my room with a little
borrowed liquor and think

about ways to be with Bryce.
It wasn't so hard when school
was still in. But this week
will offer many challenges

as far as spending time
together. Sneaking out
when Grandfather passes
out is the only way I know.

PILFERING BOOZE

Sneaking out.
        Hooking up with
                Bryce for sex.
I can't believe this
        is me I'm talking
                about. It's like I'm
on a runaway train.
        I want to jump off
                but it's not slowing
down and taking
        that leap would
                kill me for sure.
And the wonderful
        irony is I used to
                think about dying.
Maybe even by my
        own hand, if things
                turned too, too bleak.
But now I want to
        live. Want to love.
                Want to be loved.
I have to keep on
        riding this train
                for that to happen.

TRAINS LIKE THIS

Generally wreck sooner or later.
So far so good, though.

Grandfather has not missed
the short pours of whiskey

I've indulged in lately. They say
liquor is quicker, and whiskey

is definitely quicker than champagne
when it comes to a good buzz.

A shot or two, nothing scares me,
nothing hurts me. I like how that feels.

The weird thing is, Grandfather's
own drinking has waned. It's as if

the wedding planning has reduced
his stress. I don't understand why.

I do know I'll have to find a way
to replace what I've taken from

the liquor cabinet before he swings
the other way again. Bound to happen

after tomorrow. Once the wedding
is over. The reception done,

and Aunt Cora and Liam go off
on their honeymoon, return

to their new house in Austin.
They decided to live there, near

his family instead of hers (mine), go
into business together. Massaging

the uptight of Austin. That thought
is good for another swallow. Hot

liquid amber down my throat. Better.
Almost good enough to deal

with lingerie shopping. Aunt Cora
should be here to pick me up

any time. Okay, just a quick nip and
then I'd better use some mouthwash.

The worst thing about whiskey
is the smell it leaves behind.

LISTERINE ROCKS

Aunt Cora doesn't notice a thing
on the drive to the mall. I close
my eyes, lean back into the seat,

> absorbing radio music and traffic
> music and the music of Aunt Cora's
> voice. Something about *dresses*.

> Something about *the hotel where
> you get to stay tonight.* Something
> about *pick you up at eleven sharp.*

> And something that really grabs
> my attention. *So, okay. Are we going
> to meet your Bryce tomorrow?*

Just the name makes me smile.
"Last time we talked, he promised
he'd be there. On time, even."

> She laughs. *You didn't give him
> a hard time, did you? I mean about
> being punctual. No wedding starts*

> *exactly when it's supposed to.
> There's always some sort of delay.
> Don't know why that is, but it is.*

"If you say so." Not like I'd have
a clue. "I've never been to a wedding."
Not like she doesn't know that.

"Yours will be my first." And hopefully
not my last. I want one of my own
before too very long. The amazing

thing is Bryce hasn't even asked
about protection. Maybe he wants
me to get pregnant too.

"Are you going to have a baby?"
Her smile drops away. "I don't
mean right now. But ever?"

                    She looks like she has something
                    she wants to tell me. But the mall
                    has suddenly reached our line

                    of sight. She perks up and says,
                    *Who knows what the future might
                    bring? Let's start with underwear.*

UNDERWEAR SHOPPING

Is likewise something I've never
            done. Well, I mean Wal-Mart undie
shopping is one thing. Upscale
            bras and panties is all new.
And radical. There are even

salesladies who are trained to
            fit you right, and tell you what kind
of bra will flatter you best. It's kind
            of embarrassing. If it wasn't for
the whiskey, I'd be freaking out.

Only problem is, now that it's
            wearing off some, I'm getting
a headache. Hope it doesn't
            get worse. Anyway, Aunt Cora
and I take our fancy understuff

up to the counter. In her pile:
            three stretch lace thongs, two gel
underwires, and a teeny purple teddy,
            for the honeymoon. In my pile: red
velvet panties, matching push-up bra.

BOY, DOES THAT ADD UP

Almost one hundred fifty big
ones! "Uh, are you sure you can
afford that? I can wear my old—"

> Aunt Cora stops me. *This day
> is only going to happen once.
> Besides . . .* She reaches into
>
> her wallet, fishes out a shiny new
> credit card. *Liam's mom gave me
> this. Said to get anything my little*
>
> *heart desired. She knows Daddy
> doesn't have a bottomless bank
> account. I guess she does.*

I think back to Thanksgiving and
the Cregan place. Big house.
Nice furniture. Pretty backyard.

Pricey (if unremarkable) neighborhood,
the same one where Aunt Cora
and Liam will live, thanks to a big

down payment wedding gift.
Aunt Cora will be well cared for.
Do I feel good about that?

THE QUESTION NAGS

The rest of the afternoon.

Through manicure.
Pedicure.

(And just who wants a job
dealing with scaly feet?)

Trousseau shopping.
Christmas shopping.

(And why does Aunt Cora
think Liam wants pj's?)

Makeup shopping.
Window shopping.

(And by now I'm getting
totally sick of shopping.)

Stuffing the car with
packages. Gassing up.

(And I majorly wish I had
an ibuprofen in my purse.)

Driving the eighty
miles to Austin.

(And now the nagging
question really gets loud.)

Am I happy that Liam will
care well for Aunt Cora?

(And will she be happy when
Bryce is taking care of me?)

STUPID FANTASY, I KNOW

But at least Bryce is a real guy, not
a vampire or something. Fantasy
minus the fangs. Sounds good
to me, especially if there ever
is a baby involved in this story.

Meanwhile, we have arrived
at the hotel, and it is not
what you might call a dive.
"Wow. Pretty fancy. How can
we afford to stay here?"

> Aunt Cora rattles her purse.
> *Credit card, remember?*
> *Whatever my heart desires,*
> *remember? I wanted this to*
> *be a memorable experience.*

The Mansion at Judges' Hill
is quite impressive, with an
obvious history. Later I'll find
out what it is. Right now, I just
want to check in and find ibuprofen.

I GET MY OWN ROOM

It isn't huge, but it is beautiful,
all done up in restored antiques.

I get a couple of ibuprofens
from Aunt Cora, go looking

for something to wash them
down with. Score! Minibar.

Pricey water, soda, and yes,
liquor. Very pricey liquor.

But hey, the credit card
is buying, right? Three-dollar

Coke. Six-dollar miniature bottle
of Dewar's. Never tried scotch

before. Ugh. Not great. But too
late to turn back now. Nine

dollars' worth of refreshment
later, I lie down on the bed.

The headache fades and I close
my eyes to rest up before dinner.

NEXT THING I KNOW

A thumping brings me around.
No, not thumping. Knocking. Loudly.
On the door. I sit up, too quickly.

My head feels like a merry-go-round,
and I think maybe I have to throw up.
"Who is it? Hang on, I'm coming."

> *It's me.* Aunt Cora, of course.
> *Are you about ready? Hurry up.*
> *I'll wait for you in the lobby.*

Ready? What? I glance at the clock.
Almost five. How long did I sleep?
Bathroom. Quick. To throw up or not

to throw up? I give it the old college
try. Nothing. Not even a dry heave.
Guess I'm okay. No time for a shower,

I splash my face. Makeup? No time.
I make time for mouthwash, stay
in my rumpled clothes. Not trying

to impress anyone, anyway, right?
Room key in my pocket. Out the door.
Twenty-four hours, it will all be over.

THANKS TO ME

Aunt Cora and I get to the church
            ten minutes late. Everyone else
                        is already there, waiting. Pacing.

Talk about nerves! Liam looks
            green, although he's trying to
                        hide it. He and the preacher

stand off to one side. Aunt
            Cora goes to join them. Let
                        the rehearsal begin! The wedding

party gathers as the minister starts
            a blessing. I bow my head, close
                        my eyes. Someone taps my shoulder.

Micah! Why didn't I make time for
            makeup? Suddenly, midst long-
                        winded prayer, my breathing goes

shallow and my hands tingle.
            I haven't done this in weeks.
                        Micah sees. *Is it me?* he whispers.

I need air. How do I get out
            of here? But just as my feet start
                        to move, the *amen* stops them.

I suck in oxygen, concentrate
            on a mental picture of Bryce so
                        Micah's cool steel eyes don't

pierce so hard. I can do this.
                        Okay, everyone, says the pastor.
                                    Let's get this over with. I'm hungry.

A half hour later, we're all pretty
            sure of our roles for tomorrow.
                        Through the entire instruction,

Micah managed to either be
            very close to me or to let
                        me know most definitely that

he was watching me. If I didn't
            know better, I'd say he was hitting
                        on me. Impossible. No makeup.

BUT, MAKEUP OR NO

Micah finds a way to sit next to me
at dinner. His leg rests against mine,
and despite willing myself to think *Bryce,
Bryce, Bryce*, I don't push it away.

I like how it feels. Warm. Protective.
Still, just to be fair, when the conversation
around us is loud enough to cover it,
I say, "I have a boyfriend, you know."

> Micah keeps chewing his chicken
> Marsala. Finally he swallows. *I would
> have been surprised if you didn't.*
> God, he is just so smooth.

Bryce would never say something
like that. My face flushes. At least
it will have a little color now.
Pop! goes a champagne cork.

Pop! And another. *Pop!* Three.
Around come glasses, and this time
I don't hesitate to take one, despite
the way the preacher is looking at me.

Micah sees that too. He laughs.
You're on the path to hell young,
he says. But he isn't much older,
and he has a glass in his hand too.

No one else seems concerned as
the toasts begin. Plenty of wine
for all. Including me. I like the bubbly
stuff okay. But am starting to crave

something stronger. Something
to take my mind off losing Aunt
Cora tomorrow. Something to make
me forget all about Micah and how

his hand feels exploring my knee.
I like it. I do. But this time I summon
my courage, push it away. "Stop,"
I whisper hoarsely. "Please stop."

He does. And that makes me want
another glass of champagne. And
I know that isn't good. I'll stop after
tomorrow. I'll stop when I get pregnant.

WEDDING DAY DAWNS

Heavy with impending rain.
It's going to storm crazy.
Wonder if it's an omen.
Wonder if Aunt Cora's
aura has gone all gray.

> I want sun on my wedding
> day. But in Texas, anything
> goes, weather-wise, on any
> given day. So an indoor
> thing is the way to go.

Still, indoors or out,
a sense of foreboding
weighs me down. I want
to float in this soft bed,
with the curtains drawn.

> At least I'll get to see
> Bryce. The thought buoys
> me from under the covers.
> Lots to do before then.
> All in the name of beauty.

Shower. Makeup. Hair,
courtesy of the hotel's
fancy stylist. Low-cut dress.
Flowers. Hope I can be
as pretty as the bride.

EVERYTHING ACCOMPLISHED

And as pretty as I'm going to get,
Aunt Cora and I arrive at the church.
It's filling already. Most everyone,

of course, is either related to or
a friend of Liam. Our herd is much
smaller. I'm glad Bryce will be there

on the Shepherd side. There he is,
in fact, standing alone, in back.
Aunt Cora goes off to the dressing

room, gown hidden beneath a plastic
bag. "I'll be right there," I call. Then
I go over to Bryce. "Glad you made it."

> His eyes light up. *You look great.*
> *But I feel like a fish out of water.*
> *I guess you can't sit with me, huh?*

"I have to stand up in front and hold
Aunt Cora's bouquet. But I'll sit
with you at the reception." I should

introduce him to some people.
There's Micah, too handsome
in his tux. No, not him. Not sure why.

IT'S AN EXERCISE IN FUTILITY

First, I'm having a hard time
          remembering everyone's names.

And as I struggle to label faces,
          Micah comes over to, uh . . . help?

          First he gives me a major once-
               over. *Whoa now. Don't you look*

          kind of amazing? He ignores
               my intense blush, turns to Bryce.

          Don't believe we've met. You
               must be a friend of the bride?

But before Bryce can respond
          (and say what? Sort of? Not exactly?),

          Grandfather's semi-feeble
               screech interrupts, *Holy shit*

          on a shingle. Look who's here.
               Can't believe they had the nerve.

Conversation skids to a halt
          as everyone assesses the new

arrivals—a stately older woman,
        dressed to the nines. Her face

is familiar, but I would struggle
        to place it, if not for the younger

man beside her. I haven't seen
        him in years. But I know who he is.

And if he is Trey, she must be
        his mom. I've seen Maureen in Aunt

Cora's photo album, her face
        less creased then, and her hair

the color of mine. It's gray now.
        They approach Grandfather warily.

The three pull away into a corner.
        The room echoes angry drifts of

accusation. Explanation. Denial.
        I should go mediate. I should go tell

Aunt Cora trouble's brewing.
        But what I really want to do is run.

RUN, FLEE, FLY

The attack is sudden.
I am a rabbit, surrounded
by starved coyotes.
And like the hare,

        certain

death is near, my pulse
guns. Accelerates,
hot flame in my veins.
Nears the point

        of misfire.

They say, when facing
the onslaught of tooth
and claw, a creature's
heart can simply quit.

        My heart

issues a warning, and
though I keep my feet,
my brain disconnects.
A black ghost swirls,

        threatens

to suck me inside.
Voices. All around me.
Can't see who they
belong to, but I want them

        to stop.

Stop. Slow. Silence.

GENTLE SHAKING

I am swimming up.
Voices make me want
to dive back down.

> . . . *you all right?* Bryce.

> . . . *coming out of it.* Micah.

> . . . *be okay now.* Grandfather.

> . . . *freaking weird.* Anonymous.

I am making an awful
scene at Aunt Cora's
wedding. Oh my God.

> . . . *family resemblance.* Maureen?

> *Hell, yeah. Just like me.* Trey.

> *Leave her be.* Grandfather.

> *What's going on here?* Preacher.

I am lifted. Supported.
Directed to a chair.
Someone hands me water.

> I am mortified.

I AM ALSO CLAUSTROPHOBIC

With all these people clustered
around me. I feel like a grape,
being squashed into juice.

"Could I please have some air?"

Everyone takes one step back.
I can't help but stare at Trey.
His dark hair is shot through

with silver. More salt than pepper.

The skin on his face is deeply
etched with a web of lines.
His eyes—black walnut—

are familiar. They are Grandfather's.

> He takes my interest as an invitation
> to move closer again. Bryce stops
> him with a hand to the arm. *Excuse*
>
> *me, but she asked for a little room.*

> Trey shakes Bryce's grip.
> *Excuse me, boy, but I haven't*
> *seen my daughter in a long time.*

I'm just taking a little inventory.

Bryce looks at me with eyes
brimming confusion. *Daughter?*
Autumn, is he saying he's your father?

Because you told me . . .

I told him my parents were dead.
Why did I ever say that? Because
I never believed I'd have to tell

him the truth. "I—I'm sorry. It's just . . ."

Grandfather, who has no idea
who Bryce is, or what I said to him,
nevertheless attempts rescue.

He's never been a father to her.

Trey steps toward Grandfather,
on a collision course. *And you,*
old man, were never a father to me.

THINGS ARE MOVING

Light-year speed toward implosion.
            Guests are turning around in their seats,
wondering what the commotion is.
            The ushers push closer, suspecting trouble.

The minister bobs this way and that,
            unsure of what to do next. Grandfather
and Trey are close to blows, and
            Maureen is clucking like an old hen.

Bryce and Micah are measuring each
            other, and the situation. Liam sputters,
then runs off to tell Aunt Cora that things
            are going to hell. "Stop it!" I plead.

"You're ruining Aunt Cora's day. Can't
            all this wait? Can't we at least pretend
to be a family, for her sake?" Silence
            swells. Fists unclench. People return

to their places. Still, as the organ
            begins to play, anger looms louder.
Aunt Cora appears, beautiful despite
            the worry stamped into her face.

Maureen and Trey give her hugs,
              then allow Micah to usher them forward.
Grandfather takes Aunt Cora on his arm.
              Liam follows his best man to the altar.

That is my cue. I turn to tell Bryce
              I'll see him after the ceremony, but
he is nowhere in sight. The wedding
              march begins. No time to look for him

now. I play my maid of honor role
              exactly as rehearsed. As the ceremony
progresses, I steal sideways glances
              toward the guests, but cannot spy Bryce.

What did I expect? That he'd never
              discover the truth? That the shadows
of my messed-up life would never
              appear in the face of his sunshine?

Through the pounding surf in my ears,
              a watery, *You may now kiss the bride.*
My eyes overflow. Tears of joy for Aunt
              Cora. The usual kind of tears for me.

WEDDING RECEPTIONS

Are good for one thing specifically.
Liquor. Mostly champagne, usually,
but Liam's parents kindly paid for
a hosted bar. Now I'm definitely not
old enough to fool the bartender.
But I've got the sympathy thing

> going on. Micah has talked his older
> siblings into providing us both
> with stiff drinks. *Just think if your*
> *father showed up after eight years.*
> *Wouldn't you want a nip of stress*
> *reliever too? Anyway, we're celebrating.*

> Aunt Cora issued strict orders:
> *No matter what, there will be no*
> *fights. No arguments. No name-*
> *calling. Plenty of time to sort*
> *this out tomorrow. Right?* Yeah.
> When she's on her honeymoon.

Trey tried to make conversation.
So did Maureen. I asked for some
time to think things over. So far,
they've respected that. Makes me
happy. Or maybe it's the mojitos.
Micah and I are sloshing them down.

THE MORE I THINK ABOUT BRYCE

And how he left without giving me
a chance to explain . . . how he left
without even saying good-bye . . .
the faster I slosh. By the time

Aunt Cora and Liam shove cake
in each other's faces, I am completely,
amazingly, dizzyingly drunk. You
might even say I'm smashed.

I want to laugh. I want to cry.
Neither appropriate for where
I am right now. "I think I better
get some fresh air," I tell Micah.

        He is sitting very close to me,
        leg hooked in front of mine.
        Why didn't I notice that before?
        Good idea. I'll come with you.

I'm a little unsteady on my feet.
Micah slips his hand under one
elbow, steers me toward the door.
No one notices our exit. Good.

The cool December air clears
my head a little. Also makes me
shiver. Micah slides an arm
around my shoulder, pulls me

        against his warmth. *Better?*
        Weird day, huh? Sorry 'bout
        your boyfriend. What was up
        with him, anyway? He stops walking,

waits for me to answer. Not
ready to talk about it. "He just . . .
was overwhelmed, I guess."
He. Bryce. I should pull away.

But he isn't here. He left me
behind. And I like how I feel
under Micah's arm. This is messed
up. Oh God. I am going to cry.

        Here, now, don't do that. He kisses
        the tears from the corners of
        my eyes. His lips are soft as they
        move over my cheeks. And suddenly . . .

WE ARE KISSING

And this is not like any first kiss.
There is no love here. Only want.

He wants me, but that's not what
I want. Not now. Not with him.

And my head is spinning. And his
hands are all over me. "No. Wait . . ."

> *Ah, come on. You want this as much
> as I do.* And he pushes me against

a wall. Dark here. No lights.
I could . . . But I can't. Bryce.

I love Bryce. "No. I don't. Stop,
please." But he doesn't even slow

> down. *You little prick tease.*
> His breath is rum and his hands

are rough. And he is strong.
Too strong for my drunken struggle.

Just as I'm sure he'll do exactly as
he pleases, a male voice interrupts.

Take your hands off her, you little
shit, or I'll kick your lily-white ass.

It's Trey. I never thought I'd
actually be happy to see him.

Micah acts like I'm burning him.
He lets go so fast, I sway without

his support. *Uh. Okay. Sorry, man.*
We're just a little d-drunk here, a-a-and

I . . . guess we got our signals crossed.
Not looking for trouble. He whips

a U-turn, heads back toward
the party. "I, uh . . . Thank you."

It's all I can say to Trey before a half
pitcher of mojitos comes boiling

up my throat. Talk about burning!
I turn my head and let it fly.

Summer

CONDEMNED

One thing I've learned.
Life isn't fair. Even when
you try to do the right thing,
someone else's wrong
thing bites you in the ass.

Dad drives drunk. Stoned.
The judge throws the book
at him. Still, it's me going
away. He'll be out of jail
long before I escape foster

care. Maybe if I hadn't
been such a smart-ass to
her, Kortni would have
agreed to keep me in
her care. Probably not.

*The State of California
is concerned about your
welfare,* Ms. Shreeveport
said when she delivered
the good news. *I wish it*

*were possible to leave you
here, but your safety is our
prime concern. Drug use and
driving under the influence
cannot be tolerated. We've*

*found you a new placement.
Unfortunately, it's in Fresno,
so you'll have to change
schools. But at least you'll
have the vacation to settle in.*

New home. New foster
parents. New school. Just
when everything was going
kind of okay right here. Dad
and I were communicating.

Kortni and I were in truce
mode. I was getting good
grades. Excelling, in fact.
Will they even have AP
classes in my new school?

And what about Kyle? He
and I were hanging strong.
I don't want to be without
him. My life will be a well,
drained to gravel and dust.

TELLING HIM

Was something like getting a cavity
filled. Without Novocain. Evil pain,

the words drilling through the roof
of my mouth to deep inside my brain.

It was raining that afternoon, the world cold
and gray. I haven't yet shaken the chill.

Ms. Shreeveport gave me a three-day
reprieve, time for an early Christmas

celebration. So much to celebrate
and all. I didn't tell Kyle when I called

him. Wanted to do that face-to-face.
We were actually belly-to-belly on

the seat of his truck when I started
to cry. "Hold me. I don't want to go."

> *I can't hold you much tighter.*
> *And you're not going anywhere.*

"Yes. I am. They're taking me
to Fresno. To a new foster home."

> *He looked down into my eyes.*
> *When? How long have you known?*

"Day after tomorrow. I just found
out yesterday. It's because of Dad."

He brushed the hair away from
my face. Dried my cheeks with

the back of his hand. Shook his
head. *I can't let you go. Not now.*

You make life worth living.
If you leave, I have nothing.

I lifted my face. Kissed him.
"I don't have a choice. It's all set

up. I start school at Roosevelt
after vacation." He slumped down

on me. Heavy. Weighted. Then
he started to cry. *This is fucked up.*

Which made me cry more too.
We cried together for a long time.

Finally I said, "Make love to me.
I need to remember how it feels."

It felt rough. Like punishment.
Punishment for his own pain.

I REMEMBER HOW IT FELT

All the way to Fresno.
Ms. Shreeveport tries
to make conversation.

For about fifteen minutes.

> I surround myself with
> a silence-bricked wall.
> Finally she gets it.

> *You've got a lot on your mind.*

Well, yeah. Like not
knowing what's coming
next. Like wondering why

my life can't remain static.

Like thinking about
Kyle and me, on the seat
of his truck, learning

how much real love hurts.

> Like remembering what
> he said, when our tears
> had dried. On the surface.

> *Don't worry. I'll figure something out.*

I WASN'T IN LOVE

With Bakersfield. (Only

with a guy who lives there.)

But I already hate Fresno.

It may be the gateway

to Yosemite's stark glory,

but unlike the Sierra

sneaking up behind it,

the city of Fresno is an

ucking fugly collection of

east-leaning buildings,

blade-bare lawns, and

half-digested asphalt.

Cool enough now, almost

Christmas, but hotter than

Sahara sand in summer.

Really can't wait to live here.

RIGHT TURN, LEFT TURN, RIGHT . . .

Do that a dozen or so times,
you end up in the broken-down
neighborhood I now call home.

The houses are fifties era. Built
around the time kids still did
duck-under-your-desk drills,

as if that could protect them
from nuclear bombs. Ha! Maybe
that's what happened to this

neighborhood. Wonder if I should
worry about radiation. Maybe
wrap myself in aluminum foil.

At last (so soon?) we pull up
in front of a totally inconspicuous
place. (Not!) "It's fricking pink."

Salmon pink, with rotten red trim.
"You've got to be kidding me, right?"
Who paints a house like this?

> *Doesn't matter how it looks*
> *outside. It's what's inside that*
> *counts. You'll like the Clooneys.*

so says she

What else would she say,
anyway? She opens
the trunk, and I

grab my

bag. Not much in it, but
only one thing matters—
my cell phone. My

lifeline

to the real world.
The one I'm about to
walk into is

pretend.

The uneven sidewalk
tries to trip me. The step
sags beneath my weight.

I don't

want to see what's
beyond the door, but
it opens at the bell. I

need it to

be nice inside.
I need something
solid to

hold on to.

CAN'T SAY IT'S "NICE" INSIDE

But it isn't horrible. My nose
says so. It smells of cinnamon
apple room freshener—fake
but not bad. You couldn't call
the place neat, but it isn't dirty.

Everything shrieks "seventies."
Red/purple shag carpet. Thick
velour drapes. Linoleum in
the hall (and, no doubt, kitchen
and bathrooms). Dated. Used.

I notice all this without stepping
foot through the door. Too many
people in the way right now.
Ms. Shreeveport has to work
her way past a short, too-perky

blonde and a bear-sized, bear-
colored man. Brown hair.
Brown skin. Brooding brown
eyes. George Clooney,
he ain't. Wonder who he is.

FINALLY, I'M IN

Introductions are passed round.

> Blonde, with a loopy smile.
> *Hi, Summer, I'm Tanya.*

> > Bear remains quiet, so Shreeveport
> > says, *And this is Mr. Clooney.*

> > > Bear finally opens his curtain
> > > of silence, corrects, *Call me Walter.*

I stand in wordless defiance.

> > > Bear asks Shreeveport, *She's
> > > not, like, a mute, right?*

I am so loving him already.

> > > Shreeveport says, *Of course
> > > not. Say something, Summer.*

I use sign language: "Hi."

> > Blonde (Tanya) takes the high road,
> > giggles. *Ha. Hi to you, too.*

Shreeveport does not find it
funny. *Please don't be difficult.*

        Bear (Walter) asserts control.
        No such thing as difficult here.

I push back with a silent "Bet me."

        Tanya ignores my defiant look.
        Come meet the other girls.

I shrug, start to follow her.

        Shreeveport doesn't quite drop
        it. *Cooperation is important.*

I grab my bag, turn shadow.

        Walter goes all syrupy.
        There's a good little girl.

I try not to notice the way my skin crawls.

I NOTICE THE WALLS

Are eerily bare. No photos. No
paintings. No cheap ceramics.
Apparently Tanya isn't much into
the Martha Stewart school of
homey decor. Fine by me.

Even the Christmas tree, leaning
into one corner of the living
room, is noticeably bare.
I can't not ask, "What, did
someone steal the ornaments?"

> Tanya giggles (and I'm starting
> the hate the grate of her laugh).
> *Oh, no. I've just been so busy*
> *we haven't put them up yet.*
> *Maybe we'll do that tonight.*

Sorry I brought it up. The last
thing I want to do is hang gaudy
crap on a fake evergreen and
pretend like I'm part of a fake
family. Fake. Fake. Fake.

I pad along the fuchsia shag,
thinking about the tatters
of my real family. Dad in jail.
Kortni, happy not to have me
there. Mom. Mom. Where is she?

A RIPTIDE OF SADNESS

Pulls at me, but I will not cry.
Must not show weakness as
I meet my new fake sisters.

> *This is your room*, Tanya says.
> It is not much bigger than a closet.
> *Take that bed over there.*

She points to a small twin under
the window. The matching bed against
the wall is currently unoccupied.

> Tanya gestures toward it. *You'll*
> *bunk with Simone. Not sure . . .*
> *Simone? she calls. Come meet Summer.*

A door (bathroom?) opens
somewhere and a wraith—
pale as death—appears suddenly,

followed by two darker-skinned
girls, probably sisters. Real sisters,
part of my new fake family.

> *Good, you're all here*, says Tanya.
> *Summer, this is Simone, Eliana,*
> *and Rosa. Get acquainted.*

SHE GOES TO SAY GOOD-BYE

To Shreeveport. I maintain silence,
cross the room in three steps, claim my bed.

I guess I should unpack my clothes.
Having been on both sides of the "get

to know your new foster sister" dynamic,
I choose the respectful route and turn

to Simone. "Are there empty drawers?"
All three girls drill me with their eyes,

and the air, hanging thick with unasked
questions, prods my temper. "What?"

> *Nothing*, says Ghost-girl. Simone.
> *Lainie had the right side of the dresser.*

Her voice is wimpy, and I'm not surprised.
She sounds like she looks—washed out.

I suspect the answer, but ask anyway, if only
to break the insufferable silence. "Who's Lainie?"

> Young Rosa (maybe ten?) rushes
> to respond, *She used to live here,*

but she ran away. Walter says
good riddance, but Tanya . . .

Shh. You talk too much, scolds Eliana,
who is thirteen or fourteen and definitely

carries an air of older sibling. *Lainie*
had . . . issues. She spits the last word.

I can't help but laugh. "Don't we all?"
That shatters the iceberg, or at least

chips it heavily, as everyone contributes
to a chorus of giggles. We're not exactly

friends, and trust will never happen
here, but at least we don't hate one

another. And while the mood is halfway
relaxed, I might as well ask, "So what's

with Walter?" Tanya is easy to read.
The communal amusement vanishes.

And though no one says a word,
I have all the answer I need.

WE CHANGE SUBJECTS

And within twenty minutes, I know
        most everything there is to know about
                Eliana and Rosa Garcia Famosa.

Their father came from Cuba to
        the United States via Mexico, where
                he met some very bad people who

he later went into business with.
        In Texas, he fell in love (my take:
                lust) with their mother, Irena, and

together they came to California,
        where the girls were born. Irena
                Famosa expected her husband to work

in the lush fields of the San Joaquin,
        but Ignacio Garcia chose easy
                riches, moving methamphetamine

for a Mexican cartel. One day
        he went away and never came back.
                Irena grieved for a time, but met

a new man. A very jealous man
        who suspected her of things she
                never did. He killed her anyway.

END OF STORY

Except for the fact
that this happens to be
the girls' fourth foster home
in six years, and Rosa can't
remember her mother's
face. Sad, I suppose.

But "sad" is a main
ingredient in every foster
kid recipe. We must choose
to accept it, or go off the deep
end ourselves. I could
easily dive in

over my head right
now. The others wait for
my story, but this will not be
a straight exchange. "I've been
with my dad, but he just
went to jail for DUI."

Familiar excuse. Nods
all around. And Mom? Why
is it always easier to talk about
Dad than her? "And my mother
has pretty much written me
off." The truth bites.

I KEEP UNPACKING

As I talk. It doesn't take long.
                              My history or unpacking. Everything

I own pretty much fits in three
                              drawers plus five coat hangers.

Too aware of the three pairs
                              of eyes, inventorying every article

of clothing and five favorite
                              books, I find a way to keep my

cell phone discreetly stashed.
                              Some things need to stay secret.

All I want to do at this moment,
                              though, is pull out the phone, dial

Kyle's number, hear his satin
                              voice promise he's waiting for me.

Is he waiting for me? Or has he
                              completely forgotten me already?

IMPOSSIBLE, I KNOW

But even considering it makes me
        want to pace. My heart accelerates,
like something wild, snared. Caged.

        I can't let the others see it. As nice
as they seem, if they intuit weakness,
        I have rewarded them with a weapon.

I deliberately plop down on the bed,
        calm my arterial stutter. No pacing
now, damn it. Now or ever, not here.

        Instead, like an imprisoned wildcat,
I lock eyes with the human just
        beyond the bars. The one staring

at me with interest I cannot tolerate.
        "What about you, Simone? Why are
you here?" Come on, Ghost-girl. Tell

        me your story, although I'm half-afraid
to hear it. Half-afraid. Half dying to, because
        the eyes mine are locked to are haunted.

ZERO RESPONSE

So I prod just a bit. "Come on.
I told you my sordid little tale."

                              Nothing.

I look over at Eliana and Rosa.
Both are wide-eyed, silent.

                              Nada.

Hmm. This one must be good.
"Is your dad, like, a serial killer?"

                              Zilch.

She shoots a dry-ice glare.
"Okay, fine. I don't care, anyway."

                              Empty.

I wish I were rooming with *las
cubanitas*. Even three to a room.

                              Vacant.

THANKFULLY

Tanya calls from way down the hall,
Girls! I need some help. Hurry!
There is some sort of a muffled crash.

The tension in the room, god-awful
heavy just two seconds ago, falls
away, like shedding a heavy robe.

Eliana and Rosa rush out the door.
I start to follow and suddenly Simone
transmutes, phantom into flesh. *Wait.*

I can't tell you, she whispers. *Ever.*
She is human after all. Real. As real
as the fear alive in her eyes.

I nod my head. "I know." I know
because I never told either. Her
story is mine, only with a different "he."

I understand as only someone who
has been there can understand. We
have something in common after all.

APPARENTLY I MADE TANYA FEEL GUILTY

Because by the time
Simone and I
reach the living room,

she and the girls are
elbow deep in red and
green and gold.

> Rosa's eyes are wide.
> *Ooh. Look. Can*
> *I hang this pretty one?*

> > *Lights first,* commands Walter,
> > untangling a long
> > strand. *Then ornaments.*

It all looks so normal—any
family anywhere—
it's almost enough to

make you forget
how abnormal this "family"
really is. Two

artificial parents; two
orphans. One
total mystery. And me.

LIGHTS, GARLAND, AND ORNAMENTS HUNG

The tree still looks sad to me.
It's not that the decorations
are old (and they are). It's that
they were all arranged without love.
This isn't the first loveless Christmas
I've spent. Foster homes, however

solid, are all barren of that emotion.
You don't dare care about someone
you probably won't know in a year.
But I've had beautiful holidays
with both sets of grandparents—
Carl and Jean. Scott and Marie.

The ones with Grandma Marie
were especially special because
Hunter was there too. My brother.
The one I hardly ever get to see.
But when I do, he's always pretty
much amazing to me. Because

he gets to be with his sister (me).
The one he hardly ever gets to see.
Those Christmases I understand
the power of family. My three
brothers will be there this year.
I so wish I could be there too.

THE ONLY PLACE

I'd rather be is with Kyle. He's all I can
think about as I help make dinner,

> Tanya chattering away about how much
> *you'll love Roosevelt* and *church on Sunday.*

>> All I can think about at the table, Walter
>> griping about the *goddamn power bill.*

>>> All I can think about as Simone and I
>>> load the dishwasher in total silence.

Wonder what he's doing, as I brush
my teeth, get ready for bed. Wonder

> if he's thinking about me, too, as Eliana
> borrows one of my well-loved books.

>> Wonder if I'll ever see him again as Rosa
>> practices for her Sunday School pageant.

>>> Wonder if he's written me off already
>>> as I crawl between the scratchy sheets.

IT IS WALTER

Who comes to handle the lights-out
bed check. He knocks, but doesn't
wait for an invitation to enter.

Simone, in a short, gauzy nightgown,
barely covers her long legs, and Walter
is all eyes. I swear, he starts to salivate.

> No. No way. Not her. And not me.
> *Good night, ladies.* He flips off the lights,
> closes the door. Did Simone notice

> the demon-wolf in his eyes? Her voice
> drifts toward me on dark wings of night.
> *I hate him. He reminds me of my brother.*

Without telling me, she has shared
her secret. A half-dozen questions
pop into my head. Real brother? Step?

When? How? Who told? Why did
that mean she ended up here? But in
the long run, the answers don't matter.

BEFORE TOO VERY LONG

Simone's breathing falls shallow.
Rhythmic. She's wandering deep
within some sort of dream. A good
dream, I guess. She laughs softly
in her sleep. Do I ever find happiness

in my dreams? I rarely remember
them. Sleep will not come easily
for me tonight. Not in an unfamiliar
bed, in an unfamiliar room. The night
itself is a different shade of dark.

Loneliness strikes suddenly,
a cobra sinking its fangs into my
heart, venom pumping. My eyes
spill into the strange, lumpy,
bleach-perfumed pillow. Salt soak.

I should be used to this by now.
Should expect the slow opening,
the hollow place inside. I am oddly
not afraid, though I recognize
the thirst in Walter. Who knows

how he might try to quench it?
I swear I will never let him, or
anyone, take a long swallow of me
unless it is my choice. And I only
choose to be water for Kyle.

HOW LONG WILL IT BE

Before living here
        becomes unbearable?

How long before the
        Bear pays a call on me?

How long before I have
        to find a way to flee?

        Sometime before dawn
                my eyes finally close.

        And though I'm not quite
                asleep, I feel myself drift.

        Float toward that hole
                behind the bridge of my nose.

                If I can just fall in,
                        I think I might find Kyle.

                If I can just reach in,
                        I know I'll touch his face.

                If I can just take his hand,
                        will we leave together?

FOR THREE DAYS

I try to settle in, try to feel
like part of this not-family,
to ignore my gut feeling.
                                    Three days of
listening to Eliana and
Rosa argue and laugh.
Real sisters
                                    acting like
all real sisters do,
I suppose. Who knows?
Maybe, just maybe,

                                    everything
would be different
between my real sister
and me. The fact
                                    is,
it could very well be
hate at first sight.
The fact is,
                                    just
because you're related
doesn't mean you
want to be. So,

                                    fine.
Forget that ridiculous
fantasy. Who needs
family, anyway?

DAY FOUR

Tanya has taken the girls Christmas
shopping. We drew names to get gifts
for. Stupid, if you think about it. None
of us has any money. It's all pretend.

I drew Rosa. Figured a Barbie would do
for her, but couldn't stomach the idea
of traipsing around Wal-Mart. So I faked
sick. Asked Tanya to pick one up.

Walter is puttering around the garage,
playing with his tools (or something else).
This is what I've been hoping for—a few
private minutes to try and call Kyle.

> But when I dig out my cell, there's
> a message waiting for me. From him.
> *Summer. Call me. Please. Can't stand . . .*
> *Can't stand not having you with me.*

His voice trembles. Crying? My own
tears start to fall as I think about
his arms around me. The comfort
of his kiss. All this love, wasting . . .

> I speed dial his number. He answers
> almost immediately, as if waiting
> for my call. *Summer? How are you?*
> *Oh God, I've missed you so much.*

"I've missed you, too. I'm okay. . . ."
We spend a few minutes talking.
I tell him about the blonde and the bear
and my faux sisters. He tells me about

> coming to Fresno to visit his aunt
> for the holidays. *I have to see you.*
> *Maybe we can get together*
> *while I'm there. What do you think?*

Get together? How? I'm pretty sure
dating is a solid foster care taboo.
"You know I want to, but I don't
know how to make it happen."

> *You can sneak out, right?* His voice
> trembles. *I have to see you, Summer.*
> *I'll come early. Tomorrow. Give me*
> *the address there. I'll MapQuest it.*

I hear a door close, bear-heavy
footsteps. "I've got to go! Call me
when you're getting close." I hang
up, just as Walter clunks down

the hall. His face pokes through
the doorway, all feral eyes and licking
lips. I pretend I'm waking up from
a flu-induced nap. "Ugh. Gotta puke."

THE REST OF THE DAY

Is filled with

    excited squeals
    peals of laughter
    sisterly whispers
    Bear growls and
    Tanya squeaks.

I lie in bed

    trying not to listen
    trying not to get up
    trying not to obsess
    about seeing Kyle
    in just a few hours.

My head spins

    dizzy with love
    dizzy with hope
    dizzy with strategy
    dizzy with dreams
    of tomorrow.

ALBUQUERQUE JOURNAL

Working with the FBI and the Bernalillo County sheriff's department, Albuquerque police accomplished a major sting, arresting five members of a marijuana smuggling ring. Lieutenant Rocky Schneider said if not for an unrelated incident, the smuggling operation might have continued unimpeded indefinitely.

"It started with a simple speeding ticket," said Schneider. "The officer noticed a definite odor of marijuana and upon questioning the driver, discovered a quarter pound under the front seat. Rather than face a more severe charge, the driver decided to cooperate with authorities."

Albuquerque resident Wayne Allen Snow led police to a house in Rio Rancho. Upon entering, officers found almost ten pounds of high-grade marijuana, imported via runners for a major Mexican cartel. Arrested there were Adam "Buddy" Grimoir; his wife, Lince; and three Mexican nationals. All five were bound over to await trial.

"This is only a small glimpse of a much larger picture," Schneider said. "Nevertheless, it was a righteous bust, and perhaps the beginning of a positive trend."

Hunter

BACK HOME

Indefinitely.
Nikki won't
even talk to
me, let alone
forgive me.
She pisses
me off. My
fault? Maybe.
But I deserve
a chance to
explain. I

could say it
isn't so bad.
But that'd
be a lie. I'm
home, yes,
but with the
boys still in
my old room,
I'm in the
guest room.

White
on
white
with
white
trim.

I HATE WHITE

The sun through the south window
makes it much too bright in here
by day, and at night, artificial

light glares, wall to wall to wall.
If this move ends up permanent,
I'll have to talk to Mom about paint.

My plan, though, is to give Nikki
time. Then gently wear down
her defenses. She'll have to forgive

me eventually, right? There must
be some way to make that happen.
I can't believe how much I miss her.

And not just the way she fills my bed
with velvet skin and satin hair and
warm spice scent. Without her,

I am incomplete. The worst thing
is, I have no excuse for what happened
with Leah. The message that bitch

left on my phone gave no room
for misinterpretation. Nikki knew
for sure I had betrayed her. And how.

SO FOR NOW, IT'S WHITE

And not just in here,
        but outside, too. It
                started to snow four
                        days ago. And it just
                                keeps on coming down.
Semester break, no
        classes for three weeks,
                I only have to worry
                        about driving for my
                                air shifts. Holidays
mean the "stars" go
        home too, so I'm
                pulling a few extra.
                        But mostly, if for no
                                other reason than to get
out of the guest room,
        I'm helping Mom with
                her Christmas stuff.
                        Decorating. Wrapping.
                        Baking cookies, even.
That's what we're doing
        now. She tried to get
                the boys to help. But
                        Donald thinks it's lame.
                        And David prefers the pup.

GOOD THING

Someone wants to play with Sasha,
I guess. She's at that gangly stage—
all floppy feet and squirrelly tail,
wagging into the cupboards while
Mom and I measure flour and sugar

and butter. *David,* says Mom,
would you please put on your coat
and take Sasha outside to play in
the snow? If you wear her out, maybe
she'll take a nice long winter's nap.

David is willing, so off they go.
Donald and Scott are shoveling
the decks. I've got Mom all to
myself, a rare thing around here
lately. We haven't talked much

since I came back. All she knows
for sure about Nikki and me
is that we had a little fight.
I've got a lot more than that
to tell her about, though.

I watch her cross the kitchen
floor. Graceful, like a dancer,
and fit, especially for a woman
her age. Still working out at sixty.
Wonder if I'll have her energy.

SHE TURNS

Finds me staring, gawking in
admiration like a regular fan boy.

What? A booger or something?

"Nope. Just wondering where
you get all your energy from."

Can't slow down. Too much to do.

I have to smile. "You've been
saying that since I was a little kid."

Yeah, and? Nothing has changed.

Still dealing with the fallout of choices,
not her own, made twenty years ago.

Anyway, slow down, you grow mold.

Another favorite saying. "But don't
you ever get mad about . . . stuff?"

Hunter, I used to live "mad." Didn't help.

I REACH WAY BACK

Into memory, to another
        Christmas. I must have been ten.

Kristina was here with Donald.
        He would have been three.

Ron was supposed to come
        with them that year, so Mom got

        them a hotel room. *That man*
                will not stay under this roof.

        She didn't give a reason, and
                I wondered why she was so angry.

On their way out of Vegas,
        Ron was arrested. Kristina claimed

it was an outstanding traffic
        ticket. We found out later it was

for a domestic violence warrant.
        Kristina came alone, checked into

her room on Christmas Eve,
        and when she didn't show up for

        our usual family dinner, Mom
                was mad. *You can't ever rely on her.*

But she was also worried
        and sent Dad out to look for her.

Turned out she was in the ER.
        She claimed it was food poisoning.

Poor little Donald hadn't had
        a bite to eat all day except for a candy

                cane a sympathetic nurse gave him.
                        You'd think a nurse would know better.

I didn't understand until I watched
        him bounce off the walls all night.

Kristina came over the next
        morning. Spent Christmas Day, and

I mean all day, on her cell phone,
        talking to Ron, who was already out of jail.

                Mom stewed big-time. *She's using
                        again. Six years clean for what?*

I overheard her tell Dad. I thought
        she was wrong. Turned out she was spot

on. The ER visit was bad dope.
        And Kristina was pregnant with David.

MOM WAS ANGRIER THEN

Is anger something
you can outgrow?
Can anyone do it
with practice? Dad
has never quite
mastered the talent.

Maybe it's a gender
thing. I think I take
after Dad, carrying
anger like he does,
tight in my muscles,
unable to quite let go.

I don't feel like I'm
mad most of the time,
but it isn't hard to let
all that stored anger
come rippling out.
I should get help.

But it's hard to talk
about resentment,
bottled up inside.
I have it easier than
most people. So why
feel sorry for myself?

Not like very many
people have intact
families. One parent
or the other is likely
absent. Shacked up.
Knocked up. Fucked up.

Looking at it that way,
I'm pretty normal. So
why do I feel like some
sort of a freak? Bigger
question: Why take it
out on people I love?

476

ALL THIS FILTERS THROUGH

My brain in the time it takes
Mom to cream two cups of
butter with two cups of brown

sugar, add two eggs, and beat
well. And despite every warning,
once the mixer noise stops,

I have to spout words I swore
to keep to myself so as not to
hurt her. "I met my father."

> *Well, of course you met your*
> *f—, she starts, back to me.*
> Her shoulders tense, and very

> slowly, she turns toward me.
> *Your father? Are you sure?*
> She studies my face intently.

I nod. "Pretty sure . . ."
And I tell her the story, starting
with noticing piebald eyes

in the crowd at the Christmas
parade and ending with the X
holiday party. Deep breath.

I DIDN'T THINK

Talking about it would bother
        me so much, but my hands quiver
            and my breathing falls shallow.

        Mom notices, comes over to
            me. She takes my hands in hers,
                presses gently. *You okay?*

I wish I were little again so
        she could wrap me in her arms
            like she used to. I remember

how, growing up, I wanted to
        be taller than her, always kept
            measuring. Then one day, I was.

It was better before. I look down
        into her eyes. "Yeah. I'm okay.
            I just never really expected

to meet him. Or that I might
        actually like him. It was easier
            hating him for what he did."

        Mom tugs gently, sits me
            at the table. *Resentment is*
                always easier than forgiveness.

SHE SITS BESIDE ME

Pulls her spine straight,
making her still nowhere near

as tall as me. Yet her presence
seems larger than life.

> *Do you have any idea why*
> *Leigh isn't here yet?*

I shake my head. Smile.
"Didn't want to ask. I figured

once she got here, I'd end
up sleeping on the floor."

> She laughs. *Futon, remember?*
> Then she gets serious again.

> *You know Leigh has never really*
> *forgiven her father, right?*

> *Well, Wayne was recently arrested*
> *for a large quantity of marijuana.*

> *He cooperated with authorities,*
> *and they left him on house arrest,*

which turned out to be a good
thing because he just had a major

heart attack. It wasn't his first, and
they don't think he's going to make

it. Leigh flew back to Albuquerque
to basically say good-bye.

Wow. I'm sort of stunned.
He is my grandfather and now

I'll never get to know him. Not
that I ever wanted to know him,

because of the things that happened
a long time ago. Things that will

never be rectified. God, why does
my life continue to be defined

by other people's decisions? "Why didn't
he ever try to be a part of our lives?"

Mom shrugs. *Maybe he didn't know*
how to say he was sorry.

Or maybe he was afraid
we wouldn't believe it.

SUDDEN COMMOTION

As a wet puppy bounds into
the room, followed by an excited
David. *Come back here, Sasha!*
Fuβ. German for "heel."

Surprisingly, Sasha obeys,
coming round to sit at David's
left side. *Good girl. Good Sasha.*
When he moves, she moves too.

"Wow. I'm impressed. You
going to work Sasha, David?"
Before Mom's life got too busy,
she used to work her dogs, Schutzhund

fashion. Police-dog-style training
is incredibly demanding on both animals
and trainers. Might be really good
for David. Donald, too, if he'd do it.

> *There's still a club out here,*
> Mom says to me. *Scott has taken*
> *David and Sasha to a couple*
> *of sessions. I think they like it.*

> *I do,* agrees David. *They say*
> *I'm kind of young, but I'm not*
> *the only kid. Sasha likes it too.*
> *And she's kind of young too.*

SMART KID

It's good to see him so engaged.
Donald, on the other hand, really
worries me. Mostly he just sits

around, playing computer games
or watching TV. Except when Dad
makes him get up and do something.

Dad, in fact, seems to be the only
one who can convince him to
behave even halfway civilized.

Mom has him in therapy. "Severe
emotional detachment," was
the diagnosis, "probably caused

by early childhood trauma."
Yeah, like his parents' (one or
the other or both) meth-fueled rages,

resulting in fists to his face.
I remember him visiting us once,
decorated with knuckle-shaped bruises.

Such treatment can only erect walls
inside a kid. One between him and pain.
Another between him and love.

WHEN DID I BECOME A PHILOSOPHER?

I've got my own walls, and they
were not built by abuse or neglect.
I should probably go into therapy
myself, try and figure out why
I would so willingly sabotage
a relationship that means everything
to me. What am I, fucking stupid?

>Okay, I am totally fricking stupid.
>Here I thought I was using Leah, and
>she totally used me. Set me up
>completely. When she programmed
>her number into my phone, she also
>called herself, so she'd have my
>number too. Like I said. Stupid.

And now I'm mad all over again.
At her. At myself. I get up, kiss
Mom on the forehead. "Let's finish
those cookies." Mindless activity,
that's what I need. Maybe by not
thinking at all, my brain will come up
with a way to get Nikki to forgive me.

COOKIES IN THE OVEN

Mindless
        activity finished for now,
        my brain has failed me completely.

        Dad and Donald are in the front
        hall, shaking snow off their boots,

        hats. Almost unbelievably, Donald
        is laughing. A new wall goes up.
Jealousy.
        Weird. Really, really weird. Why
        do I feel that way? Maybe because

        Dad and I haven't talked in years,
        at least not about stuff that matters.

        And the last time we laughed
        together? I really can't remember.
I want
        us to be close again. We were
        when I was young. Then, I guess,

        I made him into "the enemy,"
        the one who said no to giving me

        money (for weed) or borrowing
        the car (to party). What I forgot was
his love.

GOD, I'M MAUDLIN TODAY

Must be all the obvious Christmas cheer,
and how it doesn't cheer me. Mom has
always been big on making the house
look *Good Housekeeping* gorgeous.

Electric trains. Ceramic villages.
Multicolored garland and lights,
strung on banisters and door jambs.
The tree, a twelve-foot blue spruce,

is hung with ornaments collected for
almost forty years. Wreaths. Poinsettias,
in four shades and varied heights.
Candles in holiday colors, scented

cranberry and bayberry and vanilla.
And outside? Colored lights and white
icicle lights and a giant lit Santa's sleigh.
You can see this place clear across

the valley. When I was a kid, I loved
it. Now it seems a little ostentatious.
Wonder if Mom and Dad would have
gone so all out without the boys here.

SAID BOYS

Disappear into their (my) room.

Mom vanishes into her office
to write. New book. Fantasy.

Dad decides to work on dinner,
something he often does even
when Mom is home. Chef Dad.

I sit at the table, munching cookies,
watching him season the roast.
Here is a chance to talk about
something that matters. Like?

"So, Dad . . ." Do I dare ask?

Oh, why the hell not? "Have
you ever cheated on Mom?"

> He looks up, humor in his eyes.
> *Is this some sort of a test?*
> *Do you have a hidden recorder?*

That makes me smile. "No,
no. This isn't about blackmail.
And you don't have to answer.
I just wondered because . . ."

Because of what happened with Nikki?

And here I always thought Mom was
the psychic. "Uh . . . kinda . . . yes."

       He lines a baking pan with foil.
       Nestles the roast inside. *I thought*
       that might be it. One of your listeners?

Oh my God. He *is* psychic.
"Yeah, that's right. And I swear
I don't even know why I did it.
But how did you know?"

       Hunter, I used to be in radio,

       remember? I know how it is when
       a pretty girl throws herself at you.

Good. He gets it. God, I'm glad
he's been there, except . . .
"But you never got caught."

       No, Hunter. See, I never said
       okay, not once I'd made a solid
       commitment to your mom. I just
       couldn't take a chance on losing her.

THIS COULD TURN INTO A LECTURE

And it sort of does.

Believe me, there were
plenty of willing women.
Some really didn't want
to take no for an answer.

I nod. Because I know.

But your mom came to me
already wounded. I had
to win her trust. Destroying
that trust was unthinkable.

Dad and the moral high road.

Even beyond my time in
radio, there have been plenty
of temptations over the years.
I'm sure for your mom, too.

Mom? Women are tempted?

But with as much as she has
to travel with her books,
if either of us had to worry
about that, where would we be?

Has Nikki been tempted too?

We're married, of course.
That is a stronger commitment
than living together. Although
Nikki would probably argue that.

NO DOUBT ABOUT IT

For Nikki, living together meant
every bit as much as having a piece
of paper giving us the legal right.

I still have no idea what my next
move should be. How can I make
this up to her? Dad puts the roast

into the oven. Washes some big
potatoes. Wraps them in foil.
"Do you ever wonder where

you would be if you hadn't met
Mom? She told me once that when
you first met, your dream was

to be the next Johnny Carson. . . ."
I didn't know who that was, so I looked
him up. He was pretty famous back then.

"Does it bother you that you're not
a late-night TV host? Or that Mom got
to be the famous one instead of you?"

      He keeps working but laughs softly.
      Hey, I've still got time. Seriously,
      though, sure, it's bothered me.

But we don't always get what
we want. I didn't get to be a star,
but I did get to be something

special—your mom's husband.
And your father. Those things mean
more to me than hosting late-night TV.

"Seriously? Because sometimes
you seem resentful. Not that I blame
you. You didn't ask for me."

The potatoes join the roast in the oven.
You're right. We didn't ask for you.
But I have never resented becoming

your father. Your mom and I made
that choice willingly, with our eyes
wide open. Yes, sometimes I get mad

about things beyond my control.
Not that it's useful or changes
anything. It's just human nature.

Anger is a valid emotion. It's only
bad when it takes control and makes
you do things you don't want to do.

I GUESS I CAN'T BLAME ANGER

For the Leah incident.
Lack of self-control isn't
always about being pissed.
Sometimes it's sheer greed.

Something Dad said filters
back to me now.
*Not once I'd made a solid
commitment to your mom . . .*

"You said you never
cheated on Mom once
you committed to her.
How about before that?"

He decides how to answer.
*I was dating a couple
of other people at the time.
So, yes, I guess I did.*

Okay. This could quite
possibly be useful. "So did
Mom find out?" She had to,
right? She's not exactly dense.

*Actually, she did. And
when I saw how hurt
she was, it really made
me think. She was the one*

I loved. I didn't want to
lose her. That's when I
decided playing around
just wasn't worth it.

Dad got Mom back, so
there's hope. But, "What
did you say to make Mom
give you another chance?"

He smiles. *I told her if
I ever messed around again,
she could cut off my balls.*
At my horrified expression,

Dad amends, *Not really. Look.
There's no secret formula here.
Give it a few days. My guess is,
once Nikki cools off, she'll be*

*missing you. Then go to her and
tell her you know you screwed
up big-time, but you love her too
much to let things end like this.*

*It may not work. But Nikki loves
you, and if you love her, too,
what have you got to lose?
Just be sure to follow through.*

FEELING MARGINALLY BETTER

And semi-jacked-up on chocolate
chip cookies, I think maybe I'll

ask the boys if they want to break
out the sleds. The driveway is perfect,

as long as we build up a berm across
the bottom. Not that there will be much

traffic out in a storm like this. I am
considering digging around in the garage

when the phone rings. Once. Dad
and I look at each other, some strange

kind of understanding building between
us. Suddenly David dashes into the room,

> Sasha nipping at his heels. *Mommy's
> coming for Christmas!* he shouts.

> Mom follows. *Her public defender
> argued illegal search and seizure,*

> she explains. *The judge agreed. All
> charges against her were dropped.*

Kristina talks her way out of another
predicament. Christmas drama to come.

LONELINESS AND LIQUOR

Are best friends. Too bad I haven't
had any liquor since the wedding.

                    Loneliness is eating me alive.

No more Aunt Cora. No word from Bryce.
Grandfather in bed with some ailment.

                    Much too much time on my hands.

If there were any alcohol in the place,
I'd be dropped-on-my-knees drunk.

                    Instead I keep cleaning. Organizing.

There isn't a speck of dirt anywhere.
Except, no doubt, in Grandfather's room.

                    I avoid going in there. It stinks.

Stinks like old man. Stinks like a feeble
old man, flat on his back for three days.

                    Farts and sweat and medicine.

I only go in to take him soup. Hot tea.
Water. More water. But not much me.

WHEN I CALLED BRYCE

To apologize, he was Arctic cool.
I don't understand. Why did you
tell me your parents were dead?

"I'm so sorry," I said. "It's just . . .
well, there are things about them
I'm not proud of. I was afraid. . . ."

Look. No one's parents are perfect.
And whatever is wrong with yours,
lying to me like that just sucks.

"I know. I was wrong. Can't you please
forgive me? Will you come over so
we can—wait. Grandfather's sick."

He warmed up a little. *Listen.*
We're heading out to California.
I'll be back after Christmas.

We'll get together then, okay?
But we can't have a relationship
built around lies. Love is honest.

495

AT LEAST HE USED THE WORD "LOVE"

The "built around lies" part,
however, has me worried. I wish
I would never have made up
that stupid story about my parents
being dead. But hey, for all I know,

my mother is dead. Not like I've
heard a single word from her.
And my dad isn't a whole lot better
than dead to me. I never really
expected to see him again.

Certainly not then. Did he pick
Aunt Cora's wedding for shock
value alone? He couldn't have
timed it worse, with Bryce right
there as he made his grand entrance.

At least Bryce is willing to let me
explain. But even if I fess up about
the circumstances of my birth, what
about my deeper dishonesty?
How much truth do I want to tell him?

MY STOMACH STIRS

And I'm pretty sure it has nothing
    to do with the thought of lies.

Hope I'm not coming down with
    Grandfather's bug. Wonder if it's cat

flu or dog flu, or some other
    new, improved, unidentified strain.

He's actually a little better today,
    and seeing as how he's a member

of one of those "high-risk populations,"
    I guess that's a really good thing.

I wander down the hall to check
    on him, but he's in the bathroom.

God! The smell coming from
    his bedroom is going to make me . . .

Quick. Run to the other bathroom,
    reach the toilet just in time for

my stomach to jet a horrid stream
    of oatmeal and yogurt. Breakfast.

I HEAVE

And heave,
      sweat breaking
           out on my forehead.
Gut clenching
      and letting go.
           Clenching. Great.

Who will take care
      of Grandfather   if I get sick too?

Who will take
      care of me?   No Aunt Cora to

tuck me in bed.
      No Aunt Cora to
           bring me soup,
steaming cups of
      tea. Ugh. Soup.
           Just the thought

makes me hurl
      again. I hurl till
           I'm food-empty and
there's nothing
      left in my stomach
           but putrid air.

ALL HURLED OUT

Shaky. Drained. I poke my head
        through Grandfather's door, see
he is dozing. Sounds like a plan.

I wander into the living room, turn
        on the TV. Lie down on the couch
to not watch the History Channel.

Some boring show about some boring
        monarch in some boring century.
My eyes, weighted, close and I slip

toward some deep pocket of dark
        space. Warm here. Comforting, with
a low buzz of canned boring voices.

Ringing now. Ringing? Bell. Doorbell?
        Bell? I swim up into a bay of flat,
gray light. Doorbell. Who? Bryce!

He came? I jump up way too fast.
        My head is so light. Did my brain
shrink? I steady myself. "Coming!"

The door is so far. Oh, God. Don't
        leave. Don't go away. "Be right
there!" I reach for the knob, jerk

the door open. "Bryce!" But no,
           he's too tall. Too dark. Too old.
Trey. Perfect. The anti-Bryce.

                    Sorry. Not Bryce. Can I come in?
                            He doesn't wait for an answer,
                    though. Just pushes on past me.

"W-wait. I'm not sure . . . uh . . ."
           Not sure of what? Think, Autumn.
"Uh, Grandfather has been sick."

                    That's okay. I'm not here to see
                            him. I'm here to see you. We've
                    got a little catching up to do.

I follow him into the living room,
           watch him flip off the TV. I start
to tell him I don't feel so hot either,

notice I'm actually better. Strange.
           I figured I'd be on my back for days,
like Grandfather, who I should tell

we've got a visitor. Then again,
           he's asleep and I'm a big girl.
I can handle this on my own.

AT LEAST I THINK I CAN

When it comes right down
to it, I don't know very
much at all about

the man

sitting on Grandfather's
recliner, claiming it as if
it were his own. I think he

is

probably dangerous.
Aren't all armed robbers?
And yet, would he be

a

threat to me? For all I
really know, he could
be a serial killer, a

total

whacked-out pervert,
stalking his next victim.
He is nothing but a

stranger.

A black hole. Will he suck
me in? Burn me up? What
does he want with me?

HE STUDIES ME

For several minutes. Finally says,
You look a lot like her. Your

mother. Her hair is darker.
You got the red from my mom.

Straight for the jugular.
"I wouldn't know. I never

met my mother. I don't
even know her name."

He looks at me like I'm crazy.
No one ever told you her name?

I shake my head. "For all
I know, the stork delivered me."

His mouth twitches slightly.
No, you were born at Washoe

Med in Reno. Your mom's name
is Kristina. She lives in Vegas.

"Why should I care? She never
cared enough to contact me."

*Not exactly true. I just talked
to her a little while ago. . . .*

He talked to her? About me?
"She doesn't even care if I'm alive."

*That's not so. She's tried to find
you since she got out of prison.*

What is he talking about? Anger
stings, hot in my cheeks. "No way.

No calls. No letters. Definitely
never came ringing the doorbell."

*Because she didn't know where
you were. I didn't either, not until*

*Mom got the news about Cora's
wedding. Why do you think*

*everyone was so surprised when
we showed up?* He sets his jaw.

"I don't understand. How could
you not know where I was?"

HIS EYES LIFT

Then they settle somewhere
over my shoulder, grow cold.
He points. *Ask him.* Grandfather

has come into the room, silent as
still air. I don't have to turn to feel
him there. The tension is solid.

His trembling voice falls, a bag
of marbles, over my shoulder.
You. Get out of my chair.

Trey does not comply right
away. But as Grandfather starts
to move, he stands. *Tell her.*

Grandfather limps slowly
toward his chair. He is pale
as paper. I stay silent as

he sits and meets my eyes.
*We were just trying to protect
you, Cora and I . . . we . . .*

He pauses too long, so Trey
expands, *They kept moving
around when you were little.*

THINGS FALL INTO PLACE

Suddenly. Frequent
moves to different
little Texas towns.

Different schools.
Different friends.
Different boyfriends

for Aunt Cora. Phone
numbers. Addresses I
could never quite recall,
and if I did, there were

frequent reminders
frequent lectures
frequent warnings

not to share them,
because a stranger
could get hold of
them, might come
kidnap me away.

Hidden photos.
Hidden paperwork.
Hidden stories

about my family.
To protect me from
my mother. Father.
And who else is out
there? Who else might
want to know what
has happened to me?

SUCKER PUNCHED

I can't find air, and it has nothing to do with illogical panic.

It's shock. Pure. Simple. Rational. "How could you?"

How could they make me believe I was a throwaway?

      Grandfather is completely white, and the folds

      of his eyes crease with pain. Good. I want him to hurt,

      like he and Aunt Cora have hurt me. *I'm sorry*, he says.

"Sorry? Do you understand how it feels to believe

your parents don't want you? Don't tell me they didn't

deserve me. I already know that. This isn't about them."

The look I shoot Trey withers him slightly. But his eyes

glitter defiance. A desire so different from any I've

known before strikes suddenly. "I want to meet her."

TREY STRAIGHTENS

I can see the wheels
creak-turn in his head.
He looks at Grandfather,

> says to me, *I'll take you.*
> *You should meet her.*
> *Just don't go thinking*
>
> *she's going to be like*
> *some perfect mom. Kristina*
> *is all about Kristina.*

Far as I can tell, that pretty
much goes for everyone.
"Really? You'll take me?"

> *Why not? I'd like to see*
> *her again myself. I used*
> *to love the bitch. Maybe*
>
> *I can figure out why. She's*
> *on her way to Albuquerque*
> *to see her dad, but will be*
>
> *at her mom's for Christmas.*
> *Plenty of time for a road*
> *trip. You'll be a nice surprise.*

GRANDFATHER IS SHAKING

Anger. Fear. Goat flu. Not sure
which is to blame. Maybe all three.

> *You're not serious,* he says. *You
> can't take her. I won't let you.*

I want to go over. Give him a hug.
I want to go over. Slap him. Hard.

That's the indecisive part of me—
well-known. A strange, new take-

charge part jumps in, "Yes, he can.
If I don't go now, it may never happen."

> Grandfather crumbles. *You're going
> to leave me alone on Christmas?*

I could thaw if I let myself. But no.
"Austin isn't so far. Call Aunt Cora."

My heart flip-flops in my chest. I might
meet my mother. It may very well turn

out all bad, but how else will I know
that? "I'll go pack some clothes."

BY THE TIME

My suitcase sits, barely half-full,
by the door, my anger has mostly
subsided. Grandfather slumps,
wounded, in his ratty recliner.

"Did you call Aunt Cora?" I ask
him. When he doesn't reply,

> Trey says, *He wouldn't, so I did.*
> *She said she's on her way.*

Which means we'd better go
before she gets here and tries
to make me change my mind.
She could probably do it.

I go over to Grandfather, put
my hand on his cheek. "I'll be back."

> He refuses to meet my eyes.
> *I'll be right here, waiting.*

WHEN I OPEN THE DOOR

I'm surprised to see the car
parked at the curb. It's a late
model Cadillac. White. Pin
neat. Wait. This can't be Trey's.
Suddenly I understand how

little I really know about him.
Am I making an awful mistake?
Wasn't he in prison for grand
theft auto, among other things?
"Uh. Nice car. Whose is it?"

> He pulls the key from his
> pocket, waves it in the air,
> pushes a button that opens
> the trunk, puts my suitcase
> inside. *Actually, it's my mom's.*
>
> *Get in.* He waits for me to
> make up my mind. It takes all
> of two minutes before he says,
> *Well? Are you coming or what?*
> He starts the car. Exactly

the motivation I need. I slink
into the front passenger seat,
fingers tingling. Plush white leather
sucks me in. The stereo plays
metal and my heart drums along.

My nose wrinkles at an overpowering
stench of stale tobacco. The ashtray
practically overflows. "Will
you empty that, please? And you
won't smoke with me in the car?"

> I meant it as a question, sort of.
> He takes it another way. *Kind*
> *of demanding, aren't you? I don't*
> *have to do this at all, you know.*
> Still, he opens the door, dumps

the ashtray into the gutter,
replaces it. Nice. Really nice.
I should haul my butt out of
the car, back into the house
where I belong. But I don't.

MAUREEN IS AT A HOTEL

A nice enough Best Western.
Not the Ritz, but not a dump,
either. I'd forgotten she was
part of this equation. A big part,

as it turns out, the Cadillac
being hers and all. I trail Trey
down a long hallway. "Should you
have talked this over with her?"

> He doesn't slow. *No doubt.*
> *And she can always say no.*
> *I don't think she will, but maybe*
> *you should wait out here.*

I lean back against a gold
flocked wall, sink down it,
sit on the yellow/brown swirled
carpet. Wait. Listen, as beyond

> the far door, conversation
> becomes animated. Not loud,
> not really, so if they're arguing,
> it isn't with much conviction.

It takes quite a while before
the door opens and Trey
gestures for me to come on
inside. Once again, I get an urge

to turn and run. But I don't.
The room is neat, except for
a collage of empty bottles—wine,
beer, gin, Coke, and mineral water.

It's enough to make my mouth
start to water. I could use
a gulp or two of liquid courage.
I look at Maureen. "Hello."

> She stares back curiously.
> *Are you crazy?* The question
> is so matter-of-fact, it catches
> me completely off guard.

"Wha-what do you mean?" Panic
attacks? OCD? She doesn't
know about those things, right?
Or is she just talking genetics?

SHE SITS QUIETLY

For a couple of seconds. Finally
says, *Why do you want to stir up*

a mess of trouble for yourself?
Is your life so god-awful now?

How to answer? Not bad. Not
great. But headed steadily toward

god-awful, mostly because of
the sudden appearance of the very

people in this room? TMI. "It's okay,
I guess. No real complaints. But I have

a right to know who my parents are.
Even if I end up disappointed."

We both look at Trey, who throws
his hands in the air. *This is your idea.*

Maureen shrugs. *I guess you do.*
And you very well may end up

disappointed. It's against my better
judgment, but I'll loan Trey my car.

On one condition. When you come
back through California, you stop

in Sacramento and visit me for a few
days. Don't forget, I'm your family too.

And so it's decided. Maureen will
fly home. We'll take the Cadillac

on a long, boring drive to northern
Nevada. Reno. Where I was born.

Will it feel like home? Does the city
or town where you're born imbed

itself in your psyche? I only lived
there three years. Will the altitude-

influenced temperature better suit
me? Will I breathe the air easier?

Will the scent of high desert
Nevada trump Texas prairie?

Will I come running back to Grandfather
or find solace in rediscovered family?

IT IS LATE AFTERNOON

By the time we actually hit the highway.
    First, long, straight stretches of Interstate 10.
        Through Arizona, New Mexico, into California.

        North on I-15, to 395, north to Carson City.
    More than seventeen hundred miles. Alone with
a stranger. Straight through, more than twenty-

four hours. The longest ride of my life, through
    mostly unremarkable country. Flat grassland.
        Dry desert as yet unkissed by winter's

        soft wet lips. At least it's not ungodly hot
    in December. When we get out to stretch,
it's rather comfortably warm. At least it will be for

the first part of the trip. We hear there's
    a blizzard warning from Bishop, north.
        Blizzard? I've never even seen snow, not

        that I can remember at least. I'm excited.
    Scared. Chilled through to the bone, and
we're only two hundred miles toward cold.

IT TAKES THAT TWO HUNDRED MILES

And more of tedious small talk—school,
extracurricular crap or lack of it, friends
or lack of them—interwoven with long bouts

of silence, before I finally get up the nerve
to redirect the conversation away from me.
"What's she like?" I ask, then add, "My mother."

Trey thinks for a minute, reaches over,
turns down the radio. *I wish I could tell
you. But I'm not sure I ever knew Kristina.*

*The real Kristina, that is. I saw traces
of her once in a while. That girl had
a heart. The Kristina I met was still*

*pretty, but not nearly as beautiful
as the pictures I saw of her when she
was younger, before she started . . .*

"Started using meth? With you?
Grandfather told me about that.
He said you were different before too."

His jaw clenches. *Dad doesn't know
everything. Kristina didn't start using
with me. She already had a history.*

He tells me about Albuquerque.
How she met a guy there who first
turned her on. Tells me about

partying with her father. Hiding it
from her mother and stepfather.
How she probably would have

> kept right on smoking it up then
> except, *But then she got pregnant*
> *and mostly quit until Hunter was—*

"Wait. Hunter? I have a brother?"
I've always believed I was an only
child. Not sure why, in retrospect.

> *I'm sorry. I forgot you didn't know.*
> *You have three brothers and a sister.*
> *But you're the only one who's mine. I—*

"Stop. I have to think." I turn up
the radio. Close my eyes. Dive into
the music as best I can. Ride the metal

current. None of this makes sense.
The only thing about myself I know
for sure is that I don't know anything.

OFF-KILTER

Canted. Listing
        to one side,
                a rotting hull.
Nothing will ever
        be the same in
                my world—careful
            order
   twisted.

Tossed
        into chaos.

            I don't even
        know how to
              feel about that.
   Relieved?
              Terrified?
Hopeful?
        Suicidal?

How does

   this define

        (or redefine)
              me?

WELL PAST MIDNIGHT

We stop for sleep in Las Cruces.
New Mexico is supposed to be
pretty. Maybe I'll agree, come morning.

So far it looks like Arizona did
at night. Miles and miles of
dark emptiness. A starlit vacuum.

Trey pulls into a dive of a motel.
Hope the beds have clean
sheets. The room is claustrophobic.

And ice-cube cold. I flip on the heat, go
to pee in a closet-sized bathroom.
Trey's going out for fast food, asks for

my order. I beg off. "Too tired to eat.
And I don't feel so hot. You could
bring me some bottled water, though."

I throw back the covers for inspection.
The sheets look okay, so I crawl
into bed. Tired. Real tired. So why does

it take forever to fall asleep? How do
I shut off my brain? What have
I done? What will tomorrow bring?

A THIN BEAM OF LIGHT

Ray guns my eyes, and I jump
up into early gray morning.
Where am I? I'm not alone.
Someone is snoring? Oh. Trey.

It all comes tidal waving back.
New Mexico. Cheesy motel room.
Cadillac outside the door. Smell.
What's that smell? I glance around

the room, notice the Taco Bell
bag, and wrappers, gooey with
hot sauce and bean detritus.
Suddenly I seriously need to toss

what little is in my stomach. I run
to the bathroom. Heave until I hit
empty. Get up, rinse my mouth.
Wash my face. When I exit the room,

Trey is awake, sitting up in bed,
looking more curious than worried.
"Sorry," I say. "I think I might have
caught Grandfather's flu bug."

Hope that's all you caught,
he says, half smiling. *Puking,*
first thing when you wake up?
Sounds like morning sickness to me.

Morning sickness? Oh my God.
Is that why I've felt so lousy lately?
He could be right. Pregnant?
Why does the idea shock me?

Can't admit it, though. Not to him.
Righteous indignation swells. Who
the hell is he to even suggest it?
Trey Shepherd has never been

anything but the sperm donor
whose semen maybe jump-started
me. I shake my head. "Can't be that.
What? You don't believe me?"

The tone of my voice warns him
off. He shrugs. Goes to pee. I fall
back into bed. What have I done?
And what will Bryce do when he knows?

Summer

LABELS

Hate 'em. Mostly, I guess,
because I've worn one label
or another pretty much forever.

Loser.

Because when I was little,
Grandma Jean and Grandpa
Carl couldn't afford the cutest
clothes or designer backpacks.

Loner.

Because foster kids don't make
and keep friends. Might as well
brand their foreheads: FK.
For foster kid. Or freak.

Stoner.

Because even if you don't get
stoned, hanging out with stoners
makes you feel like you belong.
Somewhere. Anywhere.

Stuck-up.

Because when you close yourself
off from questions, erect walls
around pain, unlocking the gate
to let someone in is unthinkable.

Fuckup.

Because it's easier to let others
believe you have no plans. No
dreams. No future. Nothing
worth taking away from you.

AND NOW A NEW LABEL

Probably the worst one ever
affixed to me. Not because

of the word. Because of what
it means. To me. To Kyle.

To our tentative today and even
shakier tomorrows, despite

how good it is to be together
again. Despite how good it feels

to be sitting here, close to him,
skin to skin, absorbing his heat

by osmosis. Inhaling the scent
of him. Tasting the salt of him,

whenever we chance taking the time
to kiss. Time being of the essence.

Driving south. Looking over our
shoulders, back at Fresno.

Holding the speed limit, wanting
to go faster but not daring.

He, doing this to be with me, despite
my brand-new label: runaway.

SNEAKING OUT

To meet him was harder than
I expected. Not because of Tanya
and Walter. Because of Simone,
who, for some unfathomable reason,
decided she wanted to bond after all.

> That day, after I talked to Kyle,
> started planning a little AWOL jaunt,
> Simone softened. She had drawn
> my name for our gift exchange.
> *Hope you like what I got you.*

This was after a fabulous
beans-and-hot-dogs dinner.
We were in our fart-fragranced
bedroom, listening to the radio.
Simone is a huge hip-hop fan.

Can't stand the stuff myself,
but I wasn't going to argue.
All I could think about was Kyle
and how to escape the house
to meet him the next day.

> Out of the blue, Simone
> decided to open up. *You want
> to hear about my brother?*
> The creepy voyeur in me did.
> But I kept my mouth closed.

Simone started to talk, anyway.
He was really my stepbrother,
and it started when I was eight. . . .
It wasn't a pretty story, but
I couldn't not listen to the sordid

details of late-night visits.
Bad touch. Very bad touch.
Threats to keep her quiet.
And when it all became too
much and she told, anyway,

her stepmother called her
a liar. And her father, who
was totally not going to disrupt
his new marriage, refused
to believe his own daughter.

It took a trusted teacher to
call in the authorities. Proof
wasn't difficult to come by.
Yet it was Simone whose life
was disrupted. Simone who

had to move out of her home,
into foster care. Simone whose
childhood was stolen. Innocence
eroded into nightmare. All because
of very bad touch. Love, corrupted.

NOT EXACTLY A NEW STORY

But it was Simone's story, and once
she shared it, she felt more than
connected to me. She felt chained.

Like if I left her sight, her secrets
might go with me. Like once she gave
them away, they weren't hers anymore?

Not like I wanted them. Not like I asked
for the responsibility of keeping them.
I've got enough secrets of my own.

One of which was on his way to me
from Bakersfield. And I really needed
the opportunity to head out the door

undetected. I had a couple of choices.
Confide. Or hide. I didn't really think
we had bonded close enough to tell

her about Kyle, his impending arrival.
I wanted to hold that close. Thank God
I still had the "you don't want to come

in the bathroom now" excuse going on.
Eventually she tired of shadowing me.
Stuck her nose in a book, kept it there.

I HAD MY CELL

With me, set on vibrate,
so no one but me would
know when it rang. I hid
out in the bathroom for
more than an hour, expecting
the buzz against my thigh.

I had almost given up by
the time it came. When
it finally did, it made me
jump. Good thing I was
only pretending to need
the toilet. I spoke in a low

whisper, hoping Simone
had, indeed, vacated the
hallway outside the door.
"Where are you?" It came
out a serpentlike hiss.
He was down the block.

Luckily, Walter was at
his day job. Tanya and
the sisters were crashing
around in the kitchen,
baking cookies. Leaving
was a piece of cake.

NOW I SWEAR

I didn't have running in mind
     as I slipped outside, sprinted
     along the sidewalk to where
Kyle had parked. It still was

not my goal when I jerked open
     the pickup door, bounded
     into Kyle's arms. Hadn't even
considered the idea when I buried

my face into his chest, inhaled
     his well-loved scent, turned up
     my eyes, begging him to kiss me.
But when our lips met, starved,

something stirred. And when
     his skin flowed like a warm tide
     over my own, whatever had stirred
whipped up, crazy. And when

our bodies linked, woven in
     heated rise and fall, every tatter
     of loneliness dissipated into
the ether of memory. And then

     he said, *Oh my God, I love you*
          so much. I can't be without you
          ever again. Come with me,
     Summer. Let's get out of here.

529

NOT MUCH TIME

To think it over. Still,
my first reaction was, "I can't."

>   *Yes, you can,* he said. *I need*
>   *you. Don't you understand?*

I sat up. Glanced around.
No sign of bear nor blonde.

"We can't just go. I love you,
Kyle, I really do, but . . ."

>   *If you really love me, you'll say*
>   *okay.* He reached out, grabbed

>   my face, turned it so I had to
>   look into his eyes. *Okay?*

I started to protest. But then
I remembered something Dad

had told me not long before
Shreeveport took me away.

We were on the porch, and as
usual, he was smoking. I watched

a narrow stream of smoke lift
into the cold morning. Rarely

before had the idea of separation
stung so much. I guess because

of the relative closeness we had
lately discovered. Finally I asked,

"If you could do anything over, take
something back, what would it be?"

> He thought for a minute or two,
> and when he finally spoke, his
>
> answer surprised me. *I guess*
> *I would have tried harder to*
>
> *convince your mother to stay*
> *after she got out of prison.*
>
> *I loved her enough to hope she*
> *might fall back in love with me.*
>
> *We were together for a while.*
> *You were like two or something.*
>
> *I would have done anything for her.*
> *Maybe I didn't let her know that.*
>
> *I should have fought harder to keep*
> *her. I'll never love anyone else.*

NOTHING TO LOSE

Unless I stayed. I think I surprised
both of us when I said, "Okay."
I started to open the door.

Kyle stopped me, with a hand
on my arm. *Where are you going?*

"I have to get my stuff. Everything
I own is in there." Not that it
amounted to a whole lot.

No. *We have to go right now.*
We'll get you whatever you need.

He was right. Going back inside
would have been a mistake.
I settled into the seat. "Let's go then."

His eyes lit with excitement.
I love you. He kissed me sweetly.

Started the truck. Our adventure—
and neither of us had any idea
exactly what kind of adventure

it was or will be—had begun.
I only hope it means no regrets.

AS WE DROVE AWAY

I'm almost positive I saw Simone
glance out the bedroom window.
Not sure if she noticed me or not,
and can only hope she didn't run

and tell right away if she did. Would
she have had the presence of mind
to take down the license plate?
Would she have seen the happiness

written all over my face and kept it
to herself? I feel sorry that she gave
me her secrets now. Sorry she won't
have someone to whisper to in the night.

But you can't get attached to anyone
in a foster home. I learned that lesson
a long time ago. Get close, get hurt.
She might as well learn that too.

LESS THAN A HALF HOUR

Away from Fresno, the weight
    of our hasty decision hits me.
        "Any idea where we're going?"
            Deceptively simple question.

    Kyle sighs heavily. *Nope. I was*
        kind of hoping you might have
            an idea. Any place you've
                always wanted to see?

I slide my hand into his. "Lots."
    It is kind of exciting, just picking
        a place and aiming for it. Except,
            "What do you think they'll do?"

    He shrugs. *Depends on if they*
        think you were kidnapped or
            split on your own. Hey, do you
                suppose they'll do an Amber Alert?

God, I never thought about that.
    Kidnapping? "I don't want you
        to get into trouble. Maybe you
            should just take me back."

    Zero hesitation. *No damn way.*
        I'm not sure where to go or how
            we'll get by, but one way or
                another, we will be together.

APPROACHING THE FLAT FIELDS

Of Bakersfield, I can't help but think
        about home—Dad's sorry old place.
Empty right now is my guess, with

Dad in lockup and Kortni most likely
        working. Just in case, I make a test
call. No answer. "Take me home, okay?"

      I don't think that's such a good idea.
           Why do you want to go there? But as
we near the exit, he slows down.

"I want to leave a note, tell them
        I haven't been kidnapped. And I know
where Kortni stashes her mad money."

      He hesitates, considers the note.
           Just say you're okay. Maybe that
      you were afraid living back there.

Good idea. Even if Walter didn't
        do anything, making them think
he might have is a good excuse

for taking off. And it just might
        keep him from taking a chance
on future bad behavior. Ka-ching.

KYLE EXITS THE FREEWAY

Swings in the correct direction.
"What about your dad?" I ask.
"What are you going to tell him?"

We are bumping along the dirt
by the time he answers. *He won't
even know I'm gone for a week.*

Any other week, maybe. But,
"Uh . . . Christmas. Remember?
Anyway, your sister would notice."

He thinks for a while, and I see
his shoulders slump slightly.
Forgot about Christmas.

Sadie will miss me for sure.
Then he brightens. *At least
I'll get to spend it with you.*

*Anyway, holidays bring out
the asshole in my dad. He starts
drinking at breakfast, goes*

*all day until after dessert or
until he passes out. And every
drink just makes him meaner.*

536

AS WE PULL INTO THE DRIVEWAY

I think about my own dad's drinking.
He starts early, finishes late. But
he doesn't very often get mean.
Maybe that's 'cause he mostly
drinks beer. But I don't think
his mean streak is very big.

Maybe when he gets out of
jail we can figure out how to
grow closer. That would mean
coming back from . . . wherever
Kyle and I end up. It would also
mean forgiveness on both sides.
Forgiveness isn't my best thing.
Easier staying pissed. But I'm
tired of being pissed all the time.
Tired of feeling hurt by stuff that
can never be fixed because it is
an indelible part of the past.

KYLE STAYS IN THE TRUCK

While I circle around back, where
I know a certain window has a broken
lock. I left my house key in Fresno
with the rest of my meager possessions.

I shimmy up the dilapidated vinyl siding,
squeeze through the smallish opening,
drop into my old bedroom. An odd pang
of homesickness presses, weight

enough to make my eyes water. Why
am I so sad? I hate this place. Hate
what it represents—the threadbare
remnants of my childhood, few enough

happy memories woven into that cloth.
A strange foreboding chills me, and
I creep into the hallway. "Is someone
here?" I call, though I know the place

is empty. Ghosts. That's all. They smell
of old tobacco. Dribbled beer. Cheap
perfume. Detritus-caked dishes left
to molder in the kitchen sink. Trash.

I sneak into my dad's bedroom, a thief
who has already cased the place. I know
where the spare change jar is kept beneath
the canvas liner in the clothes hamper.

Sometimes there's more than change
in the jar, and this is one of those times.
Kortni's tips have been good lately,
and without Dad's bad habits to support,

she has squirreled away almost four
hundred dollars. I take a fistful, leave
the rest to help replace the clothes
I borrow. She's a little bigger than me.

But baggy is better than nothing, and
nothing is what I have now. Two pairs
of jeans. A couple of sweatshirts.
A plaid flannel shirt. Underwear.

That's the creepiest thing, but panties
are expensive. At least they're clean.
I help myself to five pair, trying not to
think about what has worn them.

Finally I go to the kitchen, find paper
and a Sharpie, write a note: *I am okay.*
Have not been kidnapped. I had to
leave Fresno because Walter scared

me. Tell Shreeveport to keep an eye
on him. I had to borrow a few bucks
and some of your clothes. Promise
to pay you back. Love, Summer.

I GATHER UP

The fragments
                    of my shattered

          dignity. Exit through
                              the front door, paper

bag filled with
                    pilfered necessities

          heavy in my hand.
                              I look at the horizon,

hung low with charcoal
                    clouds. Storm gestating.

          Kyle waits, fingers
                              thrumming impatiently

against the steering
                    wheel. Can't say

          I blame him. We
                              really must go. Need to

run. One chapter closed.
                    Another almost begun.

THREE HUN IN HAND

We chance a quick stop at Wal-Mart.
*I've been thinking about which way
to go,* Kyle says. *I think we should head*

*up Highway 395. No one will expect us
to take that route. Not this time of year.
There are lots of places we can camp,*

*and I could probably find work at
Mammoth, once the ski resort opens.
But I think we'll have to sleep in my truck,*

*at least until I can make enough money
to get us a place. It's going to be cold up
there. We'll need two good sleeping bags.*

*A little food. Cereal. Jerky. Nuts.
Or maybe trail mix. Water. Flashlight
and spare batteries. Toilet paper.*

Toilet paper? Seriously? Logistically,
this is terrifying. I'm not exactly
a mountain man (woman?). But I go

along, hoping we don't blow our entire
money stash. We hurry the cart
through the store. As we pass

the feminine products section, it hits
me that maybe it's the right time
of the month to consider tampons.

But how do I buy them with Kyle?
How do I manage a period camped
out in the bitter-cold wilderness?

My resolution to make this happen
falters. But then I look at Kyle,
who is totally determined to see it

through. I grab the tampons,
throw them into the cart. And,
knowing my body the way I do,

I add a small bottle of generic
ibuprofen. Last thing Kyle needs
is to hear me bitch about cramps.

I blush when he smiles at my
selections. But he only shrugs,
puts a box of condoms into the cart.

KYLE'S EXCITEMENT

Is palpable, obvious
in the way he moves.
Every security camera
here is probably focused
on him right now. He might
be buying Christmas presents.

Except who wants trail mix for
Christmas? Or, uh, condoms?
Oh, well. We're not doing
anything wrong. Wait.
Inaccurate. Okay, I
don't feel like

we're doing
anything wrong.
Even if we happen
to be paying for all this
stuff with "borrowed" money.
Could someone define "wrong"?

Is it wrong to take someone else's
money so you can eat? Wrong
to leave relative security in
favor of unknown risk
at the side of some-
one you love?

SUPPLIES STOWED

Kyle checks out the map, decides
        we should go by way of Lake Isabella.
        It's only about an hour from here, and
                we can find a cheap campground there.

Highway 178 follows the meandering
        Kern. We've been this way before.
        And when we pass the place we first
                made love, Kyle reaches to take my hand.

        I'll never forget that day, he says.
                It changed everything. You changed
                everything. I thought love was bullshit.
                        Something made up for TV and movies.

"Me too. Or that people just repeated
        those words to get them what they
        wanted." Sex. Drugs. Money. "You
                always say the right thing, know that?"

If he had passed "our" spot and
        said nothing, I would have seriously
        questioned what I'm doing here.
                Instead, I watch darkness descend,

a rain of night in the headlights,
        washing away apprehension. Too
        late to worry now, anyway. Might
                as well soak up Kyle, enjoy the ride.

WE FIND A FIVE-DOLLAR

Per-night campground. *Some are free,*
Kyle informs me. *But this one has toilets.*
That's worth five dollars, don't you think?

"Definitely. And since they're here,
I'm going to pee." The night air makes
me shiver. I slip into Kortni's oversize

sweatshirt, grab the flashlight to show
me the way, happy to have both. When
I get back to camp, Kyle is messing

with a campfire. *Someone left a few*
sticks of firewood, he says. Nice of
them. Too dark to be hunting for it now.

I sit on a big log, watching him work to
start it. Before long, a small flame slithers
up thin sticks of kindling, licking at a log.

Kyle's face is handsome in the building
firelight. Rugged. "You remind me of
a cowboy. Or maybe a fur trapper."

He laughs, sits next to me. *Guess that*
makes you the lonely schoolteacher
waiting for me to come ravage you.

He kisses me, and it is sweet, despite
the smell of his smoke-stung clothes.
Too soon, he pulls away. *Hungry?*

I nod, and he goes to the truck,
brings back nuts. Jerky. Water
to wash both down with. I chew

for a while. Finally I notice Kyle
hasn't touched the skimpy feast.
"Aren't you going to eat?" I ask.

He shakes his head. *Maybe later.*
I'm not really hungry right now.
He goes to poke at the fire.

I close the bags carefully. Gulp
water, wishing I'd thought to buy
a toothbrush. "Are you scared?"

You kidding? Even if we get caught,
it's worth it. Being with you like this?
Fire's low. Come on. He has already

rolled out the sleeping bags in the back
of the truck. We climb in, and under
a meadow of stars, my cowboy ravages me.

BIRDSONG WAKES ME

Loud birdsong. A regular death metal
concert of birdsong, in fact. I keep

my eyes closed, snuggle into my bed.
Hard bed. A waterfall of light. Outside.

Sleeping bag. Cold metal beneath me.
And I am alone. I jump into a sitting

position, quieting the avian cacophony.
A flutter of wings. "Kyle? Where are you?"

An acrid drift of tobacco assaults
my nose just as I hear, *Over here.*

He squats to one side of the fire pit,
trying to resurrect the dead embers.

Smoking. God. Cigarettes are, like,
seven bucks a pack. He needs to

kick that habit, and quickly. I slide
from the warmth of the sleeping bag,

into frosty December morning.
Go over to give him a kiss, steeling

myself against the stench of smoke.
But another, more insidious smell

leaks from his pores, despite
the cold. "Did you do crystal?"

His eyes, onyx-pupiled and crimson-
rimmed, are all the answer I need.

A bubble of anger rises. Pops.
Deep breath. "You did, didn't you?"

He drops his gaze to the still-dead fire.
Just a little. Maintenance, you know.

A narrow column of bubbles lifts.
Pop-pop. "No. I really don't know."

*I'm down to a taste a couple times
a day. Keeps my head on straight.*

A thick stream of bubbles. *Pop. Pop.
Pop-pop.* "Fine. Then I want to try it."

His head shakes so hard, it must
rattle his brain. *Don't want you to.*

The bubbles become a low fizz.
It makes my eyes sting. "Why not?"

His eyes float up. He is crying
too. *Because I love you too much.*

Hunter

COUNTDOWN TO CHRISTMAS

Less than two days to go.
Rick Denio being a brick
back in his native Texas,
I'm pulling a double air

               shift.

Morning drive wrapped
up, midday well underway,
I am pouring a hefty shot
of vanilla International Delight

               into

a strong cup of coffee
when the studio phone
rings. On the far end
of the line, an extremely

               high-

sounding girl inquires
if I'd like some company.
"Leah. I told you to leave
me the hell alone." I

               gear

up to say something much
stronger when I notice
the mic is on. Just perfect.
Good thing the music's loud.

               "Go

away," I tell her, mic muted.
How many ways are there
to say no, anyway?

549

I'VE TOLD HER NO

At least a dozen times
in the last three weeks.

No.

I don't want to see her,
even if I am single right now.

No.

I don't want to smoke up
with her. Sort of trying to quit.

No.

I don't want sex with her,
not even no-strings-attached sex.

Now

if I could just get Nikki
to hear me tell her no.

How

could I manage that? Strong-
arm her, maybe? My life is

full of

women who refuse to listen
to me! Is this how serial killers
are born? Whoa. Where did that

bullshit

come from? I'm not even close
to some crazed ax murderer.

Am I?

NO, I'M NOT

I admit anger is a regular visitor.

It reminds me of some alien

vine implanted through my belly

button. It seems to germinate

in the pit of my stomach,

grow at warp speed, shooting

out tendrils to snake through

my veins, into my brain, where

it blooms into all-out rage.

But that would never make

me pick up a weapon and use

it, especially never on a girl.

Not even one who refuses to

return my phone calls. Or my love.

SHE STILL LOVES ME

I know she does. Boy,
I never thought forgiveness
would come so hard to her.
I give the top-of-the-hour

station ID, say a few witty
words about shopping
procrastinators. Once the music
kicks back in, I call Nikki.

Who apparently isn't home.
Whatever. Maybe it's better
to leave her a message. She'd
probably hang up on me.

"Nik, I swear I'm not stalking
you. But please, please listen.
What I did was worse than
wrong. It was unconscionable.

I have never loved anyone
the way I love you. And I
don't think I ever will. You
are the most important thing

in my life. Without you,
I'm empty. Please forgive
me. I swear, I'll earn back
your trust. Can we just talk?"

I COULD GO ON

But that's all the machine wants
to hear at one time, and if I call back,
I'll definitely sound like a stalker.

I'd just go ahead over there,
but she is somewhere else, and
after my shift, I'm supposed

to pick up Leigh and Kristina
from the airport. They're flying
back together from Albuquerque.

I guess I should feel bad about
my grandfather being on his last
legs and all. But it's hard to care

about someone (even if that
someone *is* your grandfather)
who never bothered to get to know

you in the first place. A couple
of visits when I was a baby,
a couple of birthday cards since.

His excuse? He couldn't afford
to send real presents or make
the trip from New Mexico.

Well, how about a phone
call? Those don't cost too
much. How about an e-mail?

Or even regular cards and
letters. I would have answered
them. We could have gotten

to know each other, even if
only virtually. Sorry, Grandpa.
Excuses are a dime a dozen.

And lame excuses are more
like a nickel. No, sir. Establishing
a relationship has nothing to do

with money. Listen to me. Like
I'm so good with relationships.
Although establishing them

doesn't seem to be my problem.
Keeping them? Nurturing them?
Definitely not my best thing.

AIR SHIFT COMPLETE

As I get ready to leave, I notice
the new part-time on-air girl

coming toward me. Woot. Girl?
Babe! I can't help but check out

her long, bronze-skinned legs,
most of which are showing. Skirt.

        Is. Short. She smiles at the way
        I'm obviously drooling. *Hi, Hunter.*

"Hey, um . . ." Name? I know
her name. It's, uh . . . "Shayna."

The hall is narrow and as we
pass, her body whispers along

        mine. *Excuse me,* she says in
        a deep-water voice. *Sorry.*

"No problem." I watch her walk
away, invitation in the exaggerated

sway of her hips. I could follow.
Set something up for later.

I could. But I won't. I'd rather
stay mired in unrequited love.

TWO THIRTY-FOUR

I've got a half hour until
        the plane arrives. Hope it's on
        time, or it might not arrive at all.
Another big storm is speeding
        toward us. The roads just got
        cleared from the last one.

Mom insisted I take the Jeep.
        Good thing. My truck is a four-
        by, but the tires lack tread.
Anyway, the Jeep has more
        room for women and their
        luggage. The freeway is packed.

Last-minute Santas rushing
        to buy those last-minute gifts.
        I finished shopping weeks ago.
Mom is always easy. T-shirt with
        some pithy author-type saying.
        Ditto Dad and his Beatles.

Jake, ski gloves. Leigh, perfume.
        Kristina, a self-help book, not that
        I expect it to do much good.
For the boys, games. And all that
        barely left enough for what I got
        Nikki. Not lingerie. A promise ring.

I'M NOT A JEWELRY EXPERT

But the ring caught my eye.
Small rubies (her) and sapphires (me),
set to look like a chain—the two
of us linked together. Forever.

It's beautiful (like her). Cleaned
out my bank account, but I don't
care. I just want to see her wear
it. How can I make that happen?

I have to wait almost twenty
minutes in the cell phone parking
lot at the airport. What the hell.
I give Nikki one more try.

She answers on the second ring.
"Nik? Don't hang up, okay?
I can't believe you're actually
there." That she actually picked up.

> *What do you want, Hunter?*
> Clipped. Guess she hasn't quite
> forgiven me. Then, in the back-
> ground, I hear another voice. Male.

And not on the television. The alien
vine bursts to life, snakes its way
through me. I start to blow. Think
better of it. "Oh. Sorry. Didn't know

you had company. I just . . . uh . . .
wanted you to know how truly sorry
I am. Thanks for taking my call."
I hang up, choking back a wad

of emotions. Hurt. Surprise.
Fury. Embarrassment. Now
there's a weird one. Why am I
embarrassed? And not for her.

For me. How could she replace
me? Did she replace me? What
is she doing with that guy? Who
is he? Where did she hook up

with him? And for what reason?
Companionship? Sex? Love?
No. Not that. I can deal with
the other two, but no way could

I handle her falling in love
with someone else. My cell rings.
The ladies' flight has arrived.
I put the Jeep into gear, and as

I pull forward into the loading
zone, it hits me suddenly that
Nikki must have asked herself
the very same questions about me.

SUBDUED

That's the collective feeling
as I give Leigh and Kristina
tentative hugs, load their luggage

into the Jeep. We all pretty much
feel like shit. They, because
they're very close to losing

their father. Me, because I'm
really afraid I've lost my Nikki.
Kristina commandeers shotgun.

Leigh doesn't try to argue. We
drive along in silence for a while.
Finally I say, "Mom got you a hotel

room, Kristina. Do you want to
drop off your stuff before we go
on out to the house?" I do not

> expect her answer. *I'm not staying
> at any hotel. I want to see my boys.
> Mom can kiss my freaking ass.*

Okay. This is going to be one
entertaining Christmas. "You might
want to rethink your attitude."

Excuse me, but just who in the hell
do you think you are? You're not
my father. You are my son.

The sky opens up. Wet snow splats
against the windshield. Very much
like how her words splatter me.

That vine again. And this time,
I let it go full bloom. "Fuck you.
I might have been your zygote.

Your fetus. Maybe even your offspring. But I have never been your
son. You have no idea what it means

to be a real mother. You think nine
months of discomfort and eight
hours of labor gives you the right

to call yourself 'Mom'? Well, bitch,
you're delusional." I could go on,
but in the backseat, Leigh's discomfort,

though silent, hangs heavily. "Here's
the hotel. Why don't you check in?
Someone will pick you up later."

I PUT HER SUITCASE

On the sidewalk, come around
            to open her door, expecting
a major argument. She climbs

out meekly, eyes on the ground,
            and I almost think about saying
I'm sorry. Almost. Instead

I open the backseat door, invite
            Leigh to move to the front seat.
"So we can talk," is my reason.

            It takes a few minutes before she
                        says, *You may not believe it, but in*
            her own way, Kristina loves you.

The vine wraps itself around my
            throat. Chokes. "Kristina doesn't
love anyone, *except* 'in her own

way.' That isn't good enough.
            Love isn't supposed to be . . ."
I hate revelations. "Selfish."

A SUBJECT CHANGE

Seems in order. "So how's . . ."
I don't even know what to call him.

                  Leigh rescues me. *Dad? Not good.*
                  Linda Sue is beside herself. Scared.

"Of what?" Stupid question. I know
the answer before she says it.

                  Losing him. She really loves him.
                  I feel sorry for her, you know?

"But what about him? How do
you feel about him maybe dying?"

                  She's already thought it through.
                  I hated him for so long. For the way

                  he left us. For the part he played in
                  Kristina's drama. I don't know, Hunter.

                  I guess what I feel is guilty because
                  I don't have a need to mourn him.

Bam. "What about Kristina?
How does she feel about it?"

                  This answer takes longer. *I'm not sure*
                  Kristina can feel much anymore.

I'VE THOUGHT THE SAME THING

Seems like, no matter what goes
down in Kristina's life, the only
thing she ever feels is paranoia.

Everyone hates her. (Not true.)
Everyone distrusts her. (True.)
Everyone is out to get her. (Uh . . . why?)

Whatever bad happens in her life,
it's someone else's fault. Wrong
turns? Forced to take them. Fall

flat on her face? She was pushed.
Personal responsibility for the choices
she has made? What the hell

is "personal responsibility"? And
what about other feelings? Love?
Happiness? Anticipation? Hate, even?

All those emotions seem unavailable
to her. Like no matter how deep
she drills for them, the well is dry.

Was she born that way? Were
those things taken from her?
What I want to know is, "Why?"

Leigh takes her time answering.
*Kristina never really was the "warm
and fuzzy" type. But when we were*

*younger, she was so much more alive
inside. The meth stole that life force,
of course. You know how they say*

*it eats holes in your brain? Well,
it does. And it eats them in the part
of the brain that controls emotions.*

*But even beyond that. I think the more
she has failed at things like relationships
and parenting, the more she has cut*

*herself off from feeling bad about those
things. And if you don't let yourself feel
bad, sooner or later you stop feeling*

*good, too. You insulate yourself. Build
up layers, like stacking paper, everything
growing heavier. And when the weight*

*becomes too much, those layers compress.
Become hard. Sad, really, to think that
Kristina has turned herself into cardboard.*

Autumn

PRETTY MUCH MISERABLE

That's how this trip has been,
not that I expected better.
Long, boring stretches of asphalt.

Landscape, mostly scrubbed of life,
at least until around thirty miles
ago. Then low desert gave way

to squat evergreens, hints of real
forest to the west, along the spine
of the Sierra Nevada. So far,

the weather has done nothing
more than loom, threatening.
But we keep heading north,

toward crazy-looking storm clouds.
Clouds like I've never seen before.
In Texas, stormers are huge, black

beasts. These are big, all right.
But they're white, with giant silver
underbellies. Bellies, I hear,

that will open and bleed snow.
The threat of an approaching blizzard
is frightening. Exhilarating.

FRIGHTENING AND EXHILARATING

The words sum up a lot of what
I'm thinking about right now. A

          blizzard

seems the least of my worries.
Let's see. Closer and closer
to Reno, the thought of home-

          coming

looms like a monster, spreading
its arms in some kind of welcome.
The idea of meeting long-lost
family seemed a whole lot

          better

in Texas. Especially waltzing
in on Christmas Eve. I can hear
it now. "Would y'all just

          look

what Santa brought this year!"
Except they don't say "y'all"
in Nevada, do they? OMG.
I so don't belong here. But,

          for

what it's worth, I so want to belong
here. So want connection with
something severed. So want to find

          shelter

in the hearts
of a family of strangers.

THAT SEEMS EVEN MORE UNLIKELY

Knowing I'm probably pregnant.
Oh yeah, even better. "Here
I am. You don't know me. But
accept me, anyway. And just
in case you're wondering, I think
I'm going to have a baby."

Husband? No. No husband.
(Not yet?)
Boyfriend? I think so.
(What will he say?)

Birth control? Well, yes,
they have it in Texas. I just sort
of decided not to use it.
(How do I tell him?)

Of course, I don't have to tell
them. At least not right now.
Bryce should probably be
the first to know. God, he's
going to be so mad at me.
But he'll stand by my side.

(Won't he?)

TREY TOTALLY SUSPECTS

The truth. But so far he has respected
my wish not to discuss the possibility.

He has, in fact, been pretty darn quiet
for most of this very long ride. When

the radio dissolves into a static dead
sea, though, there isn't much to do but talk.

And since he isn't about to initiate
conversation, I ask, "What's prison like?"

> He thinks a minute, says, *Pretty much like
> you see on TV, I guess. Except until you*
>
> *experience it, you can't really understand
> what it's like to live in an oversize crypt.*

For ten years? I'd die of claustrophobia
poisoning. "What's the worst thing?"

> He thinks again. *Toss-up. The smell—people
> stink, let me tell you. That, or the boredom.*

Wow. I thought he'd have some racy
stories to tell me. But yeah, I get boredom.

BOREDOM IS AN OVERSIZE CRYPT

Or twenty straight hours
in a car (sort of a crypt on
wheels, if you think about it)
with someone you don't know.

Even if that someone might
be your father. I still can't
think of him that way. (So why
are you here? Stupid?)

I really must stop thinking
parenthetically. Carrying on
a silent conversation with
myself. Splitting the whole

of me into halves. Pushing
myself beyond OCD and panic
attacks, all the way to the realm
of probable schizophrenia.

I'm not two people. Only one,
uncertain. One, scared of the gray
space of tomorrow. But a lot more
scared of being stuck in yesterday.

WE ROLL INTO BISHOP

A small California town also reaching
desperately for the future. Maybe
this is where I should move.

> Trey decides to stop at Schat's
> Bakkerÿ. *This place is famous. Can't go
> through Bishop and not stop here.*

Famous? Never heard of it. But,
"I guess I could eat." And I could
definitely pee. Not a lot of places

to stop along 395. If nothing else,
almost six hours since leaving our
overnight layover in Indio, it feels

great to stretch my legs. We go inside,
order sandwiches, and by the time
I get back from the bathroom,

Trey has collected them and stands
talking to a couple of locals. He sees
me, excuses himself to join me.

> *Those guys just got in from Reno.
> Guess it's snowing pretty good up
> there. We'd better buy some chains.*

ALL GASSED UP

Horribly overpriced chains
        purchased and "how to install 'em"
                tutorial complete, we hit the highway.

Normally, the yeasty scent
        of the Schat's Bakkerÿ bread
                on my sandwich would strike me

as pretty much heavenly.
        Today it's making me slightly
                nauseous, a fact that Trey, who

        is inhaling his own sandwich,
                can't help but notice. *Have you*
                        decided what to do about that?

I want to sound defiant, but
        the best I can accomplish
                is a miserable, "Do about what?"

        Trey shrugs. *I can't pretend to*
                be your friend, let alone your
                        dad. We barely know each other.

        But I am a pretty good judge
                of character, and I can see
                        you're a special kind of girl.

Special kind of girl? "What
        does that mean?" And am
                I as pea soup green as I feel?

Don't get all huffy now. All
        I meant was, you've got a look.
                In prison, we'd call you a fish—

someone new to the scene.
        I figure you're new to getting
                laid. Probably how you ended up—

Before I know what my mouth
        is doing, it opens and out spills,
                "I know how it works! I wanted to . . ."

We both realize I've said too
        much. Trey is quiet for a time.
                Finally he says, *You can't keep*

someone who doesn't want
        to be with you. Not that way.
                Not any way. Believe me, I know.

ON THE FAR SIDE OF BISHOP

The highway begins
a long, lazy climb up
toward Mammoth
and June Lake. Up
toward the clouds.
Ten or so miles up
the grade, snow

starts to fall in soft
flurries. It doesn't
seem to bother Trey,
who continues, *You*
probably don't want
to hear this, but I'm
going to tell you anyway.

I was so in love with
your mother, my heart
could barely hold it
all. The crystal, yeah,
that was an issue,
right from the start.
Messes with your head.

When we went to jail
for trafficking, we had
no choice but to do
time, crashing hard.
I was glad to be clean
when they let us go.
Especially when I found

*out she was pregnant
with you. I proposed
right away, and you
could have knocked
me over with a burp
when she said yes.
It was the happiest*

*time of my life. When
you were born, I thought
nothing could tear us
apart. And then we let
the monster back in.
Part of me was so
scared for you. More*

*of me wasn't scared
of a goddamn thing.
And Kristina? She had
more balls than any guy
I've ever known. What
she didn't ever have
enough of was love.*

*Not for me. Not for you.
Not for anyone who
came before—or after—
us. She used who she
could to get what she
wanted. And then she
tossed them like trash.*

HE WAS RIGHT

Not what I wanted to hear.
                    But what exactly did I want
                    to hear? That this little reunion
was going to end up a fairy tale?

Darn right that's what I wanted
                    to hear. I sit, semi-stunned,
                    watch the snow begin to fall
harder. "Does she want me or not?"

            I wish I knew what to tell you.
                            I don't know what she wants,
                            and even if I did, I couldn't
            speak for Kristina. I know she thinks

            she has the right to know you.
                            That my father and Cora were
                            wrong for keeping you apart.
            And I agree as far as that goes.

            But I seriously doubt she has
                            the ability to take care of you,
                            if that's what's on your mind.
            Small steps, honey. One at a time.

AS HE TALKS

We crest the summit. The snowflakes
blossom, grow into half-dollar-sized
white petals, pirouetting to collect
on the ground. Despite its heavy
frame, the Cadillac begins to fishtail.

          Trey pulls off the highway, behind
          a collection of semis and other two-
          wheel-drive automobiles. *Time to*
          chain up, I guess. He gets out
          to attempt the complex process.

I stay in the relative warmth
of the car. Close my eyes.
Hear Trey say, *Small steps,*
honey. Honey? Seriously?
And, in case he hasn't noticed,

which no doubt he hasn't, up
until the last week or so, I've
taken nothing but baby steps
my entire life. And even those
were mostly guided for me.

This trip was a giant step. I'll
deal with what's on the other
end the way I always do. Deep
and deeper breaths, gathering gold
flecks to keep from going insane.

Then there's the monumental
step of having a baby. Bryce or
no Bryce, I will never put anyone
or anything ahead of my child.
Substances? No way. That includes

alcohol. I will never touch a drop.
Not as long as I'm pregnant and
not if some tiny person's life
depends on me sober. Baby?
Are you listening? Are you really

alive inside me? Oh God.
If you are, how will I ever take
care of you? My fingers go
tingly. My breath falls shallow.
Small steps. One at a time.

BISHOP TO CARSON CITY

Is about three hours in good weather.
This is not good weather. Talk about

> initiation by blizzard. Even Trey
> is impressed. *I've seen it come*

> *down pretty good, but never*
> *quite like this. Hope a plow*

> *comes through soon. Chains aren't*
> *going to help much otherwise.*

Eventually, one does catch up
to us. Trey moves as far to one

> side of the road as he can to let
> the guy pass. *Looks like just him and us.*

Late afternoon. Christmas Eve.
Snow forming a dense white curtain.

Oh, yeah. We're pretty much alone
out here. "Stay close to the plow, okay?"

> Trey laughs. *Don't worry, little girl.*
> *I won't let anything bad happen to you.*

TOO LATE, DUDE

But I don't say that. In fact,
I don't say much of anything
the rest of the way into Carson
City. Nevada's capital, all wrapped

> up in white for Christmas. *Your*
> *grandparents live just a little*
> *north of here. Maybe we should*
> *get a room and clean up?*

> We check into a Holiday Inn
> Express on the far side of town.
> *It's kind of pricey,* says Trey.
> *But hey, Merry Christmas.*

I shower first, to let my hair
dry. While Trey goes to wash
off his guy-stink, I change into
my pretty Aunt Cora skirt, top

with a jade angora sweater.
I stand sideways in the full-
length mirror hanging on
the closet door. Flat tummy.

ALL PRETTIED UP

We head out the door, where
the snowfall continues unchecked.
When we get in the car, Trey slams

the door. He starts the car, puts it
into reverse, and I begin to shake.
"Wait." Icy tentacles thread my veins,

choke-hold my lungs. They scream for
breath. And my heart punches
against my chest. "Please, wait."

Trey slams on the brakes. *What?*
His voice is taut, his eyes frantic.
Are you having a heart attack?

I shake my head, close my eyes,
concentrate on finding air.
And suddenly, it's there.

I suck it down. "P-panic attack.
I'm o-okay now. We c-c-can go."
But we can't. Because just as we

start to turn onto the highway, a big
flashing sign overhead warns:
Whiteout conditions. Road closed.

Summer

NOT MUCH ROMANTIC

About living homeless.
It's hasn't even been a week.
                              We reek.
No showers for six
days would be bad enough
on its own, but Kyle is
                              sweating
out the last vestiges of
meth in his system. For me,
he says, though as yet
                              we barely speak
about what that really
means. That he'll never
do drugs again? Will he be
                              forgetting
how much pain he's put
up with the last couple
of days as soon as
                              the tweak is
calling out to him again?
What I need to know is
how big a
                              part
of Kyle the crystal is.
And I need to know
how big a part it is
                              of us.

I NEVER THOUGHT

That much about it before. When
you're not around someone
twenty-four/seven, you
cherish every minute
together, no questions.
No "Why are you so
sweet-natured most of
the time, foul-tempered
the rest?" No "How much
of your emotion is fueled
by artificial means?" No
"What would we be
if you cut yourself
off from something
you've relied on
just to see you
through the day?"
And the biggest
of them all: No

"Who are you really,
and do I love
that person too?"

I KNEW HE WAS USING

He never tried to hide it. In fact,
offered to share. But even if he

hadn't been honest about it,
his mood swings were obvious.

I just never realized how big
a part of his life it was. Not

sure why I didn't see it. Guess
when you choose to be blind,

you really are. Don't think it
would have changed a thing,

had I known. And now, seeing
him fight his demons for me,

I love him all the more. Even
if he is a complete grouch.

It's the nature of the crash.
Better now than years down

> the line. *I never got into
> it that much,* he swore.

> *But without you, who knows
> where I might be tomorrow?*

HOPEFULLY, BY TOMORROW

We'll be in a hotel room
in Mammoth, reward enough for
a week sleeping cold in a pickup truck.
Three nights at Lake Isabella, hoping no
one would come looking for us.
Kind of surprised when

nobody did. Another
three nights camped just west of
Lone Pine, in a sage-carpeted campground, more primitive than the first.
It was there, listening to coyote
song and eagle cry, that

Kyle crashed like iron
for two days. I gave him a wide
swath of privacy, exploring the brush,
gathering firewood, and otherwise
tending camp while he slept
morgue-dweller sleep.

When he woke up,
all groggy and weird, he was
so hungry he finished off two-thirds
of a bag of jerky. His face flushed
with color and the shivering
slowed. Resurrection!

THAT WAS YESTERDAY

And when we made love
    last night, a blanket of frost
        settling over the sleeping bag,

it was different than ever
    before. Slower. Gentler.
        Less demanding, more giving.

Hearts quickening in lockstep.
    Breath like moth wings aflutter
        against moonlighted window glass.

    I love you, he sighed along
        my skin. And *I love you,*
            desert wind blown into my hair.

And when we were finished,
    we drew into each other's
        arms, warmed within our harbor.

Something happened in
    the night, happened as we
        dreamed. Something unexpected.

For on awakening, blinking into
    the murky dawning, needful love
        had transformed into blissful love.

MAYBE IT HAD SOMETHING TO DO

With sleeping under the Christmas
star. Yeah, I know it's actually a planet
or something. And I know if it were
really the Christmas star, it would

be shining tonight. But whatever it is,
this morning it looked like a platinum-
set diamond in the lightening sky.
I burrowed into Kyle's body heat,

ignoring the quite randy smell.
"If you believe in wishing on stars,
you'll never get a better chance," I said.
"That one belongs to Christmas."

> *I have to believe in wishes, or*
> *I wouldn't be here with you. Right?*
> *Then he laughed. Even if you don't*
> *exactly smell like roses. Phew!*

"No offense, *mi amor*. But I smell
a hell of a lot better than you."
> *Guess you're right. Definitely bath*
> *time. You up for Mammoth?*

586

WITH LUCK

We'll be there tonight. Sooner
is better than later. The trail mix
is stale, the jerky gone. A hot meal

is my idea of heaven right now.
I dig in my backpack, count every
penny. "Sixty-six fifty-two.

Think we could get McDonald's?"
I hate McDonald's. But I hate
stale trail mix even more.

> Kyle exits his shell of silence.
> *I think we can do better. I've
> still got a few bucks myself.*

"Enough for a room, too?
Just think . . . a hot shower.
Soft, warm bed. Reality TV."

> He laughs. *We're living reality
> TV. But yeah, we'll find a cheap
> room somewhere. Looks like*

> *winter has arrived up there.
> The resort will open soon.
> I'll put in an application.*

I turn on the radio. Not much
available out here, despite
Kyle's monstrous antenna.

> Don't use "seek," he instructs.
> Try dialing by hand. I do,
> and from a distant city, through

> > the static, I discern a familiar voice.
> > You procrastinators don't have
> > much time left. Santa's almost here. . . .

"That's my brother," I tell Kyle.
"Hunter. He works at a station
in Reno." Nostalgia whacks me.

> Really? How come you never
> told me you have a brother?
> He turns up the volume, but

the meager signal has dissolved
completely. "I have three brothers,
actually. Oh, and a sister, I guess.

I hardly ever see my brothers, and
no one bothered to tell me I had a sister
until a couple of weeks ago."

Wow. That's tough. I love my sister.
Can't imagine not . . . His voice
catches as he considers what

he's about to say. *Can't imagine not*
seeing her, let alone not knowing
she even existed. How'd you find out?

I shrug. "My dad got drunk—
that night he got the DUI, in fact—
and it kind of just slipped out."

Kyle thinks that over. Finally says,
My dad was drunk when he told
me about my mom going into the river.

Said we were better off without
the bitch. If I had been as big as I am
now, I would have made him sorry.

No wonder he hates his dad.
Mine's a major screwup, but
at least he isn't corpse-hearted.

WE STOP AT A DINER

In Bishop. Splurge on a meat loaf
dinner, the Christmas Eve special.
That's a little weird, I guess, but
hey. Special is special. And cheap,
too. I eat every bite, mop the gravy

from the plate with the last crumbs
of a big homemade biscuit. Good
thing the place is semi-empty.
I probably look like exactly what
I am—a homeless person

      who hasn't eaten much in a week.
      The waitress comes over to check
      on us. She smiles. *Hungry, eh?*
      Can I get you another biscuit?
      Then, to Kyle, *Don't like meat loaf?*

            I hadn't even noticed that he's sort
            of just picking at his. *It's fine. Guess*
            I'm feeling a little under the weather.
            He looks it too. Parchment pale
            and a bit shaky. *She'll have a biscuit.*

I WAIT FOR THE
WAITRESS TO GO

"You okay? It would be better
if you could eat something.
You're running on empty."

> *I know. I'll try. It's just the last
> of the shit in my system making
> me queasy.* He does force down

a few bites while I polish off
the butter-slathered biscuit Jeanine
returns with. "A good night's sleep

in a big ol' bed will make you
feel better," I predict. "Tomorrow
is Christmas. Our first one together."

> The thought seems to brighten
> his mood. *Our first, but definitely
> not our last. And look . . .* He points

> toward the window. *It's going to
> be a white Christmas. My first
> one of those, too.* Outside, wisps

of snow have begun to fall. "Maybe
we'd better get going. It would
be good to get there before dark."

THE LIGHT IS DUSKISH

By the time we're on the road. It's not
        all that late in the day yet, but the peaks
to the west are tall, and as the sun dips
        below them, its failing light is swallowed
up by hastening snowfall. Glad Mammoth

isn't too far. The food Kyle managed
        to get down seems to have helped
his system recover some. His color
        is better, his energy level higher.
Hurray for meat loaf and biscuits!

As we start up the highway, the snow
        begins to come down harder. It's sticking on
the pavement, and once the temps
        fall nighttime cold, it's going to be icy.
"Hope you've got tread on your tires."

        Just got new rubber six months ago,
                he says. And the truck has four wheel
        drive. Think I'll go ahead and put it into
                four-by now, in fact. It's a simple turn
of a knob, and the obvious traction

boost makes me feel slightly less
        uneasy. We start up a long grade,
making deep tracks in the road slush.
        And still the snow keeps falling.
Giant flakes, plummeting from the sky.

Holy crap! Check out this dumb-ass.
        The words are barely out of Kyle's
mouth when a black Hummer goes
        barreling by. *Hope the jerk doesn't
have to stop fast. He'll be toast.*

Intuition, or maybe subconsciously
        willing the universe to make it happen,
the Hummer's brake lights flash,
        and suddenly it is perpendicular
to us and drifting sideways, right into

        our lane. *Fuck, fuck, fuck,* says Kyle,
                hitting his own brakes and whipping
        the wheel to keep from broadsiding
                the bigger vehicle. No. This isn't
        happening. Everything seems to go

slow motion. Turning sideways
        ourselves. Floating on snow toward
the Hummer. Toward the shoulder.
        "Kyle!" I scream as we go face-first
off the highway. Over the side.

Gigantic bump. My head snaps
        forward. Back. Someone praying.
Kyle? Falling. Somersaulting.
        Can a truck turn somersaults?
Finally, no motion at all. And silence.

STUNNED

It takes a few minutes to understand
I am okay, despite hanging at an odd
angle by the shoulder harness that
doubtless saved my life. Kyle is beneath

me, against the window. "Kyle? Kyle!"
He doesn't answer. But I can hear
him breathing. Okay. What now? If
I unfasten my seat belt, I might fall on him.

But I can't just stay here, dangling.
"Help," I call uselessly. My voice is thin,
and there's no one to hear, anyway.
I test my body. Legs, okay. Arms?

Okay, I think. A little pain where
the harness caught hold of my collarbone,
but overall I got lucky. Please, God,
let Kyle be lucky too. I have to try

and help him, so I chance letting
myself out of the seat belt. With my arm
still looped through the shoulder
harness, I manage to let myself down

without falling on Kyle. Now that
I'm loose, I can assess our situation.
Not good. The truck is resting on
the driver's side, nose against a big pine.

I can't get out that way, and to
exit the passenger door, I'd have
to push it up, over my head, which
would be hard enough without

figuring in the fact that the rollover
smashed it. Maybe the window?
As I work through the logistics,
I hear voices somewhere. "Help!"

> I try again. But it becomes obvious
> they're already coming nearer. I lift
> my hands so they know someone's
> here. *Hang on! We're coming.*
>
> I manage to get the window
> open. Strong arms reach down
> through it, lift me out. *Are you okay?*
> says the man, who I refuse to let go

of. Just want him to hold me.
Let me cry into his chest. "Help
him," I stutter. "Please, get him out."
And please get him out alive.

IT IS COMPLETELY DARK

By the time I see Kyle again.
I am sitting in the warm backseat
of a highway patrol cruiser when

they carry him up over the lip of
the highway. I jump out of the car,
run toward the stretcher. "Kyle!"

> A cop stops me. *Let the paramedics
> do their job. His arm is broken, maybe
> his collarbone, too. And he's got one*

> *giant knot on his noggin. But it looks
> like he'll be just fine. The truck
> is definitely not so lucky.*

We watch two tall uniforms load
Kyle into an ambulance. Then the cop—
Officer Strohmeyer—opens the passenger

> door for me. *Might as well sit up front.*
> He comes around, slips beneath
> the steering wheel. *Gonna take*

> *a while to pull the truck out of there.
> We'll tow it to Bishop. The question
> is, who's missing you right now?*

I'VE HAD SOME TIME

To think up an answer, so it flows easily.
"We were on our way to my grandparents'

in Carson City. My mom's already there. . . ."
Which may or may not be true.

But I'm pretty sure Grandma Marie and
Grandpa Scott will cover for me.

I suppose I should get in touch
with Kyle's dad, let him know what's up.

> *You better give them a call and let*
> *them know what happened,* says Officer
>
> Strohmeyer. *I'll take you to the hospital.*
> *You should get checked out too.*

The cop starts the car, turns carefully
around, and I rack my memory for the right

phone number. When Grandma Marie answers,
relief floods through me, and I rush to tell the story

she is so not expecting to hear. I hang up.
"My grandpa will come get me in the morning."

Hunter

CHRISTMAS DAWNS SILVER

It's the way crisp sunlight
plays on the new snow,
all sparkling. Clean. The sky
is clear. Brilliant blue.
And I am up way too early.

I wasn't the first one up.
Scott was off at daybreak,
on his way to Bishop to collect
Summer. Surprise!
Guess who was coming

to Christmas dinner, only to
be waylaid by a Hummer.
Guess she and some guy
named Kyle were lucky
enough snow had fallen

to soften their rollover. Some
cop named Officer Strohmeyer
insisted on talking to Kristina.
Mom got on the phone, and
when the guy found out

who she was, he went all star-
struck and forgot about
Kristina. Mom sent a signed
book along. Hopefully, the roads
will be clear and they'll make it

back in time for the big meal.
Mom's already in the kitchen,
baking pies and kneading
the dough for her homemade
cinnamon rolls. A Christmas

morning staple around here.
That and butcher-shop bacon.
Been the same breakfast every
Christmas morning that I can
remember. And before that, too,

I'm told. The boys and Leigh
are still fast asleep. I'm sure
Kristina is too. I'll pick her
up a little later. After I make
another stop in Reno.

HER CAR IS HERE

The house is dark. Silent
in the growing light. I let
myself in with the spare key

I had made and never told
her about. Shh. In stocking
feet along the hallway, listening.

Hoping she is alone. I hear
only her breathing as I steal
down the hall, into the familiarity

of a room filled with Nikki's
presence, even as she sleeps.
About the time I get ready to

add my own presence to the bed
too long emptied of it, I realize
this could go wrong. But I am

determined to make it right.
Her right arm lies atop the thick
quilt, exposed. I kiss her fingertips

gently. Move my lips along her
cool skin to the crook of her elbow.
She sighs, opens her eyes.

She could jump up. Scream.
Run from me. Instead she says,
I was dreaming you had come.

I ease onto the bed beside her.
Kiss her. Easy. No demands.
Kiss her mouth. Her forehead.

Her eyes. Down her nose. Back
to her mouth, which she opens,
inviting me inside. "I'm sorry,"

I whisper, before accepting
her invitation. Diving in, as
into a warm spring. And before

we go any further, she says,
I forgive you. This time. But
this is the last time, I swear.

"I know." The love we make
is remembered. And it is all new.
And there is no one else in the world.

WE DOZE FOR A WHILE

And then

       somewhere, music. Loud.
       Incubus? Oh, my cell. The first
       thing I think, as I part the clouds
       of semi-sleep, is: better not be Leah!

And then

       as the mist dissipates, I remember
       it's Christmas Day, and I am on
       a mission. Besides winning
       Nikki back, that is.

And then

       I pull Nikki tighter against me.
       Have I won her back? Can it
       really be so? I kiss her awake.
       "I have something for you."

And then

       I reach over the side of the bed,
       find my jeans. Extract the shiny
       red box from one pocket, dismissing
       the phone in the other pocket.

And then

       I tell her, "Merry Christmas,"
       all hot and wobbly inside, like
       I'm the one getting the present.
       She sits up into slanted sunlight.

And now

> My angel smiles, lingers over
> the shimmery gold bow. Slits
> open the tape, carefully unfolds
> the foil. *I love little presents.*

And now

> She lifts the lid from the cardboard
> box, removes the smaller, velvet-
> flocked box, slowly, too slowly,
> opens it. *Oh Hunter, it's beautiful.*

And now

> She pulls the ring from its holder,
> starts to put it on her right finger.
> "No," I say, taking it gently and
> moving it to her left ring finger.

And now

> I explain, "It's a promise ring.
> It belongs on this finger. Maybe
> someday we'll exchange it for
> an engagement ring." Wow.

And now

> She moves into my arms. Kisses
> a long thank-you. *I love it,* she says.
> *And I love you.* And, despite my
> cell going off again, she proves it.

WHEN SHE GOES TO SHOWER

I check my voice mail. No Leah,
thank God. But there are two

                                 from Mom. *Your Grandpa Bill*
                                 is flying up from L.A. He gets in

                                 at eleven. Can you pick him up?
                                 Call me back to let me know.

I look at the clock. Ten fifteen.
I let Mom know it's not a problem.

Then I call Kristina to give her an
ETA for her own pickup. Her phone

goes straight to voice mail. Wonder
who she's talking to. I join Nikki

in the shower, admiring how pretty
her summer tan looks under white

soap foam. "Have plans, or can you
come out to the house for dinner?"

She thinks it over, some sort of back-
and-forth in her head, as if arguing

                    with herself. Finally she says,
                    I should spend the day with Mom.

Dad's in Hawaii with his girlfriend,
and I don't want Mom to be alone.

"Bring her along," I offer. As soon
as the words fall from my mouth,

I realize that could be a bad idea.
Kristina. David. Donald. Summer.

Throw in Grandpa Bill, who's eighty-
five, and all the regulars—Leigh, Jake,

Misty, and me. It's already a formula
for family disaster. But Nikki's face

        lights up. *Mom would love that.*
        Your parents won't care?

I suppose I should have asked.
But hey, too late now. "The more

the merrier, Mom always says.
We usually eat around four."

Initiation by fire, I guess. "I love you."
Hope she still loves me after dinner.

THE AIRPORT

Is busy. Weird. You'd think everyone
         would already be where they're going
                by Christmas morning. I guess blizzards
                        have a way of messing up travel plans.

I wait inside for Grandpa Bill, who
         I haven't seen in almost a year. He's
                Dad's dad, and has always been really
                        good to me. Mom says the amused

look he generally wears has to do
         with Dad getting back as good
                as he gave Grandpa Bill once
                        upon a time. Meaning I haven't

always been the perfect kid. But
         hey, no such thing as "perfect,"
                right? I'm watching a couple
                        of not exactly perfect kids right

now, in fact, running around,
         screaming and laughing while
                their poor mom looks about nuts
                        as she waits for someone too.

Maybe I don't want kids. Wonder
         if Dad will wear an amused look
                someday because I'll be getting
                        back as good as I used to give.

I COLLECT GRANDPA BILL

And his small suitcase, load them
into my truck. "We have to pick up

Kristina, too. It's going to be a little
tight in here." Sardine-can tight.

        The amused look wavers just
        a little. *I hope she can find a few*

        minutes to spend talking to me.
        His voice crackles. *Last time*

        we had a Christmas together,
        she never bothered much with

        small talk. That kind of hurt
        my feelings, know what I mean?

"Grandpa, you ought to know
by now not to let anything Kristina

does or doesn't do hurt your feelings.
Kristina is all about Kristina."

SHE'S ALL ABOUT KRISTINA

When we get to the hotel and have
to wait more than twenty minutes for her.
All about Kristina when she opens
the door, sees Grandpa Bill,

> and says, *Hey there, Grandpa,*
> *how you been? Scooch over.*

He starts to sputter, doesn't
want to complain, so I do it
for him. "You're skinnier than
he is. You can ride in the middle."

> She throws up her hands, but
> what can she say? *Whatever.*

For the next fifteen minutes,
she goes on about how Ron wants
to ruin her life. Finally, disgusted,
I say, "Try picking better men."

> That elicits a reaction. *What would*
> *you know about the men I pick?*

I have debated saying a single
word about this, but my mouth
opens and out comes, "I know
about one. I just met Brendan."

AWAKE MOST OF THE NIGHT

Sleep elusive, chased
         into the night
by fears of today.
         Christmas.

My first far away
         from the only
family I've ever
         really known.

My first, promised
         to spend with
the family I've only
         dreamed about.

What if they won't
         let me in?
What if they don't
         want to see me?

What if they send
         me away?
Why did I come
         here, anyway?

AND ANOTHER NIGGLING QUESTION

Is

        there some selfish reason
        for Trey bringing me here?
        "Out of the goodness of
        his heart" doesn't ring true.

There

        has to be a bigger "why"
        than just to make me happy.
        He never cared before.
        The need to know is

a worm

        slithering through my brain.
        I tried to bring it up last
        night, when he was fighting
        his own sleep demons,

working

        up a tobacco-infused night
        sweat. Both of us tossing
        worry, I asked, "Did you make
        this trip for me or for you?"

His

        thrashing stilled, like he
        thought about feigning
        dreamland. But then a low
        sort of growl exhaled from his

core.

HE SAT UP IN BED

A dark silhouette against
backlit blinds. And once
he started to talk, it all

came spilling out. *I've
spent the last fifteen
years hating your mother.*

*That hate came from love
left to rot in my gut like roadkill
in summer. You know why*

*I ended up back in a cage?
Because I didn't give
a half damn about anyone.*

*Rob 'em? Why not?
Rough 'em up? Hell, yeah.
Because it made me feel*

*in control. Never was,
though. What I couldn't see
was that hate controlled me.*

HE PAUSED THERE

And I thought he would stop
without telling me what I still

wanted to know. "You haven't
answered my question."

Because I'm not really sure.
I think it's wrong that Dad

and Cora kept you from
knowing your roots. Just

wrong. I want to fix that if
I can. But I also want to see

Kristina again. Maybe I can
quit hating her then. At least

I'll have a chance to tell her
what the last fifteen years

have done to me. I was dead
inside. And then I saw you.

A piece of me, so full of life.
I came a little alive too.

ALL THAT TALKING

Seemed to wear him right
        out. He settled back down
                in bed. Boulder dropped

into sleep. Guess clearing
        his conscience tuckered
                him out. I, on the other hand,

had no such reaction to
        all that confession. Strange
                voices bypassed my ears,

whispering straight into
        my brain. *Dead inside . . .*
                hating her . . . a little alive.

I remembered something.
        It seemed a memory buried
                deep in toddlerhood.

Mommy? Daddy? Glimpses
        of slat-shadowed faces,
                screwed up in rage. Screaming.

I hate you. Door slamming.
        Pillow over my head against
                the noise. Scrambling for breath.

MY HEART STUTTERED

With sudden clarity.
I'm not crazy.
The relentless feeling

of panic started there.
In my parents'
love-fueled hatred

for each other. And
me. I bet they
hated me because

I kept them together.
Drove them
apart. Reminded them

of what they should be,
and how incapable
they were of being it.

THE REST OF THE NIGHT

Was lost to the voice
of the wind calling
down over the Sierra.
Something familiar
about that keening,
too. Some part of me
longing to hear it again
after all these years.

       I listened for hours,
       until finally it calmed.
       And in the lull, doubt
       lifted, a ghost shrugging
       off flesh. Nothing stays
       the same. So how can
       you trust anything?
       How can you believe?

              I got up, went into
              the bathroom. Arranged
              the toiletries by color.
              Rearranged them by height.
              But there weren't enough
              of them to make the job
              important and in that
              way, make me matter.

IN THE BOLD LIGHT

Of morning I wonder if I count
for anything at all. Christmas.
It's early here, but Texas time

is two hours later. I find my cell,
buried in the oversize bag
holding my clothes. Later I'll call

Bryce to wish him a merry Christmas
and maybe share some special
news. But he's probably sleeping.

Instead I call a familiar San Antonio
number. No answer. Worry punches
at my gut. But then I remember.

Aunt Cora doesn't live there
anymore. Grandfather? Probably
with her in Austin. I have to

scratch deep in my brain to
find the right combination
to make the phone ring there.

> Liam answers, too cheerful.
> *Well, hello there, world traveler.*
> *Merry Christmas to you.*

Nevada is hardly the world.
But I don't say so. "Can I
speak to Aunt Cora, please?"

Liam puts down the phone
to go get her, exposing
the handset to background

noise. Off-key singing. A chorus
of laughter. Voices I know,
and some unfamiliar, a strange

blend of old and new, all
around Aunt Cora and
Grandfather. Homesickness

swells. And not a small amount
of jealousy. They are there.
I am here. Where I swore

I wanted to be. When Aunt
Cora picks up, all I can say
through the tears is, "Just

wanted you to know I miss
you. Give Grandfather a kiss
for me. Gotta go now."

I COULD LET TREY SLEEP

But the desire to escape
this room is driving me crazy.

"Wake up," I urge. "The day's
a-wasting." It's one of Grandfather's

favorite sayings, and that wave
of homesickness crests.

Trey shakes off sleep reluctantly.
But when he sees my face, etched

with expectancy, he goes into
the bathroom to shower. I get

dressed again in my one nice
outfit. Brush out my hair. Put

on my shoes, and within one very
long hour, we are ready to go.

We are barely out the door before
I decide my cute Texas-friendly

ballerina-style flats aren't exactly
suitable for snow. Especially not

snow like this. "Oh!" The word
disappears in a puff of steam.

"It's just so . . . beautiful." Everything
is carpeted white. Morning sun glints

off the clean, mostly undisturbed
drifts. Traffic beyond the parking

lot is light. Slow between the giant
piles of plow-pushed powder.

> *Definitely a whopper of a storm.*
> *Looks like it's moved on for now.*

My clothes are Texas weight,
and I shiver beneath them. But

a strange feeling floats down
over me. It's a flurry of calm

I've never felt before, and worry
dissipates. Whatever happens,

I know somewhere in all this snow
I've found a missing piece of me.

Summer

ADVENTURE OVER

Kyle's truck is totaled. And with
it, our dream of playing house.
I guess somewhere deep inside
I knew it would come to an end.
Just didn't know how quickly.

At least we're alive. Relatively
unscathed. It could have ended
a whole lot worse. Kyle will have
to stay in the hospital a couple
of days. Long enough for his dad

to collect him. Oh my God.
He was pissed. But not nearly
as pissed as he would have been
had Kyle's blood work shown
him to be under the influence.

And, despite what Kyle believes,
beneath his dad's overt anger,
a large dose of relief was obvious.
I may not be in a position to judge,
but I think he cares about Kyle.

As for me, bruises. Contusions.
But no broken bones. Nothing
punctured or torn. *You were*
exceptionally lucky, the ER nurse
said. *Good thing you buckled up.*

Damn good thing, actually. Also
good they let me stay here overnight.
Waiting room chairs aren't the most
comfortable things to snooze in,
but they're better than the kind

that come with too many questions.
Like those in police stations.
I get up from the one I've been
in for too many hours, wander
down to Kyle's room, peek through

the door. Kyle snorts in his sleep.
God, he's cute, tangled in dreams,
a thick drift of hair across his face.
Whatever happens to me, I hope
he doesn't get into too much trouble.

TWO NURSES HUSTLE PAST

Laughing about something.
The noise rousts Kyle from
wherever sleep has led him.

> He yawns as his eyes open, try
> to make sense of the surroundings.
> Finally they focus on me. *Hey.*

> He smiles. Tries to sit up in bed.
> And then reality crashes around him.
> *Come over here. What time is it?*

I point to the large clock on the wall.
"Little hand on the seven, big hand
on the five." I draw alongside the bed.

> He reaches for me, winces. *Okay.*
> *That hurt a little.* Pain or no pain,
> he takes hold of my hand. Squeezes.

And it hits me that we may not be
holding hands again for some time
to come. My throat knots up

> and my eyes burn. Kyle notices.
> *Hey, now. Everything's okay. Well,*
> *except for a couple of broken bones.*

Tears begin to fall in earnest.
"But your truck is history. So
is Mammoth. And what about us?"

> I don't care about my truck.
> Don't care about Mammoth.
> All I care about is you. If any-
>
> thing bad would have happened
> to you, I would never have forgiven
> myself. This is all my fault.

"No it's not. Anyway, nothing bad
happened to me. You're the one
with the broken bones, remember?"

> He smiles. Hard to forget. Except
> when they want to hold you.
> Kind of like now, for instance.

My entire body heats with a warm
flood of love. But the truth of things
tempers it. "What will happen to us?"

> He quiets me with a kiss. I don't
> know. But whatever happens, I swear
> we'll still be together. Somehow.

WE LEAVE THE "HOW"

To the future.

           Settle for being together
           right now. In this moment.

I'm pretty sure

           I won't see him again for
           a while. Maybe a long while.

We'll celebrate

           Christmas safe and warm,
           at least. Not buried by snow.

After that,

           and after the truth
           of our situation emerges,

we'll just have to see.

GRANDPA SCOTT

Reaches the hospital around ten.
I see him wandering down the corridor,
looking for me. Age has not

much diminished his fair good
looks, and the nurses smile
appreciatively. I nudge Kyle.
"There's my Grandpa Scott."

> Kyle locks eyes with Grandpa,
> who stands outside the door,
> assessing. *He doesn't like me.*

"He doesn't even know you.
How can he not like you?
I mean, he might be a little
annoyed. But he's here."

I go give him a giant hug. "Thanks
for coming. Sorry you had to drive
all this way on Christmas."

> He draws back to give me
> a good once-over. *Are you
> sure you're okay? We're just
> happy you weren't hurt.*

"I'm fine, Grandpa. Someone
was watching out for us, for sure."
After quick introductions, Grandpa

> excuses himself. *I'll go take care
> of the paperwork. We should
> probably hit the highway soon.
> Was good meeting you, Kyle.*

I don't want to leave, but I know
I have to go. I give Kyle a long,
sweet kiss. "I wish I could stay, but . . ."

> *No. Go on. We'll talk when you get
> back. . . .* He pauses there. Neither
> of us knows when or where I'll get
> back to. *Merry Christmas. I love you.*

ONE LAST KISS

And without looking back,
I go to find Grandpa.
He's at the nurses' station,
where he has dropped a signed
copy of Grandma Marie's latest

> book for Officer Strohmeyer
> to come pick up later. I watch
> Grandpa Scott totally schmooze
> a plus-size nurse with orange
> hair. *I'm sure we can find*

> *another copy for you. Write*
> *down your address and I'll make*
> *sure you get one. I can pull*
> *strings with the author.* He winks,
> turns to me. *Ready to go?*

Before I know it, we're out
the door and in Grandpa's new
Lexus SUV, cruising toward Christmas
dinner, me fiddling with the seat
heat control, mostly because

it gives my hands something
to do besides tremble. By some
unspoken agreement, neither
of us says a word until we're
well on our way out of town.

THE HIGHWAY IS
MOSTLY CLEAR

But Grandpa drives cautiously.
Have to be careful of black ice,

is his explanation. It is all he says
for a while. But finally he broaches

the necessary inquiry. *So we
hadn't expected you this year.*

*And Kristina didn't know you were
coming either.* He pauses. Waits.

"It was a last-minute decision,"
I try. "We wanted to surprise you."

You definitely did that. His voice
is gentle, tinged with humor. *And*

*you surprised everyone else, too.
We called your dad's to let him know*

*you were okay. Someone named
Kortni answered. She said your father*

*was in jail and as far as she knew,
you were in a foster home in Fresno.*

He lets the weight of his words sink
down around us. *Was she wrong?*

OBVIOUSLY HE KNOWS

She wasn't wrong. And I'm just
too tired of it all to try and make
up a lie. "No. She was right."

Despite the Lexus's luxury, I have
become extremely uncomfortable.
Oh, well. Fabrication is useless.

I launch the story, omitting only the parts
about making love beneath the stars
and Kyle's farewell to the monster.

Grandpa Scott absorbs it all
in silence. When I finish, he thinks
about things, then spends some

> time crafting his comments.
> *Running away is never a good*
> *decision, Summer. There has*
>
> *to be a better answer, though*
> *to tell you the truth, I'm not sure*
> *what it is. Let's get through today*
>
> *as best we can, then make*
> *some decisions tomorrow.*
> *This should be interesting.*

I point as we pass the place where
Kyle and I plunged off the highway
yesterday. Last night's heavy

snowfall has covered most
of the evidence of the accident.
"You can't even tell it happened,"

I muse. What I don't say is how
scary that is. If circumstances
were just a little different,

we could still be down there, buried
in a giant snowdrift. Suffocating.
Or left to slow starvation.

Even without my voicing
those thoughts, Grandpa Scott
gets them. *Someone was watching*

out for you, all right. You've got
something important to do
before you check on out of here.

IMPORTANT? ME?

I've never once thought
of myself as
important,
or considered
I might have a special

reason for being. I've
mostly thought
of myself
as an accident.
Someone in the way.

Something important to
do? Like what?
Guess I
don't need to
think about that right

now. Like Grandpa Scott
said, let's just
get through
today. And make
big decisions tomorrow.

Hunter

SOMETIMES I SHOULD SHUT MY MOUTH

I knew bringing up Brendan
wasn't the most tactful thing
to do, especially on Christmas.
But sometimes Kristina makes
me so mad, I want to hurt her.

It's stupid. She doesn't injure
easily, at least not when the slaps
are verbal. When I mentioned
Brendan, she didn't say anything
immediately. Finally she said,

> *I'm surprised he came back.*
> *Surprised he's still alive,*
> *actually. He ripped off a lot*
> *of people. Even worse than*
> *he took advantage of me.*

We were almost home by
then. I slowed enough to get
a few words in. "Don't suppose
you'll take some responsibility
for what happened that night?"

ANGER PUFFED

From her mouth in
abbreviated breaths.

> What? You
> want to
> blame me
> for getting
> raped?
> Oh
>   my
>   God.

And then she really
pissed me off.

> Just like
> a man.

Despite Grandpa
Bill's obvious

uneasiness, I jumped.
"All men are not alike.

And, thank God, all
women are not like you."

SHE HASN'T SPOKEN

To me since. Not that I care.
When we got home, she went
straight into the house and

retreated somewhere with
the boys. For all of ten minutes.
Then I noticed Donald join

Grandpa Bill in the family room.
He got a new game system
for Christmas. They're playing.

I am helping Mom wash veggies
when David bops by with Sasha.
"Where's Kristina?" I ask.

He shrugs. *She went outside*
to smoke a cigarette. Why
does she like those stinky things?

Mom answers, *Tobacco*
is addictive. Once you start
smoking, it's really hard to quit.

I'll never smoke, he decides.
Not if it makes you smell
like that. Come on, Sasha.

EVENTUALLY

Kristina comes back inside,
trailed by Jake and Misty,
who have just arrived bearing
gifts like Christmas magi.

They sweep into the kitchen,
Leigh close on their heels,
put the presents on the table,
chant a chorus of "Merry Christmas."

Kristina heads straight for
the brightly wrapped boxes,
finds one with her name on
it. *Ooh. Can I open it now?*

Leigh stops her from tearing
into the Santa-and-puppy
paper. *Why don't we wait
for Scott to get back?*

Kristina, who has managed
to ignore me completely,
reluctantly agrees. Nicotine
obviously can work wonders.

Jake goes into the family room,
and I hear him say, *Grandpa*
Bill! I didn't know you were
here. Where's your car?

> *Damn DMV wouldn't re-up*
> *my license. Said my eyes*
> *don't work so good anymore.*
> *Hate to admit they're right.*

The banter picks up speed in
the kitchen as Mom and Misty
and Leigh and Kristina start
yakking girl talk. Enough, already.

I'm on my way to the family room
when the doorbell rings. Nikki?
She's early, but that's all good.
I swing the door open. "Nik!"

Autumn

THIS HOUSE IS INSANE

Insane, as in beautiful.
I stand on the front porch,
staring up at the tall doors.
Oak, with beveled stained glass.

I wait for the familiar tingle
in my fingers. But I don't
feel close to panic. I reach
out. Ring the doorbell.

> The door jerks open. *Nik!*
> But I'm not Nik, whoever he
> is, and the boy who is waiting
> for him is confused. *Uh . . .*
>
> *Can I help you?* He is older
> than me by a year or two,
> with mink-colored hair and
> eyes an unusual shade of green.

We are related, but I'm not
sure how, and even less sure
of what to say. I start to back
away, but Trey takes over for me.

You must be Hunter. Wow.
I haven't seen you since you
were a baby. Damn. I'm, um . . .
Is Kristina here, by any chance?

> Hunter—my brother—nods an
> "oh, okay" nod, turns, and yells,
> *Kristina! Someone's here to see*
> *you.* Beyond him, amazing Christmas

decorations swag staircase
railings, and the scent of turkey
roasting and bread dough rising
makes my mouth start to water.

> A woman comes to the door.
> I have dreamed of this face,
> only a younger version of it.
> Kristina. My mother. Curiosity

> lights her eyes, only to be
> replaced by sudden wonder.
> *Trey,* she says. *What are you . . . ?*
> Then her eyes fall on me.

AT FIRST

There is no hint of recognition.
I could be a Jehovah's Witness,
passing out literature. But then,
         a rain:

                  Memory search
           Denial
                      Rewind
               Inquiry
         Puzzlement
                       Recognition
               Surprise
         Shock
                     Stunned
              Acceptance

     Autumn? Is that really you?
     She comes forward, hand
     extended toward my face.

Suddenly I don't want her
to touch me. I don't know why
not, except you don't let strangers

touch you, do you? I step back.
Annoyance shadows her eyes.
So much for imagined reunions.

NOW IT IS HUNTER

Who rescues me. *Autumn,*
he says matter-of-factly. *I always*

hoped we'd meet one day.
Come in. It's cold out there.

The house is full of people.
Thank goodness I've had a little

practice lately being around
a mob of not-quite-family. Lots

of introductions. Two aunts.
One uncle. A great-grandfather.

Another grandmother. Marie.
Three brothers. And my mother.

Everyone seems excited to see me.
I'm not sure how to feel in return.

Voices. Questions. Puppy feet.
Television, loud. Timer buzzers.

Oven doors closing. The whistle
of a teakettle. It's all too much.

I ASK FOR DIRECTIONS

To the bathroom. Follow them
      through a maze of halls and space.
           This house is crazy. Compared
               to Grandfather's staid white
         rooms, these are warm with wall
     color, art, and hardwood floors.
I don't know my grandmother yet,

but I feel her presence here.
      She's an author. I've seen her
         books around school, though
            I've never opened one.
         I wonder if I would have, had
      I known how much they relate
to me. I think maybe not. Surreal.

I wander down a long hallway,
      hung thickly with family photos.
         Hunter in Little League. Kristina
            as a teenager. And uh . . . me,
        as a baby. I was here all along.
     I need air. I cut through my grand-
mother's office, go out a side door.

LOOKS LIKE THE PARTY'S STARTED

The driveway is choked with cars,
lined bumper-to-bumper against

the berms of piled snow. "Did you
do all that shoveling, Grandpa?"

> He maneuvers the Lexus carefully.
> *With a little help from your brothers.*

"Brothers? Plural? You actually got
the boys to work?" That's a surprise.

> *Believe it or not, Donald has become*
> *quite a good helper. David would still*

> *rather play with the puppy, but he's*
> *getting better too. Consistency.*

We could all use a little of that.
Grandpa noses the SUV against

the garage, and as we exit the car,
the office door opens. "Who's that?"

The girl is a year or two older than me,
with thick copper hair tumbling loose

> to her shoulders. She is not dressed
> for snow. *I have no idea,* Grandpa says.

She stares up into the crackled
blue sky, lost in solitary reverie.

I am connected to her in some
unfathomable way. The door opens

again, and out comes my mom
with some guy I don't know either.

> They light cigarettes, and Grandpa
> Scott says in a stiffened voice, *Trey.*

Everything clicks into place. Trey plus
Kristina equals, "Autumn." My sister.

She pivots like a soldier on drill, goes
back inside. This day is full of surprises.

GRANDPA SCOTT SHIVERS

Cold out here. Let's go inside.
But he creeps along, trying, I think,
to understand what this development
means. Trey has materialized, a ghost

of times best left unremembered.
And Autumn? What does she know
of those times? How much does
she really want to know? Still,

the little chills quivering through me
have nothing to do with air temp.
"I didn't even know I had a sister
until a couple of weeks ago."

> Grandpa looks truly surprised.
> *Someone should have told you.*
> *But so you know, Marie has been*
> *trying to track her down for years.*

I glance over at Mom and Trey,
who stand close to each other,
exhaling smoke into iced air.
"Why didn't Mom ever tell me?"

> Grandpa shrugs. *I've never*
> *quite figured Kristina out.*
> *It's almost like she fuels*
> *herself on secrets and lies.*

GRANDMA MARIE'S KITCHEN

Has always felt like sanctuary.
Some people might think
that's a cliché, but compared

to any other kitchen I've ever
spent time in, this one is always
the gathering place. Warm.

Spice-scented. Spilling laughter
and conversation. Today there
is more. Today there is reunion.

And, for some of us, relationships
too new to quite comprehend.
Grandma Marie is at the counter

kneading dough. Aunt Leigh
and Aunt Misty play cards at the table.
Autumn hovers in a corner, trying

to make sense of what these women
mean to her. I know the feeling well.
Might as well try the direct approach.

"Hi, Autumn," I call across the short
expanse of tile. My feet follow, until
I stand in front of her. "I'm Summer. . . ."

SHE IS WARY

Like a caged cat, escaped,
            but unsure of the wild lands
beyond the bars. I understand.
            Already, we walk common ground.

It is tenuous turf, riddled with
            the rifts and earthquakes of our
personal histories. We confess
            scenes. Abbreviated clips.

With her soft Texas drawl
            and faux hippie wardrobe,
on the surface she is nothing
            like me. But just below the skin,

we find connection. I shudder
            to think why that might be, because
our common denominator is
            someone I don't want to resemble.

Autumn and I talk for an hour,
            while the house fills with holiday
cheer. I don't know where we'll go
            tomorrow, but today there is communion

here, and now I have a sister.
            There is power in that. Today
I am surrounded by family
            and affection, uncluttered by need.

Hunter

SURPRISES

Are rarely good things
around here. Today they
are kind of a mixed bag.

Good:

Meeting a sister I only
half believed existed.

Not-so-good:

Meeting a guy I always
half blamed for Kristina's
return to the monster.

Good:

Watching Summer and
Autumn test the choppy
waters of sisterhood.

Not-so-good:

Watching Kristina pay
more attention to Trey
than to her children.

Good:

Seeing how well David
and Donald are coping
despite being ignored.

Not-so-good:

Seeing that no matter
how some things change,
others never will.

THE BEST SURPRISE

Of the day was Nikki
opening her arms, allowing me
back into her life.
I have to remember how bad
being closed out felt.

I know we're young,
that we have a long way to go,
and love has a way of
fading. I can't promise her we can
keep ours alive, but

I can promise to give
it a damn good try. Temptation
is something I can't
control. Flirtation is a whole
different thing.

As afternoon slants
toward evening and she hasn't
arrived, anxiety nips.
What if she changed her mind?
Should I call her?

But then the doorbell
rings and I know it's her and
now it really feels
like Christmas. Thanks, Santa,
for the best gift ever.

DESPITE HER MOM STARING

I pull Nikki into my arms, kiss
her like we don't have an audience.
Then I notice the bags her mom
holds. "Let me take those for you."

I peek inside. Eggnog and brandy.
This could prove an interesting
afternoon. I lead the ladies into
the kitchen. "Look who's here!"

It is a busy place. Mom slices
turkey. Leigh mashes potatoes.
Misty spoons cranberry sauce,
trying not to trip over Sasha,

who sits, tail wagging at
the prospect of some offered
tidbit. David obliges, slipping
her bits of roasted poultry skin.

Autumn and Summer have
tag-teamed the table setting.
Nikki and her mom see what
they can do to help. It might

be a scene right out of a Norman
Rockwell painting. Except,
of course, it isn't. It can't be.
Because this is our family.

649

DINNER IS READY

My grandfather—Grandpa Scott,
he said to call him—has announced
that it's time to eat. We all gather

at the table, which has two large
folding tables placed at one
end, and still we'll all barely fit.

Once everyone has found a seat,
two chairs are too obviously empty.
Hunter goes to the door, calls loudly,

> *Kristina! We're all at the table.*
> *Are the two of you planning to join*
> *us? Room service is closed.*

His voice carries thinly veiled anger,
and his girlfriend shoots a warning
glance that says, *Watch your temper.*

> Earlier, I heard Hunter talking
> to Grandma Marie. *Why is Kristina*
> *outside?* he asked. *Why isn't she*

with her kids? Why can't she just
act like a mom? Doesn't she care
about them? Doesn't she love them?

Grandma answered right
away, as if she'd thought about
the question many times before.

I think she wants to love them.
Wants to love all of you. But
she can't. I told you how meth

eats into the brain. Well, the part
that gets chewed away is
the part that lets people love.

I think about that as Kristina
and Trey finally find their way
to the table. How sad if they

really aren't able to love.
It explains a lot. But it also
raises more questions.

QUESTIONS LIKE

Why am I here?
            What have I accomplished
            by coming all this way?
            I wanted to meet my mother.
            Mission accomplished.
What does it mean?
            We haven't even spoken
            to each other. My fault,
            I guess. Should I have
            run into her arms?
Do I open
            my arms to her now?
            She seems much more
            interested in rekindling
            things with Trey.
Does she care
            at all about getting to
            know me? Would she try
            harder to break down the wall
            if I radiate more gold flecks?
Will I ever find
            the courage to storm
            the wall myself? What do
            I mean to my mother? Why
            can't I open my mouth and ask?

Summer
BEEN THINKING

So much about where I might
be going, I've kind of neglected

thinking about where I came from.
Wonder how Christmas was for Ashante.

Did Santa visit? Does she still believe,
despite having her innocence stolen?

What about Simone? Did Bear and Blonde
deliver? How about Eliana and Rosa,

sisters who I never really got to know.
Sisters missing their mother. At least

they have each other. And now that I have
a sister, will we have each other too?

We will not, I predict, ever have a mom,
not the kind who we'll sit down at dinner

with. Except for on holidays, that is.
I wish Kyle were here to share this

holiday dinner. Wonder what hospital
turkey is like. Wonder if he is lonely.

NOT MUCH ROOM

For loneliness here.
The table is heaped
with food, surrounded
by four generations
of family. It's sensory

    detail, maxed. Perfume
    of Christmas feast.
    Assorted flavors, blended
    with conversation.
    Swelling. Fading. Swelling.

        Loud. Soft. Loud. Silent.
        In those scant moments
        of silence, reflection.
        Live-wire tension. You
        can feel it building.

            Something wants to blow.
            You can see it, anxious,
            in the lift of shoulders.
            You can hear it whine.
            Implosion imminent.

WHAT LIGHTS THE FUSE

Is an innocent question.
When are we going home?
asks David. Conversation brakes.

Everyone looks at Kristina,
who doesn't answer right away.
Finally she says, *I don't know.*

Donald stands, clenching
his fists. *Fine by me. Who*
wants to live with you, anyway?

He slams his chair back
into the wall, rattling dishes.
Then he stalks off into the other

room. Grandpa Scott says,
Excuse me, and follows,
leaving all eyes on Kristina.

I can't go back to our old place,
she says. *Ron knows where it is.*
Why is everyone so mad at me?

I think about chiming in, and
so does Grandma Marie. But
it is Hunter who opens his mouth.

Hunter

MAYBE IT'S THE EGGNOG

I had a couple, heavily spiked,
before we sat down to dinner.

Maybe it's just Kristina's wide-
eyed pretense of innocence.

Whatever it is, I've had enough
of her acting like she gives a shit

about anyone but herself. "Look
at us, Kristina. I mean, take a few

minutes of your precious time
and really look at what you've done."

My voice amplifies with each word.
"Every one of us at this table has

been hurt by you. Some of us have
been crushed—no, annihilated,

and all because of you loving yourself
best of all. . . ." Nikki rests her hand

on mine. I stop, not for Kristina's sake,
but because Nikki wants me to.

Autumn
HUNTER'S OUTBURST

Is completely unexpected.
The sound of yelling, so close
to me, jump-starts the race
of my heart. My fingers go numb.

I close my eyes. Concentrate
on my breathing. Deep in. Hold.
Trickle out. Deep in. Hold . . .
Nobody notices. Good.

> Eyes still clamped shut, I hear
> Kristina respond. *You're wrong.*
> *I don't love myself at all. In fact,*
> *I can hardly look at myself*
>
> *in the mirror some days. Don't*
> *you think I know what I've done?*
> *It's not that I don't care. But*
> *I can't change anything now.*

Heart still too quick, but slowing,
I open my eyes just in time
to see Kristina's tough facade
crumble and fall away with the words . . .

Summer

I'M SORRY

That's what Kristina says.
We all look at her as if we haven't
quite heard her correctly.

> But she repeats, *I'm so sorry.*
> *I never wanted to be a bad mother.*
> *Maybe that's why I kept on*
>
> *trying, kept on begging for another*
> *chance to finally do it right. But I*
> *don't have the skills, don't have—*

"Don't you dare say it!" I yell.
"Don't say you don't have
the resources. You do, or

you could have. All you had
to do was ask for help." Anger
oozes like blood from my pores.

> Her anger is greater. *No!* she
> shouts. *You don't understand.*
> *I can't ask for help from people*
>
> *I turned my back on. People*
> *I stole from. Lied to. Hurt.*
> *People whose love I threw away.*

Hunter

KRISTINA IS OUT OF WORDS

Good thing, because
that's all they are. Words
without conviction
have no meaning.

I look

down the long table,
past turkey carcass and half-
eaten pie, and ignoring
the shock-iced eyes that stare

at her,

I measure her lowered
gaze, the foreign
language of her body.

And I
find

in the cold iron set
of her shoulders,
the boulders of her fists,

defiance.

Apology without regret.
The desire to challenge,
still. And, obvious through
a red haze of my own,

anger.

Autumn

KRISTINA IS OUT OF STEAM

I can't help but feel sorry
for her. She is a bird,
too broken to fly.

I look

across the granite width
of table, beyond crystal
glassware and cloth napkins.
Notice the way Trey smiles

at her,

as if telling her she has said
exactly the right thing. But
Hunter is not swayed. Summer,
too, seems unconvinced.

And I
find

in Kristina's refusal to meet
anyone's eyes, in her knuckles
that tap without rhythm,

fear.

And in the way she hugs
her secrets close, like I must
continue to hold on to mine
for a while longer yet,

deception.

Summer

KRISTINA IS OUT OF EXCUSES

I look
          I know that's what Grandpa
          Scott would say, and the rest
          of us would no doubt agree.
          My mom has said enough.

I look

          to my right, where Leigh
          sits, drop-jawed, gawking

at her

          sister, as if she's never seen
          her before. On my left, Autumn
          seems lost in some obscure
          distraction. Wonder where
          her thoughts have wandered.

And I
find

          in the tears that drop from
          my mother's eyes into puddles
          on her dinner plate,

doubt.

          A growing desire to escape
          the confines of this house,
          no longer her home, by
          her own design. And in that,

loneliness.

Hunter, Autumn, Summer

I HOPE FOR

Trust. Joy.

Courage. Honesty.

Belief. Belonging.

> Attaining these
> things may not
> come easily.
> Because, look
> very long at
> Kristina, I see

me

me

me.

PUBLISHERS WEEKLY

The release of Marie Haskins's and Kristina Shepherd's highly anticipated mother/daughter memoir, *Monster*, was yesterday put on indefinite hold.

"We felt it was appropriate to wait until Kristina's current round of chemotherapy has been completed," said Haskins, whose novels *Crank*, *Glass*, and *Fallout* offer a fictionalized account of Shepherd's twenty-year battle with methamphetamine addiction.

Shepherd said in June of the memoir project, "We want to fill in the blanks, not only for my mother's readers, but also for my children, who still might not have all the answers they need."

All five of Shepherd's children currently reside with Haskins.

Shepherd, who reunited with her husband, Trey, after a fifteen-year separation, has recently undergone radical treatment for lung cancer. "The prognosis is about as good as you could hope for," Shepherd said. "I throw it out there to the universe, pray God is listening and that he hasn't given up on me."

Author's Note

This is the third and final part of the saga begun in my first novel, *Crank*. When that book released in October 2004, I could not have predicted its phenomenal success. The story in *Crank*, and in its sequel, *Glass*, is shared by many. But even those whose lives have never been touched by this particular monster are drawn to Kristina. Despite her many flaws, they come to care about her and her family. Especially her children.

Originally, I never planned a sequel to *Crank*. But readers demanded more of Kristina's story. I could probably write ten books about her fall from grace, but series often degrade over time, and I don't want to give my readers progressively weaker books. Rather, I wanted the final Kristina book to be the most powerful of the three. And I believe I've done that with *Fallout*.

The book is written from the points of view of her three oldest children, now teens in the book, and dealing with their own lives, which have been shaped by the choices she made when she was their age. At the time I pen this description, the real "Hunter" is thirteen, but I write him at nineteen in *Fallout*. Which means I've written the future. Please remember it's only one possible future, created from how I see these children's lives now. And also please remember that, while these books are rooted in our real life, they are to a large degree fiction.

I chose to pull out of Kristina's point of view, into her children's to give them a voice, and to give voice to my readers who struggle with their own parents' addictions. There are many. I also believe the ultimate hope of these stories lies here, with the generation that can choose to break this cycle. You will get "the rest of Kristina's story," through different lenses because "the monster" doesn't only destroy the addict. It tries to destroy everyone who loves him or her. Parents. Children. Partners. Spouses. Friends. If this describes you, take care of yourself first. Get help if you need it. You might find a sense of peace and community in an organization like Al-Anon. Above all, please know, without a doubt, that you are not alone.

A Reading Group Guide to
FALLOUT
by Ellen Hopkins

PREREADING ACTIVITY

What psychological impact might drug addiction have on offspring?

Is it possible for a drug addiction to be just one person's problem?

How else, besides drugs like meth, can an addiction manifest itself, especially in the life of a teenager?

DISCUSSION QUESTIONS

Since the birth of her first child, Hunter, how has Kristina changed over the years? How has she remained the same? How has her relationship with her parents evolved?

How are Hunter, Autumn, and Summer alike? How are they different? Which of the three has a better chance at a successful life? Why?

Why is Autumn so careless about unprotected sex? How does she feel about getting pregnant? Is she grounded in reality? Explain.

Summer has feelings for both Matt and Matt's friend, Kyle. She describes Matt as a nice guy who has never pushed her to have sex and who has never belittled her or yelled at her. However, these positive characteristics "make him boring" How can this be? What characteristics in a boy excite her? Why? What similar responses to men does her mother have? Consider her mother's relationship with Ron.

Trey and Autumn's journey to Autumn's grandparents house is also a journey through Trey's relationship with Autumn's mother and, ultimately, his relationship with Autumn, his daughter. Along the way, Trey says, "I've/spent the last fifteen/years hating your mother . . . What I couldn't see/ was that hate controlled me." What does Trey mean? Give examples. What other characters have been controlled by hate? Explain.

Anger is a recurring theme in *Fallout*. Hunter reflects on his own rage and wonders why people take it out on those they love. Why do you think those closest often are hit the hardest by rage? Is Hunter's anger justified? What about his mother's? Explain.

How might anger be self-contempt? Use Kristina as an example.

Hunter's mother remarks in the closing pages that she "used to live 'mad'". What does she mean and how has she changed? Has she found peace? Explain.

Autumn and Summer both want desperately to be loved. Explain their desperation. Why are they so quick to fall for a boy? Why are they so needy? In what ways are they like their mother? In what ways are they different from their mother? How will they need to change so that they can have healthy relationships with men?

How do Kristina's children define love? Would you say they "misname" love? If so, explain.

Kristina has hurt everyone she has touched, and she seems to know she has. How does she respond to the pain she has caused?

Will Kristina's family ever heal? What scars might remain? Explain.

Fallout ends with the phrase, " . . . look/very long at/Kristina, I see/me/ me/me." Each use of the pronoun *me* represents one of Kristina's three older children. What do all three wish for? What are their fears? Will each of them be able to stop the "monster" from destroying their own families?

ACTIVITIES

Draw and/or use computer software to generate a relationship tree, highlighting the key characters in *Fallout*.

Choose one of the following relationships to research: father/daughter, father/son, mother/son, mother/daughter. What are the characteristics of a healthy relationship between the two? What relationship difficulties might a young teen have if one of these relationships is damaged? Prepare a class presentation based on your findings.

Organize a book read at your school between parents/guardians and their children around a book with strong relationship themes between parents/guardians and teens. Mothers and sons might read a YA novel about a mother/son relationship (ex., *Bucking the Sarge* by Christopher Paul Curtis); a father and daughter might read a YA novel about a father/daughter relationship (ex., *Story of a Girl* by Sara Zaar). Adopted children and their adoptive parents might read *Whale Talk* by Chris Crutcher.

Read a nonfiction account or a biography about a child growing up in a foster home (ex., *Three Little Words: A Memoir* by Ashley Rhodes-Courter) and share your reactions to the reading with the class.

Fallout guide written by Pam B. Cole, Professor of English Education & Literacy, Kennesaw State University, Kennesaw, Georgia.

Turn the page to
discover Ellen's
greatest inspiration.

My Greatest
Inspiration:
My Readers

People often ask what inspires me. When I first got the question, it stumped me. Inspiration? Why, it's everywhere, right? It's the view of the Sierra Nevada outside my window. It's watching my children grow into adults, succeeding in ways big and small. It's listening to my grandchildren laugh, watching them build Legos and play trains. It's my husband. My pets. My friends. My home. Truthfully, all these elements have served to inspire my stories. But my greatest inspiration over the years has been my readers.

At this point in my career, between regular mail, e-mail, and a plethora of social networking platforms (Twitter, Goodreads, Tumblr, Google+, Pinterest and a handful of Facebook pages), I receive around two hundred reader communications each day. While I enjoy every "I love your books" or "You are a genius" (especially that one!) or "I'm preordering your next book right this very minute," the more personal ones speak to my heart. They come in fairly regular categories. I'd like to share a few actual messages.

YOU'VE GIVEN ME INSIGHT

I come from a town that is filled to the brim of meth users. The slogan there is "City with a Toothless Smile." I lost two of my very close sisterlike friends due to their constant usage of that dark chemical. I like to say that I tried to do everything I could to help them, but they kept digging themselves deeper and deeper into the hole of substance abuse and addiction. I think it's my fault that they ended up the way they did. I left them back in my hometown, alone, when I went off to college. How I wish I could have put them in a box and taken them with me. The feeling and memory burn my heart. Sometimes I wake up, drowning in my own tears, because of the wicked realistic dreams I have of them. Their bodies are still walking this dirt, but their minds are forever gone.

I can point out comparisons between the book and my life, even though I never touched the drug. Your books put light on the possible thoughts of "what they were thinking" when they were doing all these degrading, horrid activities. Your books always helped me realize just to let go. Users can only seek help if they want help; I can't force or lure my friends into treatment anymore. They have to want to fix themselves. It hurts to come to such a conclusion, but it's the truth.

YOU'VE OPENED MY EYES

I know you must get a million e-mails a day, so if by some chance you do actually read this, I just want to say thank you for opening my eyes. Even if you don't see it, it doesn't matter that you read it, but that I write it.

I just finished reading Glass. I read this book because I wanted to better understand addiction. It never really clicked, you know? How someone could give up so much just to get high. I've never understood. And frankly, that's what I realized. Addiction is something so strong, that if you're not caught up in it yourself, you can't quite wrap your brain around it. I put myself into Kristina's shoes. As she fell deeper and deeper into her addiction, I started resenting her more and more with every page I turned. But I also felt sorry for her, how she can't control her self.

Now I can relate to my own family issues a little more. My uncle has thrown his life away. And not only his, but my mom's, my nana's, and his son's. I know I don't have to explain to you how stressed my family always is now that he's in jail. Everyone is on edge all the time. I used to hate him for turning my mom into a different person, for making her cry every day. But now I hate his addiction. It's his fault for allowing "the monster" into his life, but is it his fault he doesn't know how to ask it to leave?

I have used marijuana for two years (I'm now GUFN, thanks for teaching my mom her favorite new word). I got caught, and honestly, when I read about Kristina, it reminds me of how I acted. I didn't really realize how heartbreaking it is for my mom to see me using drugs at such a young age, when she knows I've seen what it has done to my family. I haven't smoked in ten days, pretty good considering I haven't been clean in two years. I know it's a gateway drug. But there is no way in hell I would ever do anything hard. Especially because I see myself in Kristina. And that scares me. Thanks for teaching me enough about drugs to know that if they are offered to me, to turn and run, fast.

YOU'VE GIVEN ME HOPE

Identical *is* the most intense work of literature I've ever read. I've never felt so close to anything in my entire life. The only thing that's made life bearable this month was having the opportunity to read your books, relate to them, and realize that I'm not alone and I never have been.

First of all, thanks. A ton. You're such an inspiration to so many people. I was nervous to read about all these intense topics. And at points, I found myself in tears because everything is so real. I'm fifteen. But since I was almost ten, I've had two different sexual abuse cases opened. It started with a family member, moved to his friends. It was tough to live with for a while. It reminded me how scary it was to deal with as I read the sections in Identical that talk about Kaeleigh's fear, when she counts her father's footsteps in the hall, scared of what's coming next. I don't know if I've ever cried that hard in my life. But it was okay, because although it's fictional, these things really happen and I'm not going through them by myself.

Physical abuse came next, and it was scary. And from there, I struggled with addictions to cutting and alcohol. Alcohol is finally gone, but cutting is still near, and I think about it a lot. It's been twenty-six days since I've picked up a razor and used it against myself. Progress is progress.

Suicide is very real. Addiction is very real. Abuse is very real. But hope and faith and love are also very real. And they can often outweigh the struggles. Maybe I just want to tell you that you've given me hope and security. Thanks for listening, and thanks for turning frightening topics into conversation. Because, truly, they're important.

YOU'VE GIVEN ME A VOICE

I want to say thank you for your books. I was seventeen when Crank came out, and it helped me out by giving me a voice to tell someone what happened to me. Normally, I didn't choose to read this kind of book because it would bring back too many memories, ones that I have tried to repress. My mother was kind of like Kristina in your book. Some of my earliest memories are of me getting beaten or raped so she could get her next fix. By the time I was five, the only thing I knew was abuse.

When I got put into foster care, I was kind of like Maya Angelou, I didn't speak, I couldn't find my voice. As I got older I got better, but I only spoke when absolutely necessary. I don't know why I picked up your book, but it seemed to be the key to my voice. I found a good friend to talk to. He was all I had. He had (and still has) trouble shutting me up. The very morning I finished Crank I got up, got dressed, went to his house, and for some reason told him everything. It made me feel so good to finally have a voice. You gave it to me. You were like that lady that helped Maya get her voice, but for me.

YOU'VE SAVED MY LIFE

Impulse. *The three stories in the book will stay with me for the rest of my life.*

I have been suicidal for over a year.
I thought dying would just make everything better.
Make myself and everyone else happier.
I thought nobody would care if I died.

The end of Impulse *really affected me.*

I grew attached to all three of the characters.
I felt like they were my friends.
I loved them.
Related to them.
Connected with them.
Understood them.
Vanessa . . . Tony . . . and Conner.

The ending of Impulse *left me in tears.*
Shock.
Disbelief.

Frustration.
Confusion.

I read Impulse *a few months ago and I still feel the way I felt about the*
     ending.

I've read your other books as well.
I loved them.
They're on the top of my bookshelf, my favorite books.

But Impulse really, really touched my heart.
No book has ever made me feel the way I felt once I finished the last
     page.

I wish I could change his decision.
Help him.
Fix it.
But it's too late.
Suicide is a permanent end to a temporary problem.

I was once suicidal.
Not anymore.

You saved me.
After reading Impulse, *I realized that suicide does not have to be*
     the end.

I'm still breathing.
Crying.
Smiling.
Lying.
Laughing.

Loving.
Living.

I'm still alive.
You're my hero.
Thank you.

These are just a few of the thousands I've received over the years. You can find many more on the tribute wall on my website. How could I *not* find inspiration from readers, who share their stories with me, often in person, after book signings or school visits? How could stories like these *not* touch my heart? How could I ever stop writing real stories, inspired by real people, knowing my books have the power to change lives?

This is why I push back against would-be censors, who claim my books are too dark or edgy, when what they mean is "real." Yes, real life can be scary, and I represent that in my books. But I also write about love and hope and light beyond the darkness. And as long as I can bring a little of that light into my readers' lives, I'm going to keep on writing and keep making it real.

Turn the page to
read as the real
"Kristina" shares her
side of the story.

Kristina Speaks Up

"KRISTINA"

I'm not exactly sure where to begin, but to describe where my heart was at the beginning and how it got lost along the way. Any way you look at things, I'd like it to be known that I've always wanted to do the right thing. Even when it came right down to destruction and carnage in my wake, I looked upon myself in a kind of helpless and detached way: a flailing passenger on a tumultuous runaway train destined to destroy everything in my path, knowing my own demise would be eminent upon encountering the slightest obstacle, yet still unable to do anything but watch on autopilot and hang on for dear life.

I don't blame anyone for my actions, or try to blame a bad childhood for my faults—in all actuality I had a very privileged upbringing. I didn't really see it as such, being your typical teenager, but my problems weren't anything to put into a storybook. I believed I was "blooming" when I began acting out, and I really did create a kind of alter ego to carry the guts-and-glory part of things through. Without that part of me, I might have actually become valedictorian and gone on to college. It's a tiny bit scary that this same me could quite possibly have been a judge or lawyer and responsible for defending or condemning the very same kinds of people that I ultimately became, isn't it?

My only reason for showing little to no resistance to the dark side was yearning. Deep and mourning within my soul lived a desire so desperate to be assuaged that it consumed my dreams: I wanted to be accepted and embraced by the other kids more than anything in the world. I looked at the pretty girls and wanted to look like even the plainest of them so that I would be accepted and admired and would fit in. I longed for the cruel little tyrants to like me, but I had glasses and straight As and had not yet come into any real maturity, even by the end of the eighth grade, when all "those" girls had boyfriends and went to parties. I suppose a child of any age with a traumatized heart becomes easily malleable when her deepest desire becomes a possibility. When it comes down to a search of the soul, I suppose I would even go so far as to say that I still feel the desire for attention and approval from anyone in my vicinity. I've fought to reach a point where most of me is so far beyond that cosmetic crap, it's unbelievable, yet that one little seed remains at the back of my skull, nagging my brain like a tiny parasite. And sometimes it surfaces no matter how hard I fight it, or how far beyond shallowness I believe I have advanced.

Everyone grows up eventually, and as I became more and more willing to throw all caution to the wind, it never occurred to me to stop and take a look at myself. My transformation came almost overnight, and suddenly one day the boys began to notice me. Well, one boy at first, but after that they came almost too easily. The "bad boys" called to me like the sirens of myth and lore called to sailors, and each step I took toward them led me further and further astray. I still saw myself as the ugly duckling, and each flirtation built my confidence to new levels. I had finally found my own power and that in itself was the first and most addictive drug in my arsenal of self-destructive weapons.

Still, for some reason, I couldn't fully see that I had magically become an actual beauty. It was like some unseen force kept a shroud over the person I had become, and every flaw I possessed became magnified in my mind and heart until I reached a point where I obsessed over each tiny thing and constantly felt incomplete—always striving for greatness in the eyes of others and constantly failing to ask myself what could make me happy with myself. In the middle of my freshman year, I adopted an ironclad facade of a trendsetter. I clung to the disguise for so long that, after years of putting up a front, I actually finally figured out how to believe in the fictional person I had created. In doing so I found liberation. I realized that people didn't want a weak-minded little girl who simpered at their feet and rushed to please. They wanted "Bree," as my mother so aptly named her, the self-confident leader of the pack who wasn't afraid to speak her mind and didn't give a damn what they thought of her or anything she did. And that is exactly who I showed them. I pretended to be a self-confident, mellow "stoner" who started trends because my style was the only one that mattered.

Of course, Bree was an entirely made-up person. I decided to let surface an exact opposite of who I felt I was, and amazing things began to happen. The girls stopped trying to beat me up, and then went out of their way to make friends with me. Ironically, they fell over themselves to please me because I successfully made them think I couldn't care less if they liked me or not. I couldn't believe the difference in their attitudes and actions. That made it even more important to build my walls of smoke and mirrors so they would not find out that the only reason I "liked" certain music, clothes, hobbies, and people was because they did. I lived alone, inside myself, because I was afraid to draw attention to myself that might send my carefully mortared walls tumbling down as a result of a lack of structural integrity.[1]

So this was where my soul fretted and when I reached the first really bad decision to be made—the first of the evils that led me down a shadowed path and dragged many friends and loved ones through the depths of my abysmal undertow.

It seemed like a harmless thing to smoke a cigarette, a deliciously bad little habit to hide from my mom and stepfather, one that would immediately curry favor among the popular and make me feel as if I had taken a huge step toward liberation. Truth be told, I actually went through a kind of indescribable misery to accomplish this feat of

---

1   I think most people act in whatever regrettable ways they do because of fear—a lack of trust in the humanity of the human race. We're just all too ignorant to open our eyes to our true motivations, and too self-centered to care about anything more than our own skins first and foremost.

stupidity. I realized, after trying to fake smoking for a week or so, that I looked like an obvious poser. After all, a true smoker can see when somebody doesn't inhale. The first time I inhaled nicotine into my lungs I didn't even cough, and this, of course, boosted my confidence, and I happily smoked an entire cigarette immediately before classes began at school. I felt fine and I fit into the group like I had always belonged there. My spirits soared! The bell rang and we filed in to first period like we did on any other day, but my heart was pulsing with a kind of jubilant song. For the moment, nothing was even remotely amiss in a place where anxiety normally prevailed.

Ten or fifteen minutes into my English class, my euphoria ended abruptly. My face broke out in a cold sweat and my limbs began to shake. I got up from my chair and ran like Satan himself was at my heels. I made it to the bathroom, but I was a long way from the toilet. I spewed things I swear I ate for dinner three or four nights prior, and I bawled like a newborn as I splashed the floor and wall with filth I can't even begin to describe. When my gut was finally emptied, I felt much better, but I knew right away what had made me sick, and I dreaded the days to come. I wondered if smoking would always cause this reaction and I feared the answer yet continued on my path with perseverance. I found out in the most awful way that some people's bodies take about two weeks to adapt to the strength of the nicotine bombarding them before they develop any kind of addiction or immunity, but still I pressed on in the same daily fashion until I woke up one day and realized I needed a smoke. The whole journey to that point had kept me wondering how in the ever-loving hell people could get hooked in the first place if the price was so high.

This was kind of the way I progressed through each bumbling experiment, first with booze, which I hated, and then with marijuana, which I abhorred. I continued to misuse both with single-minded purpose, however, because I refused to be deterred.

Both pot and alcohol made me feel detached from the world. "In a tunnel" is the sensation my sister and I used to describe the experience. Being intoxicated in these ways filled me full of dread because I hated feeling helpless and out of control. I had to know I was completely in command of my mind and able to retain my sanity and my disguise or I constantly feared for my adeptness in the crowd. I was forced to carefully control my own usage while convincing others I was using far more pot and alcohol than I actually was, which is not an easy feat. I also detested feeling dizzy and nauseous and, once again, could not see what all the hype was about or why on God's planet people got off on being helpless and flailing on the carpet. They actually bragged about passing out in their own vomit, but I could not stomach the thought of showing signs of weakness. I was already lost in a world I couldn't fathom, and I didn't even realize yet that life, as I had it structured, was very soon about to crumble.

Shortly after I turned fifteen, I decided the next logical step toward destruction would be to get losing my virginity out of the way. Not because I had any desire for the sexual aspect of things, but because I was sick of being the "odd man out" when sex came into any discussion. It didn't take long to do just that, but I didn't feel any different when it was all said and done. I didn't achieve the desired epiphany. The fantasy that girls have about their entire life having meaning once they become a woman was all a load of crap, and I became even further disillusioned. There was little to no enjoyment for me in sex. Somehow I had led myself into a trap that now left me obliged to get the tedious chore out of the way before I could build any relationships or be taken seriously. I never even knew what kind of enjoyment a female could find in the whole business until I was much, much older. As a result, I sank deeper into bleakness.

By the time I was nearing seventeen years old, I had let too many things fall apart on the surface. I was careless with my schoolwork, and I aroused the suspicions and anger of my parents with almost frightening frequency. I behaved in appalling ways at parties and just in general. Even thinking about some of these things now is downright embarrassing. Suffice it to say that my mother was very ontarget with a good number of the assumptions in her story. One of the things I found most amazing was how she intuited who the "good guys" and "bad guys" were. For instance, without really knowing (and definitely without liking) "Chase," she seemed to know he really did love me and had my best interests at heart.

But there was so much more she never imagined. Like the fact that I not only trafficked meth but also manufactured it heavily for a while. Or like the time one of the guys[2] I moved in with pulled out a gun and shot someone right in the head. I was standing not two feet away, and the sight of that messed me up for years. It would take thousands of paragraphs to relate them all, and I'm not sure I have the courage to confess every secret. I do know this: at first the horror stories I had heard about crank were sufficient to keep me afraid and I swore I would never breach the line between harmless drugs like weed and dangerously addictive drugs like speed. I stayed away because I was terrified of overdosing and getting brain damage and everything else that has been attributed to any controlled substance that comes in a white or powdered form.

I truly wish that whatever genius launched the DARE program would cease whining about the dangers of pot and put some real effort into scaring the daylights out of would-be methamphetamine enthusiasts before all hell breaks loose in their lives. Because it wasn't at all hard to break my resolve when some friendly peer pressure was applied to just the right places.

In fact, considering how hard I fought to avoid breaching the divide up until that point, it was really easy. And once I crossed the line, there was no prayer of turning back. What's truly and sickeningly funny is that I often bragged that I didn't have an "addictive personality," using this

---

2   This guy was also the chemist who showed me how to cook meth.

lie as a cover for not getting completely hammered during past forays into less frightening vices. I hadn't the slightest clue how wrong I was.

For some reason, in the midst of the blurred haze that encompassed a sizable portion of my past, I remember everything about the first time I tried crank, down to the smallest detail. I sat in my friend's old Pontiac, squished in with four of my closest comrades in the parking lot of a slimy old bowling alley, and I watched as they made four smallish lines on a cracked CD case. My best friend, "Robyn," goaded me to try a little. I resisted, mostly because I was afraid of the burn, but I hated the thought of being the only one not included in the party. Finally she persuaded me to snort a tiny blast made from the remnants of the other lines. That way, if I didn't like it, the effects wouldn't be nearly so powerful.

I caved in like a virgin on prom night. I felt almost no pain from the initial impact, and almost instantly my heartbeat increased and my spirit leaped in a way that made me feel truly in control of my own destiny. I was hooked, and I wanted—no, needed—to know how far I could go and what heights I could achieve. Suddenly crank became the world's most harmless little drug in my mind, so as to more easily justify each time I dabbled in the wondrous euphoria that made me feel alive and helped me believe my uncertainties had been vanquished.

As with any addiction, at first it was a once-in-a-while pleasure, but it became an all-consuming passion before I even had time to wonder how I got lost in the grip of the monster. I found, for a time, a substance that sated my great hunger, and my common sense lost its foothold. I have countless regrets and hundreds of memories that would make the strongest man's skin crawl to hear them recounted. I may find the courage to completely purge my demons when there is more blank paper and hours of time in which to search my past. The story has not been completely told yet, and I would not want to ruin any surprises that "Kristina" has yet to relate, but just know that there is no such thing as easy fulfillment of your greatest desire. There's a reason God does not always give us everything we ask for, and that is most people don't really know what they want. Fewer still have a clue what they actually need.

I put myself through the darkest drawn-out hell anyone could possibly imagine, and I dragged people with me who should never have had to experience pain inflicted by my hand. I'm filled with deep remorse. Meth poisoned more than my body. It poisoned my life. I am ashamed of what I allowed it to do to me and to my integrity. I can only hope that I will be able to keep others from making the same mistake. If I can prevent even one person from taking the same path I have, then it all will have been worth it. No matter what the struggle these days, I comfort myself knowing that I have been through worse things, and anything else that could possibly get thrown at me from this point on will be a learning experience and nothing more. My soul is at rest and it's become a bit easier to find a smile in the tiny beautiful things that life has to offer.

There's no real way for me to travel the universe, attempting to save people or anything, but I suppose that's not my intention anyway. I just want a few people to open their eyes and see the possibilities that surround us but are overlooked more times than they are noticed—to understand more fully the repercussions that can be incurred so easily with a seemingly unimportant little dalliance. And maybe to appreciate just a little the things we so often take for granted.

I've spent years tearing at my bindings again and again only to design yet another oubliette to puzzle through until I find the chink in the bricks and can begin anew to tear them down. I travel in circles like a diabolical carousel in a horror novel. But I have finally found freedom in the ability to battle my demons and win. My world has become a lovely place because I appreciate each and every moment of life not spent in the hands of the monster. Oh, now don't get me wrong—I still dream about him from time to time. I still miss his kiss and the escape from pain that he offers. I still think about getting high just one more time so the world will make sense for a heartbeat or two, but I have found the strength to fight him off, for which I am eternally grateful.

I urge you to never forget that addiction is not easily controlled and very rarely completely beaten. If you're already in recovery, never be so sure of yourself that you take the wrong risk and get pulled back into oblivion. The hunger will hit you when your back is turned. Learn to see that life is the most precious gift and if you piss it away, you'll wake up one day and realize it's over before you ever got a chance to really live. Do your best to find joy in the sunshine or a rainbow or in the simple smile of another. If you succeed, you will feel a weight lift from your heart.

There's a universe full of endless promise. It carries many pitfalls and there is a price that must be paid, but if you look for only the good in things, you'll find that the bad won't tear you down nearly so thoroughly. Discover your wonder before it becomes too fleeting to capture long enough to know it was even there.

Turn the page for a first look at Ellen Hopkins's riveting novel SMOKE.

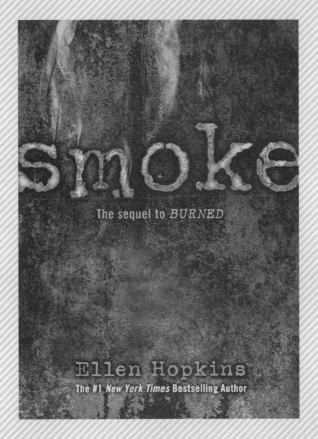

Pattyn Scarlet Von Stratten
Some Things

You can't take back, no
matter how much you wish
you could. No matter how
hard you pray to

        some

all-powerful miracle maker.
Some supposed God of Love.
One you struggle to believe
exists, because if he did,

        things

wouldn't be so out of control,
and you wouldn't be sucked dry
of love and left to be crushed
like old brittle bones that

        are

easily ground into dust.
Hindsight is useless
when looking back over
your shoulder at deeds

        irreversible.

Dear, Sweet God

Forgive me. I don't know what to do.
Where to go. How to feel. I'm perched
on the precipice, waiting for the cliff
to crumble. No way to change what

happened. What's done is done and I . . .
I can't think about it. If I do, I'll throw up
right here. Bile boils in my gut, erupts
in my esophagus. I gulp it down, close

my eyes. But I can still see him, lying there.
Can still hear the gurgle in his throat.
Still smell the rich, rusty perfume of blood
pooling around him. I so wanted him dead.

My father. Stephen Paul Von Stratten.
The bastard who beat my mother. Beat
my sister. Beat me. The son of a bitch
who was responsible for the accident

that claimed my Ethan—catapulted him
wherever you go when you die. Our unborn
baby rode into that wilderness with him.
Dear, cruel God. Why couldn't I go, too?

Eye for an Eye

If ever a person deserved to die,
it was Dad. But when I saw the bullet

hit its target square, watched him drop,
surprise forever branded in his sightless

eyes; when his shallow breathing went
silent, I wanted to take it back. Couldn't.

The Greyhound shifts gears, cresting
the mountain. Donner Pass, maybe.

Can't tell, leaning my head on the cool
window glass. It's dark. After ten. Escaping

into the night. Into the unknown. It's warm
in the bus, but I can't quit shaking. I think

I'll be cold forever. Frozen. Soul-ripping
sadness ice-dammed inside of me.

I shouldn't have listened to Mom. Shouldn't
be here. Shouldn't be free. I should be in

handcuffs. Behind bars. Locked away
forever. That's what I deserve. Instead,

I'm on my way to San Francisco.
I want to see something I've never

seen—the ocean. They'll find me,
sooner or later. Put me away in a cement

box without windows, where I belong.
I want to carry a memory with me,

bury it inside my heart, treasure, to be
exhumed when I need something

beautiful. Peaceful. Pacific. Of course,
I'll probably never feel at peace again.

Dad had ghosts who visited him often,
demons he tried to drink away. Now

he'll be my ghost. A ghost, filled with
demons. Haunting me until I'm a ghost, too.

The Bus Is Crowded

I chose a seat near the back, away
from the driver. Mistake. Too close
to the bathroom. It stinks of urine

and worse. Every now and again
someone goes in there and then it
smells like marijuana, though smoking

is prohibited on all Greyhounds.
At least that's what the signs say.
Not like the driver cares. Easier not

to interfere with derelicts, dopers,
failed gamblers, and crazies. Oddly,
I feel safe enough among them.

Like freeway drivers in separate cars,
all going the same direction at the same
time, each passenger here has a unique

destination. A personal story. I try
not to listen. Try to tune the voices
out. Don't need other people's drama.

But Some I Can't Miss

Somewhere behind me, a couple
has argued for an hour. Seems
he was up two hundred dollars
at Circus Circus. But she dropped
that, plus three hundred more,
which explains why they're:
> riding a piss-smelling bus home
>> 'stead of getting a little cooch
>>> in a cozy motel room before
>>>> catching the morning Amtrak.

Kitty-corner and a couple rows
up, two blue-silver-haired women
talk about their husbands, kids, and
grandkids. One of them got lucky
on dollar slots. Now she can pay
her electric bill and have enough
>>>> left over to put some back into
>>> our savings. Shouldn't have
>> took it out for this trip, but I
> just had one of those feelings. . . .

Behind Me

The guy takes up two whole seats.
      No one wants to sit near him, mostly
because he smells like he hasn't had

a shower. Ever. Probably homeless and
      put on the bus by law enforcement. They
don't much like finding people frozen

to death in riverside cardboard boxes.
      Lots of homeless take up residence on
the banks of the Truckee. Wonder if one

of them will notice the metallic glint
      of a 10mm. The gun that killed Stephen
Von Stratten. Wonder if the cops will

check the river. After . . . it . . . Mom
      told me to take Dad's car and go far
away. Fast away. She gave me her money

      stash, packed a few clothes. *Once
         the cops come,* she said, *they'll
      look for the car. Dump it soon.*

Driving into Reno, it came to me—
        a scene from an old movie—to park
the old Subaru in the airport garage.

I took the overhead walkway, down
        the escalator, out the front doors,
carrying the tatters of my life in

an overnight bag. Walked the couple
        miles to the bus station, much of it
along the river. Seemed like a good

place to lose the gun Ethan gave me
        for protection. It did protect Jackie
from another fist to her face. But, oh,

the price was dear. For Dad. For me.
        For the entire family. What will happen
to Mom and the kids now? Tears

threaten, but I can't let them fall.
        Can't show weakness. Can't show
fear. Can't look like a girl on the run.

Keep reading for a
glimpse of TILT.

Tilt too far and
you'll fall. . . .

tilt

Ellen Hopkins

The #1 *New York Times* Bestselling author

Should the sun beat
summer too fiercely
through your afternoon
window, you can

                        slant

the blinds to temper
heat and scatter light,
sifting shadows this way
and that with a

                              lean

of slats. And if candor
strikes too forcefully,
step back, draw careful
breath and consider the

                                    angle

your words must take
before you open
your mouth, let them leak
out. Because once you

                                          tilt the truth,

it becomes a lie.

My World Tilted

Completely off its axis the night
I hooked up with Dylan Douglas.
It was New Year's Eve—five

months ago—so maybe part of that
earth-sway had something to do with
the downers, weed and cheap beer,

a dizzying combo on an empty stomach.
What I know for sure is, when he came
slinking up like a cougar—all tawny

and temperamental—something inside
me shifted. Something elemental.
I, probably the oldest prude in my whole

junior class, transformed into vamp.
When he smiled at me—me!—I knew
I had to make him mine. I would

have done anything. Turned out, all
I had to do was smile back. Just like
that, we belonged to each other.

Love at First Smile

That's what it was. He says so,
          and I agree. What kind of girlfriend
                    would I be if I argued about something

like that? Not only that, but we
          fell in love as a new year began.
                    Symbolism there. And I didn't need

a resolution when a result had
          just occurred. All the hurt of
                    losing my last boyfriend—who was

at the same party, slobbering
          all over my ex-good friend,
                    Tricia—dissolved, shaved ice in

a cup of hot tea. Dylan is a hundred
          times the guy Josiah is. Thank
                    God I didn't give my virginity

to *him*. I didn't give it to Dylan
          right away, either. Unlike Josiah,
                    he never pressured me to. But after

a couple of months, love spoke
        louder than fear. One night
                we were mostly naked and

all knotted up in each other's
        arms. And the time just seemed
                right to say, "I want to. Please."

        Dylan was just so cute. *Are you
        sure?* He said it right before
                I stripped off my panties. And

he confirmed, *You're positive?*
        just as I pushed him inside me.
                I think I wanted it more than he did.

And all that hype about awful
        pain? Well, that may be true
                for some people. But, except for

a couple of seconds of intense
        pressure, it didn't hurt at all.
                But it made our connection steel.

Loving Someone

That much—so much he means
more to you than anything—changes
things. You lose friends, because
you'd rather be with him than with them.

I've always been popular. Cheerleader.
Junior class president. Homecoming
princess. All the girls wanted to hang
with me. One was even a stalker.

Now, they still smile and say hello,
but the only ones who I'm really close
to are Audrey and Emily. Both of them
have sleepover boyfriends, at least when

their parents aren't home. That's another
thing love changes—your relationship
with your parental units. It becomes
them versus you, as if they're afraid

of losing you. Jealous of the person
who can make that happen. News flash,
Mom and Dad. I'll be eighteen in a few
months. You've already lost me.

Now It's Summer Vacation

Definition: sleeping in. Lazy days
          at Tahoe. Parties. And that leads me to
          deception. Because here's the thing
about parents. Mostly, they don't want

their kids to have fun, at least not
          if it involves underage drinking,
          illegal substances and the possibility
of sex. This is the first party of

the summer. I plan on an all-nighter.
          Which means I can't say I'm going
          out with Dylan. So I invented a sleep-
over at Emily's. "Hey, Mom," I call

toward her bedroom. "I'm leaving
          now." I grab my backpack and keys,
          start toward the door. I'm almost there
when my brother comes out of the kitchen,

          yacking down a sandwich. *Emily's,*
                    huh? Trace checks out my shorts,
                    the scoop of my tank. *God, man,*
          you look like a Fourth Street hooker.

"When were you on Fourth Street?
        Anyway, know what they call a guy
        who looks at his sister's attributes
like that? Pervert." His face turns

the color of ripe watermelon flesh.
        Ka-ching! Got him. Trace is fifteen
        and never been kissed. At least, I'm pretty
sure he hasn't been. It's not like I follow him

around, and it's not like he'd go
        bragging about it if he had. Trace is
        the so-quiet-you-have-to-wonder-what-
he's-hiding type. Except, that is, when

it comes to ragging on me. "Tell
        Mom I said bye, okay?" I escape into
        the gentle warmth of late afternoon
June. The party won't start until after

dark. But I don't have to wait that long
        to see Dylan. He's picking me up at
        Em's. I see it as a French vanilla lie.
Not totally white. But close enough.

Emily's Parents Aren't Home

So I don't bother with the doorbell. "Hello?"
No response but a meow from Monster Cat.

Ah, now I hear giggling behind her bedroom
door. She's either on the phone or not alone.

I probably shouldn't barge in. Tyler's probably
in there, too. Instead, I text Dylan. HEY, BABY.

COME GET ME. Just as he says he's on his way,
Emily comes out of her room, adjusting clothes,

hair mussed and makeup smeared. Good call.
"I take it Ty's here?" They've been going

       out for almost a year. Serious love.
       Uh, no, actually. It's not Tyler. It's Clay.

The look she gives me is half challenge,
Half plea. Last time I looked, Clay happened

to be going out with our mutual friend,
Audrey. "Hey, I won't tell." But I can't

believe she'd cheat on Tyler. "Did you and
Ty have a fight or something?"

       She smiles. *Nothing like that. I just
       wanted to try something different is all.*

Something Different?

God, I'm glad Dylan is everything
I need. Two horn blasts tell me he's outside,
waiting. "Are you coming to the party later?"
I don't ask, "Are you coming with Tyler or Clay?"

                    Probably. She grins. *Depending.*

Whatever. All I really care about
right now is Dylan. My pulse picks
up speed as I hurry down the walk
to his shiny green Jeep. He always

keeps the Wrangler spotless. When
he sees me, he gets out and waits,
and his perfect smile spreads across
his incredible face. God, he's amazing—

bronze skin beneath too-long blond
hair that makes him look like a little boy.
Well, except for the fact that he's six
foot two and buff as hell. He opens

his arms. I give a little jump, and
he's holding me and we're kissing.
His lips are smooth and he tastes like
peppermint. And I never want to stop.

                    But he does. And he says, *I love you.*

Three Words

And everything bad in my life
        melts away. I look into the turquoise
        deep of his eyes. "I love you, too."

I tangle my hands into his hair,
        pull his face into mine for another
        kiss, this one hotter than the last.

        A passing car beeps going by.
                Dylan draws back, laughing.
                Maybe we should get a room?

"Maybe." We could probably
        get one inside. But then Dylan
        would find out about Clay.

He and Tyler are friends.
        "Let's get something to eat.
        Not good to drink on an empty

stomach." Experience has
        taught me that. Dylan agrees.
        But before he detaches himself

        totally from me, he slips a hand
                down the scoop of my tank.
                Can't wait to kiss these, too.